THE THRILL OF IT ALL

Also by Joseph O'Connor

NOVELS
Cowboys and Indians
Desperadoes
The Salesman
Inishowen
Star of the Sea
Redemption Falls
Ghost Light

SHORT STORIES
True Believers
Where Have You Been?

THEATRE/MUSIC/SPOKEN WORD
Red Roses and Petrol
True Believers
The Weeping of Angels
Handel's Crossing
My Cousin Rachel
Whole World Round (with Philip King)
Heartbeat of Home (concept development and song lyrics)
The Drivetime Diaries (CD)

THE THRILL OF IT ALL

JOSEPH O'CONNOR

HARVILL SECKER

LONDON

Published by Harvill Secker 2014

2 4 6 8 10 9 7 5 3 1

First published in Great Britain in 2014 by
HARVILL SECKER
Random House
20 Vauxhall Bridge Road
London SW1V 2SA

www.randomhouse.co.uk

Addresses for companies within The Random House Group Limited
can be found at: www.randomhouse.co.uk/offices.htm

The Random House Group Limited Reg. No. 954009

A CIP catalogue record for this book is available from the British Library

ISBN 9780436205736 (hardback)

ISBN 9781846553530 (trade paperback)

The Random House Group Limited supports the Forest
Stewardship Council® (FSC®), the leading international forest certification
organisation. Our books carrying the FSC label are printed on FSC® certified
paper. FSC is the only forest certification scheme supported by the leading
environmental organisations, including Greenpeace. Our paper procurement
policy can be found at www.randomhouse.co.uk/environment

Typeset in Sabon MT by Palimpsest Book Production Ltd,
Falkirk, Stirlingshire

Printed and bound in Great Britain by
Clays Ltd., St Ives plc

For Philip Chevron
1957–2013

Way it see it myself, there's only one reason for art: to make you appreciate that you got a spin on the planet. Picasso, the great writers, the poets, the musicians. If you can listen to the Beatles doing 'She Loves You' and not be a little bit glad you're alive, you've got an answering-machine for a heart.

FROM FRAN MULVEY'S FINAL INTERVIEW

Preface

My name is Robbie Goulding. I was once a musician. For five years in the 1980s I played guitar with the Ships. This memoir has been long in the making.

Commissioned in the opening months of the twenty-first century, it appears – at last – more than a decade late. Time is an editor, altering outlooks, italicising certain memories and blue-pencilling others, unearthing chronologies you didn't notice while living them. And the book, like its author, has changed with the years, increasing in size, now slimming, now regaining, surviving the recalibrations and unnoticed evolutions collectively known as Fate. At one point, it was angrier, out to settle a few scores, then it morphed into an assertion of lost friendship. It seems to have become the book I wish someone had given me when I started out in rock and roll. Had that happened, it would be a different book indeed.

For reasons that will become obvious, I don't remember every part of this story. So, here and there I've relied on the reminiscences of my former bandmates, who speak in their own words, drawn mainly from interviews. Inevitably there are moments when those recollections differ from mine, but life would be thin if we all sang the same notes or noticed the same goings-on. My thanks to Sky Television's Arts Channel for permission to quote Trez Sherlock, to Seán Sherlock for agreeing to be interviewed (by my daughter) for this project, and to BBC Television/Lighthouse Music Ltd for permission to quote Fran Mulvey's last interview. A brief passage comprising my daughter's own perspective is included in the narrative. She recorded this for personal reasons, essentially as a diary, and it appeared as a blog on various music-related websites in the winter of 2012. We inhabit the age in which everything is public, especially, of course, the private. When young myself, it was the other way around. Bowie sang to a public who knew nothing about him. Mystique, it was called at the time.

Some characters you'll meet in these pages are no longer with us. My late mum, Alice Blake, from Spanish Point in County Clare, bought me a guitar for my fourteenth birthday. More even than this, a life-changing gift, she tolerated the endless murderings of 'Johnny B Goode' that occurred in our home as a result. Greater love hath no woman than to endure 'Stairway to Heaven' morning and night for two years, with 'House of the Rising Sun', 'The Sound of Silence' ('if only,' Dad said) and further notables of the apprentice repertoire. Mum went on to survive the emergence of punk. I have memories of the September evening I spent learning the chords of 'Anarchy in the UK' at the kitchen table as she ironed my soccer kit for school. Beside her among the Angels of forbearance is the noble shade of a proud Brooklynite, Eric Wallace, founder of Urban Wreckage Records, whose belief kept the Ships from sinking.

I thank my daughter Molly Goulding, for editorial

assistance, and her mother, Michelle O'Keeffe, from Athens, Tennessee, for more than any love song could convey. I would have liked to write at greater length about Michelle in this account, but she has insisted on the privacy that she has always valued, and I respect and understand her wish. My father Jimmy and brother Shay are princes. I thank them for uncountable solidarities.

All errors and lapses – well, most – are my own. Nothing in the book is fiction.

Engineer's Wharf,
Grand Union Canal, London,
Winter 2012

PART ONE

Ships in the Night

1981–1987

One

Let me tell of someone I first saw in October 1981 when both of us were aged seventeen. An exasperating and charming and fiercely intelligent boy, the finest companion imaginable in a day of idleness and disputation. His name was Francis Mulvey.

So many symphonies of inaccuracy have been trumpeted about Fran down the years that I find myself reluctant to add to the chatter. Unauthorised biographies, a feature-length documentary, profiles and fanzines and blog sites and newsgroups. My daughter tells me there's talk of a biopic movie with the Thai actor Kiatkamol Lata as Fran, but somehow I can't see that working. She wonders who'd play her daddy. I tell her not to go there. Fran wouldn't want me included in his story any more. And he's lawyered-up good, as I know to my cost.

These days my former glimmertwin is private, characterised by the media as a 'reclusive songwriter and producer', as though 'recluse' is a job description. You've seen the most recent photograph available – it's blurry and five years old. He's with his children, attending the first Obama inauguration, sharing a joke with the First Lady. I barely recognise him. He looks trim, fit and prosperous, in a tux that cost more than my houseboat.

But the boy Fran, in his heart, was a demi-monde figure, more comfortable in a second-hand blouse rummaged in a charity store in Luton, the town where the fates introduced us. Thirty miles from London, in light-industrial Bedfordshire, boasting an airport, car factories and a shopping centre under permanent reconstruction, it had also, my brother joked, a time zone of its own, 'clocks stopped around the second lunar landing'. I think of it as my only home town, the place I grew up, but by literal definition we were immigrants. I was born in Dublin, the middle child of three. In 1972 – the year I turned nine – we moved to England following a family tragedy. Luton's housing estates, built after the war, were identikit, perhaps, but there were parks and further fields that my brother and I enjoyed. My parents were fond of our neighbours on Rutherford Road, whom I remember as tactful, welcoming people. It wasn't Thrillsville, admittedly, but every country has her Lutons: places notable for points of indisputable interest, one of which is the fact that they are thirty miles from somewhere else. You will find them in Germany, northern France, Eastern Europe, by the thousand in the United States. I've never seen one in Italy but I know they must exist. Swathes of Belgium seem one *vast* Luton. The best to be said for ours is that it was *good* at being Luton, in a way that, say, Malibu could never have managed. I had happy times and tough ones. There was a lot of non-event, as we marched to our own little humdrum. I tend to divide my youth into before and after Fran. The former I recollect as a series of monochromes. Luton got colour when he came.

I'm told he no longer wears make-up, not even a dusting of rouge. When I first encountered Francis, in college in the eighties, he would pitch up for lectures sporting more lip frost and blusher than Bianca Jagger at Studio 54. Apart from on television, he was the first male I ever saw in eye shadow, a weird shade of magenta he sourced by trawling theatrical-supply shops. 'They use it for murderers and whores,' he'd explain, with the insouciance of one on terms with both.

I became aware of him during my first month at Poly. Let's face it, he would have been difficult to miss. One morning I saw him upstairs on the 25 bus, asking the loan of a compact-mirror from the unsmiling conductress, a Jamaican lady of about fifty who was not a believer in light-touch regulation when it came to Luton's scholars. Supplying the mirror, she was then beseeched for a tissue, on to which he imprinted a lipstick kiss before handing both items back to her. It's a mark of Fran's innocence, which expressed itself as vulnerability, that no one kicked his teeth down his throat.

Who was this wraith? Whence had he come? My class-mates traded theories about his birthplace. China was a candidate, as were Laos and Malaysia. Oddly, I don't remember anyone ever suggesting Vietnam, his long-departed actual motherland. What was certain was that he'd been adopted in South Yorkshire as a child, looked fabulous and didn't talk much. Many regarded his habitual silence as a form of attention-seeking and determined to look the other way. The Poly had students and faculty of different ethnicities, as any college near a large English town would, but in several respects Fran was unusual. You had the feeling he was aware that there was only one of himself, a threatening signal to transmit to any group. It must also be unnerving to the transmitter, I imagine. The peacock may be flaunting through angst or plain boredom and would rather you just buggered off. What Fran had wasn't confidence. It was a million miles from flounce. The closest I can come is 'dignity'. And you want to watch out when you've dignity in England because it can look like you're taking yourself seriously.

I can't say I recollect offensive remarks. That would rarely be the form things took. But there would be that certain tentative chuckle and a rolling of the eyes, particularly among the boys, who were not exactly hostile, but who wanted you to notice that Fran didn't look like you, in the unlikely event you hadn't noticed already. Fran didn't look like anyone.

He lived in a room, though no one knew where. Leagrave, perhaps. Farley Hill. He was rumoured to have friends at Reading University, and this, by itself, gave him an urbanite's exoticism. We, at the windblown outposts of my town's Polytechnic, felt outshone by the Flash Harrys of Reading. They galumphed about their town quaffing hock, snogging doxies and shooting mortarboards off each other with a blunderbuss – huzzah! – while we fumed on the banks of the Lea.

Theatre, Film and English were Fran's courses at the Poly. Sociology and English were mine. Dad accused me of selecting Sociology in order to annoy him, and he wasn't entirely wrong. In addition I'd registered for Greco-Roman Civilisation, since it was required of all first-years to 'do' three subjects, and I reckoned, having twice seen the movie

Ben Hur on telly, that I'd a fair bit of groundwork dug. Also, I couldn't think of anything else. The college offered Musicology but this wouldn't have occurred to me. I'd been banging on a little Ibanez Spanish guitar since my fourteenth birthday, was workmanlike in the plunking of a Beatles riff or two, but studying the mysteries of music seemed to me pointless, dingbat that I was in those days. I adored the Patti Smith Group. They hadn't a degree between them. It was hard to picture Patti telling herself the key signature of C-sharp minor contains four sharps. Why would she need to know?

My hobby became Fran-watching. There are worse pursuits. I see him yet in the 300-seater lecture hall, always at the back, often smoking. There was a girlfriend for a while, a mournfully gorgeous punkette. They'd spend afternoons in the student bar – 'The Trap', we called it – wordlessly gazing at art books, the pair of them ordering 'crème de menthe frappé', not a common undergraduate's drink in Luton. Paddy, the obliging barman, would gamely produce the crushed ice that beverage requires by filling a supermarket bag with chunks from the freezer and stamping his hobnail boots on it. But by Christmas the girlfriend was no longer around, at least no longer paraded. When the college reopened in January, there was another at Fran's side, a soul-girl said to be studying Mechanical Drawing. You saw them hand-in-hand on the soccer fields at dusk, two blackbirds in the snow that lay for weeks on the campus. Then there was a boy. Predictable murmurings began. My experience of the young is that they can be intensely conservative and easily disconcerted, far less accepting than the old. If Fran was a loner, it wasn't entirely by choice. And I'm no one to judge, for I didn't approach him myself, preferring to be intrigued from a distance.

He contributed articles to the Students' Union newspaper. I found them odd, enticing and very, very bold. Joy Division released the compilation album *Still* not long after their vocalist Ian Curtis took his life. Fran's review termed the sleeve 'corpse-grey'. I felt that was close to a boundary but not the right side of it. He went through a thankfully brief phase of signing his pieces 'Franne', attracted, I think, by the Elizabethan connotation. Evidently he loved the melancholy ballads of Dowland and Walter Raleigh, for an article on that subject appeared beneath his name. An unusual, clever boy, he'd endured a childhood of savagery. I don't know how he was alive. Many years after I met him – in what turned out to be the last television interview he'd ever give – he made public some of the biographical details.

From Fran's Final Interview, Michael Parkinson Show, April 1998

Yeah, I'd rather talk about boxing, any night of the week . . . I love Herol, man . . . That's my idol . . . Herol 'Bomber' Graham . . . From my part of the world, and yours . . . Up Sheffield.

Where am I from? Well, Yorkshire, like I said. Before that . . . you know . . . Vietnam. I was born in a place called Dầu Tiếng over there. Rural, it is, in the Sông Bé province . . . I'm probably not saying it right . . . I've been in touch, you know, with the authorities down there. And I found them very helpful. But it's hard with the records . . . Beautiful country, is Vietnam, I was over there last year, very gentle people, and curious, and welcoming, but the place is still messed up. My dad might have been a soldier. American, yeah . . . Anyroad, I was abandoned. A foundling . . . I ain't sorry for myself, you know, I've done all right . . . But that's what it was . . . Not the best.

Yeah, the war was still on. But you know, you're a kid. So you don't understand what's going down is a war, it's all you been used to, like weather. Violence? Sure. I saw bad, bad stuff. Nowt to say about that . . . Because this in't the forum. Talking to you now, we're on telly, it's fine, and I've a respect for you personally, always have done. But I've limits . . . Which makes me unusual.

All I know: some farmer took us as a baby to a convent in Tây Ninh City . . . And I'm told I was there until four years old . . . I've looked into it. Because yeah, I'd like to know more . . . It's a natural thing, in't it, you wonder where you come from . . . I've a researcher working for me now, she helps, she speaks the language. And there's incredible folk out there, in the States, in Vietnam, trying to put all these stories together. Because there's thousands of Vietnam-born children have a background like mine. Canada, the States, all over Europe. You get to thinking you're alone. But you're not.

First thing I remember is the heat, you know, that heat you get in Indochina. Humid. Then the sound of French. Because the nuns looking after us, they were French. Funny, I remember two of them had the same name, Sister Anna. There was a priest often come to visit, Father Lao, Vietnamese. And soldiers about. Big Yanks talking English. A huge rubber tree – you could see it from the window. And a yard, where there was a bell, and animals and people selling stuff. I mean farm animals, roosters, and these small, black potbellied pigs. And we'd play with the pigs. Me and the other kids. And often I get to thinking, what happened them kids? Break your heart to see 'em. Break your heart.

One day this European woman's come and she's give us a cup of milk. Some diplomat's wife. You could see she didn't want to touch us. Nothing against the woman, she was doing her best, but I won't never forget that. Couldn't bear to touch us. That's the West, right there. Mix of kindness and condescension. And fear. Because pity's the cousin of fear. And to me, the whole thing about aid . . . it wants changing. Going further. Dole 'em a cup of milk? Deluding yourself, man. The crumbs off your plate in't enough.

Whatever happened, I dunno, they've took us down to Saigon. To this massive great orphanage, like, eight mile from the city, with fifteen hundred kids. Frightening place. Like a nightmare. Poor kids who've been maimed, and blind, and deformed. I was there a couple of months, and the night came when they took us away, me and a dozen others. They've put us on a bus, give us Red Cross parcels, bottle of juice, pack of sweets. And you're a kid, all you're thinking is Christ, what's this? And now we're at the airport. Told us, get on that plane. This adoption society, a Catholic charity, they're taking us to England. And nobody's ever asking if you wanted to go. But you're going. Decision's been made.

A plane, man. Imagine. And I'm proper scared of planes. To me, right, a plane is dropping bombs out the sky. I don't want to be in no plane . . . Eighteen hours later, I'm on the ground in England. Cold. Foggy. I in't never felt cold. And there's snow. What's *that*? You don't even have the words . . . And there's no one to ask. So you're scared.

This woman and her husband, they've took us away. Told us I'm now an English boy. 'Stop speaking that language.' They were cruel-hearted bastards. That's all. Less than human. I won't say their names. Wouldn't sully my mouth. Animals. Thugs. I hope they rot.

At seven I was taken by social services and put in a home. Then at nine, I got fostered by this Irish couple up Rotherham . . . Prefer not to say where exactly. Just private . . . It's been put about by the tabloids that they treated me bad. They never. They were proper decent people. But we didn't get on. Fell out when I was a teenager. I left at sixteen. Got nowt against them, no. They'd limitations. Who don't? I don't blame 'em for not being able to handle me, I was broken inside. You can't fix that brokenness. All you do is cope. No, I wouldn't want to see 'em again – anyway my foster-dad died a couple of years back – but I wish them an easy conscience. They did their best. You know? It's something. And they give us my name. Francis Xavier Mulvey. And that was my Irish foster-dad's name. God rest him. That's a boxer's name there, right? Francis X. Mulvey. Not as cool as Herol Graham. But I like how it sounds. He's won twenty-eight fights, man. I never won *one*. But I'm hopeful, you know? For a pessimist.

This isn't the place to continue Fran's childhood story. When I met him, he never spoke of his upbringing directly, although of course there were hints – if you wanted to see them – but I was as shocked by the full revelations, when many years later they came, as were most of the tabloid-reading public. In his student days Fran was good at setting up smokescreens of irony and indifference, even to those who loved him. You didn't take it personally. In truth, you rather admired the smoke, tinged as it was with the brilliant glow of his magnetism. Yes, you noticed he'd fall silent when the subject of family was discussed, but you assumed he wasn't listening, or perhaps had misheard, or simply had other things on his mind. In conversation he asked a lot of questions, always a sign that the asker doesn't want to be questioned himself. But I only understood this with hindsight.

I see him in memory, dawdling the draughty corridors of the Arts Block or asleep in one of the bare brick alcoves of that inhospitable building. The college had a cohort of rural Irish students, pursuing degrees or diplomas in Agricultural Science, and it surprised me to notice Fran at one of their discos. Not that he stayed too long. He was beautiful even then, before he'd grown into his beauty, scrawny and kissable, like some teenagers are, a ragged organza scarf around his throat on a wintry morning, a Judy Garland bonnet on his head. In all my life I never encountered a thinner individual. You'd have seen more fat on a chip.

It is not true, as has been written, that he'd come into the college wearing 'a dress'. The days of the frock came later. But certainly, his look was unusual even then, among the raggeries of denim and collarless cheesecloth we conventional souls went in for. On his long, slim fingers were profusions of rings, scavengings from the junk shops of the town. He turned the pages of a book as though someone was watching, which most of the time someone was. There was oldness about him. His eyes were cold lakes. He reminded you of those ruined chapels you see in the north of countries, weather-blasted, still hanging on. He had a part-time job washing dishes in the canteen. You'd glimpse him through the grille where students placed dirty plates, Fran wearing the only spangled hairnet ever made. You didn't reckon that the professors so barely aware of his existence would one day offer seminars on his work.

It was as though he'd been lifted out of *The Threepenny Opera* and dropped into Stanton Polytechnic and Agricultural College by some sardonically smirking god. In one of his articles he wrote that society's esteem for accomplishment was 'brutalising, murderous', that 'the artist has a DUTY to fail'. This was beyond the usual beslobberments of undergraduate drivel that nearly all of us parroted at that innocent time. He actually seemed to believe it.

In those days, the man that sold him drugs had a question: 'One-way or return? I've both.' Fran, when we were students, was a stickler for day-tripping. Indeed, he had an intolerance, which seemed to me strange, of drug use when witnessed in others. He could become puritanical if some Arts girl in the Trap took a pull on a jazz-fag. Even drunkenness, which most of us indulged in, as he did himself, could purse those frosted lips to a scowl. His mode at a party was to stand in a corner, observing from the shadows as the odour of lager and mildew sanctified whatever writhings ensued. I was astounded when he told me he never missed Sunday Mass. I suppose I shouldn't have been.

That conversation, our first, I am able to date, for I know it took place on the afternoon of Good Friday 1982, which fell on the 9th of April. The holy day tended to unleash a viral panic through the undergraduate body, for it was one of only two in the entire year when the Trap, being administered by an observant Catholic landlord, was closed or at least shut early. Several pubs in the town were unavailable for the same reason. Others did not welcome students. The unease would commence at the start of Easter Week, rising to full-blown hysteria as Spy Wednesday approached. There would be *no drink*. What would we *do*? CHRIST, THERE WILL BE NO DRINK. In some realm of re-enactment Our Lord's departure from the corporeal zone was imminent, but we had more immediate devastations on our minds. By Holy Thursday night, you could have sodomised anyone in the college in return for a six-pack of Harp.

The form was to stockpile and repair to someone's flat, in one of the many crumbling old houses partitioned into bedsits for students or the not-quite-destitute. There, the Zeppelin wailed and the wallpaper peeled. Christ's tears spattered the windows that the ratepayers of some rural county had arranged for bright youths to live behind. A nice girl studying Accountancy would end up weeping into the communal toilet on the landing, puking like a fruit machine, her hair held aloft by some monster out of Poe, his other paw working its way into her tights. Scholars in a wardrobe chewed at one another under damp coats. The corrugated kacks of the lessee or his cousin dried by an electric fire. Some wurzel would start fisticuffs and get kicked down the stairs, only to return, an hour later, eyes raging for forgiveness, the bottle of Blue Nun he'd stolen from the 24-hour minimart in the town his passport back into the pleasure-dome.

Rebel-yells, drunken gropes. Lachrymose talk. Backroom fingerings, declined lunges, Black Sabbath's 'Paranoid', stale bread in the toaster at dawn. My Purgatory will be a thousand years of Good Friday, circa 1982, reeking of chips, old carpet, crushed sexual hopes and unlaundered nylon bedsheets sprinkled with Brut aftershave by a student of Agricultural Science. Sad songs say so much, as Elton once told us, but the Bedsitter Blues be bad.

It was at the original bleak lock-in that I first exchanged words with Fran, emboldened by the pint of snakebite I'd pretended to enjoy. He was wearing a kilt and scarlet-lensed sunglasses. A kilted youth was a rare enough sight in Luton – well, maybe on St Patrick's Day, but he wouldn't have fishnets and a parasol, as Fran rather noticeably did. His polo-blouse was in the colours of the Italian soccer club A.S. Roma, the only sporting association he ever admitted to liking. I felt the slogan he'd embroidered – 'Up the Romans' – was either deliberately provocative or grossly tactless in the general context of Good Friday.

'Fakkin queer,' remarked a boy, later an adviser to New

Labour, passing by. 'In your dreams,' Fran nipped back at him, toeing a cigarette out on the lino. With difficulty, I took a step forward.

'I'm Robbie,' I said.

He nodded.

I waited.

He raised the crimson shades as though curious. I suppose it isn't possible that he didn't blink for ninety seconds but that was the way things seemed. Then he reached into his sporran and tugged from it a naggin of transparent liquid, opened it without averting his gaze from my own, took a docker's deep slug, wiped the rim on his cuff and offered it unsmilingly. I sipped. Gin-flavoured paint stripper was now on the market. Who knew? I downed a belter.

The first sentence he ever slurred to me was in the Gaelic language, '*Labhair ach beagán agus abair go maith é*', a proverb known to every alumnus of the Irish Christian Brothers. 'Speak but little and say it well.' It was clever of him to address me in Gaelic, a twitching of his antennae. Fran was always good at codes, at sounding you out. My answer, being in Gaelic, seemed to admit me to the nightclub. His watchfulness lowered one notch.

Well, then he switched to English, or his own version of that language. This party was 'a droolery', he averred. Our host was 'a shitehawk', the guests were 'lottery spittle'; enduring them was 'an emotional groin-strain'. The college we attended was 'a nest of illiterates', training 'flunts' to be 'hirelings' and 'couch-jockeys'. Bombing it would increase the average IQ of the Bedfordshire hinterland by no insignificant percentage. Vivisection should be the fate of most of its professors, but they lacked the properties of a lab mouse so what would be the point? I was flummoxed by his accent, which turned out to be heavily Yorkshire tinged with Connaught, when I'd expected a bored poet's drone. Fran sounded like the son of a Mayo-man, which in one sense he was, a fact I learned only later. Strange solecisms peppered his conversation, yet you knew what they meant. That student, 'a fukken facecloth', had a girlfriend 'a hanky'. The pair of them would give you 'the butt-plugs'. The thug now urinating into the sink was 'a stonewash Jerry', Fran's term for a boy whose mother buys his jeans. The problem with most people was that they 'never rang themselves up', a phrase I took to mean that they acted without thinking. I did my best to present myself as an urbane and inveterate self-dialler. I don't know how convincing I was.

It was hard to conceal disquiet at his defamations of our lecturers, of the college community generally. Dipsomania and impure practices were imputed to some, incontinence of ghastly varieties to others. Professor X was 'an eel-faced sadist', Dr Y 'a pimple-nippled klutz', the Dean of Humanities, in all truth the nicest of women, 'a piñata waiting to happen'. Father Z, the Catholic chaplain, was 'cottage cheese on legs', his curate 'a midget on stilts'. Great was Fran's ire for the triumvirate of elderly scholars helming the Department of Comparative Religion. A puddle-eyed, ignorant, self-spanking fop, a mule-eared turd and a monk-sucker. Their achievements in bastardry, sloth and betrayal had considerably exceeded their scholarship. The writer in residence was a 'turtle-necked rat', the porter 'a dug-up Troglodyte'. The Adjunct Professor of Architecture had put the grope into Gropius, and any elevator containing only the Moral Tutor must be avoided. The texts required to be read by candidates for the degree of Bachelor of Arts (English Literature, Hons) were 'an anthology of degraded chimps' bumfodder'.

Did I box? Why not? 'You should.' In his Yorkshire adolescence, three posters had adorned his bedroom wall: Jean Genet, Grace Kelly, Herol Graham. 'Kid standing out needs to box,' Fran said. 'Look like me up north? You boxed or got shat on.' He had spent many hours in Brendan Ingle's gym in the Wincobank area of Sheffield as a boy. 'Didn't have the hands. But I could fight a bit, yeah. Nothing like Herol. You look strong.'

I didn't 'stand out'. Nor did I look strong. But it's arresting to be offered a compliment by way of induction, even when you don't believe it.

Not a syllable about music was spoken by either of us that evening. We swapped clichés and inanities about the early novels of John Banville, to whose works Fran attributed significance for they rarely troubled the bestsellers lists back then. Anaïs Nin and Brendan Behan he mentioned with similar mercy, at least I think it was mercy, it might just have been drunkenness. Elias Canetti, winner of the 1981 Nobel Prize for Literature, was 'passable, if you like being bored'. Jane Austen? 'No.' Dickens? 'A perv.' George Bernard Shaw? 'A peeved vicar.' Only one of the Brontës didn't make you want to kill yourself: Branwell, the pisshead brother. I must surely know the writings of Czeslaw Milosz? I didn't, but I said that I did. It was difficult, given my condition, even to say 'Czeslaw Milosz'. Try it next time you're soused.

Soon he reeled off a prospectus I hadn't actually sought, the list of authors enjoying his imprimatur. Rimbaud, Verlaine, Kathy Acker (who?), Kerouac, Neal Cassady, the

Lake Poets 'bar Lying Billy Wordsworth'. Elizabeth Bishop wasn't bad; she'd rung herself up. Keats and Camus rarely stopped. But Dylan Thomas, 'a fukken soup-tureen', was wildly overrated; he 'couldn't write "cock" on a shithouse door, not without several attempts'. A piece of pulp erotica called *Hot Dames on Cold Slabs* was 'the only important American novel since *The Beautiful and the Damned*'. Banned here in England, of course. Fran always made a speciality of esteeming banned writers, because he knew you wouldn't have read them.

If I'm honest, he struck me as something of a disappointment that evening, silly and a bit predictable and spoiling for a quarrel, neither as brilliant nor as dark as I'd imagined him from afar. In 'Subterranean Homesick Blues' Bob Dylan advises against following leaders. But at eighteen, who wants advice? And come on, don't be judging me. When young, you were grandiose yourself from time to time. If you weren't, you loved someone who was. And it isn't as simple as the attraction of opposites, more a matter of half-glimpsed recognitions. Friendship is a Venn diagram, not an inhabiting of the same space, and the philosopher Montaigne had it right: 'If you press me to tell why I loved him, I can say very little. It was because he was he, and I was I.'

I didn't see him for a fortnight or so. Indeed I remember thinking he must have abandoned his studies, the better to contrive the destruction of the college with a thermonuclear device, for he didn't show up at his weekly tutorials. I'd made a point of watching out for him. But then, towards the end of April, I noticed him at a lecture, alone, as was his custom, at the back of Theatre L. Mild scoffs issued forth from him as it was alleged from the dais that the literary works of Gerard Manley Hopkins repaid study or gave any sort of pleasure. Students turned to glower at his gum-chewing sternness, an Easter Island statue in heart-attack pink. To one he offered that gesture of sexually tinged aspersion involving the right hand's middle finger. Soon afterwards he appeared to be feigning sleep or actually sleeping, forehead on the desk before him. He approached me when the talk was over, and I was surprised to see he was carrying a black plastic refuse-sack from which he produced a guitar.

The departing lecturer was denounced, somewhat unfairly, as 'Harry the Talking Haemorrhoid' before the matter at hand was raised. He'd been teaching himself Stranglers riffs, he explained with some reticence. The instrument was a bass. He'd found it in a skip on Gordon Street in the town. A 1970s 'Violin' Höfner, spray-gunned green, white and gold by no craftsman, so that jags of its original black scowled through the tricolour here and there. It lacked its original pick-ups and the action was so wrecked that to hold down a high B made your wrist and knuckles ache. Poor navvy, it looked as though it had been used to smash down a door. He had stolen a set of strings for it, but hadn't an amp. Would I know where to score one, cheap?

In truth, I was so fiercely flattered he thought me worth asking that I blushed to the meats of my teeth. It is the only blush of my life that I actually remember. Once or twice, it has coloured my dreams.

As it happened, my brother Shay had recently quit a band, a long story that would embarrass several people if I went into it here. Taking up space in the dustbowl of his bedroom was a Marshall JCM 800 bass amplifier. It was the size of a washing machine and into it had been stuffed Shay's hopes, along with every red cent he scrimped ten months to pay for it from his part-time job cleaning the toilets at Luton Airport. He had a degree in English and Politics but the employers of Bedfordshire weren't looking for that. A girlfriend was on the scene and so he didn't wish to leave the town. Also, although he denied this, he was something of a home-bird. He was never a good bass player but had resolved to be loud, one admirable and far from unique compromise.

I had nothing to barter with Shay but I wanted to impress Fran. I sought a loan of the amp, but my brother's refusal was stern, for even though it was a now silenced reminder of gruesome failure, he didn't want to let it go. I've noticed this curious stubbornness in many people of Irish heritage. We like to hang on to the evidence that something didn't work out: wedding photos, a miraculous medal, a passport.

Undaunted, I asked if we might buy it on credit, the repayments to come weekly, interest added. This amounted to seeking a loan from my brother in order to buy something from my brother, a commodity I didn't need, except for the status it would confer on me: not a wise or sane model for progress, you might think, but actually, years later, in the era of the Single Currency crisis, all Europe was run on this Company Store basis. My thinking was that if I skipped a pint or four on a Friday night in the Trap, my sacrifice could be put to use. Asked by Shay what I intended to supply by way of collateral, I found myself puzzled, outdrawn. I wasn't entirely sure what collateral was, but I suspected I was in no position to supply it.

He pointed out that the loan I had in mind would take seventy-two years to be repaid, by which point he was planning on being dead. It became a weird contest between us, a matter of pride – even of ideological skirmishing. Shay professed Trotskyism in those years, sullenly, beadily, with absolutely no concession to the realities of human nature, as all religions ought to be professed. Property was theft; the Workers' Republic would abolish it. From each according to his abilities, this was his credo, to each according to his needs. But when the contention was turned back on him as a demand for the amp, he would out-Thatcher the *Daily Mail* with his scalding refusals and his defence of private ownership. 'That amp is fukken *mine*, you work-shy fukken spazz,' he'd roar, the vein in his forehead a throbbing purple glow-worm. Worse were the occasions when he shooed you away wordlessly, never looking up from his *Collected Speeches of Lenin* as you slunk to your pit of furies.

Our wranglings went on for a tortuous fortnight, to the amusement of my Dubliner dad and the grief of my mum. A farmer's only daughter from the loveliest part of County Clare, she found arguments in the home upsetting. Her own family was the mildest and closest I have known, possessed of that sensitised and intelligent courteousness country people sometimes have. Shay and I didn't give a jot. Onward we fenced. His method of awakening me was cruel. He'd creep into my room before dawn, slip over my ears the headphones now connected to the amp, then BLAST out the brutal triangular riff of Deep Purple's 'Smoke on the Water', fleeing before I could recover sufficiently to strangle him. Once, in my later life, I had the privilege of meeting Jon Lord, Purple's matchless keyboardist, a Paderewski of the Hammond Organ, and I was honoured to shake the hand that played the mesmeric blues solo on 'Lazy', but back when I was a teenager I adopted the stance of my peers: Deep Purple were lumbering dinosaurs, mired in sludgy pomp, sinking to deserved extinction. They would wallow in the Hades of the twenty-minute drum solo, where mules and apes cavort. Shay insisted I was wrong, they'd outlast all the fads. He wouldn't collaborate with any fan of punk and New Wave. It would offend the dark lords of rock. Elvis Costello, whom I admired, 'looked like an accountant doing four years for fraud'. Siouxsie Sioux was clearly 'mad in the head'. Adam and the Ants? 'Fuck me wept.' To loan me his amp would be handing a shotgun to a toddler. The consequences could be awful, even lethal.

I'd totter home from the Trap to find Shay already polishing his denunciations, his tactic being to get in early with the sucker-punch of his NO before the question had a chance to be restated. He'd call me a scrounger. I'd call him a contra. Icons of Che and Fidel scowled down upon his bed, over his neatly shelved childhood collection of Airfix fighter bombers and battleships, but his mercenary little heart belonged to The Man, I chided. 'Boil my cock,' he'd retort. The high-water mark of my outrage came one memorable midnight, when, almost tearful with anger at being so long denied my quarry, I drew myself up to the full feather of my outrage and bawled, '*What would Nelson Mandela do?*' The excoriation of his laughter still scorches.

My sister Molly had been killed some years previous to these events, suddenly, in an accident in the Dublin neighbourhood of Glasnevin, where we lived at that long-gone time. The driver was drunk. Molly was crossing the road.

The presents for her seventh birthday were hidden in my mum's wardrobe, and there they remained many months after the funeral because no one could bear to throw them away. You can imagine the grief. I've no words to describe it. To see a woman cradle the body of her seven-year-old girl a last time, a father knelt weeping at the lip of a grave, is to know that certain lives meet the undeserved cruelty that can never be overcome, only survived. My dad worked as a keeper in Dublin's beautiful Victorian zoo, a job he adored, but he couldn't do it any more. For a time he was unable to leave our house at all; he couldn't forgive the road, or the town. Similar work came up in England. My mother was reluctant. But my father felt that England was his only option now. The shop steward at his union, which was organised across the two islands, put in a strong word, and we went. Dad's brothers were in England, and three of my mother's sisters. All but two of my thirty first cousins were born there. My mother, numbed by pain, and by broken, shipwrecked love for him, agreed to the move while fearing it. Molly, to my parents, and to my brother and me, had not disappeared – how could it be possible? – but subsisted in the air of our family's life like dew on the apples of autumn. We could scarcely even bear to mention her name. But her absence sat to every meal, every little event and great, every silence of Sunday morning or Christmas night. She rained on our windows and arose from the sweet william and meadowsweet Dad grew in our new home's garden. My parents had been through the worst hurt on this earth. Molly must have looked from our eyes.

What I'm about to say is ridiculous, but the fact is the fact. Something in the tussle about that amp wasn't funny.

The youngest child is often the centrifuge of a family. Molly was one of those objectively gorgeous and mischievous kids for whom siblings, especially brothers, are drawn to compete. Whenever Shay and I had stupid fights – and we fought all the time – I felt we were still fighting for my sister's approval, that one of us would gain the prize and the other would be shamed. It was perhaps a means of not forgetting her while learning to say goodbye, a realisation I was beginning to approach in the month I met Fran. It's but one of the ways in which his appearance in my life revealed what had long been there.

In the end, I stole the wretched thing, one rainy Sunday afternoon when Shay was away addressing a meeting of the Cambridge University branch of the Socialist Workers' Party. (Yes I know.) They were empathising over canapés with the working class of El Salvador or passing resolutions demanding of President Reagan that he, like, totally resign, as the rusted supermarket trolley I'd unearthed in Dad's garden shed trundled from our house, heavily burdened. An Agatha Christie fan, I'd broken the kitchen window to simulate a burglary, but Shay, no fool, wasn't fooled. Trotskyites can be sceptical, even in the face of evidence. Hence the story of the 1980s British Labour Party. Shay didn't speak to me for nearly two months and would eventually get his vengeance by melting holes in my Buzzcocks albums with a cigarette lighter. Later we managed to parlay our battle into a joking kind of truce, not without the shedding of tears. He emigrated to New Zealand in 1991 and rarely comes home any more. He's a research officer for that country's National Council of Trade Unions, was a speechwriter for Prime Minister Helen Clark, and hopes to stand for

election next year. But whenever I hear 'Smoke on the Water', my brother's in the room, the sweetest and funniest man I've had the blessing to know, and one of the smartest, too. His Christmas card two years ago featured an improvised speech bubble coming from Baby Jesus's cradle. It said 'Deep Purple rock, you thieving Tory sod.' My daughter is 'Molly Shay' for my sister and brother, whose haughty, Iberian looks she has, like many with West of Ireland blood.

Forgive me. I run ahead of myself.

It wouldn't be fair to accuse Fran of giving me the impression he was a brilliant musician. But oddly, that was the impression I had. Wilde wrote somewhere, 'I have set myself to music', and I assumed Fran was doing something similar, or trying to. But when I unveiled the stolen amp, he seemed peevish and afraid, challenged as he would now be to produce. Having sought so long, he was reluctant to find: a recurring motif in the outlook of all maddening people. You could no more predict Fran's behaviour than sculpt a statue of the sky. Doing the obvious was not in his kit. Instead he told me he'd been feeling 'pangsious', an adjective he'd invented, a compound of 'anxious' and 'pang'. The bass guitar was not his instrument, he had come to discern. He was ringing himself up on this matter.

He got rid of the bass, acquired a cheap Takeharu-copy acoustic, and I hefted the amp into the artificial lake on the campus one night, in a rainstorm of guilt and fear. I was convinced that if I tried to sell it I would be arrested and end up in court and that the resulting criminal record would bring the horror that I would never be permitted entry to the United States. It was Fran who told me this, and who helped me ditch the amp. Emigration was my only ambition

at the time – well, the only one I ⌐
in public. We crooks with a past haσ
The college was demolished some yea⌐
remains, now centre of a leafy Business Ⴑ
that lake has ever yet been drained. Perhaps tι
gists of the twenty-seventh century will find an aη
the sludge and marvel at the strange rites of those pε

Amp sunk, Fran began offering me snatches of his lyrics, screeds of disconnected fustian and euphonious platitudes that sounded for all the world, if I'm absolutely honest, like well-meaning advertising copy. 'Hope is a Breath Away'. 'Love is a Home'. Unobjectionable burbles, yes, but a tad Eurovisionary in outlook, hardly the effusions of a rebel. At best you imagined them accompanied on synth by an eyes-closed Rick Wakeman or one of that Moogy fraternity. Had you been involved in the marketing of toothpaste, life insurance or cholesterol medication, Fran's luminescent visions of couples running hand-in-hand through poppy fields in the rain would have set your cash-flow projections ablaze. As it was, they seemed to me vacuous and queerly unoriginal, produced, as they were, by a youth who had a self-pierced nipple and claimed an addiction to three-way sex. You wondered who he was trying to impress. Himself, perhaps.

The way I saw it at the time was that the world had an ocean of songs. We'd bob across it in our grubby boat, making for nowhere in particular, having a little fun and fishing on the way. In any case, nobody wants to hear original material from a busker. That's like listening to music made by someone else's toddlers: nice, even admirable, you'd bang your tambourine if asked, but really you'd prefer Stevie er. The sooner Fran abandoned what I saw as a phase, the better. Of course, I didn't say this. He was my friend, so I listened. Further spillages of numbing nothingness issued forth from his pen. But one day, something small and important changed. A lyric of Fran's made me laugh.

It was by no means Cole Porter. But it had something, all the same. Call it juice, personality, a sense of itself. It reminded you of talking to him at a bus stop, had a sardonic ordinariness I found pleasing, and also a certain stance. It was Fran put into metre and nothing much more. John Lennon said the secret of song-writing is no secret at all: say what you mean and set it to a backbeat. He read me the lines and I chuckled.

> *Rang myself up.*
> *But the answerphone threw me.*
> *Telephone screamed.*
> *I was pangsious and blue.*
> *Mummy was out.*
> *I was weird and self-conscious.*
> *Rang myself up.*
> *Beast who answered was you.*

'Who's it about, Fran?'

He looked at me strangely.

'There are times, Robert Goulding, when your shallowness has hidden depths. Come – thou shalt buy me chips.'

Two

The Humanities Building at the Poly, now long gone to rubble, was a stomach-punch of 1960s modernism. Some architect who lived in Perugia or a converted rectory in the shires had reckoned that a neo-Stalinist tower block was just the setting required to get your youthful creativity spurting. Here and about were abstract sculptural works of frightening repellence and brutality, on which students hung coats or hats. The lifts didn't work. The toilets rarely flushed. I've no doubt it won many awards. Fran's nickname for the campus – 'Bucharest Airport' – will give you a sense of the scene.

On the ninth floor of Humanities was located the Department of Ethics, Comparative Religion and Theology, for obvious reasons a rarely visited place. The tumbleweed drifting the landing would very occasionally be disturbed by God-bothering students, an endangered species, even at the time, and by trysting undergraduate couples with no other venue for their ardour than those corridors hung with posters of popes and Michelangelo's 'David' and Jonathan Livingston Seagull in uplifting silhouette.

Pious readers will know of the Stations of the Cross, a

series of representations, sculptural or pictorial, depicting fourteen important moments during the last earthly hours of Our Saviour. I'm sorry to say that the student body had sacrilegiously appropriated the terminology of the Stations into the euphemism of its erotic slang. In B9, getting to 'The First Station' meant holding hands while French-kissing. Arrival at the Fifth involved manual stimulation through underwear (preferably someone else's). Six was unzippering or de-knickering. Seven I don't wish to go into. Gaining the Eighth meant you'd persuaded your co-conspirator of the time-honoured biblical injunction that it's better to give than to receive. Fortunate to progress beyond Nine, your gratitude to the heavens was deep. Not that I myself had ever forged so far along the road. On this pilgrimage I was a Four, if that. The only person I'd ever gone to bed with was myself. I suspected that my self and I would be better just as friends. But we were finding it hard to split up.

There was an almost impressive view of the car factory from the landing's wall-sized windows, which had never been washed since the day they were installed. They were splattered on the outside with asterisks of guano, on the inside with obscene graffito: blasphemies, oaths, defamations of the innocent; rude diagrams, commemorative boastings. Beyond the town, the fields of mushroom-tunnels and the airport might be seen, and the trading estate where most of my school friends worked or pushed prams. It wasn't a vista that filled you with hosannas. But if you were willing to tolerate the sighing, the glimpsed entanglements in doorways, the assorted sounds of slobbering and ecumenical sucking, all the tingle-tinged soundtrack of teenage erogeneity, B9 could be a poorboy's oasis.

Fran and I started to go there in breaks between lectures, armed with our guitars and my grimy copy of *Bert Weedon's Monster Chord-book*, Fran with his jotters of lyrics. By then, there were few major scales in which I couldn't twang around, with the possible exception of B-flat. G, C and D are good keys for the developing guitarist, their chord progressions easy and related minors doable, their dominants and subdominants attainable by any human being with normal levels of motor skill, and you can sophisticate with a little blues lick or a nifty jazzy sixth as confidence grows in the fingers. B-flat is a nightmare, since it involves you in D-sharp or a capo, which latter I was always forgetting or mysteriously losing, often because it had been stolen by Shay. Fran's natural key was B-flat.

His baritone was hesitant, as though he was apologising for it. You couldn't have called it powerful. That would all come later. But its combination of rawness and reluctance was like nothing I had heard, except maybe in Aretha Franklin's early recordings for Atlantic, a collection of which glories my dad once disappointedly received in return for his Green Shield stamps. The Christniks came and went, and increasingly stayed, as Fran paced the charmless corridor that overlooked the Science Department car park, shaking his fist at the lake and the recently erected student gymnasium ('Asbestos Towers'), as though he resented the existence of both. He trembled when he sang. He clutched at the air. He pushed his hands through his fringe, the great tart. I didn't know that I would one night see him on the stage of the Hollywood Bowl, on his knees like James Brown, pleading with the spotlights, my frantic fingers scurrying what felt like the ten-mile length of my fretboard while the crowd chanted his name in roared unison. They'd want him to whirl the mic by the flex, lasso it, make it scream, smash a tambourine against the floor. All this would happen. But not yet. He was eighteen and a few months when he first sang in my presence. You'd think the moment would be burnt into my memory but it isn't. What I remember is my hope that he'd sing like a hero. Which by Jaypers he did. Yes, Fran always had the pipes. It just took him a while to locate them.

FROM FRAN'S FINAL INTERVIEW

I play guitar better than most, but I don't rate myself much of a singer. I can do it. That's all. It's not much. Singing in't about singing, it's about what you got to say. Or what you see. Singing's just looking. If you can talk, you can sing . . . Elvis wasn't the singer Sinatra was. It's context. People say Dylan couldn't sing. To me, that's balls. His diction's perfection. His phrasing. His breathing. Dylan leads to Patti Smith, leads to John Lydon. And on you go. I'm a very average and limited singer in a technical sense. I'd have loved to be Roy Orbison. But I weren't. So you do what you can. And that's all I done. What I could. You know? And then some . . . And this thing about everyone saying I worked hard to connect with the audience? It's cool to get a compliment but I never. People think you're the cat's miaow. But it's only breathing, nothing else. What it was, I shut me eyes and went somewhere private. That's all. Billie Holiday's a singer. Etta James. Johnny Cash. Townes Van Zandt. Tim Hardin. The folk singer, Odetta – she's a genius, to me. But then singing's only a part of the game, not even the main one. Lou Reed can't sing at all. But can he *sing*? Damn straight. Perfection's too easy. I like flaws.

Singing can change things. It's a lowering of borders. You'll have noticed that you croon like Ole Blue Eyes in the shower, that you yodel in the car while the traffic lights watch, or do your Jagger for the chorusing dishwasher when the house is empty. But many of us, invited to serenade a cluster of upraised, kindly faces would rather be poked in the eye. Hardest is to sing to one person in a room. Lovers might risk it, or parents and children, but if your colleague at the office said 'sing to me, damn you', you'd back towards the door, smiling tensely. Perhaps because singing is the only music made by the body alone, a lack of wariness is required for any adult to sing before another. And oddly, once you've sung, how you see one another is recalibrated, particularly if you've managed to get through an entire song. Three minutes is an immensely long time for someone to listen. Even spouses don't listen uninterruptedly for three minutes. If they did, we'd have a lot more divorce. You've done an intimate thing. And the listener has, too. You've shown who you are – who you wish you were, maybe, Thus, with Francis and me.

My daughter once asked if it's possible to tell when a boy is secretly insincere. I told her: ask him to sing to you. If he won't, he's a waste. If he does, he's a might. Simplistic, perhaps, but it's not the worst touchstone. If a person won't sing, he's hiding.

I had rarely sung to anyone. Neither had Fran. But the fact that I wasn't great at it diminished no possibilities. I remember his gentleness, that strange, new colour. 'Sing, Rob. It's nothing. You'll feel seven years younger. Sing like there's nobody listening.' My voice was a croak, but with practise it improved. The bleat pressing up from my lungs was itself. Resistant to the air it was meeting, admittedly, but still, *my* bleat, my own. There was also what singing was doing to my friend. It's hard to find the metaphor. Say it took off his masks. Fran was becoming possible.

Trust. Reliance. Call it what you will. The opposite of no isn't yes, it's maybe. Songs ended, began, were abandoned, reworked, and somewhere in the changed weather Fran began revealing details of his childhood. His early years in England with his adopters were horrific. Taken from them and placed in an institution, he 'kept quiet and read books', hoping he'd 'live there for ever'. He told me more of the Rotherham couple that fostered him at the age of nine from the residential home. 'West-of-Irish', from the isthmus connecting Loughs Corrib and Mask, the place where *The Quiet Man* was filmed. They showed him photographs and postcards, taught him little songs in Irish. They tried to be kind. It confused him. Long accustomed to dread, he found silences terrifying. By the time he came to know that he wouldn't be beaten for speaking, that he didn't need to steal food or hide himself before sleeping, other pains and separations had grown. His foster-parents were religious and they found themselves unable to deal with the teenager he became: his clothes, his feelings, the particular writers he was drawn to, the music he adored, 'the sex thing'. His foster-father, a night watchman at Maltby Colliery, was 'a good man, but we didn't like one another'. The quarrels grew violent. At sixteen Fran left, hitching south, sleeping rough, begging or thieving around the town of Boston, Lincolnshire before making an eventual way down to Bedfordshire, where he'd hoped to find casual work on a farm. A librarian at Luton Library caught him stealing a book. A woman of compassion, she didn't call the police but gave him the price of a meal, helped him apply for welfare and encouraged him to enrol at the Poly. She tried to make him contact his fosterers back in Rotherham but he wouldn't. To me he never spoke of them bitterly, but always in the past tense. They came from the village of Cong, County Mayo, had brought him there on holiday the year he turned twelve. Cong was beautiful, he told me. The people 'talked quiet'. They were gentle to a frightened boy who didn't look like their own but who bore an Irish name. They had let him milk cows. Taken him out on the bog. 'You're a grand little maneen, God love you.' Sometimes the children in Cong had looked at him curiously, but never with hatred, not once. It was clear that these few days had been precious to Fran, that he clung to them as a rare memory of uncomplicated peace, and was grateful and, in an odd way, proud. In later years, when baffled journalists requested a definition of his nationality, he'd sometimes give the answer 'Viet Cong'.

Here I apologise to the scholars burdened with penetrating my cranium. They deserved better than I was wired to give. The novelist Seamus Price was Professor of English, the peerless Amina Ali my Sociology tutor, a woman of such knowledge and tactful kindliness that words crumble in describing what I squandered. I bow before the executioner for the desert of wasted chances, but I have promised to be honest in this chronicle of my crimes. Essays went unwritten. Assignments weren't met. The library, centrally heated and comprehensively stocked, was untroubled by my malodorous presence. Had I all to do again, I can't promise it would be different, for there was an unhappiness in my heart that was driving me towards music, and what's anyone to do, thus driven? Soon, I came to realise that pretty much the only reason I was going in to the college every day was to play the guitar and listen to Francis Mulvey sing, and, funds permitting, to get slaughtered.

Shakespeare, Scott Fitzgerald, they were pleasant enough interruptions, coordinates through which you had to pass in order to reach a destination, but no longer the point of the journey. Words on a page were only words on a page but a song needed someone to love it by singing. I counted every minute, every millisecond, until lunchtime. Fran and I would adjourn to the lofty Parnassus of B9, each of us pretending a casualness I don't think we felt. It was like wandering into a confetti storm of song-scraps and traded hopes. Whatever discomfiture and self-recognition the songs were aiming at became the reason for existing at all. Most love stories begin with a Krakatoa of irrationality. Mine is no exception.

Scrawny cherry trees stood sentry along the walkway that led from the Arts Block to the canteen. Dr Ali said that when they flowered it was time for serious revision, because the exams would be fast approaching. Alas, their blossoms fell on my indolence and doom. I hocked my textbooks for a motorbike jacket, bleached my hair with lemon juice, pierced my earlobes with the needle previously used by Dad to mend punctures in our footballs, even contemplated shaving off my eyebrows because Fran bet me I wouldn't. By mid-May, we started cutting lectures, then abandoning them completely. The wider world was beset by troubling events: Britain and Argentina at war in the South Atlantic, Duran Duran riding high in the charts. All of it passed us by.

Mum and Dad had scrimped hard to give me the start they never enjoyed. I'd made a mess of applying for a local authority grant, and the small scholarship I was grateful to have received from Luton Town Council covered only half my tuition. Books were expensive, and then there was my keep. I earned a little by collecting glasses and emptying ashtrays in the Trap but it was really only pocket money, a few pounds a night, and it was spent at the very counter over which it was paid. I wish I could say I made more of my chances. But the facts are the facts. Fran and I were cutting loose. We didn't so much bite the hand that feeds as devour it right up to the armpit. We'd often remain in B9 for ten straight hours. We came to regard it as our private Cavern Club, our place of first hopes. Mum, I'm so sorry. I know what you gave me. But, presented with the chance to sell my soul to rock and roll, I didn't think about it long. I lunged.

Secretly, somewhat guiltily, I admired many genres of music. My dad's Benny Goodman albums meant as much to me as did Slaughter and the Dogs or the Clash. After Patti Smith's *Horses*, the record that set my dreams ablaze, the soundtrack of Lionel Bart's *Oliver!* that we had in the house was my desert island disc. I was dizzied by the way Nelson Riddle's blowsy brass lit up Frank Sinatra's 'Fly

Me to the Moon', still the sexiest song I know. *My Fair Lady* I preferred to *Exile on Main Street*, not a thing you admitted back then. But Fran was the least prejudiced singer I'd ever met. He adored the Mud number 'Lonely This Christmas' but was nuanced on all post-Ziggy-Stardust-Bowie: a treasury I worshipped with such eye-popping intensity that I'd have genuflected before 'Ashes to Ashes' and 'Fashion'. But it wasn't a pose, an empty-headed eclecticism; it was simply that he was like a child when it came to a song. When he reckoned it sucked, he wouldn't sing it at all, no matter the hipster that made it. He'd do 'Stranded in the Jungle' by the New York Dolls, or a tornado of rocket fuel from Iggy Pop and the Stooges, segueing into 'You Sexy Thing' by Hot Chocolate or Shakin' Stevens' 'Green Door' by way of The Pistols' 'No Feelings'. The most evocative love song ever penned, in his view? 'Love Me Like a Reptile' by Motörhead. He raved of Tony Bennett, loved his 'loosey-juicy' style. He pledged allegiance to T-Rex, ordained Nina Simone the greatest soprano since Callas, bigged the diction of Christy Moore. I disliked all synth-bands. He praised Depeche Mode. Meat Loaf, an unlikely hero for a punk fan, perhaps, he loved with apostolic fervour. He thought *Bat Out of Hell* a more consistent achievement than *Sergeant Pepper*. I thought it a parody of Springsteen. Disco was regarded by student cognoscenti as naff, but Fran would do a Donna Summer or 'Stayin' Alive', chucking slices of The Trammps, Chic and Imagination into his blustery covers of Blondie. I've seen idiot hacks write that he learned his exquisite falsetto from 'the counter-tenors of grand opera'. He learned it from Barry Gibb.

For an absent-minded boy – he regularly forgot what day it was – his memory for lyrics was remarkable. Rockabilly enthralled him; he'd gibber like Elvis on speed, clawing at the air as he belted out Gene Vincent's 'Be-Bop-A-Lula' to the audience of filing cabinets and pigeonholes. Fran had a slight limp, the result of an injury sustained as a child, but often he claimed a brotherly empathy with Gene, whose motorbike accident in 1955 left him in lifelong pain. 'We cripples have to stick together, Roberto.' He'd have a crack at a traditional ballad when the mood was upon him, which surprisingly frequently it was. If you've never seen 'Scots Wha Hae' sung by a Viet-Yorkshire-Irish boy in tartan bondage trousers and a Dead Kennedys T-shirt your youth was poorer than mine. Robert Burns he announced 'the Baudelaire of glam rock', magnificently rolling his r's in the manner of a person who has never actually been to Scotland but has seen it on the television while stoned.

We ransacked my dad's collection of American country records, learned whatever songs lit our candle – usually plunky three-chord heartbreakers about cowboys dumping waitresses – and then hocked the albums in a hippy kip called Pet Sounds, a basement smelling faintly of cooking oil. They demurred at the idea of offering us anything for the rare Luther Perkins and Merle Haggard. Those we flogged in Brereton's pawnshop in the town. Fran was avid to spend the loot on a couple of Chinese rocks so we could get pigged out of our tits while listening to Richard Hell and the Voidoids, but I was very afraid of heroin, I am relieved to say, and anyway, I felt he was only testing me. With the dough, and some of his own, we bought a second-hand microphone and a little Vox AC30 amp, a cutie that worked off a car battery and even had a built-in echo that gave you a touch of Sun Studios. We nailed down 'Blue Moon of Kentucky' and 'That's All Right, Mama', Fran substituting a satanic screech for every Presleyean *uh-huh-huh*. I began to see in him a seriousness I'd never noticed before. Maybe 'seriousness' is not the right word: more a patience. What I mean is that he revealed himself as a stickler for getting it *right*, for going at a song any number of times, sometimes literally scores, whatever it took, to drill to what he felt was its heart. Playing a song was easy. *Playing* it wasn't. He taught me what little I ever knew about the mysteries of dynamics, playing quiet on the bridge, sometimes not playing at all, or shifting up a key for the final chorus to 'whaang the mother on home'. Tempo drops, up-strums, dropping out the bass. He'd make me listen to blues or gospel tapes he'd stolen in town: Son House and Muddy Waters, Mahalia Jackson, Sister Rosetta Tharpe, the Louvin Brothers' version of 'Cash on the Barrelhead', Dylan's *Slow Train Coming* and *Saved*. Patsy Cline's recordings he adored for the sparseness of their production. 'Nothing is wasted. *Listen.* You're not *listening.* That's a snare and a *pedal steel.* And a fiddle on the middle eight. There's *nothing* on that record in't needed.'

I still remember the whole day it took us to learn the Stones' 'Brown Sugar'.

Yeah, yeah, yeah. WOOO.

My glimmertwin buddy. My Fran.

The most striking thing about him? He just didn't care. It was a stage of his life when he couldn't tell a lie. The lies would all come later.

FROM FIRST YEAR EXAMINATION PAPER, DEPARTMENT OF ENGLISH LITERATURE, STANTON POLYTECHNIC, 2nd JUNE 1982

Q: *Write an essay of 1000 words responding to William Wordsworth's poem 'Composed by the Side of Grasmere Lake' (1806). What is of value in the poem? Why is it regarded as an important text in the evolution of the Romantic Movement? Support your answer by appropriate quotation.*

Answer given by candidate Francis Mulvey:

WHAT I SAW BY THE LAKE NEAR MY VILLAGE, VIETNAM

CLOUDS, vomiting flame, reflect on
    mirrored lake
Through the gold west, and hell-copters flit
By death-splintered air to scuttered murder,
    spit
Upon the naked orphans, forsaken.
Sleep on, Wordsworth, saint of rainy
    nowheres,
As I hid among the reeds, quaked,
    concealed
At speechless distance, you sang, fey
    hypocrite
Of daffodils and Dorothies, of tea and cake.
Poetry a mirror? To blinkered men in
    libraries

Choking on similes. Metaphor-beguiled.
And still you teach what only seems,
But never the screams of a motherless child.
Be thankful, thou, for Worthless Words.
They pay the rent, feed England's dreams.

It was my custom, as a lad, to inflict myself on a diary. The punk rock Pepys, I was not. I started it on the night of my sixteenth birthday but I'll spare you my existentialist gloom. I think I kept it going for one reason only, which is that Dad always told me I couldn't persevere, that I was doomed to be a perpetual starter. I wrote it to spite him, a more common reason for artistic endeavour than is sometimes understood. Poor Dad. He was a compelling muse.

It's because of that diary that I know the date on which Fran and I first offered ourselves to the public: 16th of June 1982, 41st birthday of Lamont Dozier, the Motown song-writer we both reckoned the *primus inter pares*. Fran felt that this anniversary would prove auspicious, and I allowed him to persuade me, though in truth I was petrified. Lacking even the money for the bus fare, we walked the three miles from college into town, hefting our instruments, amp and car battery on our girlish backs.

'It was the hottest day ever recorded in Luton,' my journal informs me. Many of the town's youthful goddesses were wearing not much. There is no sexier bower in the world than a municipal park in summertime, its lawns bedecked with flocks of maidenly allurement, abdomens bared to the rays. By the time we got to St George's Square I was in a miasma of piggish sweat, produced, I think now, by the lust and the nervousness as much by the merciless sun. Even Fran appeared uptight, which he almost never did. I had on jeans with a lumberjack shirt I'd stolen from Shay. Fran's look was Pretty in Pink. We unbagged the guitars, smoked a joint in a doorway and downed a preludial naggin of vodka.

At that point, an extraordinary thing happened. Our family GP, Dr Shillibeer, emerged from the splendid art deco town hall, looking stately and plump and open for business. He was clad in a blazer with a rose in its lapel. In his wake followed a party of persons with notebooks. Dr Shillibeer saluted me amiably, asked after my parents, and mentioned, as though this were the most unremarkable of occurrences, that his companions were psychiatric nurses from East Berlin. What they were doing in Luton he didn't explain. Wishing they weren't, perhaps. As Fran began to tune up, and I began to tune out, they clustered, led by Dr Shillibeer, in a frightening crescent around us. One of them produced a camera.

I have played Wembley Arena, Elland Road and Yankee Stadium, Knebworth Rock Festival, the Budokan, the Fillmore San Francisco, before the endless meadows of Glastonbury and hundreds of thousands in Central Park. The hands typing these words have held Rory Gallagher's 1961 Stratocaster, and the manuscript of William Faulkner's *As I Lay Dying* in the late genius's Oxford, Mississippi mansion. But I can promise you that I never felt a knot of apprehensiveness so terrifyingly pure as the one those psychiatric nurses tied in my throat.

David Mamet says the purpose of theatre is to create 'cleansing awe'. That's what seemed to come over me. Fran started into a twelve-bar boogie played with feline sloth.

My hands were so sodden with perspiration that for a moment I couldn't find purchase on my strings, and silently I faced the verdict that I must slink from the scene, scorched by my father's mockery. And then Fran belted into 'Blue Suede Shoes', his right foot stomping time, a snarl about his lips, every sinew in him honed to assure anyone needing persuasion that a mean-eyed gunslinger had arrived. Lightning flickered in the snake-pit of my bowels. I strummed. The tourists yah'd. Fran turned to me and bellowed in Gaelic: '*Scaoil amach an boibilín*!', an exhortation politely translatable as 'Get out the little fella', although *boibilín* has ruder meanings. When you hear it, you are being encouraged to go for broke. I tried. But my *boibilín* wilted.

You've seen teenagers busking. They're often adorable but rarely the genuine stuff. 'Lola' by the Kinks and 'Blowin' in the Wind' and butcheries of Don McLean. Into this category I place my eighteen-year-old self, buds of toilet paper affixed to my neck where I'd cut myself shaving, tufts of recalcitrant fluff on my upper lip. I must have looked the sorriest virgin in all the south of England, which believe me is saying something. But Fran was already home. He'd everything he needed. Hiccuping like Buddy Holly, throwing pouty scowls at passing shoppers, he pawed at his crotch and swivelled like a stripper and karate-kicked the air before him. The crowd began to grow. By the time we hit the middle verse where the solo is meant to happen, he was jitterbugging with a woman who looked like a plain-clothes nun, so nobody was listening to the Scotty Moore licks I was murdering. Fran clambered a goodly way up a lamp post and gave a valedictory benediction to the throng before being persuaded back down by a constable. For one hideous moment I thought we were about to be nicked. Fran said it was a pity we weren't.

Neither of us had thought to bring a hat. Fran ordered me to remove a sock and pass it around, but even though I was ragingly jealous that the punters had preferred him to me, I felt no one deserved my sock. Dr Shillibeer, peace be upon him, gave us his boater, insisting we put it to use. Luton has a proud tradition of hat-making, so perhaps he didn't want to see us embarrassed before the German visitors. Four quid in coppers and two pfennig coins were all we collected, but our elation roared like a fever. We'd performed only seven minutes. Our prospects were good if you averaged them out, which, youthful and foolish, we did.

The whole of that afternoon we spent busking in the precinct as the sun blazed down on our initiation. Our clothes were sodden rags and our faces got burnt, and our throats grew sore from howling. From time to time we'd rest and enter the McDonald's for sustenance, counting out tenpences into hot little stacks translatable into burgers and water. Then back we would speed to what we now felt was our pitch, where we'd belt out the 'Blues in a Bottle', a song with three chords, like a lot of the killers. It says nothing very significant about human existence. But I can never hear it without experiencing again the intense pierce of longing that attends all memories of transition.

That night, Philip Larkin spoke at an event in Reading University, for which I'd obtained two tickets. I'd been wowed by his work since discovering *The Whitsun Weddings* in Luton library at the age of fourteen, and the thought that he was coming to read within a hitch-hike of our town had literally kept me awake. When I imagine the evening, as I sometimes do, even now, I see ranks of packed seats and hear *shush*-peppered silence, as the Elgar of bicycle clips and rain on the window is led to the spot-lit lectern. He was elderly by then. He died in '85. I pan around the hall as he opens a book. Below him, in the front row, two empty chairs gape.

'Poetry is over,' Fran slurred, in the Trap. He was always trying to shock you like that.

Three

M y guitar-playing improved but I failed my First Year exams. Dad clarified to me with a visual aid, his enraged and scarlet face, that if I didn't catch myself on and stop acting the maggot I could betake myself from the protection of his fatherly armpit to 'live in some dosshouse with winos'. It drove him berserk that my brother and I had begun to address him as 'Jimmy' and my mother by her own forename, Alice. Naturally, seeing his disconcertment unfurl into fury only served to encourage the over-familiarity. We kept it up, undaunted.

'Yo Jimzer. Hey Jimbo. ¡Ola, Jaime! Mon Jacques? Wee Shaymus!' My brother, on retiring to bed, would call Waltonistically 'Night, Jim-Bob.' This resulted in the increasingly resigned paternal valediction, 'Take the back of my arse and boil it.' I don't know how Alice could stand us.

Having refused to answer the examiners' questions on his hate-figure Wordsworth, Fran was invited to continue his studies elsewhere. A kindly tutor, Declan Kiely, was interceding on his behalf, but the Prince of Perfumed Grandiosities hitch-hiked to Paris. I was left to spend the summer being supportively bawled at by my father as I sweated for the August retakes. Worse, Dad secured for me a part-time position at his workplace, Whipsnade Zoo, I think as a means of teaching me the lesson he reckoned I sorely needed, that menial labour of the kind that must be endured by ingrates who mock their elders' efforts can be monotonous, tiring and dirty.

When you face at nine in the morning a flock of 130 unbiddable Chilean flamingos that are to be shepherded into the new enclosure they do not wish to enter, it doesn't matter as much as you might imagine that they are pretty. Dad would hand me a shovel. 'Wakey-wakey, College. Stop daisying around. The buffalos want mucking out when you're done.'

A postcard arrived from Le Fran wishing me 'bonne chance' in an irritating way. He was writing this outside Samuel Beckett's apartment building in the Boulevard Saint-Jacques. It was only a matter of time before 'he meets me'. I wondered what Monsieur Godot would make of Stanton Poly's *grand fromage*. I'll be honest. I was glad he was gone.

I learned a few songs, kept up at my practice, and with Shay attended the Rolling Stones concert at Ashton Gate stadium, Bristol. I can't say that musically it was the greatest event in history, but battling our way up the front for 'Satisfaction' was fun. To be within twenty feet of the chain-smoking scarecrow that turned out to be Keith Richards was to feel the joyous thunder that a summer day can bring when you're young and at a gig with your brother. The repeats came around, and I scraped the grades I needed. In congratulation, Jimmy and Alice bought me a second-hand electric guitar, a gorgeous cranberry-coloured Epiphone modelled on the Gibson ES-335. My daughter has it now. Second Year began. There was no sign of Fran. I fell in love.

G O'C, a dark-eyed student of Educational Psychology, chatted with me sometimes as we waited for the bus. Her parents had bought her a pony. It was clear that G and I were not of the same socio-economic stratum – Jimmy regarded horses as animals you backed at Kempton Park, not as pets to be ridden by sensitive teenage girls – but we clicked all the same, albeit briefly. She played dulcimer, knew a lot of English and Scottish traditional airs, and they gave us something to talk about. The death of my sister, to whom I was close, had taken my dearest female friend. I'd spent my teens attending a school where all but two of the teachers were at least technically men. I was tongue-tied around girls and I lacked Shay's handsomeness.

We'd been talking music at the bus stop now and again for a week when G invited me to her brother's 21st. This took place at the mother's vast house in Marston Moretaine – Daddy wasn't on the scene, having discovered adultery in Radlett – and to crunch my way up its gravel drive and enter that many-windowed restatement of the Tudor-cum-Georgian sluiced me with glinting dread. A professional DJ was inflicting the criminal works of Haircut 100 on the vulnerable young, and the cake was the size of Alice's fridge. I was the only boy in the marquee who had attended a soccer-playing school, but everyone was welcoming, especially G, who revealed to me the rudiments of how to approach 'a fork supper' before blushingly playing her dulcimer for the company over dessert, at Mum's somewhat sherried insistence. We walked in the garden. Well, one of the gardens. There were others, for roses and statuary. I still remember the sweetness of our hesitant little intimacies, the teeth-bashing, palate-licking, tongue-sucking, vacuum-creating, dare-I-open-my-eyes teenage kisses. She loved Joan Armatrading, *Mansfield Park* and *Pride and Prejudice*. Dear G, if you're reading this now, as who knows, you might, I send belated abjections for my gormlessness.

Asked to choose the setting for our first proper date, I opted for the dramatisation of *The Elephant Man* at St George's Theatre, Luton, thinking to impress my girl. 'People like ourselves' did not attend the theatre, Jimmy advised darkly. He employed this phrase with such frequency and certitude that Shay and I, to mock him, abbreviated it to 'PLO'. We were English kids by then. We thought this Irishman funny. But it was impossible to dislodge his scripturally detailed and finely calibrated credo, his personal Leviticus of prohibitions. The PLO washed their hair in the bath once a week, anything more being suspect. Male PLO members visited a proper barber's, not 'Peter's Hair Fashions' on Bute Street, a place we enjoyed telling him was 'unisex'. Ladies went to Mrs Ogilvy at Dion Creations on the roundabout for a blow-dry and set, and bought the Sunday roast in Freddie Baxter's coming home. Their men opened doors for them and regarded all females with knightly respect, hence no 'bra-burner' could ever emerge from, or belong to, this tribe whose women knew only the unending contentment that any 'normal woman' could want. The PLO did not eat vegetarian food, go on skiing holidays, vote for the Social Democratic Party, enjoy ballet if male, sports if female, practice transcendental meditation, name children after non-saints or geographical features such as rivers, drink wine or 'cocktails', listen to BBC Radio 4, read *The Times* or any broadsheet newspaper, wear any item of clothing usually associated with the opposite gender, play tennis, or watch it on the television, or even mention it in his presence, and they did NOT frequent any non-pantomime-offering theatre unless they happened to work in its cloakroom. 'Getting above yourself' was a grievous danger, Jimmy felt, since it invariably led to unhappiness, even suicide. The PLO ought to be grateful for being the PLO. I dismissed him as a reverse-snob. I should have listened.

During the opening moments, the distinguished actor Derek Chapman strode stark bollock-naked on to the stage and began assuming one by one the hideous disfigurements of unfortunate Joseph Merrick while an unseen narrator enumerated them. A sound issued forth from the velvet darkness beside me as he started flopping his head and drooling. It was the sound of G O'C exclaiming in horror 'Sweet Jeeeeeeeezis'. The next tryst I organised was to Peter Shaffer's *Equus*, a piece I thought she'd like, given her interest in ponies, but it turned out to be a somewhat shriek-inducing work in which a mentally unhinged boy called Alan discovers he wants to fuck a horse. The last bus to Marston Moretaine was quiet enough that night. G, usually a good sport, was disconcerted. I had sensed a little friction between us in recent weeks and was hoping there'd be more of it before the evening was through, perhaps in Mum's hydrangeas. But no. G explained that the trouble wasn't me, it was her. She'd love us to be friends. No, she really, really would. We didn't see each other again.

Fran returned from his boulevarding, sporting a goatee and cape, like some species of bebop-loving vampire. Inexplicably he was permitted to resume his studies, but it would be required of him to repeat First Year and apologise in writing for disrespecting his teachers, one of whom had all but threatened a departmental strike were Wordsworth ever traduced again. You can imagine Fran's private response, wretchedly ungrateful boy that he was, but I won't repeat it here. He penned the necessary apologies but refused to repeat, instead offering – yes, 'offering' – such was the arrogance – to sit all the First Year examinations the following weekend. This was allowed. To the fury of some, he scored A's and high B's in every paper.

Over the summer he'd been listening to George Brassens, Jacques Brel and *des chanteurs comme ça*, and claimed to have punctuated his idleness with polymorphous fornications, the consumption of absinthe, visits to Oscar and Jim out in Père Lachaise Cemetery, and narrow escapes from the pox. Paris offered *'diablerie'*, his new favourite word. ('Knucklehead' was his favourite old one.) He had enjoyed a married Russian air hostess in her hotel room one lunchtime and a Jesuit in civvies the same night at Les Halles. As for the evening, he'd gone boating with the bisexual twins from Grenoble – his eyes crossed in Proustian recollection. For a while he tried to persuade me that we should 'busk in French', since 'Luton was ready', he felt.

There was a view among the student body that Second Year didn't matter too much, that you could cruise your way along and no one would notice, so intent were the professors on caning the freshers and cramming the soon-to-be graduates. I'm afraid Fran and I took to that view like trout to the fly. By the end of October '82 we were up to our old ways, spending many more hours on the busk around town than on library, lecture or literature. One afternoon, while playing a solo outside Cavendish's shop, I saw Mum approaching down George Street with our neighbour, Mrs

Bavister, with whom she sometimes went to the pictures. I wouldn't have thought it possible that Fran and I could leg it so fast, ardent smokers and committed layabouts that we were. We even left our collection-hat behind on the pavement. That evening, over tea, she looked at me meaningfully before sliding a handful of coins across the table. The hat she kept and perhaps destroyed. Thank God, she said nothing to Jimmy.

By now, Fran and I had put together what a forgiving person, perhaps a social worker, might be prepared to call 'a set', a collection of numbers we were able to perform without actual murder being done, merely grievous bodily harm. We were the sixth-best buskers in Luton.

Occasionally the subject of forming a band would arise, since the sonic possibilities of two guitars are limited enough. Fran, initially, was reluctant. He'd get into one of his head-wrecking sermons on the dangers of 'ambition'. But even then, I knew this was camouflage. The busking thing was, well, a thing: an activity between us, a means of asserting the friendship. He'd never dream of stating it directly but he didn't want a stranger coming in. Other kids of that age reveal themselves in great lolloping doses, as though they're spraying you with a fire hose. Fran used an eyedropper. For a while I went along with his non-verbalised insistence that we maintain the little circular fort we'd built against the world. But you know what it is to be young. You're a taxi-light lit. And then, of course, there was Trez.

She and I disagree about the first time I saw her. She insists it was in Freshers' Week of 1982, that we were briefly introduced in the Trap by a couple of classmates, but of this I have no recollection. I know she began attending the

Poly that month, having dropped out of Harlow Tech. What is certain is that I was alone in the concourse on 3rd November '82, trying to put together an essay about Chaucer's *Canterbury Tales*, a work described by Fran as 'norvacious'. Strictly speaking, this adjective meant possessing the admirable qualities of the Stranglers, more precisely of their music, derivation being from the title of their album *Rattus Norvegicus*. But other things, and other persons, could possess norvaciousness also, an all-round peerless excellence. ('Bach is proper norvacious, I'm telling you, Rob.') For some reason I glanced up as the wind blew leaves down the corridor. It was my nineteenth birthday. Life was about to change.

A posse of boisterous Agricultural Science students – brilliantly, we called them 'Aggies' – had erected a stand near the commemorative bust of John Bunyan and were soliciting for membership of their society. 'Ag-Soc', they called it. Fran called it 'Goat-Soc'. They'd accuse him of being the leader of 'Quare-Soc'. Many were in that particularly creepy form of fancy dress comprising Afro wigs, 'comedy' breasts and granny's bloomers. Vulpine howls and unpleasant music involving the spangling of banjos added to the unimaginable sordor. They looked like an Appalachian novelist's first wet dream as they battered their bodhráns and twirled their shkirts and tweaked their polyurethane nipples. The compulsory inflatable sheep had been borrowed from Uncle Pat in the care home and was brandished at passers-by or offensively stroked or subjected to unprintable indignities. Drink had been taken, you felt. A 'blow-up rubber woman' clad in full Sligo Rovers strip was seated on one animal-handler's shoulders like a girlfriend at Woodstock.

It's at moments such as this that you wonder in your heart if universal suffrage is wise.

Anyhow, there I sat, steely, urban and superior, when the most inspiritingly lovely human I had ever seen in my life came walking down the corridor like a vision. Many student girls of the era dressed in her mode: layers of charity-shop puffery, adorned with crucifixes and rosary beads, unmatched Doc Martens, leather jacket. Early Madonna was the icon and the look was attainable on little money. But no one did it like Trez. No one ever would. I had died and gone to Oslo.

A very firework display of lewdnesses arose from the peasantry as she approached. Would she care to join Ag-Soc? The craic was only feersh. They'd give her an oul ride on the thractor. 'Go home and wank Dobbin,' she smiled, sweeping by. I took 'Dobbin' to be the name of a horse.

Yeats says that his muse Maud Gonne had 'beauty like a tightened bow'. Brother Clarence, the drunken fossil who taught us English at school had once seen her crossing O'Connell Bridge in Dublin and he'd tell us how right Yeats was. But I never knew what the words meant until I saw Sarah-Thérèse Sherlock. A stunner. An Oxfam Fatale.

FROM INTERVIEW WITH TREZ,
DECEMBER 2012, SKY ARTS TV

. . . I was nervous of Fran and Rob, to be honest. I mean, I fancied Fran, of course. Who didn't? The prettiest boy in the college. He'd this incredible self-confidence and seriousness. He walked like a model. I had a Saturday job in Bayliss Wright's, an art supplies shop in the town, and I'd sometimes see him come in and look at the books. One day I saw him buying this beautiful poster, a Marc Chagall drawing. I wanted to tell him it was lovely, just, you know, to say hi. But somehow I hadn't the nerve. It amazed me that he bought it, because he always looked really poor. You'd see him in the canteen, when no one was looking, taking leftover food off the plates. It'd break your heart. Hard to know what to do. I'd be buying an extra sandwich just to leave it, so he'd take it. You're young – y'know – you don't have the words. I should have gone over and just said hello. But I didn't. I don't know why.

Someone told me he was born in Vietnam, adopted over here. There was a bit of racism in the college, yeah. Definitely there was . . . I wouldn't want to overstate it, things were changing by then. But maybe that's too easy. You'd have to ask Fran. I don't think he likes to talk about it.

Then I remember one night there was an Anti-Apartheid disco in the Student Union Common Room. Fran was there with Robbie and he was dancing away by himself to this James Brown record. Fran I mean. Poor Robbie didn't dance. I remember thinking Fran was a star just from the way he was dancing. Ridiculous, I know. But I did. I knew he'd be famous. Daft, but that's the truth. I could picture him on *Top of the Pops*.

I had a little crush on him, for sure. But it didn't last long. I reckoned he was far too 'out there' to look at me twice. Also, I thought he wasn't interested in girls, I think everyone did. Maybe he thought that himself, I dunno. He wouldn't talk to you much. He was, what's the word – reserved. Always measuring. There was an astuteness about him that Rob didn't have. A girlfriend of mine used to joke, 'There goes Sly and Robbie.' Which wasn't accurate at all. What Fran had wasn't slyness. It was more, he wouldn't talk until he knew he could trust you. I didn't think of him as an extrovert. I still don't, now. He was one of those kids, you'd hear the cogs whirring away in his head. The cogs and the sound of the rain.

Did I think they were an item? Fran and Rob? Oh no way. I can see why you'd ask, but that wasn't the vibe. It was more that the two of them had this aura they'd be kind of transmitting: we're, like, serious heavy musos, don't be coming our way, we might be discussing, I dunno, guitar tunings. They'd finish one another's sentences, be laughing at jokes you couldn't make out. You'd see them sat in the canteen for about fourteen hours at a time, smoking, or reading the *NME*. Or they'd sit there saying nothing, which wasn't something you saw. Two males able to say nothing was pretty rare in my experience. Still is.

. . . Rob was absolutely lovely if you bumped into him by yourself. So clever and shy, and he listened to what you were saying, which wouldn't be a strength of most boys in those days. He was a nice-enough-looking lad but I don't think he knew it. He'd this beautiful head of curls. [*Laughs.*] You'd want to sink your fingers into them. There was a sadness around him, I guess, because of what happened with his sister. He didn't talk about it much but it was there all the same. There's this Irish poet, Paula Meehan, has a book called *The Man Who Was Marked By Winter*, and the title reminded me of Rob . . . His mum and dad were amazing people. Darlings, the two of them. His dad was a zookeeper in Whipsnade.

I was nominally a member of Declan Kiely's group tutorial that term but had missed all but one of its meetings. Well, why squander time discussing literature with the wisest scholar on the campus when you could be busking to glue-sniffers in the precinct? Trez, having completed First Year at Harlow, changed her mind about journalism and was permitted to enter Second Year Humanities at our Poly, doing English and History of Art. Told she'd been assigned to Declan's tutorial, I contracted a dose of the Prodigals. I wrote a note to my tutor that he's often quoted back to me. 'Dear Dr Kiely. I am sorry for my absence. The reasons were compelling and remarkable.'

There were ten of us in his group, but I looked at only one. Had you been there yourself, you'd understand. Let me contextualise by noting that in order to qualify for the Economic Journalism programme at Harlow Technical School you needed to have scored five high A Levels, including honours-level Mathematics and at least one language. I knew. I had tried for it, and failed. You didn't abandon this course to study paintings and novels. It made you unusual if you did.

She was rumoured to be from a London-Irish family,

had won prizes as a kid for fiddle and Irish dance. Years later she told me that she'd deliberately worn her shoes on the wrong feet as a child, to make her toes point out more while dancing. For days after a competition she'd be barely able to walk. But she always won the prize, or came close. I've sometimes been asked by a journalist to sum up Trez. That story is the one I tell.

There she was, seated beside me, while Declan talked books. She made notes at astonishing speed. The tattoo on her right forearm read 'Million dollar hero in a five and ten cents store', a line from a song by my favourite band of the era, the magnificent Radiators From Space. Sellotaped to the cover of her notes-folder was a portrait of David Bowie, the artwork from the sleeve of his godlike album *Low*. I think you're getting the picture.

It was a requirement that we write a major essay that year, on 'The Idea of the Sympathetic Imagination in Romantic Poetry.' Declan asked us to begin our pieces with a single short quotation that would sum up the idea in question. Most of us supplied dutiful drivellings from Shelley or Charles Lamb or from poor old Keats's dreary letters. But the epigraph chosen by Trez was a statement no Romantic could deny. It was taken from the writings of Felice and Boudleaux Bryant, 1952, as sung by the Everly Brothers.

'All I Have to do is Dream.'

TREZ

My brother Seán was a part of it. See, it was a time in my late teens when I was looking again at music.

Saying 'what do you want from this beautiful thing?'
You know? Is there something you could give it? Or
are you just wasting time? I couldn't see myself in
an orchestra or, you know, a string quartet. The life
of a professional musician can be seriously hard and
you couldn't face the uncertainty unless you loved
that music to death. And I loved it. But not to marry.
There were other things I was thinking about, professionally, for the future. So what do you do with your
music? Give it all up? Or play something else? And
there was other music I liked but I felt – I don't know
– a novice. Like that moment at a party when
someone stops singing because they've forgotten the
words, and you think, I'd love to join in. But would
everyone laugh? Sounds mad to say it now but I
figured I'd left it too late. All these questions – I
reckoned I should have asked them younger. I was
only eighteen or something. But that's how I felt.
'Age-rage', I call it. Ridiculous . . . But I thought, if
I don't find – some *vessel* I can put music into, then
all the hours of practice meant nothing, so my childhood meant nothing. So I started looking about. And
Seán was into really different stuff than me. He'd
say 'Sis, you want to hear this. Just give it a listen.'
He'd be coming home from the flea markets with
these boxes of scratchy records: the Small Faces, the
Action, the Creation, the Smoke, John's Children,
the Skatalites, the whole Mod thing. A lot of it, I
didn't even like. I was mad into classical, and then,
you know, the folk. But there's stuff you put in your
head lights no fires at all. The Who gave me

something to burn. Like Mahler. Or the blues. When you're young, you've a flame-thrower for a heart . . . Rob always thinks I was totally sussed around the time we met. But musically not. I was lost. Bless his heart, he could be a bit silly around an okay-looking girl. He thought, if you brushed your hair, you had life worked out. And that was a thing I got from my mum. Now, she *was* beautiful. If you'd seen her. Total smasher. And she'd say to me and Seán, take an interest in your appearance, looking nice doesn't cost, it's an armour. But no. I was lost. At a cross-roads, you know? And I'd say it was the only reason I ended up in a band. Without it, my childhood would be, I don't know, a chapter nobody needed. All my mum's efforts to pay for my lessons, all the rest of it, too, the thousands of hours. And I couldn't let that happen. No way.

She'd jingle the coins in her pockets in three-four time. She was cleverer than anyone you knew. Perhaps you remember the actress Nastassja Kinski. Trez had something of her invulnerable cool and her saucer-sized umber-brown eyes. Often, on the bus, in the library or the lecture hall, the seat beside her was empty. 'Cheekbones', the girls called her, or 'Warpaint' or 'Legs', their resentment so obviously arising from envy as to make it endearing. 'She thinks her shite's chocolate.' 'Dr Lipstick'. 'Lady Muck'. She was the only student in the college accusingly reputed to 'wear perfume'. You forgave Fran the innocent floridness sometimes seen in gifted young poets when he remarked, in those days of well-meant exaggeration, 'That girl makes Debbie Harry seem

Rod Stewart in drag.' Most of us, when young, were out of someone's league. Few were out of everyone's. Trez was.

Let me fast-forward to the evening, near the close of November '82, when she came up to me in the student canteen. We'd nodded at each other now and again before Declan's tutorial, had sometimes murmured agreement about a novel or poem being discussed there, but had never, to my recollection, exchanged a word of extramural conversation. I was 'Fran's friend', wasn't I? I confirmed that I was. Could she join me for coffee? I swallowed.

The coffee at the college was a mixture of sputum and beard-shavings, but I drank as much as I could hold down. I think I did this because Jimmy regarded coffee as suspicious. Like Russia. It presented itself as innocent but must be treated with stern scepticism, no mere beverage but the counterculture in a cup. A zookeeper of distant infamy, a man of coffee when the others were of tea, had brought shame upon the brotherhood by running away to Brighton with someone's spouse not his own, specifically someone's husband not his own. There they openly lived the grind-your-own lifestyle, it was whispered, and lolled about in togas arranging wildflowers. Coffee was the fuel of the bawd, the satyr and revolutionist, the uppity, the malcontent and the rakehell. In our kitchen was a jar of horrible brown powder that had perhaps once been in the same factory as a coffee bean. If you wanted to annoy Dad, and I usually did, you would suggest that he drink the reeking wolfsbane that occurred when the granules met boiling water. *Tassste*, you might hiss, giving your impersonation of Mephistopheles to Faust. 'Ask my bollocks,' he'd retort.

Well, Trez sat down across from me, 'coffee' in hand,

evidently one of the libertines like myself. Her hair hung over one eye, like Veronica Lake's, and her earrings were Anarchy symbols. Did I like Dr Kiely? He was brilliant, we agreed. What was that novel I was reading? It was Salman Rushdie's *Midnight's Children* and I was finding it sticky oul going but I forbore from telling her this. Could I spare her a smoke? She'd owe me. No problem. Our talk was a little reticent as we circumnavigated and halted and gazed at our cups and the novel. What did I reckon the finest guitar solo in the history of New Wave? I answered that John Perry's work on 'Another Girl, Another Planet' by the Only Ones would have to be up there, and she nodded. Robert Quine's on 'Blank Generation' was technically more daring, she said, correctly, but Perry was epic, too. Then there was silence. I asked the obvious question.

She'd given up on Harlow because her heart wasn't in it. The teachers back in school had railroaded her a bit. She didn't blame them for doing their best. But journalism was something you couldn't profess without 'a passion'. It shouldn't be a matter of scoring A's in exams but of wanting and needing to do it. She'd made the right choice. Her passion lay elsewhere. She wanted to be an art historian, to study in New York, eventually to earn a doctorate, to write. I'm fairly certain it was the first time anyone had ever spoken the word 'passion' to me in a non-religious context. That the speaker was someone of my own age was strange. She mashed out her cigarette in a saucer on the table and pulled a battered, coverless paperback from her bag.

'That's for you,' she said. 'You mentioned it in the tutorial. I saw it in a charity shop and just got it.'

It was *Babel* by Patti Smith, a chapbook of her poems.

Someone had scrawled across the grubby frontispiece an inscription in red pencil. 'NYC '78. I'm a believer.'

Everything was quiet. There were tears in my eyes. I don't know why. I was floored.

She took off her glasses and peered through the lenses at the ceiling. Then she asked if it was true that I was in 'a band' with Fran. I said it wasn't exactly a band, we only busked. She looked at me appraisingly as I fell slowly through space. Love-bees buzzed around me. Rocket-men zoomed. She was 'into music' herself, she said.

When did we practise? Could she maybe 'sit in'? She played cello and fiddle. 'A little bit of bass.' She didn't mention that at the age of twelve she'd won a Royal Academy scholarship for composition and counterpoint, and the London section of the *Fleadh Cheoil*, the foremost competition for Irish traditional music, going on to win that title a further four times. No genius ever tells you she's a genius. It wouldn't have mattered had she done so, for there were other things on my mind. I was already wondering how to break it to Fran that the interloper busting up our citadel would be a *cellist*. But I'd find the form of words. His resistance would be crushed. Had she confessed herself a xylophonist, a banger of spoons, an admirer of the J. Geils Band or the Brotherhood of Man, a hater of every sort of music ever made in this world, I still would have piped her aboard.

We went for a pint and we talked about novels, which is always a way of talking about other subjects. Had I a girlfriend? No. Had she a boy? 'Not really.' The Trap boasted a Pacman machine and we played it a long time because Trez knew a way of cheating. Supper was a cellophane sandwich and a packet of pork scratchings. At eleven o'clock she cycled home.

I had missed the last bus, so I set out to walk the four miles to Rutherford Road. At mile one, the rain came on. It surged steadily, viciously. I was drenched to the underwear. The wind was a mad dog kicked out in a storm, shrieking like Siouxsie Sioux. But in all the great conurbation of Luton, there was no happier boy that night.

I didn't know that I had just begun the most continuous conversation of my life. You don't, when you're a kid. The novels get it wrong. The past *is* another country, but at least you were there. The future has latitudes of its own.

Four

O ut the back of our house was a good-sized, dry-lined shed built by Jimmy. There he pootled around, fixing household appliances, or sometimes enjoying the surreptitious cigarette my mum pretended not to know about. In the very distant past, it had been a kind of aviary, planned headquarters of the pigeon-breeding empire he felt would smash the competition. But the birds had been noisy and the gentle complaints of the neighbours had prevailed, and his dreams had flown away. Still, the 'chalet' – you didn't call it 'a shed' – was his place of private resort. He'd spend time there of a summer's evening, reading his cowboy novellas or practising the cornet, which he played in the Jim Connell Memorial Trade Union Silver Band. He had his wood-turner's lathe and he ran up pipe racks and back-scratchers and Christmas tree decorations for the annual British Legion sale of work. There was perhaps that simple pleasure I assume any amateur must feel in a structure put up by his hands. This was no splintery obscenity bought in a flatpack, but a thing he'd drawn out with care. I remember, in the year my sister was killed, helping him saw and plane. The spars were dug down, and the windowpanes painted.

Often, we worked in silence. One night when I happened to look in his direction I saw him weeping into his paint-stained hands. It was among the most terrible sights of my life.

Beyond the shed, he grew tomatoes under sheets of polished glass, and gooseberries in huge bushes where the butterflies were lovely. He told you their names with an insider's joy. They seemed a kind of music. They dazzled. He also raised that vilest of all plants, rhubarb, and my poor mum, who didn't like it any better than I did, out of love for him found many ways of cooking it. The Grace Before Meals would be oddly touching on those evenings. Forgive me, I wander again.

It was a perfectly sound structure, if a little cold by autumn, but he permitted Fran and me to practise there. This would have the advantage of 'ridding the house of that arse-aching racket' and giving us a zone of our own. We spent many, many hours there, trying to write songs, amid the mossy, loamy aromas of teak dust and potting compost, the sweetness of sanded-down pine. The black-and-white television Jimmy couldn't bear to euthanase sat on its shelf like a respected old relative draped in her spider-spun veil. Sometimes it uttered a strange *click* from the depths of itself, as though enjoying the transmission of oblivion.

On the first evening Trez was to 'sit in' I gave the place a bit of a sweeping. Fran was surprisingly helpful, proving handy with the squeegee and enjoying the pink rubber gloves that my mum insisted he wear. ('You've beautiful skin, dear. You don't want to ruin it.') His eyelids were besmirched with kohl, so that he looked like an Arapaho mop-woman. Well, we dusted and broomed, fetched a chair from the kitchen. But Jimmy's chalet was a venue Trez would never see. I suppose that shouldn't have surprised me.

She pitched up a bit early, cello on her back, fiddle in its case in a knapsack. She was wearing a broad-brimmed bonnet, silken poppy in its band, lace veil covering only the eyes. What threw me was that she had a bunch of lilies for Alice, wrapped in a fold of newspaper. This was by no means an era in which students bought flowers for their elders, especially if said oldsters were unknown to them. Alice had recently gone working part time in a secondary-school canteen and was not accustomed to kindliness from teenagers. She looked at these flowers. I thought she was going to embrace the caller. She led her into the kitchen, while Fran and I watched, confused. He was staying with us at the time, owing to a number of painful difficulties. Encouraged by me to make contact with his foster-people back in Rotherham, he had written to them but the response was a final rejection. They wished him well, so they said, but didn't want him back. 'What's done is done.' It hurt him. Also, he'd been evicted from his room in the town, the landlady having discovered that she didn't like his 'type'. She had nothing against him 'personally' and didn't 'believe in prejudice'. 'But I don't want your *type* in the house, love.'

'Carry in that poor girl's cello!' Alice commanded. 'Dear God, do you call yourselves gentlemen?'

The chances of anyone calling Fran or me such a thing were remote, but we did as were told, grumbling slightly. Our estate wasn't one in which you saw a cello too often, and to leave one on the front step, guarded only by Jimmy's garden gnomes, might be a high-risk venture. When we returned, cello borne lengthways between us like a coffin containing a heavy president, Alice and Trez were seated at the kitchen table, Trez reading mum's tea leaves, predicting happiness. 'You're a beautiful and sensitive woman,' she was saying. Which was true. 'You find it difficult not being listened to, am I right?'

'God preserve us,' Alice replied. 'What else? What else?'

Apart from at Shay's graduation ceremony, where she wept with fierce, embarrassed pride, I'm not sure that I ever saw my mother in such a moment of uncomplicated happiness. Here in our house was an embodiment of the most wondrous creation to have ever lighted this earth: an ordinary, human, teenage girl. All parents of a daughter will know what I mean. Our home had been a monkey-house of maleness for so long: the grunts and smells and fondnesses expressed through coarseness, the burps and gibes and joustings and grumbles, the shavings in the sink and the loo seat left up. Here, perhaps, was that most unsayable of absences, the young woman my mum would have loved for a daughter.

Presently Jimmy arrived home from work, on his face the visor of unaffectionate cheerlessness that Mum insisted made him look handsome. It was clear that he'd lost in his little flutter on the ponies, for his greeting to the dog was of Nietzschean glumness. 'If I backed the fukken tide, it wouldn't come in.' He glared bleakly at Fran, whom he enjoyed pretending to dislike, and performed the bitterly ironic 'jazz hands' gesture he often employed to mock what he saw as our showbiz aspirations. Then he started uttering low imprecations about the peacefulness of the house being disturbed yet again by the infernal bloody rock and roll racket. For some time it had been our habit, Fran's and mine, to start 'rehearsing' in the kitchen after the evening meal supplied to us had been cleared, our efforts punctuated by Jimmy's scoffed curses and aggressive rustlings of his *Daily Express*. 'Feck off to that chalet, for the love of Sweet God.' Against our self-penned lyrics he mustered his favourite mask in the arsenal: a stare of pitying incomprehension. In truth he rather liked having us about the place because it gave him something new to grouse about, and there was amiability in his Irish brand of derision. 'Youse pair of bukken bangers. Do you want a cup of tea? Christ almighty, listen. Have a biscuit.'

Also, to be fair, he was privately a man of compassion, a quality he had in common with my mum. When they heard my friend was an orphan – I told them what little I knew of his childhood – they were incapable of being anything but kind to him. The weeks after his eviction were hard times for Fran. He'd show up at the house unannounced. They'd always let him in, no questions. Mum would feed and water him, even if I wasn't on the premises, or permit him to watch the television while he awaited my return. One night I came home late and half-cut from college to find her quietly tearful in the kitchen. When I asked what was wrong, she said 'nothing'. It was many weeks afterwards when she told me the truth. Fran had called up earlier, was asleep on the sofa, thumb in his mouth, 'like a baby'. It hurt her that his birth-mother had met whatever was her fate, that the people charged with caring for him had now turned their back. 'He's only a boy. Another woman's son.' Darkness was fighting the light in him, she said. Of all the evaluations of Fran I would hear down the years, I never heard a more accurate one.

It didn't stop Jimmy ridiculing his clothes, hair and make-up, or calling him 'a funny tulip' or 'a daisy'. But that evening, the first Trez ever called to the house, we were into some new realm of Jimmydom.

Jimmy's glance met her face. And a silence fell over him. She stood graciously from the table and accepted his hand as I made the required introductions. She had on a cardigan and a blue knee-length dress she must have found in a charity shop, a waif from the '40s, perhaps. It was cinched in at the waist and had buttons up the front; a horse-shaped brooch adorned its pocket. Her hair was tied back, every freckle on her face beseeching you to kiss it, and her eyes were the auburn of pine cones.

Jimmy didn't actually genuflect and touch the hem of her frock to his lips but you reckoned it was an effort for him not to. He was floored, poor man. It was touching to see. She said how nice it was to meet him, that I'd spoken often of him fondly, (a lie), that she hoped she wasn't inter-rupting his 'private time' with his wife, whom it had also been a pleasure to meet. By the time she'd finished speaking, I had the feeling Jimmy wanted to run away with her. He was knocked-out loaded. He was Trezzled.

'Would you have a cup of coffee or a sandwich, Sarah?' he croaked. Coffee? From *Jimmy*? The beverage of the devil? I wanted to say 'Who *are* you, alien being, and what have you done with my father?' But no point. He wouldn't have heard.

No she didn't want coffee, many thanks all the same. She'd be grand with a drink of water, 'if possible'. Jimmy thrust out his hand towards the sink with the speed of a hostage at gunpoint. *Water, I command thee. Bow down*

and be served. I am Jimmy, Lord of Elements, fear my power.
Alice hurried over and filled a teacup at the tap. You felt
she was about to kiss the saucer she fetched from the press
while traversing the lino between them. Unless Mrs Prior
who led invalids to Lourdes or some other personage of
high eminence happened to call, saucers, in our house, were
usually employed as ashtrays, except at Christmas, when
they were persuaded to hold gloops of cranberry sauce or
the spat-out pips of satsumas. The idea of bringing one into
play as foundation for a cup to be held by any person under
fifty would have been seen as affectation. But then Trez.

'You've lovely manners,' Jimmy said with a smile of
dazed adoration, 'not like these two Comanches here.' Trez
had indeed, and has still, 'lovely manners', a quality you
don't think is hugely important when young. As I've aged,
I've come to the realisation that things like drive-by shoot-
ings and wars can only start without it.

'And Robert tells me you're from London, Sarah. I don't
hear it in your accent?'

Who was 'Robert', I wondered for a moment.

The divine visitant confirmed that she had assumed
human form in London, very mention of which Gomorrah
would habitually inflame Jimmy to subvocalisations of guff
or have him looking up exorcists in the phone book. But
here he was, nodding admiration and fetching out the chocolate biscuits, and remembering a pleasant trip to the capital
he claimed to have made with my mum some time in the
late 1300s. ('That wasn't me, Jimmy.' 'Sure of course it was
you.' 'Some fancywoman I suppose.' 'It was *you*.') Excellent,
the city of London. It would never be bettered. One could
travel the world ten thousand years without meeting someone

finer than the Londoner. Like all Irish people, Jimmy had a great talent for making an exception. It was as though Princess Diana had dropped in.

'And I'm told you're a musician. I see you play the voilin?' This little sonic tic was a feature of his speech, the pronunciation of all 'io' sounds as 'oi'. There were roits in Belfast, the zoo was rebuilding the loin cage, the Midwestern United States contained Oiwa. My brother and I enjoyed tormenting him about it, little bastards that we were, frequently driving him to the threat of voilence.

We knew he idolised us. How we punished him.

'And what are you studying at the college, Sarah?'

'Boilogy,' I said.

He managed not to punch me in the throat.

Alice gently remarked that Jimmy's tea was beginning to grow cold and that the young people should now be left to their fun, to go down to 'the chalet' and play music.

'The what?'

'The chalet.'

'Is it that dirty oul shed? Sure you couldn't have a, a' – he waved his hand at Trez –

'Voilinist,' I suggested.

'You couldn't have a visitor in a dirty oul shed.'

Well, nothing would do him then but that we practise in 'The Good Front Room', a place of hallowed sacredness in the house. 'It would be nicer for Sarah,' he reminded my mum, who by now was looking at him strangely. Like many Irish couples of their era and milieu, Jimmy and Alice maintained a 'Good Front Room', into which you were rarely considered good enough to go. It contained items of Waterford Crystal and other little fancies given them as wedding gifts, a Chappell upright piano with several broken keys, and the many trophies won by Jimmy for ballroom dancing in his oft-recalled youth with his partner, one Bernie Foy. It was fun to subject him to an occasional tease about Bernie, who had emigrated to Canada with her chap, a plasterer by trade, thereby denying my future progenitor the All-Ireland title for rumba/cha-cha-cha and who knows what darker pleasures. 'A poignant farewell,' Shay and I would say. 'Did you ride her down to the docks on your crossbar?' Alice didn't like this, but Jimmy sort of did. The intimation that he'd been a bit of a lady-slayer was one he found pleasing, though he'd always command you to stop. Almost to the end of her life, Alice felt Bernie Foy was about to come wiggling up the rhubarb patch in her scanties and haul Jimmy away by his cummerbund. 'That girl' had been 'a certain sort', she once confided to our neighbour Mrs Park, as Shay and I eavesdropped, chuckling.

Into The Good Front Room we were led by my dad, Fran and I hefting the cello. By the time we put it down, he was showing Trez his trophies. 'Oh those old things, dear me; you wouldn't want to mind those. No, I wasn't a bad dancer, Sarah. Only amateur, of course. Dublin silver-medallist mambo and bolero, mind you. But the knees went baw-ways on me. It's all in the knees. If you don't have the knees, you're bunched.'

Then he switched on *both* bars of the electric fire, *mirabile dictu*, while Fran exchanged little bits of initially guarded but amiable girl talk with Trez, about where she had bought those lovely tights, he buying his own in Primark. It was nice to see him make the effort, and she returned it appropriately, complimenting him on his footwear but wondering aloud did he ever get a heel stuck in a grating. And then a marvel happened that I wouldn't have believed possible had I not been there to witness it.

Jimmy didn't drink, being a member of the Poineer Total Abstinence Society, but *occasionally* from some hidden keep a dusty bottle of Guinness might be produced for the visitor. It could happen on Christmas Night, say, or if war had been declared or a loved one raised from the dead. Well, he turned to doe-eyed Trez, and forth from out his beak came words of unimaginable strangeness.

'I believe it's permissible nowadays for a young lady to enjoy a little refreshment. Would you take a glass of beer, Sarah, love? Since it's a special occasion. The first, I hope, of many future visits.'

Trez considered a moment or two before smiling her acceptance, if he was certain it was no trouble at all. He nodded, sage scholar who feels progress must be allowed. Had she told him she fancied a couple of buckets of meths, he'd have cantered down the chemical factory to get them.

'And I suppose youse two Balubas might force down a drop?'

Fran and I supplied the required whinnies of gratitude.

'A nice pair of flibbertigibbets, aren't you now? Sure liquor never sullied them lips.' He chuckled at his witticism and ruffled our hair. Well, Fran's was hard to actually *ruffle* because of the lacquer and the gel but he sort of patted it before wiping his hand on the antimacassar. 'You're good lads all the same. Not the worst, not the worst. Do you know what youse should call yourselves? If this "band" of yours takes off? Two Mules for Sister Sarah.'

And away he quietly backed, the man who threw the zinger. Trez unzipped the cello. Off we went.

Playing music with someone you barely know can be embarrassing in its way, like getting naked with a lover for the first time. Everything's suddenly out there. You're hoping to impress, at least not to cause a scream of horror. Even when fondness and trust have been haltingly established, the awareness that what you're offering might prove a disappointment can sometimes be the ghost in the wardrobe. Trez was pretty quiet as Fran and I strummed our chords, the opening sequence of Roxy Music's 'The Thrill of It All'. It was my favourite song at the time and we'd worked it out carefully. I will never be able to put into language the bolt that shot through me as Trez began nodding along.

Now (Christ!) she was playing, her bow in strutted blurs, mouth set in what I can only term a snarl of excitement as she sawed out great buzzes and groans. Fran crossed to the piano and vamped out that demoniac riff, hunching like the boy who never had a lesson, stamping on the sustain-pedal as though it would give him back a drumbeat and shaking his head at the ceiling. The cello was too loud, my guitar was out of tune, and Fran's fingers had all the wrecking-ball finesse of Jerry Lee Lewis and none of that master's skill. But I was gone. I wanted to weep. I don't know how I didn't. Fran began to sing. Trez *thwucked* an evil bass. I thrashed that innocent guitar, the closest friend of my youth, and I stood to my reflection in the black rainy window, asking it if such joys could be.

Had the Horsemen of the Apocalypse ridden up Rutherford Road at that moment, I'd have felt we could kick their gloomy arses back home to Hell or, better, charged them admission to the show. Trez picked up her fiddle and coaxed from it a screech that made me want to shove my guitar through Jimmy's display case and decapitate every piece of Waterford in the room. I didn't even mind the way she was smiling across at Fran. Well, I didn't mind much. Well, I did. But there was a moment when she winked at me, and nothing else mattered. 'I *love* your playing,' she said.

Hope is like Abba. It never goes away. In the days and weeks that followed, she would sometimes link my arm as we waited at the bus stop or walked by the lake. We talked of music, of our childhoods, of Fran, of one another, with an openness I'd never known existed except in great songs. She had one sibling, a twin brother, whose jokes she often quoted. But much of what she said wasn't funny. She'd had sufferings to contend with: no father in her life, a mostly shit school, a mum who'd been hurt, anti-Irish graffiti on the door of their flat whenever the Provos bombed England. What had got her through was music. I knew what she meant. Every song I heard on the radio was about Sarah Sherlock. You know what it is when you're nineteen.

FROM ROBBIE'S DIARY
Sunday 5th December 1982

SONGS THAT REMIND ME OF SARAH

What I feel when I see her? On the Street Where You Live.
What I feel when I don't: Blue Monday.

Her eyes: Brown Sugar.

Her smile: Here Comes the Sun.

That frown she sometimes has: Ruby Tuesday.

All the poems she's read, all the novels she knows, all her lightness when talking, her gestures, her clothes, and all her insistences, laughing You're wrong. And the moon is eclipsed by her song.

What I don't want her to be: My Best Friend's Girl.

What I'd do if she went: Cry Me a River.

Way she walks? Rebel Rebel from Devil Gate Drive.

How she dances: Rock Lobster by the B-52s.

What she sometimes makes me feel: Send in the Clowns.

What she never makes me feel: Pretty Vacant.

The way she laughs at something irrelevant: Pennies From Heaven.

But the expression on her face, that morning in class: Don't Look So Sad. Sea of Heartache.

Music on her Walkman: Tainted Love, Soft Cell. Beethoven's First. Jimi Hendrix.

Her favourite song ever: Famous Blue Raincoat.

Runner-Up? In the Bleak Midwinter.

And her kind, sweet laugh. And the way she shakes her head.

What she sang when I bribed her with my second-last smoke: Cum On Feel The Noize.

First single she ever bought: Puppy Love by Donny Osmond.

A classic she dislikes: Reet Petite.

Her greatest stanza ever in the history of poetry? There is a house/in New Orleans/They call the

Risin' Sun/Thass *bin* the ruin of many poor boy/
And me, oh Lord, I'm one.
Fave Dylan song? Watchtower, Lonesome Death of
Hattie Carroll. Masters of War. Only Bleeding.
What she actually does own: A leopard-skin pill-box
hat.
My *favourite Dylan song?* Sarah.
How she looked at me, then: Sad-Eyed Lady of the
Lowlands. Bell Bottom Blues. Sound of Silence.
What she'd like us to be: 'Really good mates.'
What I feel right now: Nowhere Man.
I'll Never Fall in Love Again. Crying in the Rain.
Take a Piece of My Heart. So Lonely.

Five

F ran and I pinned up an ad in the music pubs around
the town, because we couldn't afford to place one in
What's On In Luton. TRIO SEEKS UNBEATABLE
DRUMMER. ANY GENDER. NO MESSERS. GIGS LINED
UP. SERIOUS OUTFIT. I pointed out to Fran that the word
'any' should properly be 'either' but he accused me of provin-
cial small-mindedness and lack of imagination. Like all the
great insulters, he knew the truth hurts.

Having shoplifted a litre of vodka, we betook ourselves
to a Billy Bragg gig at the Blessed Matt Talbot Hall up the
street. The BMT, as it was known, was a gruesome little
hovel, having for most of its existence been administered by
the Religious Sisters of Mercy, a body that once pipped the
Democratic Republic of Zaire to the Oscar for World's Most
Ironically Named Entity. Why they needed a dance hall may
only be imagined. A venue for public frightenings, perhaps.
By the early 1980s, those pious days were receding but the
building, like many bishops, was somehow avoiding demoli-
tion despite deserving it. It smelt of mould, rising damp,
sinking hope and old facecloth, and had statues of the
Catholic martyrs, chipped, dismembered or facetiously

defaced, in the grottos of its crumbling alcoves. A shockingly bloodthirsty mural of a half-naked Lord Jesus Christ being scourged by personages who looked like Ron Moody as Fagin adorned the wall behind the mineral bar. A sign on another wall warned 'Jiving is Forbidden', you traitorous slut of a wannabe-Protestant, you murderer of the Virgin Mary. Manchester's finest, the Smiths, would play their first southern gig at the Matt Talbot Hall, a venue whose aura of melancholic ruination seemed, at least to me, the perfect frame for their canvas. Fran said the problem with Morrissey was that he wasn't sexually ambiguous *enough*.

The night Billy Bragg played Luton was bleak and thundery and I was feeling more than a bit querulous. If you are an admirer of what Fran used to term 'Panglo-Irish literature' you will understand that in any town with an Irish community the rain surges down without the tiniest respite, not quite as evocatively as it does in a novella or short film but quite a lot more wetly. Well, the night of which I write was a first-class pisser. Bilious roars from the heavens. Horizontal sleet. Zeus was dispensing the thunderbolts and lightning. Luton looked like a Judas Priest album cover.

The previous week had not been a happy one. Fran found himself a room and moved out of our house. A late essay led to a written warning from my tutor. Far worse was a private failure that was scalding my conscience. Julie Hyland from across the road had asked me to her school-leaving dance but the evening failed to go well. Signals misread, badly paced and anxious drinking, the stupidity of the 'round-buying' system. I had made a fool of myself and was ashamed that I'd upset Julie, who had shown a child's uncomplicated kindness to me when my sister was killed and our family came to live in Luton. She had grown into the smartest and loveliest young woman. The fact that I'd ruined a night when she deserved so much better was following me like a bloodhound incubus.

I took it into the BMT and it squatted on my back, while we waited for Billy Bragg to come on. The fucked-up grimness, the aroma of elderly priest, was not conducive to cheer. I was and will always remain a strong admirer of the Braggster, but, as with any other musician, you'd want to be in the mood. Drunk, in wet clothes, listening to Barking's own Woody Guthrie was doing little to raise the spirits. How in the name of Christ could the English call a town 'Barking'? Given the aggression with which he sang, it wasn't entirely inappropriate. But still. That name annoyed me. I sat in my soak, occasionally bum-shuffling for warmth. There seemed an *awful* lot of songs about girls who didn't want you. An awful lot of songs about Trez.

Well, then there were songs about the wickedness of the tabloid press, and then there were songs about Missus Fatcha. He flailed with tight-jawed fervency at his gloriously loud electric, this one-man Clash, this hammer out of Essex, sweating, apparently on cue. The oppressing of Winnie Mandela, a widely admired personage (outside of Soweto), was condemned in rough four-four. Integrity in a polo shirt stomped and proclaimed and head-butted the mic and pogoed. I agreed with every denunciation busting forth from the PA, but I sensed a growing tension beside me.

Fran always avowed a loathing for any music that had, or thought it had, a political message, especially if he shared its politics. Personally, I feel the converted are entitled to a sermon now and again, and there are times when fish in a barrel require to be shot, otherwise what is the point of *having* fish, but he didn't see it that way at all. He was hard to bore in those days, but ardency bored him. Billy was beginning to burble, he felt; Billy was 'bellying on'. Fran's response was to start boring *me* nearly to violence by communicating his boredom, repeatedly, with nudges, as I tried to focus on the torrid ballads of lonely rebuffings that I'd entered this place to enjoy. Well, by now we were being reminded in jangling G-7th that fascism is not a good thing. The audience, not wanting to be outdone, howled accordance. 'Intolerance' was an evil, Billy Bragg announced, and the punters, stoked on lager and rereadings of op-eds in *The New Statesman*, bellowed for the intolerant never to be tolerated, to be strung from the lamp posts in their pants at dawn and buried in quicklime afterwards. 'The Trade Union Movement' was, contrariwise, most excellent in every way and must be supported by all non-Nazis. Again, I agreed. Power to the People. But the cold and the wetness and being told of Fran's boredom were stirring some drunken resentment. The windmills getting speared would still be there in the morning. What was the point of our presence? I felt like one attending a meeting of kind-hearted grandmothers who were being invited to concur that, generally speaking, little children are preferable to Satan.

He, Fran, kept threatening to sod off, and I told him to sod off if he wished to. One of his immaturities was that he didn't realise you were not going to beg, that you had a fragile but calculable investment in yourself to maintain, no matter how his neediness might provoke it. You want to go? Fine. Close the door on your way. Did I ask you to remain? Did I fuck. Among the compromised, pretending indifference is a means of saving face, a tactic our friendship had taught me. Anyway, he had annoyed me by dressing in a provocative manner that evening; culturally not sexually provocative. One irony of rebellion is that it wears an extremely prescribed uniform. It was *de rigueur* for male youths at an event of leftist tenor to sport either black second-hand donkey jackets or denim dungarees and a bobble hat – perhaps with a little badge professing allegiance to the ANC or beleaguered Chileans/whales/Laotians/Ken Livingstone pinned where someone would notice it, like on your tit. But Bucko had pitched up in his powder-blue belly-top and pixie boots, his face like the cake in 'MacArthur Park' that someone left out in the rain. It was wearing thin. The attitude, not the make-up, although actually that was wearing thin too. *Obviously*, they were looking at him. How would they not? Lutonians are a curious people. But he resented the very mild and fleeting glances his deportment had been conjured to stir. He was in this era one of those bohemians whose constant cry is to be *left alone* and *not stared at* while sashaying down the street in tiger-skin thong and ball-gag with a nipple-clamped gimp in a nappy. I exaggerate, of course. Yet this was his view. And you can't have it both ways. But he tried to. The only point during the concert when he stopped his whispered decrials was when a party of drunken Trots started heckling Billy Bragg for not supporting the IRA, or perhaps for singing too many songs about girls who don't want you, or likelier for not singing enough of them. A great deal of stolen vodka had gone south by then. Jamaica's second-most-famous export after reggae had also been consumed in hefty measure, along with a flagon of cider. The Trots were calling Billy 'a Tory', which in those days wasn't good unless you were the majority of the British electorate.

By the time I got home that night, Jimmy was in a state of what used to be called, by him certainly, 'high dudgeon'. With the chilly summons 'Oi, Bollocky Bill', I was beckoned to the kitchen as I tried to creep up the strangely reversing escalator that my drunkenness made of the stairs. His visage appeared at me kaleidoscopically, revolving in quartet, like the faces of Queen in the video for 'Bohemian Rhapsody'. Alcohol is a terrible thing.

Not only had he opened the electricity bill, the monthly arrival of which he feared and detested, blaming me for turning on the immersion deliberately for no other purpose than to enrage him (largely true), but the phone had been ringing like that of 'a whure-house in the Vatican'. Telephones, in those less advanced days, used to ring when they rang, not bleep, chirp, play the riffs from 'Dancing Queen' or 'Gangnam Style' or recordings of Simon Cowell disappointing a child. He was angry, tired, hungry, vengeful, and scarlet as an aroused baboon's arse. Bad enough that I should treat his home 'like a fukken hotel' but now I was treating it 'like a fukken office for daisies' and he wouldn't stand for it, did I hear, no he wouldn't. Who did I think I was? Colonel Tom fukken Parker? The image of 'an office for daisies' was threatening to make me laugh, Quentin Crisp dusting the photocopier, Oscar Wilde typing invoices, the noted female-impersonator Danny La Rue high-kicking about the works canteen in taffeta. And it was always hard not to laugh when Jimmy gave out to you if he was wearing his zookeeper's uniform and when he used the noun 'daisy' in that way. But I tried not to. To him, the word meant directionless layabout rather than effeminate person, not that these categories were mutually exclusive in what he often called his way of thinking.

'Some daisyboy, aren't you? Clueless O'Reilly. The varsity man in my hole.'

With no small effort, I managed not to chuckle.

'Backchat me, Mister, and I'll put you on that road! You may up and pack your bags and away to some gin-shop with my foot up your transom as you go.'

Again, I suppressed any bleat of mirth. I was afraid I might befoul myself if I surrendered at all. There was a technique I had perfected of grinding my fingernails into my palms and staring impassively at the wall behind him. The small pain produced by the grinding I had found a way of translating into a steely-faced, sullen, shark-like coldness, an unreachable Arctic of teenaged contempt with igloos of malice in its glare. But I was hoping to Holy Jesus that he did not address me as 'Bridget', a thing he often did when in the windstorms of his annoyance. It could reduce me to bawls of uncontrollable laughter, and I didn't want those to happen.

'A nice gentleman I am after raising in this misfortunate house and the whiff of drink off you enough to floor a fukken racehorse. Chomping Polo Mints, were we, beyond on the bus? Well, the jig is up, Bridget. I know that game. When's this do you think I was born?'

I was going to say '11 BC' or something easy like that. For the moment, I held my powder.

My fukken tea was fukken ruined, he continued, accusingly. My parents were of that Irish class and generation that had its dinner at lunchtime and its tea at six o'clock in the evening following 'the Angelus bells' on the radio. Point out that they were 'pips', not actual bells, and Jimmy would warn you not to upset your mum by further displays of smart-arsery. If you hopped the ball by telling him that 'dinner' was a repast taken in the hours of darkness, he accused you of fancying yourself a member of the British Royal Family, an entity he disparaged while being magnetised to its marriages, its comings and multiple goings. The word 'supper' would have got you veritably flogged by his mockeries. I knew. I had tried it out and was building up to 'luncheon', saving it for a wintry Sunday when amusement might be needed in the house, one of those sad little windswept cabin-fever Sabbaths when *Only Fools and Horses* wasn't on. He yanked open the under-sink bin to show me the congealing or coagulating remains of my meal. It was, had once been, beans and a rasher. There were hungry souls in the world this night, he thundered.

'Send them that, so.' I nodded.

That was lovely talk now, God forgive me for a reprobate. Had he dared to disrespect his own father, Lord have mercy on the same, 'the cunt would have killed me stone dead'. It was down on my ignorant knees I should fall, for the mercies of the Deity and His providence. The peoples of Ethiopia would give their every graven idol to be me, fed by caring elderly parents of martyric unselfishness whilst I dandied about the town like a playboy. To awaken in 57 Rutherford Road would be the summit of their dreams. Gratefully they would clear a table to earn their board-and-lodging about the place and would not assume the words 'dishwasher' or 'chimneysweep' meant his wife. If male they would take out the rubbish or mow the fukken grass and would sometimes bring the dog for a walk. They would go to Mass when told to and not be shaming the household. Unlike my brother and me, they would shrink from belief in a supernatural presence called 'Captain Daz' whose purpose was to gather besmirched garments or bed-linen from a reeking clump in the wardrobe and convey them to the laundry basket. These unfortunates would *use* the antiperspirant and foot-powder my mum had bought for them in Boots and be thankful for the insole deodorant. The bedroom charitably provided for them would not be 'a slag-heap' or 'the County of Bedfordshire Dump'. But what had he and his espoused saint received by way of appreciation or acknowledgement? (A slap in the kisser for their troubles.) What was it a mortal sin to waste? (Good food.) Where and when would I burn? (In Hell, one day.) Who, precisely, did I think I was? (Depends how you're framing the question.) Jimmy was such a good-natured man that seeing him lose his temper was ridiculous, like watching the Dalai Lama do the Twist. My 'comeuppance', his favourite word, was coming soon. When was I last to Confession?

'I don't believe in Confession.'

Here I had the Jimster rather against the ropes, because I knew he didn't believe in it either. But it was interesting to see how he'd fight his way out. 'Oh, he doesn't believe in Confession. Wonderful, tell us more. What else do you not believe in, Mr Daisy?'

Any symphony of Jimmy's fury would include this *allegro spiritoso* passage, where he'd repeat your most recent utterance of daisyfication to some invisible magistrate in the room. I listed some of the other things in which I didn't believe: deep-pan pizza, the likeability of the seaside, the posthumous apparition of holy virgins to pubescent girls in grottos, the fretless bass guitar, the too-frequent cutting of my toenails, the capitalist system, hummus, optimism, Western civilisation, Spandau Ballet. *Some* daisies believe Miss Piggy will eventually marry Kermit, I expounded – generally the more imaginative of the flora. Sooner or later, we got around to the immersion heater, as sooner or later the Arabs and the Israelis get around to the borders of Palestine. Clearly the fukken immersion was something I *did* believe in, since my devotion to it was fukkenwell frenzied. He produced the electricity bill from the pocket of his epaulette-gilded tunic as though it were a piece of revolting pornography he had found beneath my mattress. Mum didn't have a pair of pincers among the accoutrements of her kitchen. Had she had them, he'd be using them now. His glower was fierce and avenging as he twirled that gruesome document, evidence of my lizard depravity. 'Love does not rejoice in the wrong,' the Good Book tells us. In the case of Jimmy Goulding, it did.

How many baths a day did I think I needed? (Five, I said. No more.) Was I of the view that his money grew on the trees? (Did it not?) I must be the cleanest fukken student in the greater Luton area. (Not hard.) Did I think him a fool? (In which sense?) How often did I think he had bathed when a boy back in Dublin? (Biannually.) What had he done to deserve this abuse? (Difficult. Maybe blame it on the boogie?)

That was nice talk indeed I had learned at the college, an institution he imagined as conducting seminars on insolence and perversion before everyone 'minced off for a coffee'. Mrs Burchmore across the road had witnessed me 'spitting in her rockery'. I had given 'a funny look' to Mr Prior down the newsagents. Where would the infamy end? This led back by no circuitous route to the question of the telephone, my overuse use of same, for no Christian purpose, but for organising my indolence and debauchings (if only), now for auditioning drummers. Well the gravy train stopped here. I must reckon him 'a tool'. The piss would no longer be taken. I was treating him as the PAYE department of the Inland Revenue treated him, viz, a muggins mcbride to be soaked. Well I'd milk him no more. He was 'nobody Rosie'. The milk truck done shut down.

I pointed out to the several Jimmies assailing me that someone ringing the house did not cost us, i.e. him, any money, but as always when confronted by rational opposition he insisted this wasn't the point. After a day spent hefting carrion into the vultures, chasing an escaped tapir throughout the immensity of Whipsnade Zoo's bus park and shouting at disreputable Scousers in the penguin enclosure, he was entitled to the peaceful enjoyment of his home. The telephone his labours provided was not my individual property. My mother, he continued, was being driven out of her mind. 'And she doesn't have far to go!'

'I . . .'

'Tell you this, Mister Lip, there's a new sheriff in town. Your daisying days are over.'

'But . . .'

'Don't you answer me back! Enough of your smartness, my gosser. Am I running a fukken employment exchange for your daisying friends, you twittering impudent maggot? I'll give you fukken drummers. Up your sainted idle hole! Do you know what I was doing tonight while you were fannying around like a Mary? I was bottle-feeding a poor little pygmy marmoset whose mother abandoned him. *Imagine* what he'd give to be you and your brother. Get up to that sty of a bedroom and study.'

'I did a lot of study today,' I countered when I had finished gnawing my lips. 'I wrote an essay on William Blake's imagery.'

'Oh Jaysus, stop the lights. You poor lamb.'

'There's no need to be sarcastic about it,' I said, deliberately riling him. Jimmy was a large man in those days and had a tendency to sweat a lot when angry, and this, combined with his cue-ball baldness, could sometimes produce the remarkable effect of the perspiration on his scalp being evaporated by the heat of his ire, resulting in what looked like smoke pouring from his head. When this happened, and it happened not infrequently while Shay and I were in our teens, it was a sight for which queues would form. Jimmy when angry went stark, staring loco. Shay termed it '*in loco parentis*'.

'An essay on Blake's imagery. Boys oh boys.' Notwithstanding that it didn't mention sociology, a study Jimmy defined as 'the science of destroying society', the phrase encompassed everything he found suspect in third-level education, a system he felt had only been put in place to give bigamists something to do for a living. Every time he repeated the sentence, he vocally italicised another of its hated words. 'An *essay* on Blake's imagery. An essay on Blake's *imagery*. It's exhausted you must be. Rest your brains.'

'I'm a little tired, yes,' I said, cunningly. I had seen that Shay had entered the room clad only in ill-fitting underpants

-96-

and was silently urging me on. Jimmy did not look at him but continued to regard me as I rubbed an eye and pretended to yawn.

'Sure lie down, would you not? Will I pull off the young master's wellingtons? Would he like a cup of tea *in the bath*?'

'I'd prefer cocoa. Or maybe a coffee?'

The finger that had comfortingly stroked a runt pygmy marmoset's belly was extended in my direction, shaking. 'I'll coffee *you*, Mister Bucko. You see if I don't. *An* essay on Blake's imagery. And they call that fukken work. And you wonder why the English laugh at us.'

'I don't,' I said.

'Oh they laugh at us in England. They are breaking their shites laughing. And why *wouldn't* they laugh? An essay on Blake's imagery.' I will spare the reader the Second Movement of his Wagnerian denunciation, but blasphemies were many and sacrilegious oaths plentiful, as were impracticable suggestions of a picturesque nature touching the late William Blake (1757–1827) – surely a strong candidate for High Queen of Daisydom – as well as myself, the college authorities and my associates. Jimmy's own imagery was vivid and pungent, if sometimes contortedly expressed. It was clear that he didn't feel a grounding in the literature of the English-speaking archipelago would have many practical applications in the marketplace. In this, of course, he was not entirely wrong. 'Damn the essays on Blake's imagery *I* ever wrote in my day, I'll tell you *that*, Your Majesty.'

'I'll read it to you if you like? Want to pull up a chair?'

'Oh terrible smart, aren't you. Prince Fucky the Ninth. And you arsing your way through the world like a – like a –'

'Daisy?' I suggested.

At this point, perhaps mercifully, Mum entered the kitchen, looking weary and glancing conspicuously away from my brother's investigations of his southerly person, to say there was an individual calling himself 'Bongo' on the phone in the blessèd hall – 'blessèd' was the nearest she ever came to a curse-word – and he had recently departed a group with a name of almost libellous unpleasantness and he was only one of a profusion of drummers to have telephoned that night and for the love of the Living God and Our Holy Virgin Mother could I not make it stop and where had I been till this hour?

'In the library, writing an essay,' I slurred. 'On Blake's imagery.'

'I know what library you were in,' Jimmy said coldly. 'A library called Sheerin's pub.'

'I have never been in Sheerin's pub in my life,' I responded, lying in the sake of the cause.

'A library with a "discotheque" going on in the basement. And an abortionist handing out contraceptives to schoolgirls.'

'I don't go to discotheques. Whatever those are.'

'My hairy sainted aunt you don't. You forget I have friends.'

It was easy enough to forget, since he didn't have any friends at all, but Jimmy in supervisory mode liked to conjure up the spectre of himself as commander of a legion of zoo-keeping spies that was tracking you through the sulphurous alleys and opium dens of Luton and noting your every judder. 'You were seen,' he would say, as he did on this occasion, and the more ardently you replied that you could not have been seen, unless perhaps by some unfortunate wretch suffering the delusional effects of para-noid schizophrenia, the more he would assure you that you had been.

'You were seen.'

'By whom?'

'Never you mind by whom.'

It was cruel making him say 'whom', a word no Irish person ever uses unless giving an impersonation of a gobshite. I made him say it a few more times but then I felt I should stop because Shay's attempts not to laugh by stuffing a tea towel into his mouth were beginning to frighten me a little. Jimmy whipped around and glared at him, like an owl in a mood. Then slowly he revolved the orb of his head back towards me. It was by now a hellacious shade of red that no English adjective could describe. Ensanguined and fierce, it was redness itself. I felt I was being observed by a huge Japanese flag on to which some vandal had crayoned a scowl.

'Go up and get the bible, Alice,' he commanded my mum.

'I will in my hat,' she said.

'I am going up that fukken stairs. And I'll be back with the bible. I swear to the living Jayzus, I will get that bible, God forgive me. Are you telling me you will put your filthy paw on it and swear before Almighty God that you were not in a pub this evening?'

'I won't swear on the bible, no.'

'Hah!' he exclaimed. The dog woke up, startled, and began doing to itself what my brother's then girlfriend reportedly refused to do to my brother. Mum looked a little uneasy as she toed it.

'I have quit the Catholic Church and become a Quaker,' I told Jimmy, a bit of a tongue-twister when you're sloshed out of your tits and trying not to look at an auto-fellating greyhound whose showbiz possibilities are occurring to you. 'My people do not take oaths.'

'I'll Quaker you in a minute. With the tip of my boot. Do you know *your* trouble, Fellow-my-Buck?'

'Yes,' I said, to disconcert him. But it didn't work.

'Idleness. And ingratitude. Oh go on, that's right, *laugh*. You're good and able to swig Guinness and talk shite by the yard, I'll give you that. You and your brother there. Shay Guevara himself. A nice pair of intellectuals I'm after raising in this gin-shop. Laurel and fukken Hardy, only you wouldn't know who was who.'

'Whom,' my brother interjected.

'If there was doctorates in bollocksology and scratching yourself in bed, the two of you'd be professors by now. Pair of loafing, idle thicks. You couldn't find your arses in a dark room.'

'Jimmy, love,' said Mum, in mildest admonition. 'Don't be too hard on the boys.'

The remark, though gently spoken, stirred a poker in his coals. Jimmy adored and respected his wife as the personification of all goodness, his and everyone's moral better by a distance of furlongs, and to receive her disapproval would always send him scats, as it did on this occasion. The eruption of Mount Goulding was close, one felt. He blamed me for his shaming but continued what had caused it, bad words raining on the corner of the room in which I tried not to snot myself with laughter. I was the daisyest fukken daisy in the bunch, he assured me, 'a daffodil', 'away with the fairies'.

Please call me a violet, I was silently beseeching. I wanted to hear him say 'voilet'.

'I'm vay shorry, Shimmy,' was the best I could manage. 'Vay vay shorry indeed.' A sudden charade of penitence could make him pause and rev the engines. But he opted to accelerate at the speed bump.

'Oh, he's *teddibly* sorry. Oh, lardee-dar-dar. He's teddibly, *fraightfully* soddy.' It was his practice when angry to falsely imitate my accent as though it belonged to one of the actors in the televisualisation of *Brideshead Revisited*, a programme that both enraged and beguiled him. By now I was quacking back hot tears of mirth, low honks bursting forth from my nose, as he flailed me with a florilegium of fucks.

Well, there followed his lament on the recession then beset-ting the kingdom, but how none of her people should be worried. Their days of tribulation were numbered, thanks be to God, for the international bond markets would rejoice at the tidings that my brother and I, when eventually we deigned to enter the workforce, would go armed with a know-ledge of poetry. Lesser nations had committed the grave error of educating their young persons in skills that might prove of some remote use. Pity the poor Germans with their clattering factories. How they must be envying us nowadays. 'Hallay fukken looyah. A degree in readin pomes.' He shook his head in what he must have thought was a gesture of abject aston-ishment, like a lawyer resting his open-and-shut case.

Kindly woman, my mum remarked on the excellence of the college library staying open until midnight on a Monday and could she poach me an egg on toast.

'Would you not get him a fukken lobster and a drop of champagne, no? I can send the fukken butler out for chips.'

'Jimmy, please.'

'It's you I blame! You should have reddened their arses. *Look* at him. Fukken daisy can barely stand up. Streeling into my house stocious from some pub full of whures.'

'He was writing an essay on Blake's imagery,' she continued placidly. 'And that's a very nice thing to be doing.'

'I know damn well what essay he was writing,' Jimmy said. 'An essay on the imagery of MY HOLE!'

'That would certainly make an interesting theme,' I said.

'Especially for a sociologist,' my brother added, crucially.

Moments later, smoke. And goodnight.

Six

We saw drummers of passable ability and some who could barely hit a skin. The former tended to glaze over when they heard Fran's songs, the latter to try outbanging the competition. But loudness was not what we were after. Some candidates wore wire-rimmed glasses and listened hard when you spoke, which slightly put you off them, for some reason. A creepy grinner in his mid forties, clearly a sex-case, pitched up in a leather jacket like a pervy Fonz. Rhythm was 'rooted in the body', he kept saying to Trez. We all had 'cycles', women especially. We suggested he cycle on home.

You'd have reckoned in a burg only thirty miles from the world capital of rock and roll that recruiting a drummer would be easy enough, like unearthing a welder on an oil rig. Admittedly, the remuneration was unexciting, i.e. nothing, but this was the early 1980s. We had nothing ourselves. If anyone wanted a quarter of it, we were happy to agree. But sometimes, talks broke down.

It proved a difficulty that our advert exaggerated, not to say lied, about the group having gigs lined up. I'd warned that this was foolish but lost the vote two–one. Only a fool wouldn't have suspected Fran of a certain creativity when it came to the truth, but I was surprised that Trez acquiesced in it. Her reasoning was that the gigs would surely follow once a drummer came on board. Fran didn't bother with reasoning.

We saw thrashers, smashers, belters, welters, thudders and twelve-cymbal jazz-boys. Groovers, whompers, rinky-dink stompers, a chappie who banged on a box. Flailers with Taekwondo sweatbands engirding sodden brows. Metallers with biceps of oak. Knockers-on-woodblocks, glockenspielers in docs, cowbell-abusers galore. A young woman – how we would have *loved* a young woman on drums – who found three-four time a challenge. Bless her, she bashed the hi-hat like granny at the seaside playing Whac-a-Mole on her way to the bingo. Folksters with bodhráns. Flunters with *gongs*. A stoner on washboard and thimbles (I swear to Keith Moon), recently released from prison in Wales. All we wanted was a kid of our own age with the essentials and a look. But it was like asking Jesus to disco. They'd turn up to impress, talking paradiddles and flams, in their bleached 501s and ironed NYU tank-tops, wanting to give you their *ideas* about the nature of rhythm, as though anyone ever danced to an idea. Sweeping fingers across a chime-tree, they'd ask you to listen, *really think*. You found yourself thinking of hitting them. Others had been to the hairdresser in a lamentable attempt to look like quiffed Larry Mullan, handsome drummer with U2, or that outfit's bemulleted vocalist.

Umcha, umcha, umcha, UM. Thus, my dreams resounded. Badda-badda bum bum, opening figure of Ann

Peebles's 'I Can't Stand the Rain', was one pattern we'd asked candidates to keep playing while we tried jamming. One morning at the breakfast table Jimmy happened to idly rap it out with his fingertips. It was the closest I ever came to parricide.

These were difficult days. Busking as a trio was not without its challenges, particularly because Trez was adamantly committed to her studies and insisted our public appearances be timetabled around them. Also, she liked you to play in tune and bothersome things like that. Ah the straitjacket of the classically trained. Any monies we gained from flouting the Vagrancy and Solicitation Act (1853) went immediately to hire the little audition room on Cumberland Street in the town, and I found the effort of feeding this monkey exhausting. Weeks cranked by. Luton's Ringo eluded us. The dread spectre that would never be a rock band began to possess me. Doomed to be acoustic, drummerless, undanceable, our future was as Bedfordshire's answer to Peter, Paul and Mary. With two Marys. That wasn't a good place to be in the early 1980s when Stewart Copeland of the Police was pounding his way to American number ones while peroxide-headed Sting, looking like a pouty fugitive from *A Clockwork Orange*, skanked and thwacked and *thunked* on the bass, saying mine is a band with *a drummer*. An eternity shorn of rhythm would be my desolate fate. I'd be filed under Easy Listening.

Pattern. Periodicity. Call it what you will. The percussion of the world never stops. Without it, music is pretty, a distraction, nothing more. The sea without its tides would be a puddle. The void from which our species oozed will always be a void, and our way of defeating it is to clap. Some Neanderthal smeared in wode eyed the lightshow of the stars and smacked his belly in halting four-four. In the snap of a finger, the jitterbug arrived and the apes learned to walk on the moon. All of which is touching. *But we couldn't find a drummer.* It was what Fran termed 'a pain in the oysters'.

In the end, Trez stepped in, as she might have done from the outset. My diary records an absurdist conversation that took place in the Trap on the night of Wednesday 2nd March 1983. Funds being low, we were sharing one pint, not a unit of capacity that is easily trisected in any context involving youth, human nature and alcohol. The beer tasted soapy. We'd no cigarettes. The feeling between us was fractious.

'My brother plays drums.'

'Your brother, Trez?'

'Yeah.'

'This in't the fukken Osmonds,' Fran clarified.

'Your brother plays drums?'

'Rob, that's what I *said*. Do you have to repeat it? Sweet Jesus.'

'He repeats your every word because he's into you.'

'He isn't.'

'He's smitten.'

'No he isn't.'

'*Ask* him, why don't you?'

'Leave him alone.'

'He'd like to be your cello.'

'I said leave him alone.'

'Purring betwixt your thighs.'

'Your brother plays *drums*, Trez? Why didn't you tell us?'

'Because he works, Rob.'

'He what?'

'He works for my uncle Jack.'

'He plays drums for your uncle Jack?'

'No he doesn't! He works.'

'So, he works for your uncle.'

'Jesus, that's *what I said.*'

'What's he do? For your uncle?'

'He works,' Fran said.

'I . . .'

'My uncle repairs washing machines. My brother helps him out. *Stop drinking my share, Fran, you mouldy fukken scab.* And he also plays drums. It's his hobby.'

'His hobby's playing drums?'

'Merciful Christ.'

'So you're saying . . . he'd like to be in the group?'

'He *wouldn't* like to be in the *group.* Because he *works.* For my *uncle.* A fact I have *mentioned four hundred bleeding times.* But he also plays drums. And he's good.'

'What's he into?' Fran asked her.

'Musically?'

'No sexually. *Of course* fukken musically. You never *fukken listen.* It's beyond me why acne-boy fancies you.'

'Sod off, Fran, okay?'

'Well, she's deaf. It's annoying.'

'From *you?* I don't listen? Hypocritical flunt.'

'What kind of washing machines?'

'Shut your hole, Rob. Okay?'

'Anyone any money for a pint?'

'No.'

FROM INTERVIEW WITH SEÁN SHERLOCK, NOVEMBER 2012, CONDUCTED BY MOLLY GOULDING-O'KEEFFE, ROBBIE'S DAUGHTER

See, where your auntie Trez and me was brought up, that's what you heard. That part of south London, there's people from everywhere. West Indians, Ghanaians, Nigerians, Congolese. Like, our neighbours in the flat upstairs was a family from Guyana. Steel bands and stuff. Same in school. There was black kids and white together, couple of Irish, Pakistani. You didn't think about it or nothing, [it] was your parish, that's all. I mean, yeah, you'd have your National Front selling papers down the High Street now and again, but they was dumb as a box of rocks. They'd be all 'Keep Britain British' but you didn't pay them no mind. There's an arsehole in every town. That's the law.

Old neighbour of ours, Ernie Ballantyne, had a second-hand record stall up Lewisham market. He'd let me help on a Saturday. So there was always records around. The old teddy-boy stuff, then your glam, your country, jazz, the pop stuff, rocksteady. Ern didn't care, he'd sell anything. He was into the old Gracie Fields, the wartime songs. 'White Cliffs of Dover', all that. He knew Ian Dury a bit, you know, of the Blockheads. Dury's dad drove a London bus and so did Ernie for a while. And he knew the blokes from Squeeze because they come from Deptford down the road. Nice man, Ernie. Brung me to my first ever gig. 19th February 1975. Chuck Berry at the Lewisham Odeon. And he'd take me down the wrestling, Kendo Nagasaki, Giant Haystacks, all that. First time I's ever in a pub was with Ernie, the Bridge House, Canning Town, to see Dr Feelgood. Another one I remember was the Greyhound in Chadwell Heath, outfit called the Spinning Wheel was on. I think he felt sorry for me and Trez because we hadn't no dad. And I liked helping him out on the stall.

But the ska done me in. Dunno why. Just clicked with it. The Skatalites and Desmond Dekker. Prince Buster. The Dragonaires. Bluebeat stuff. Delroy Wilson, all that. I dunno, I liked the sunniness of it. The way a kid will. The English ska was more down, you know, gritty, in your face. I liked the Jamaican stuff better . . . 'Hard Man Fe Dead' . . . 'Oh Carolina'. . . 'Monkey Man'. . . And to me, there's music just in people talking. So I'm glad I's born in London. That's a choir, right there. Get the Tube from Whitechapel over to Acton Town, you'll hear every language in the world. Know what I mean? To me, that's give a sweetness to London like nowhere else around. Like, I love New York and LA, but it ain't London, never will be. The place you come up is special.

Regular little rudie I was from ten or twelve [*Laughs*]. There's pictures of me doing the moonstop the day I made me Confirmation, little porkpie hat, the works. I didn't have no consciousness of the Irish thing at all. Well, I tell a lie, like I heard it, what with me mum and that. She come from Sallynoggin, in Dublin.

Mary Sherlock. She'd be giving you earhole about the Four Green Fields. And she was a beautiful singer, don't take me the wrong way. Mum won medals for singing, all the old Irish songs. 'Wrap the Green Flag Round Me, Boys, to die were far more sweet.' But it weren't my thing, see. Well it ain't when you're a nipper. Stands to reason you wouldn't go for the music your mum would be into . . . My mum had it hard. I'm not much of a one for the good old days. For a while she cleaned house for a nice family, Jakobovits, they was Ashkenazi Jews, and Mrs Jakobovits was very good to my mum, but then they moved. She was a cleaner in a light-bulb factory down Bexleyheath for a while; after that she worked in Lewisham Hospital, in the laundry. Your single mum didn't get much help or understanding, not back then. There'd be remarks, all the rest of it. Kids can be toe-rags. She spoke with an Irish accent and they'd be taking the piss. She was tough, you know. But she idolised us. That's truth. And she always had this thing – you'll get your education, that's that. Wouldn't take no argument. You better not start one. Catch you bunking off school, she'd rip off your arm and beat you to death with it. [*Laughs.*] She'd say music's well and fine but it ain't no education. [*Adopts 'Irish' accent.*] 'De music's fer feckin chancers and rogues!'

Personally I don't give a monkeys about politics, being honest. To me, they're all the same. I don't give 'em headroom. Kiss your arse till they're elected, then tell you 'kiss mine'. But it weren't a stroll for

Irish people in England my mum's generation. You was a bit second-class. Not always. But they felt, you know what I mean, that the old place thrown 'em out and the new one only wanted 'em if they was prepared to be micks. Twats laughing at them in sitcoms. Like at black people, or Pakistanis. Funniest thing to do in your comedy sketch was stick in a foreign johnny. Fuzzy-wuzzies, darkies, Paddy on de dhrink. 'Lawks, there's a Nigerian moved in across the street! Says he's a doctor! Hide the silverware!' *Black and White Minstrels* on telly – swear to God. Look, it was what it was, and I'm glad it's gone away. You'll get ignorance everywhere. What you do is fix your own. Read a book. Look about. Grow up. The other bloke's music, see it might be worth a listen. That Bob Marley single? You like it? What's he saying? Try Nina Simone. Get informed. There's history, geography, everything in music. See, it paints you a picture. Take a look.

But it was a different time in England, still stuck in the past. England's mellower now. More chilled. All I'm saying, it weren't a cakewalk for people like Mum. And then you had your Provos. It made things hard. Bombs up in Woolwich and Birmingham, all the rest. Mum'd be afraid to go to work. And ashamed. That's truth. And I'm, 'Mum, it ain't us.' But after a while, you stop bothering. Fucked if I'll apologise for the stuff I didn't do. None of this shit's down to me.

But it ain't that simple. Comes and bites you in the bum. There was a time when I was sixteen, I fancied going in the army. See the world. Learn a trade. I'll have some of that. I go down the recruiting depot in Greenwich, tell the sergeant my name. He says 'Your own lot won't like you taking the Queen's shilling.' Me own lot? Who's that, mate? You talking about the Mods?'

I literally don't know what he's on about. Then it clicks.

'I'm London born and bred.'

'Son, there's London and London.'

Is he having a laugh? I'm looking in his face.

Never been in Ireland, support Charlton Athletic, Ray Davies in his Union Jack suit on me bedroom wall. I mean, listen to me voice, mate. I ain't Brendan Behan.

He's a nice old geezer, he ain't being funny. But he's gimme a piece of advice, which I'm very glad I took. He ain't saying no, but go home and talk to your mum. And that was the end of the army. They missed the chance of Drummer Sherlock in the Royal Marines band. I'd have grooved 'em up good. There you go.

Seán was whipcrack handsome, with his sister's huge eyes, a close-cropped, jaw-jutting Gary-Cooper-like fellow like you see on posters in old barbershop windows. You could imagine him as the Marine who kissed the girl in Times Square the night victory in Japan was announced. Although he was skinny in those days, you often pictured him as muscular, probably because he had none of a thin man's birdy nervousness but tended to be silent in a room. He smoked roll-ups he seemed to form with one hand. He drank bourbon-and-Coke and owned a car. It had a hundred thousand miles on the clock and was rusty, with fag-burnt leatherette seats, but to be the possessor of an internal combustion engine of even basic functionality wasn't a thing you encountered in our circle. Endearingly, Trez referred to him as 'John-John', a pet name from their childhood. He called her 'Sis' or 'Mugsy' or 'Blags'. He spoke in what I later learned was a south London accent, though at the time I had it down as plain cockney.

In he strode to the audition room as though he were the owner, blowing kisses to the aged cleaning lady as she left. Yep, he'd been here before, had drummed in several bands, had even done a bit of recording. 'All right, Robbie? How you doing, mate? Yeah, I bang the old skins. No Ginger Baker or nothing. Just an 'obby.' Rendering his speech in bad phonetics reduces him, as that cheap literary tactic always does, so I'm not going to be doing it a lot. My point is that Seán spoke like the born Londoner he was. For some reason it added to his authority from the start. I can offer no explanation. He wowed us.

I've seen it written with scriptural authoritativeness that Seán and I 'attended the same school' and were 'childhood friends' as a result. But that isn't so, and I don't know how this nonsense got going. It occurs to me now that I don't know *where* he went to school. He was like someone who never had: clever, articulate, uncomplicatedly good-natured and self-assured, entirely without the brokenness-dressed-as-gaiety you saw in kids my age. Trez had many of those qualities, too, and an irony all her own. But I'd never met anyone as disconcertingly likeable as Seán. I wasn't quite sure how to handle him.

We talked history. He rated the Who, was a Small Faces completist. His heroes were Ray and Dave Davies. Yeah, the Stones were the nazz. Charlie-boy could *drum*. But Metal gave him a pain in the jacksie.

'You're not a poorpler?' Fran asked.

'A what?'

I translated: an admirer of Deep Purple.

'Mean, Paicey's an ace drummer. And Gillan on the vocals, he'll scream down your house. Axe-man like Blackmore's gonna bring you the fireworks. It's just Metal ain't my cup of tea. Like, nothing *against* it or nothing. Each to his own way of thinking.'

What he loved was a deadly drummer playing clean as a razor, 'making a hard thing sound easy, that's the gig'. There were technically greater drum performances than that of Al Jackson Junior on 'Green Onions' by Booker T & the MGs but this was Seán's favourite. Fabulous track, really. More complex than you thought. 'Fackin thing's in chromatic minor with a fifth as tonic chord,' he pointed out.

'An *open* fifth, John-John,' Trez said with an admonishing laugh.

'Yeah, obviously. They know that, Sis.'

'Amazing, the way you see it in the blues,' Trez continued. 'The open major tunings that the old black guys came up with. D modal, Joni Mitchell uses that a lot.'

'And then your open G,' Seán agreed, 'D G D G B D, with the fifth string removed, which is pretty much all Keith Richards plays in. Sodding *brilliant*.'

Silence came down. I sensed Fran's unease and my own.

We enjoyed thinking of ourselves as 'instinctive musicians', a phrase that, whenever I see it now, makes me reach for a Taser-gun. If all you're offering is instinct, close the door on your way out. I have instincts myself, as has every shite-hawk in the world, and have spent much of my life trying, and failing, to be rid of them. But back then, one saw matters differently, or pretended to, or something. Unquestioning believers in the myth of amateurism, false gospel of popular music since about 1956, Fran and I tended to assert quiet superiority to – even punchable pity for – anyone who knew what a treble clef was. By this means, we proved our idiocy. A-7th resolves to D, from Palestrina to dubstep, and it will continue to do so long after you've gone, because it's been doing it a damn long time. It does that because people *like* it to do that, and what they like is presumably the point. If you think Robert Johnson and Bessie Smith weren't aware of this, listen again. You wouldn't permit a surgeon who boasted that she didn't know a scalpel from a hacksaw to slice you open and whip out your kidney. Only in the arts do we see pig-ignorance as a qualification. It's the worst form of snobbery I know.

But since Trez's arrival into the scum-speckled swamp of our dilettantism, that well-documented pose had been harder to maintain. You did your best to maintain it, but you didn't do so publicly, and any pose not publicly main-tained becomes its evil twin, a hang-up. Now here came Seán too, wading through the morass of our complexes, like some lolloping St Bernard who didn't realise he was saving you, impossible to dislike, although I tried to. He is to this day the only adult I've known who really *can* pull off a Paul-McCartney-style thumbs-up-with-cheeky-grin and not make you want to disembowel him. Well, Macca can do that, too, obviously.

Seán confirmed to us that he was working with his uncle in the town, mending washing machines, tumble driers, fridges, cookers, 'all your basic white goods, also lawn-mowers'. He found the repairs trade 'all right', enjoyed 'the people side of it', was aiming to have a van of his own on the road one day. If it didn't happen, didn't matter. He'd do something else. Maybe open a 'Mod boutique' or 'a bakery'. He intended being his own boss – 'see, that way, you survive. Know whose kids ain't never hungry? The boss's.' The electrician's qualification he was working towards at night school would always be a help. In the meantime, he had 'a goal and beer money'. He wasn't like us, he continued, smiling fondly. Music was just his way of passing the time. Some people drank, or played footie, or went to church, or were interested in politics. He drummed. Banging on drums was only 'dancing sitting down'. You didn't want to take it 'too serious'.

At this point I plunged into the depths of my defensive-ness and said Fran and I took things way serious. That was pukkah, Seán said. His sister was the same. He could see why she 'thought so highly' of us, he remarked, a statement that made me blush like an over-blurbed novel. Trez was also blushing, even harder. I don't exaggerate when I tell you that up to that moment I suspected she regarded Fran and me as messers.

Well, Fran continued asking questions, but with a newer intensity, like a voter on a doorstep seeking the views of a candidate. A strange thing to do since Seán had expressed no interest in being elected. His only reason for being at the studio was to collect Trez and drive her home. But suddenly his manifesto was sought.

His position on the Specials? Strongly in favour.

His views on the Queen? He dug Freddie.

Where did he stand on Duran Duran?

'Ard to say, really. On its throat?'

Fleetwoodmackery? Opposed.

Yes? No.

Andrew Ridgeley of Wham? The lesser of two evils.

Early Roxy Music? Magnificent beyond words.

Later Roxy Music? Hmm.

Status Quo? Again hmm. One really shouldn't like them. And yet.

'Fade to Grey' by Visage? Vice versa.

'Keep on Loving You' by REO Speedwagon? Only in cases of capital murder, but the Geneva Convention should be consulted.

The Beat? Mighty sweet.

The Sweet? Very much.

Genesis? You 'avin' a laugh?

'Since you're here,' Fran said, 'play us something if you would?' I had rarely seen him address anyone with what appeared to be courtesy. Seeing it now made me scared.

'What you reckon, Mugsy?'

'Why not,' she replied.

'Won't do no harm. Where's Black Betty?'

'Black Betty' turned out be familial slang for Trez's cello. My growing unease flared like dropsy. These people spoke in *nicknames*. Was this Walton's sodding Mountain? I reached for my last cigarette.

What they played was a traditional planxty by the

seventeenth-century harpist Turlough O'Carolan, a lumi-
nously gorgeous thing full of Italianate harmonies and
strange swoops you weren't expecting. He scarcely touched
the snare or the ride with his brush but every time he did,
it made a difference. Nodding with priestly gravitas, his
shoulders swaying time, he'd give her a shy smile or glance
up at the ceiling as though the bare light bulb was listening.
You didn't often get to hear a brother and sister performing
music. To observe it was to know your limits. She would
nod, he'd give a roll, she'd raise an eyebrow, he'd fill, and
you understood you were looking at people with a closeness
born of years, that there was something in the particular
way he shimmered a cymbal that his sister was telling him
to do. It was beautiful music and I hated every moment.
The monster of envy was here.

I was young at the time but I realised one truth: no
quartet can comprise two duumvirates. Fran and I had been
engaged on something small of our own. Then had come
Trez. Now her brother. What next? Granny Sherlock and
her excellence on the banjo? I didn't want to join the fucking
Family von Trapp or have its London-Irish offshoot annex
me. As Seán grinned and departed the room, accompanied
by his sister, having wished us to 'be lucky' with a cheery
bump of fists, I was already making up my mind that he
wouldn't do at all, but would one day make something like
a very nice suicide counsellor whom the mums at the school
gate secretly fancied.

Amazingly, it was Fran who demanded we enlist him. I
was convinced he was joking. He was serious. Seán must
join the group, if only on a temporary basis. 'Any semi-sane
bugger' would agree that this was essential. In the Franningrad

Soviet, there was only one Chairman, no matter the expedient pretence of democracy, and as happens in every dictatorship, personal or political, lunacy was imputed to naysayers. In addition, it was put to me that I was being 'a fukken Wilbur', Fran's term for a person taking his relatively small sufferings far too seriously (from the names of the poet William Butler Yeats). Worse, I was a 'Mimi': one whose only conversational topic is himself (from the Beatles' 'I Me Mine'). Also, a 'Wisty', a person of hysterical and unmerited self-importance (Wystan Auden). Fran knew how to throw a low punch.

We began the kind of ding-dong you see in a bad soap, where we paced and furiously smoked and took seven kinds of umbrage, denouncing one another with competitive silences when violent words failed, as they do. What I resented was the way he was subtly changing our roles. I had always been Felix, he was meant to be Oscar, the pip-spitting, chain-smoking hammer of the respectable, the lush with his boots on the pouf. Suddenly the wretch was lecturing me that I was becoming 'impossible'. This was Vesuvius accusing you of volatility. You didn't happen across a musician like Seán every day, he pointed out, as though anyone with functional eardrums wouldn't have realised this fact about four seconds after Seán started playing. 'Guy knows his stuff, too. All I'm saying, Gimpy? He'd give us another arrow in the quiver.'

Well, that was where I lost it. The red mist beset me. I said I would give Fran an arrow, but not in his quiver, unless that word was new slang for the utmost and most previously unexplored (even by him) rafters of his satanic hole. Well, that isn't how I put it. But I definitely said 'hole'. Jimmy had started to influence my vocabulary.

'It's me or him,' I said.

Fran gave a short laugh. 'You're wonderful when you're angry.'

'I mean it.'

'Tell you what, we'll have an arm-wrestle. Whoever wins chooses.'

'Roll up your sleeves,' I said.

Seven

SEÁN

Yeah, they asked me to join. Stands to reason. They had to. Funny though. Now you mention, I don't never remembering them asking. Way I recall, the deal was I'd sit in till they found some other schlub. A week or two, a month. But that ain't the way it went.

Quit the day job? No way. I's happy as a trout. Well, I'd had enough of bands, see. Been in and out before. Wedding band, session work, bit of this, bit of that. I'd me eyes on the prize, love. Electrician. Imagine. Good solid trade and your money every week. The missus says I should've stuck at it. She's right.

See, I didn't take music serious. Music's just a laugh. You're doing nothing else, you'll give it a go. And Fran was a piece of work. Like, imagine meeting Fran. I'm nineteen years old, here's the Prince of sodding Denmark. Mouthy. In your face. But you couldn't help loving him. He's banging the piano-lid against the upright in rhythm. Limping like Richard the Third. Full of pig-iron, you know? Razor-boy meets Madame Mao. You ain't likely to forget him, put it like that. You didn't see his likes back in Lewisham.

I liked Rob from the off. Good boy. Always was. Sweet, low-key kid. Give you the shirt off his back. Not that you'd want it. No, he wasn't no soul-boy. Absolutely not. He dressed like a geezer the Undertones chucked out for being too scruffy. But intelligent. Sharp. We was mates in a shake, we'd have a drink and a natter down the Great Northern, near the station. He's gimme a lot of blather down the years, says he didn't like me at the time. But that ain't the way I remember, straight up. We never had no bother, it's a little thing he does. Why? Ain't no clue, love. He's a pillock [*Laughs.*] Me and Robbie go back. Long time ago now. Nice kid he was. Good friend.

Bit slow on the uptake when he had a few beers down, mind. Tells me one night – playing pool in the Northern – 'I thought yourself and Trez was *identical* twins, you know, before we met.' I said 'How the fuck could a boy and a girl be identical, mate?' He's pondered a sec. 'Oh yeah.'

And Mugsy, she was great. When you're twins, things is different. Music in a family, well it makes life sweet. Little squabble, you play music. Christmas night, you play music. It's a way of having a conversation without having to talk. I say to my kids, that's the thing about music. It's there when you need it, like a mate you can trust. Mightn't reckon you need it now, but the tough day comes. Music's give me everything. I love it.

The problem was Fran. See, I couldn't understand him. He'd be using these expressions, like a slang of his own. Not being funny, but you wouldn't have a monkey's what he was on about half the time. He'd be yakking about the news or an article he's read in the paper and you're scratching your head, looking on. Frannie was one of them kids, his brain went faster than his mouth. If he couldn't put his finger on a word, he'd just make it up. And then sometimes he's come up with a word, just for privacy, or naughtiness. See, music again. Look at rap. Like a personal slang. 'One up' was G-major, 'two up' was D. Robbie'd write them down. Like a translator. He'd collect them. But me, I wouldn't have a breeze what the two donuts was on about. Off they'd go again. Speaking Frannish.

FROM ROBBIE'S DIARY, APRIL 1983

The following usages have been noted in the speech of subject Francis Xavier Mulvey.

Handball, Starman, Stoutheart, Spatchcock, My decent sombrero, Good Morning Nurse: salutations connoting approval/affection.
Snow White and the Seven Dwarves: the Governing Academic Council of Stanton Polytechnic and Agricultural College.
Gropecunt Lane: the Department of English Literature at Stanton Polytechnic and Agricultural College, particularly the corridor where that Department is located.
Flunt-monkey: a roué or satyr. A mercurial libertine. A person given over to the appetites, e.g. Lemmy from Motörhead, Charles Haughey, former Taoiseach of Ireland.
The Cat in the Hat: His Holiness, Pope John Paul II.

Thing One and Thing Two: Daryl Hall and John Oates.

Cruella de Vil: the Prime Minister of this country.

Pangziety: the alternating current of sadness and rage that one feels when abandoned by a sweetheart or the Labour Party.

Claptonistically: adverb describing winces, gurnings and other facial emotings while lost in a long guitar-solo, eyes closed.

Big Jean from Accounts: satirical term for any large, jolly person overly keen to 'fit in'. Fran's name for Father O'Reilly, the chaplain.

Zippy and Bungle: Jimmy and Alice.

Glimmertwin: a blood brother, an ally, a lifelong friend. From 'The Glimmer Twins', collective nom de guerre of M'luds Jagger and Richards.

Woollyback: (1) unfair term for rural dweller. (2) any Irish-born student of Agricultural Science at this college. See also **Hedge-Biffer, Bog-Wasp, Slurryist, Uddermensch, Mad Pat**, the latter not a person's name but an unruly condition: 'The night Celtic beat Borussia Mönchengladbach, he went Mad Pat altogether. We couldn't get him down off the roof.'

Popocatépetl: an active volcano in Mexico. Also an onomatopoeic sound uttered by Fran during rehearsal to illustrate to drummer what he should be playing.

Catweazle: a man or woman of frightening, cross-eyed or unkempt appearance, e.g. the Professor of Industrial and Organisational

Psychology. The collective noun is 'a whinny'.

Raspberry Rippled: pleasantly drunk. See also, **Hornswoggled, Baw-faced, 'Up for the Match'**: very dangerously and offensively drunk.

Shishkebabble: late night drunken conversation occurring in takeaway.

Faggiography: the art of persuading strangers to give you cigarettes. Faggi*ology* is the study of this.

The Brothers Grim: Lynyrd Skynyrd.

Happy Jack: a song by the Who. Also the name of Fran's favourite plant.

Crazy Phil's Mobile Disco: insulting term for excessively cheerful person. 'I've never liked that Mary. Always 'up for the craic'. She's a bit Crazy-Phil's-Mobile-Disco'.

Sex-mechanic: a seducer, a jade, a promiscuous person.

New Balls Please: expression indicating desire to change subject of conversation.

Shirley: name inflicted on drummer by Fran.

Mother Shipton/That twat: vice versa.

This planet is home to few persons that I love more than Seán Sherlock, the most loyal and empathetic of comrades you could ever hope to meet. Aged nineteen, he was already more quietly wise than your granddad. Decency informed his every act. What image could encapsulate a prince such as this? If in the realms of a Kafkaesque nightmare you were arrested for some horror you didn't commit, and your torturers made the mistake of allowing one telephone call before they sparked up the batteries, Seán's would be the number to dial. He'd know what to do. I have never seen him panic. Even as a teenager, he was a person so solid that addressing him was like talking to a flagpole in a parka. You wanted to *salute* him, God's truth.

Here was a boy with his act together so utterly that he didn't have to point it out by telling you. A fellow earning *wages*. A man. With a girlfriend. He'd paid for his own drum lessons by doing handyman jobs around his council estate after school. He understood drills. He'd built people's bookshelves. He never knew his father but shrugged it off when you asked him. 'We was lucky to have a mum and a gran.' At sixteen, he had what amounted to a part-time business, a wedding-band he managed from the public telephone box near his home. He would tell you that one of his ambitions was to buy the council house in which his mother and grandmother lived, so they wouldn't have to worry (a thing he achieved at the age of twenty-two). How deeply I disliked and begrudged him. He pretends not to believe me, but it's the shameful truth. I feared and coveted and fumed. This is what happens when emulousness goes mad. Why had I not been born Seán?

I begrudged the debonair bowling shirts, the neatly pressed worsted suit – the only one he owned but it always looked new – with its three-button jacket and the double pleats in the pants, and the Northern Soul crests on the cufflinks. When he eulogised Martha Reeves or Geno Washington and the Ram Jams, he assumed you had the faintest idea of the highs he was on, and this I *deeply* resented. He scoffs when I tell him, always thinks I'm joking, but if an unfrightening method of murder had revealed itself to me at the time, I might have been tempted to ice him.

He'd arrive into rehearsal, bring coffees, bump fists with us, make pleasant and inclusive remarks, somehow get the decrepit electric radiator going, and sit at the kit with all the infuriating cheeriness of Santa-In-His-Little-Drum-Shop. No suggestion was too preposterous for him to call it what it was, no key-change too jarring, no lyric too pretentious. Songs whose recollection make me blush to the earlobes, he would praise as possessing 'the suede'. But that was Seán. He wouldn't even know he was lying. Having put in twelve hours in the service of his uncle, he gave the steadying geniality of his evenings to his sister's friends, with the talent he'd been honing for eight years. Through all of it, he'd insist he wasn't *in* the group but was merely helping out until 'a proper drummer' came along. What is to be done with a person such as this? Van Diemen's Land would be too easy and too close.

Trez was the most naturally gifted musician I'd ever have the honour to know, a 24-carat prodigy, playing since she was five. Fran would unfurl over time into an artist so unique that he may have gone on to rewrite the rules of his medium. But Seán Sherlock, and no one else, turned us into a band, eight to the bar, the hard way. Here was a boy who could chop time into beautiful slivers, turn rhythms upside down, careen them inside out, while the thudding, insistent stomp of his matchless right foot bashed out a vicious bass-beat. You could argue that Everett Morton was smoother and faster, but I'd give you the argument back. There will never be another drummer like Seán's god, Ginger Baker, but even in that hungry and feverishly exciting era, on a fourth-hand kit, in a stinking basement, with some trio of Crass-loving punks waiting to slink in when your session was finished, elbowing you out of the way, finishing your butt-ends, Seán could coax thunderstorms from a Roland drum that would stand you in drop-dead awe. We thanked him, Fran and I, by abusing his ears with our sonic pollution, and by laughing at him when he and his sister had left the room. He was then, and is still, a person of private kindnesses, but he'd equipped himself with a ridiculous tough-guy image which meant you weren't permitted to mention them. At the risk of his displeasure, one truth must be noted. When, some years later, my drinking wrecked my marriage, the mercy that kept Seán and Trez Sherlock in my life, through anguish, destruction and bitterest failure, was the only reason I surfaced. I never said any of this to Seán at the time. But I think he knew. I hope so.

TREZ

. . . And then our first actual gig would have been what, in the Student Union Common Room for end of exams, June '83. It was a fundraiser for the Nicaragua Solidarity Society. We were pretty well rehearsed. We weren't too bad . . . The main act was a crowd called Thatcher on Acid, heavy, heavy punk, I loved them . . . From Somerset . . . God, who else, let me think. It's so long ago now . . . We hadn't a name at the time. We'd gone through about five thousand possibilities. The Changelings. The Inklings. The Tatterdemalions. The Hair. Seriously – John-John wanted to call us 'The Hair', I think because the Who were called that when they started . . .

FROM ROBBIE'S DIARY

The Phlogistonics, the Brittlestars, the High Numbers, the Stress-Dreams, the Milliners, the Blockers, the Cloudberries, the Modest Proposals, Shoolbred Works, Stockwood a go-go, the Loggerheads, the Borstal Boys, the Lost Causes, Desolate Shade, the Stone of the Heart, Daydream Farouche, the Takeaways, the Pangur Bawns, the Pretty Young Things, Herol Graham and the Bombers, John Banville's Chinese Orchestra.

TREZ

. . . And I'm fairly sure it was Robbie came up with 'The Thrill'. After that Roxy Music song 'The Thrill of It All'. Yeah. I bumped into him in town on the afternoon of the gig and he ran it by me as a suggestion because we needed a name by tonight. So I said fair enough and the lads didn't object. So that's what happened. Last-minute baptism. The lads, being lads, always felt your name really mattered, but I didn't. Like, 'The Beatles' is a God-awful name for a band, when you think. And 'Bob Dylan' sounds like a guy who sells second-hand furniture. A name's only a name. I mean 'The Doors'? That's a band?

But the boys loved making their lists and having arguments about them. It was kind of a big dick competition for a while, who'd come up with the name, be the daddy. I suggested we call ourselves the Handbags or the Big Girls' Blouses, just for badness. Or maybe the Tool-belts. Dear boys.

It was end of exams so the audience was fairly hammered. The room had these granite slabs on the floor and bare concrete walls – like a toilet cistern, the echo. Really bad. The stage was made of tables. It wasn't the Fillmore East . . . But they gave us a proper sound-check, well, as proper as it gets. They'd hired in an actual PA system, even a couple of disco lights. We were on first, we played all covers, maybe for half an hour. I'd say there were thirty people . . . Al Green's 'Take Me to the River', then 'Dear Prudence', the Siouxsie and the Banshees version, a couple of Iggy Pop things. The Monkees' 'Stepping Stone'. Patsy's 'Walkin' After Midnight'. Robbie was a bit nervous. I remember he wore his guitar very high on his chest, like Gerry Marsden from the Pacemakers used to do, so he could see the fretboard when it came time for a solo. The cool thing at the time was guitar around your knees. But fair play, he put substance over style. [*Laughs*] John-John was mad keen to do 'Cum On Feel the Noize' by Slade just for badness, so we did. It's actually a fun song to do, especially when the audience are stocious and most of them are your mates. It was amazing to see people dancing and punching the air. Wow . . . There's nothing like playing music and seeing people dance. We did a couple of Patti Smith things, 'Redondo Beach' and 'Dancing Barefoot'. Funny, Fran was the most nervous of us, which you'd never have imagined. He was dressed like, I don't know

. . . miniskirt and leggings. Poor baby was sweating, so his mascara ran. A couple of numbers in and he looked like a bisexual panda. This mob of pissed Aggies arrived and started giving him grief, but that was when he got into his mojo. The more they slagged him off, the better he got. That's Fran . . . One of them gozzed at him, which was a thing you'd see at a gig back then. Disgusting I know, but that's the way it was. And I remember Fran saying in this beautiful camp voice: 'Darling, you proved you've a head full of snot. Well done!' And everyone was in the palm of his hand from then on. Even the Aggies started bopping.

It's compulsory for every band to say their first gig was a disaster, but ours actually wasn't. I'd say we were competent. No Thatcher on Acid or anything, don't be getting me wrong . . . [*laughs*] . . . But we certainly didn't disgrace ourselves. We were thrilled. What was sweet was that Rob's dad and mum pitched up with his brother Shay. They were dead proud of Robbie. You could see it. He was chuffed. And my mam came along and my aunties and the neighbours. It was actually a lovely night, a very nice memory. They all went off for a drink and we stayed for the other bands and the disco.

Funny, I remember there were these two miners from Durham or somewhere. There was all this stuff at the time saying the NUM might have to go on strike. Some American, MacGregor, had been hired to start closing down the pits. I took an interest in it because my uncle Stephen was a big trade unionist. He was a steward in the Merchant Navy, then he joined the Communist Party when he left. And there weren't many lifelong Communists born in Dublin. Interesting man, Stephen. Self-educated, left school at thirteen. But that's another story. I think these lads were in the college for a Labour Party meeting or something, you know, to make a speech. And they got dragged along to the Common Room after. Well, they got a fair bit of attention, not just because of what they were saying but how they looked. We'd this dense image of miners as kind of grimy and put-upon. Little ferrety fellows in overalls. You know, with lamps. But this pair were massive hunks of about twenty-five, incredibly handsome, with necks thicker than their heads and muscles the size of mountains. They looked like they should've been in the Human League.

It was a lovely occasion. Our first proper gig. And let's face it, it's not every night you cop off with a miner. Which certain people did. I'm not saying which ones. Pardon my blush. Where were we?

FROM FRAN'S FIRST INTERVIEW, *WHAT'S ON IN LUTON*, AUGUST 1983

. . . We've been gigging over the summer but not much. Just pubs now and again, like the Castle . . . We've played the Brewery Tap a few times . . . Do you know it? . . . On Park Street . . . There's all this nonsense about how we're an Irish band . . . We're so much more. Sarah-Thérèse, our bassist, is actually French . . . Robert, our guitarist, has an interesting history. Really, music saved him. I can't say any more. A guy that age in prison, it isn't going to be easy when he's sensitive and pretty. . . . You ask what's the reason our group is establishing a reputation? Oh I assume because not everyone in this town has a cowpat for a brain . . . We're going in for this *City Limits* magazine Battle of the Bands Competition in October and I expect we'll win that. And then we'll move to London. Brian Eno wants to produce us. But we're looking at options. Got a light? Ta. Got a fag?

FROM *CITY LIMITS*

Scumbag Picasso + Handmade Chairs + the SK Alligators + the Suburbans + Busted Flush + the Barbed + the Sacred Hearts + Gauloise de Beauvoir + the Anti-Dance Men + the Brainstems + Remember the Porter + Clusterfuck + the Ships in the Night + Outdoor Jacks + Death + Vorsprung Diphtheria.

The Earl's Arms, St Albans, 'Battle of the Bands' Beds Herts and Bucks heats, October 1983.

> . . . Seventh-placed Luton outfit, the Ships in the Night, lived down to expectations, serving a pungent, viscous sludge of leftover Bowie with lumps of folkish gristle and pepperings of whiteboy reggae (yawn), under a

coagulating skin of faux Moddery. Num! Num! Nope. Their version of Goebel Reeves/ Woody Guthrie's 'Go To Sleep, You Weary Hobo' made you do just that. Frontperson Francis Mulvey is not unable to, er, sing but spent most of his time haranguing an audience that could scarcely contain its indifference and sluttishly blowing on his nail varnish. Tasty work from Sarah Sherlock on cello and five-string Hardanger Norwegian fiddle (no, we didn't know either) meshed with less accomplished strummings from Bobby [*sic*] Goulding on guitar. (Yikes! *Tune* it, young jedi. Might help.) Solid drumming from looker Seán Sherlock did its best to underpin the effort. But nothing you haven't heard, oh, forty million times before, apart from the little you wouldn't want to hear again. They used to be called 'The Thrill', but there's naught to thrill here. File under Going Nowhere Fast.

Eight

Down the years, I'd see Fran spin lurid fabrications on the subject of how we raised the cash to make a demo. We did not 'sell our blood by the pint' (*NME*) or 'win the South Yorkshire State Lottery' (*Oregon Post*). As for his claim that he, Seán and I 'worked as gigolos in the posh areas of Luton' (*Daily Telegraph*) – I being especially popular because of my skills at something the men of Bedfordshire were reluctant to undertake – I've probably established that I wouldn't have been very successful on the game. Any restless hausfrau admitting me to her bungalow while hubby was away on the golf links would have been likelier to offer me a cup-a-soup than to lead me upstairs while wriggling out of her tights. Oliver Twist went to London to make his fortune. Ours was made before we got there.

In 1980s Ireland, taxis were required to display a metal badge listing the identity number and other credentials of the driver. This item, 'a taxi plate' was thus a sort of currency, a means of selling or buying the licence. That postcard-sized oblong of pressed steel was worth thirty thousand punts, a preposterous amount of money in Ireland at the time. Thirty grand would have bought you a house, or a member of parliament.

How does this relate to the singer of what was by now called the Ships in the Night? Indeed you might wonder. But it does. A Dublin taxi-man died that spring and bequeathed his two plates to relatives in England. Those beneficiaries were the pair of sewer-hearted thugs that had adopted the six-year-old Fran on his arrival from Vietnam. I believe they're now dead. It's sad there's no Hell. I'm told they were publicly the very model of oily propriety. Anyway, they had suddenly two taxi plates.

Unfortunately for these low-lifes, Fran was contacted by a social worker in the north, who informed him of their unexpected inheritance. At the time, he told me that they'd offered one of the taxi plates 'for his future'. The truth I discovered years later. My poor friend, worldly at nineteen, had gone to a lawyer in Luton. Before her, he swore an affidavit from which I'm not going to quote. She sent copies to those wretches, threatened to expose them to the police if the outcome her client demanded were not reached. The boy that would jail his parents is not to be fucked with. They sent what was required, by return.

I tell of this in order to cross-hatch the scene that took place in the Coffee Inn in Luton the night Fran produced his taxi plate from his pocket. For a moment I wasn't sure what it was.

'Take a goo',' he said. 'Touch it if you like.'

He looked at me coolly. And outlined his plan.

The intention was to sell that taxi plate for as much as he could garner, to a number of different purchasers, none of whom would know about the others, and then disappear with the proceeds. A complex system of post-office-box numbers and aliases was being devised to this end. He began sketching it out on a napkin.

'Disappear? Where?'

'Down London. Where else?'

'But that's fraud.'

'So?'

'You could get four years.'

'Not if I'm in London.'

'I'm told they've police in London.'

'So what? I'll change me name.'

'Don't be dense.'

'It's foolproof. I'm telling you. *Ring yourself up.*'

'You're moving to London? But what about the band?'

'In't that what I'm telling you? We're *all* moving to London.'

'You've discussed this with Trez and Seán?'

'Of course,' he lied.

'You're lying,' I said.

'How dare you?'

'There's no way they'd let me move to London.'

'Who?'

'Zippy and Bungle.'

'Balls to Zippy and Bungle. They wouldn't mind at all. They *told* me they wouldn't mind. Swear to God.'

'Fran, listen – I'm serious. I'm supposed to be in college. I've *finals this year*. So do you.'

'You hate it,' he said. 'That Poly is killing you. You've not been to one lecture this term.'

The term was only weeks old, but his accusation was

true. Still, I told him I didn't want to upset the folks. I couldn't leave home. Not yet.

'Butch up, for fuck sake. Don't be such a poof.'

Iron Man had on a chiffon blouse and mauve beret as he uttered these words. There were times when he rioted in ironies.

At this point, I should share a note of social geography. My dad loved Luton and everything about it. Rebuilt in the post-war years by Irish immigrant workers, numbers of whom remained when the work was done, the town was 5 per cent Irish but no ghetto. What he saw as its modernity of balances pleased him. He wouldn't have liked to live in an all-Irish place. Kilburn would have driven him mad. At the same time, you wanted your customs and little ways respected. Luton was the perfect solution. An amiable settlement, confident and forward-looking, open-hearted, generous to all. We'd live politely together, in tolerance and fellowship. English and Irish would put away old misunderstandings, in the happy town where good people of all heritages were welcomed with warmth. Mr Ali who worked at the Crown Court was a wise and scholarly man, married to a dentist from Wales. Mrs Chaudri, Shay's one-time teacher, must be counted a living saint. The town's meals-on-wheels system for elderly residents would implode without Mr Khan's involvement. Father O'Connor was friendly with the vicar, Reverend Jennings from Dorset, these two holy men playing golf at the weekends with Dr Czerwinski, a son of Poland. Our neighbours were family people who deserved the unstinting courtesy that all fortunate Lutonians must afford to the world, as example to the citizens of wretchedly miserable hellholes like St Albans,

Flitwick or Cheddington. Given the frailty of humankind and the existence of Original Sin, Paradise on this earth can never be possible. But how blessed to have come so close. We had markets and parks and a magnificent public library, and cows in the fields beyond the station. God be praised, the municipal swimming pool was *free*, on Sundays and most bank holidays. There were wholesome and likeable girls who might snuggle his grandchildren. There were jobs at the airport or in Harpenden. Being the nice Irish family on our road wasn't only a status; it was a serious, an awesome burden. Luton wasn't a town but a self-respect he'd achieved. In NO way was Luton like London.

You won't believe me, but in the eleven years of my life in England, I'd visited the capital on only five occasions, four being allegedly educational trips with my class, the fifth a Thin Lizzy concert at Wembley Arena with Shay. To Alice but especially to Jimmy, London was a metropolis to be feared: a nest of cutpurses, highwaymen, cheats and low persons, fallen women, strange fashions and noise. Seventy minutes from Luton station, it was nevertheless another country. I don't remember Dad ever going there or wanting to do so. There were pubs up in Soho, Jimmy would tell you, where MEN went to meet MEN and NO WOMEN on the premises. That sounded like most of the pubs in Luton, my mum would reply. He'd look at her darkly. Poor Jimmy.

'I'm going,' Fran said. He'd sell the plate legally ('if you insist'). A small-ad would appear in tomorrow's Dublin *Evening Herald* inviting bids. His mind was resolved. He asked me to make my choice.

'I'm staying,' I said. 'So should you.'

Now tearful, he pulled his rucksack and guitar from beneath the dirty table. And he pushed through the door of the Coffee Inn without closing it, like a boy who wouldn't be seeing any of this again, not the rain or the flower-girls or the beggars in the alley, not the prophet selling *What's on in Luton* outside the Regis Café, not the streets where our apprenticeship began. I sat alone two hours, shocked and upset. Then I walked around the town, looking in the record shop windows.

I went to the Poly library, hoping to bump into Trez, but she wasn't around that night. I opened a scholarly journal that was lying on a table. It contained a sixty-page article on Graham Greene's use of punctuation in *The Power and the Glory*. Someone spent many months writing that.

I'm a stayer, I said. My father has me wrong. It hurts right now. But I'll stay.

Eleven nights later, I took the coach to London with Seán, Trez having refused to join us. She was adamant about it. She wouldn't quit college. Her mother had made too many sacrifices to get her an education. I mustn't drop out. But I did.

One of Fran's biographies says I 'ran away', but that isn't the truth. Leaving would have been easier if I had. Jimmy accompanied me to the coach depot, the two of us crying as we went, as though I was emigrating to America or Mars. It was October 1983. I was a month short of twenty. It was snowing that night in Luton.

I would break my mum's heart. Please could I stay and finish college? It wasn't too late to reconsider. The tenner he pressed into my hand just before I walked through the gates with Seán, I never could bear to spend. My daughter has it now. One day my grandchild might look at it, the faded greens and blues, strange as the currency of any country from the past. A portrait on a crumple of paper.

SEÁN

See, what happened, I was going for an apprenticeship at Hayward Tyler, engineers in the town. And I didn't get it. That's all. Pissed me off. Nobody's fault, but it well pissed me off. Uncle Jack and the washing machines, it's all fine and nice, but I was bored of it, being honest. Had enough. You're working fourteen hours, coming home shagged to buggery. He's handed you six quid for your pains. Nice feller, Jack. But he wouldn't spend Christmas. And the girl I was seeing, she's give us the elbow and all. Same week, as it goes. So imagine.

I'm low as the corpse in a cut-price funeral, and me mum's always worried and the rain's horizontal. The place was depressing. Trez in a mood. I'm Luton'd right up to the tits. Plug in your fucking kettle and the street lights dim. Monarch Airlines up the airport have a job cleaning planes, and the money'd be steady and it's union. But I ain't cleaning planes forty years till I peg. Sod that for a game. Pull the ripcord.

Scoot down the smoke, look about, play the drums, pick up a bit of work over there in a while, never know. There's always work in London, least there was back then. I'd a bob or two saved. And I fancied a change. Rob was off anyway, and Fran was there already, so balls to it, count me in. Go west young man. Why not?

I didn't think of it as permanent or nothing, just a walkabout, being honest. London wasn't no place I wanted to settle for good. Well, what happened, I'd a bit of bother with the law down there, as a kid. My mum don't like me to talk about it even now, so I don't . . . And of course I'm a reformed character. [*Laughs*]

No, look, all it was . . . sorry Mum . . . I shouldn't say it. But I'd a mate back in school, Nelson Johnson, good boy. The two of us was twelve, right pair of little toe-rags. We've mitched a bit and robbed, the way a couple of kids can do. We thought we was all that. Couple of yardies, me and Nelson. Smoking. Breaking windows. Stealing dirty magazines and selling them to classmates. Tryin' to pay girls' fares on the bus. All that. Harmless enough, some of it. Good clean fun. We wasn't, like, shooting nobody or stabbing old ladies. We was just being horrible little bastards. You'll chuckle, but Nelson's a very successful structural engineer in London now. Got a beautiful family, we're still in touch every Christmas. I tell him, 'Rudeboy, I remember when you wasn't so Babylon.' And we have a good laugh. But the story.

There's this National Front geezer outside the Labour Exchange every Saturday. And he's giving it large through a bullhorn like a twat. 'Send "the coloureds" back home.' Um, where, mate, to Peckham? 'English Culture is White.' Do what?

Here's a genius you give him a copy of The Complete Works of Shakespeare he'd tear out Hamlet for bog-roll. And usually you wouldn't even look at him, the stupid dozy mare. I'm proud to come from London, greatest city in the world, and there's the decentest people in Lewisham you're ever gonna meet. But there's always one arsehole, that's the eleventh Commandment. Anywhere you go. One arsehole. It's there in the bible, mate, look at the apostles. There is always one arsehole. That's the only thing I know. Spot the arsehole. He's there. Look again.

And you don't waste your time on him, well I know that now – but back then, things was different. Here's this moonfaced drooling berk outside the Army and Navy Store in his hat. I remember him good. A vicious, bullying, genuine, first-class, fully certified bell-end. So here's a Saturday we're mooching along, Nelson and me doing nothing, when Goofy from the Front says a certain word as we pass. He's looked at my mate and said this certain word. 'Go back to fakkin Africa, you dirty little blank' – it's a word I ain't never gonna say, me mum raised me better. So I won't say that word. But you know it.

I'm twelve years old. And this geezer's two hundred. But I've given it the full Clint Eastwood, right up to his face. Because you ain't gonna talk to my boy like a dog. I'm a Sherlock. Won't have it. Never did. 'Oi, John? Muppet? What you say to my mate?' He's looked at me and said it again. And Nelson's pulling me away. 'I've called your mate a little blank. And you're one and all. Only some is from Africa and some is from Mickland. But you're all blanks in the end. You and your slag of a mother.' So I've kneed him in the family marbles, just once, very hard, and give him a nice little head-butt as he's toppled. And I can tell you it ain't possible to twist someone's bollocks right off, cos I'd have done it that day if it was. Well he ain't best pleased. Which ain't no surprise. And he's big as an ape and he's battered me. It's only this nun passing by yanks me away by the earhole. And she's dragged me off home, up the stairs to the flat, and Mum's slapped me the length and breadth of the gaff for me pains and 'Sacred Heart o' de living Jaysus. I'll murther him!' Yeah. She didn't like no trouble so she's gone a bit Vesuvius. Seán O'fucking Casey ain't in it.

These days, I live in California and the wife's got me on the Yoga. And I like it out there. Nice place. Anything a London bloke my age would enjoy doing is illegal, but there's a tax exemption for juicing your wheatgrass. I'm well into the mindfulness and I listen to Enya. Cut me up on the freeway, I'll call you a twat, but I'm smiling. You know? Relaxed. I'll give you a traditional London hand gesture just to prove I'm alive but it's meant with affection, straight up. Bother me and I will recommend your immediate departure. But I won't break your legs. Not at first. Lewisham days, I wasn't so mellow. Back then, I wasn't no Buddhist.

Boy grows up a fan of The Who, he ain't in touch with his feminine side, put it like that. Mr Townshend's a chappie whose idea of stagecraft is demolishing a drum kit with a mic stand. Enya gonna do that? No she ain't, my dear. And I Won't Get Fooled Again.

I've sworn vengeance on that tosspot. And I meant every word. So I've waited and chilled and been a good little bleeder. Into school every morning, early Mass on a Sunday. Cherub in a pac-a-mac. Sweet. I remember our Trez saying to me 'What you up to? Mum'll kill you.' But all I done was smile. Innocent little angel. One thing you learn when you come up in south London is smile. Confuses your victim. Little tip. Never fuck with an Irish. He's patient, is Paddy. He'll balls you right up. Know your history.

Well, it's come to where the arsehole's car had a little mishap one night. Vauxhall Astra it was. Goofy's proud of it. You seen him tootling up Lee High Road to the meeting of the Masons, polishing it on a Sunday morning having shagged his poor old Eileen while pretending she's Eartha Kitt. Nice motor, the Astra. Handsome. Holds its value. Me and a certain party whose name I won't mention, well we follows him up to the Masons one Monday night, late, and we've smashed every window, every light, every mirror, scraped a naughty word or two across the bonnet with a fifty-pence piece, then filled the driver's seat with a bag of dogshit from a very sick dog. And dropped a match down the fuel tank for afters. Which I don't recommend no aggrieved person to go doing, by the way. But that's what I done. Oh dear.

Only this copper's clocked me haring up Lewisham

High Street ten minutes later, reeking of petrol and reefer and me eyebrows scorched off. Good sprinter, that copper. Bang to rights. Magistrate's said to me: 'What the fuck you do that for, torch a geezer's car, you villainous little horrible toe-rag?' Well, she didn't put it that way, but that's what she meant. I've said 'To watch it burn, Your Honour.' Wrong answer.

Off to Ellesmere nick, [an] institution for Young Offenders. See, I'd a little bit of previous. Shoplifting mainly. Glue, now and again. Stealing mopeds. Year before I got done for a 'taking and driving away', which is nicking a car, which wasn't too clever, but I was underage so they let me off with a bollocking. But still, I'd a name, and you don't want a name down the court. The Bill and yours truly got acquainted here and there and we wasn't too fond of each other. And funny, I wouldn't be here talking to you now if that hadn't of happened. See, [there] was an old bloke worked in Ellesmere, one of the officers there, had a thing about music for kids. There was recorders and a xylophone and a nice little piano he's blagged from a kindly old-dear in the town. A box of them kazoo things, couple of chromatic harmonicas. He's big into the harmonica because he says it's the only instrument in the world you can play while riding a bike. But I couldn't get with no recorder. If there's a worse sound in the world than a roomful of juveniles blowing recorders, that's a torture I wouldn't wish on Joe Stalin. And I didn't like the xylophone. Still don't. Dunno why. And my hands was too clumsy for the piano.

But this bloke, Mr Jenkinson, he doesn't give up on me. He's well into his Sinatra, even classical stuff, Beethoven. He's brung his records in from home, stuff you never heard. He sang carols in a choir with his missus I recall, and he'd play you a bit of Handel they was learning. And he'd ask you what you reckoned, like you knew what he meant. Gentleman, he was. Humane. Like your uncle. Give you a bit of dignity. Meet you halfway. Because you'll get that in England with a working-class person that generation. There's more cock talked about those people than anyone else on God's earth. 'Racist' this and 'ignorant' that, because they don't read The Guardian and eat Brie. They're the people won the war, mate, while you was lying in bed. You're 'anti-fascist'? Lovely. Have a frappuccino, we're impressed. But you didn't lose an arm at Anzio like Frank Jenkinson done. Top bloke, Mr Jenkinson. I owe him.

So one morning I've come into the day room and there it is by the window. Handsomest thing I ever seen in my life. Five-piece drum kit. Second-hand. Kicked to bits. Cymbals all dented. Z-shaped rip in the snare. But to me, that kit was beautiful.

Mr Jenkinson's got it off a showband in Liverpool was packing in the game. 'The Corsaires' they was called. Name in glitter across the bass. He's handed me the sticks. And I've sat on the stool. And all I'm here to tell you – I hit them skins hard.

I hit them like I meant it. I beat them drums up. Mr Jenkinson, bless his heart, takes off his uniform jacket and starts blowing 'Land of Hope and Glory' on his Funtime kazoo. I've eczema sores on my knuckles at the time but I hit them drums so hard [that] the sores broke open and bled down my wrists. That ain't a thing you see every day of the week. Little kiddie with blood on him from the drums.

And that's all I got to say. That's how it happened. There's days in your life when the whole story changes. Usually, in my experience, they're the days you wouldn't think it. Walk into a room. There's a drum kit by the window. Every friend you'll ever make, every country you'll ever see, the wife you didn't know you'd have, your beautiful kids, your whole life. All of it goes back to the day you first hit a drum. Scary thought, it might never have happened.

[The] morning I come out of Ellesmere was my thirteenth birthday. Mum told me we was moving to Luton. And I told her I'd go anyplace in the world where you could learn the drums proper. She said they had 'em in Luton. Off we went.

And I didn't think I'd be back to London at the age of nineteen. See you just never know. That's my point.

Nine

For a couple of weeks Fran and I stayed in East Finchley with a college acquaintance of Shay's, but it didn't work out too well. Paul worked in insurance, and while he did his best to be hospitable, I don't think it suited him to wend home at seven or eight and find the two of us had been on the sofa for most of the day watching tapes on the VCR he'd paid for. You didn't see a VCR back in Luton in the early 1980s. Having one at our disposal was like waking up in Graceland. Fran's ability not to go out or even twitch was astonishing. Crocodiles in the reptile house have moved with more vigour.

There was also the question of the particular tapes Fran favoured. By mail order he'd purchased a work entitled 'Three Men in a Boat', but it turned out not to be a dramatisation of Jerome K. Jerome. Personally I had nothing against the lads enjoying themselves, as clearly they were, just it wasn't my own end of the dance hall. Paul didn't see things in quite the same way. He was by nature a tolerant sort, quietly each-to-his-own, as most English people are, in my experience. You could be having it off with a trouser-press and no Englishman would mind, once you don't expect him to drop around and watch. But Fran had the thoughtless habit of leaving about the communal areas the boxes in which his erotica was packaged. Noticing 'Jockey-Room Bi-Boys' on your living-room carpet and saying nothing about it is hard.

'Dolby?' Paul enquired, with heroic insouciance. But a point had been made all the same.

His mates were sound enough, suity guys from the office, and they knew what do with a joint when you offered, but they had a way of talking about football that I couldn't quite get. *Everything* was football, even the girls they'd be rating. Anna was Arsenal, Meg Bristol City, Jenny was Everton, Vicky Man U. Boys will be boys, and it was innocent foolishness, but foolishness not your own grows tiresome. Fran could be taciturn with our host, whom he clearly didn't like. There was a disagreement about the phone bill, I seem to recall. Fran was calling chat lines and I was calling my cousins in Auckland, who can talk at great length when surprised. Also, I'd been keeping in touch with a certain young woman in Luton, on every ludicrous pretext imaginable. Could she return the book I'd loaned her to the college library? Would she like to have my locker? I didn't need it any more. 'Trez, I noticed the Open University has a programme tonight that you might find pretty interesting. On the statistics for neurofibromatosis in Yuan Dynasty Tibet.'

Fran supplied a tenner or two, which I think covered the damage. But he had a way of settling debts that made the recipient feel small for having asked. Post-Celtic-Tiger Ireland could do with him.

One morning I awoke to find he'd gone out. There was a note saying he'd be back 'in a couple of days', he was visiting his 'girlfriend Louise' (his WHAT?). Unless wooed by some mysterious process involving looking out a window in East Finchley, it was hard to know how Louise had been met. In any event, he didn't return for almost a week. When he did, he answered no question as to where he'd been wandering, merely offered that he and Louise had spent the entire time in bed. Not that you pressed the point.

Trez arrived in town wanting to talk about the band. I was delighted to see her, but things weren't quite clear. She explained that she intended continuing her studies, the group must take second place to her pursuit of a degree, but Third Year required her to be in London a bit, visiting galleries and the British Library. It was a strange conversation. I wanted her to be our full co-conspirator. Fran surprised me by insisting he understood her position. The group would never compromise her in any way, he promised. We got drunk over a curry he bought us.

Next morning she went to Deptford, where Seán was gaffing with their uncle Stephen, a nice old cove, full of stories. The distance between us seemed vast. It sounds ridiculous to say so now, but the Tube put me in convolutions of thundered paranoia, a maze of illegible connections, body odour and claustrophobia, its roaring, fetid tunnels and cage-style elevators an amateur Freudian's field day. I'd like to give you a hymn on the neon delirium of London, the small-town bumpkin singing 'Bright Lights, Big City'. But it wasn't like that. Most days I hung out in East Finchley, trudging its estates, marvelling at the sheer variety of pebbledash and carriage lamp available to the English self-improver. Occasionally I'd go mad and look about the garden centre down the road. Hail hail, rock and roll.

Somewhat to my surprise, Louise proved to be real, a flame-haired, laconic but amiable Goth, of many byzantine tattoos. She came from Haslingden in Lancashire, I seem to recall, and began showing up at the house with her drugs and a dog, a mutt whose name was Richard. It was clear that Louise and Fran were fond of one another. Their love-making was frequent and loud. Feeling prudish, among other things, I would take myself out, with Richard on a string, and we'd walk the leafy avenues until we felt it seemly to come home. Thoughtfully, one afternoon they invited me to join them in the shower, not, I feel sure, because of any huge sexual attraction but they didn't want me feeling left out. Maybe they just thought I needed a wash. The gesture was appreciated. Well, politeness costs nothing. That I declined is to this day a tiny regret.

I don't remember the band playing any music at all for at least the first month in London. We'd meet up now and again in a pub on the border of Chinatown, a Dutch joint that sold lager of frightening strength to frighteningly strong Australians. I'd fume and feel aggrieved, resenting their muscles, despising their backslappery and chummy braggadocio, the glow of antipodean snazz. Their laughter had a triple-X surfer-beach suntan, and even their silences boasted. I hailed from an island where teenagers were ritually warned by sworn celibates that taking off your underwear made the Virgin Mary weep. But these dudes transmitted pheromones with omnidirectional cheerfulness, a megahertz of detestable brio.

Midst the howls and how-AH-yahs sulked the Ships in the Night, anchored in immigrant glum. Three pints of Oranjeboom and a point-scoring squabble would flare between us. A whiskey, we'd be trading the barbs. The politics of the kingdom, our disappointment with the electorate, the disappearance of the ozone layer, the war on the unions: these controversies of the era were sullenly rehearsed, each of us trying to catch out the others in an admission of less than North Korean ardency. As though the advent of Margaret the Mad was the fault of your friend, who was secretly offering satanic sacrifices for her victory. *You're saying you're not totally crazy about every track on the Clash's second album? Take that back, you fascist!* Like leaking water, private anxiety will always find an outlet. Trouncing each other was our plumbing. If Trez was among us as Seán and I got into an argument, she and Fran would exchange the what-are-they-like look used by girls since the dawn of creation when boys are starting to bore. That would annoy me further. One night the pub's TV happened to flash a shot of a woman in a skimpy bikini, plugging bingo in a tabloid newspaper or perhaps foreign holidays. Seán, the most courteous and chivalrous of youths, uttered some mild remark into his beer about what he saw as her attractiveness. I think he called her 'Leeds United' or 'Stoke'. Fran and I rose up like a pissed Cerberus of self-righteous hypocrisy and outdid ourselves with denunciations of his shameful sexism, so viciously that he was dumbstruck for an hour. In our circle, to call someone a sexist was like calling him a Klansman. Young men were feminist at the time, or, if they weren't, often pretended to be – in my view, a damn good thing. But that Seán, of all people, was a recipient of our disingenuousness is a sign of how unhappy we were.

It was a difficult month, our first in London. Since the age of fourteen, I'd had a map of its songs in my head: I'd sauntered Abbey Road, gone Down in the Tube Station at Midnight, loaded the Guns of Brixton, done the Lambeth Walk, roamed Gerry Rafferty's Baker Street, knew how many holes it takes to fill the Albert Hall and marvelled at the Waterloo Sunset. But the wintry city was not the one of my teenage dreams. Carnaby Street, in my bedroom, was a yellow brick road, where pop-eyed Johnny Rotten and sultry Marianne Faithfull got it on with the Artful Dodger. The real metropolis, on the other hand, had the Northern Line and gridlock. It's not that London was unexciting. But I didn't understand it, felt lost. Its amp went up to eleven.

Trez was in Luton a lot of the time, which meant I didn't see her too much. Whenever she and I got together, we spoke only of her studies, almost never of music or the group. Seán, too, seemed to have his own life. Phoning Uncle Stephen, you'd be told the twins had gone out and he didn't know when they'd return. With bugger-all else to do, I began teaching myself to cook, out of an Elizabeth David book I found in the house while tidying. Anyone can learn to roast a chicken with trimmings, as my mum always said, and a basic omelette or cassoulet isn't hard. The housemates developed a liking for my Light Salade aux Lardons and announced me the Michel Platini of cuisine.

But I was drifting and aimless. Louise was by now off the scene but Fran continued to absent himself for days at a time. I pretended not to know the reason.

This isn't the place to go into his using. But you didn't need to be a genius to see it was increasing. Faced with a direct question, or as direct as I could make it, he'd insist he wasn't an addict, would never dream of injecting, that smoking heroin was safe. As though the means by which you take it is more of an issue than the substance you're taking, and why. He grew secretive about his circle. That troubled me. Here was a boy who didn't work but had thirty grand in a bank account. His taxi plate was taking him on journeys it might be hard to come back from. It occurred to me to shop him. The twins said I shouldn't. Seán told me he'd speak to him, and I know that happened. But it bothered me that I'd left it to Seán.

There grew in me the bad feeling that we'd made this move foolishly, that the band would fall apart before long. If I'm honest, I suspected we weren't 'a band' at all, just another collection of misfits with instruments. That seems an adult and retrospective thought, I know, but it assailed me even then. Maybe the effort of leaving home had taken all I had. I walked East Finchley a lot.

In the end, it was Trez who kicked our asses into something like a shape, as perhaps we'd always known she would. December froze up London and she told us it was time. The 'fuckaboutery', a favourite word – she'd learned it from one of the Oranjeboom Australians – would have to stop right now. She'd written two songs. We were going to record them. We hadn't come to London for nothing.

FROM FRAN'S FINAL INTERVIEW

Trez is a remarkable person. Nobody knows how much. Me and her was never the closest but I always admired her. Single-minded. You know? Nobody's fool. Kids, you know, they talk ten kinds of nonsense. But I never heard Trez say a stupid thing in her life. Innocent, sure. Never a cynic. But sceptical.

Questioning. Watchful, all the time. And I'd say I learned to be watchful from Trez. Don't give it all up. You know? Sometimes watch. And it put us at odds, because that weren't how I saw things at the time. She had seriousness. Poise. And none of the rest of us did. You don't when you're a kid. You're insane. My thing was, they call me effeminate, I'll put on a dress. She said to me one night, you know what you should do? Go on stage in a three-piece suit. And actually she was right. Totally on the money. She was always a great one for staying ahead of the audience. Clever, clever person. Kept 'em guessing.

Trez suggested we get a flat, the four of us together. When necessary, she'd commute back to Luton for lectures. Things needed to change. 'So we're going to bloody change them.' She'd been looking through *City Limits* and had options. An 'amazingly sunny basement' (is there any such thing?) was available in Brickfields Terrace near the Bayswater Road, a neighbourhood where life was grittily experienced back in those days but it meant the rents were cheap. We pitched up to look it over, Trez, Seán and I, Fran having refused to involve himself with a member of the landlord class. Perhaps it was just as well. His mode at the time was full-on Boy George with a seasoning of Alice Cooper and the Damned. He'd got hold of a sewing machine and begun making his own clothes from garments he rummaged out of bins – a chef's checkerboard trousers he daubed with silver furniture-paint, a 'naughty nurse' uniform he slashed with a cut-throat razor. He'd go to nightclubs in a peephole bra accessorised with Winchester College Old Boys necktie and Carmelite wimple dyed scarlet. He'd asked me if I thought it practicable that his entire head be tattooed with a map of the globe; failing this, with a hammer and sickle. I told him I thought it would hurt like blazes, and he desisted, thank God, but his notion of himself as a Miro lithograph in knickers continued. He loved telling bikers in the bars we frequented that his 'clitoris was pierced' and offering to show them the evidence. Trez, as the only member of the band who was in a position to know, advised that you wouldn't necessarily want it pierced, or displayed to drunken wastrels if it were. But Fran would rejoin that art ought not to be withheld from the masses. It's possible that his mascara budget exceeded his expenditure on drugs, and in daylight the effect disconcerted. Also, he was listening a lot to the early Velvet Underground. It became part of his messing to address strangers in the croaky German accent fans of Nico will recollect with affection. Bayswater had a fair bit of prostitution in those days – every phone box in W2 was papered with lurid invitations – but whatever Fran might be offering the more exploratory of west London's married men wasn't something you wanted occurring in your basement.

Into the decidedly non-Velvet Underground we moved, on a bone-chillingly freezing night. It's tempting to ladle on the mildew-and-creeping-squalor of it all, as one or two of my former colleagues have done, but in truth our little subterranea wasn't so bad. Naughty Seán once told the *Christian Science Monitor* that where we lived was 'a former S and M dungeon' with 'mice the size of puppies' and 'whips in the wardrobe', that johns would knock on the windows pleading to have unspeakable things done to them, but I don't remember any of that. It was tenebrous, and the block could be noisy, admittedly. There were Colombians next door, amiable fellows, but they did love a late-night fiesta. You'd drink yourself into a slumber and hear the cha-cha-cha in your dreams, and occasionally what you told yourself probably wasn't gunfire. But we each of us had a mattress, and there was technically speaking a kitchen, and a bathroom that sort of functioned, at least sometimes, usually Mondays. As for the view, one is reminded of an immortal line from Trez. 'It's improved since they painted the gasworks.'

To live with your friends when you're young is pleasant. Fran, in particular, seemed to like the little routines, the rosters for shopping, the domesticities. Nearby Porchester Library had a collection of cassettes, not vast but it had been put together by someone who cared about music. Fran started getting into Mahler and the Irish composer Seán Ó Riada, both great favourites of Trez. He grew fond of the Sunday night world-music show on a pirate station broadcasting from Tower Hamlets, a programme offering everything from complex-rhythm Balkan stuff to Youssou N'Dour and the Super Étoile de Dakar. I came into the flat one evening to hear something so strange and clean and beautiful that it made me stand and listen. Fran told me it was Vietnamese folk music, Hát chầu văn. He explained that it was based on the Five Notes Scale, 'Ngũ Cung' and that he remembered someone in the orphanage teaching him the names of the notes: Hò, Xự, Xang, Cống, Liu. In truth, I don't know if it's possible that this was a genuine recollection or something he'd learned from the radio. But to witness his awe as he spoke of this music was touching. The instrument sounding like a zither was called Đàn bầu. The oboe-like timbre was Kèn bầu. That extraordinary shimmering lament was produced by a k'ni, a one-string vertical fiddle with a resonating disc held in the player's mouth. 'Listen,' Fran whispered. 'Shhh. Don't say nothing.' Trez came home, and Seán with a mate. We sat there, dream-blown, listening with Fran, while the sunset made the floorboards glow.

It was in the following weeks that Trez started trying to speak with him about his infancy in Vietnam. He remembered words to do with food, and the names of the days. Monday was 'ngày thứ hai', Friday 'thứ sáu'. Fran could be gently playful, and it became one of his endearing routines to teach us the days by referencing them to pop songs. The Rolling Stones had a hit called 'Ruby thứ ba'. Hearing the juicy tones of Lewisham contend with those words was sometimes a music in itself. As always while joking, Fran appeared serious. He would scold us for mispronunciations, accuse us of 'not trying'. He could also be very mischievous. One night the four of us went to a Vietnamese caff on Praed Street as a little test of our progress in the language. The waitress listened in mild surprise as Seán, Trez and I gave our orders for Bún bò Huế and Cơm chiên Dương Châu in a passable Hanoi accent. She then turned to Fran, who glanced up from the menu and said in broadest Yorkshire: 'Could tha do uz an egg and chips, luv? I hate this foreign grub.'

Strolling Queensway on a Friday night, you felt you were in a show, but the street itself was the showstopper. Lebanese restaurants, Turkish bars, Egyptian traders. Balti-houses, a bierkeller, bodegas, *churrerias*, a tiny Islamic bookstore, Greek barbers. Thai and Saudi newspapers in racks outside the minimart, with the *Longford Leader*, *The Kerryman* and *Pravda*. That street was a song, but we had songs of our own to get down. It was hard to turn away from the dazzle.

Six floors above a kebab shop on Bishop's Bridge Road was an attic of almost perfect decrepitude and filth, rejoicing in the moniker 'Santa Monica Studios'. The balding, rat-faced owner had placed advertisements in the windows of the area's newsagents, among the cards offering FRENCH MAID MASSAGE and SCHOOLBOY CORRECTION, proclaiming his possession of a 16-track recording system. The rate was thirty quid cash per hour, a 'lunatic price' which 'must end soon'. Thirty quid wasn't nothing. It would have purchased you quite an amount of schoolboy correction, enough to do you till the end of term. But having shopped about the quarter, we soon came to discern that the Santa Monica was a relative bargain.

Up those 72 steps we'd hike with our gear, weighed like pack-mules, thirsty and hot, past bricked-up partitions, the torched remains of armchairs, past a freezer cabinet Fran quipped was employed by the *chef-de-kebab* downstairs for hiding illegally imported cadavers. As you managed to ascend further, the walls displayed posters of grinning inebriates, perhaps at some former time musicians, and helpfully cartooned arrows. Summit gained, you'd press onward and stagger into 'S.M.S.' (I kid you not), inhale the heady aroma of piss, chips and sadness, congratulate yourself on not having died of disgust, and wait for your creativity, which had fainted along the way, to follow you up the stairs.

But he didn't make it simple, that balding, rat-faced man. Balding, rat-faced men rarely do. Out he'd toddle from the back room where he spent a suspicious amount of his time, now blinking and rubbing his palms and adjusting his underpants through his baggies and lying that it was good to see you. He had the wariness of one perpetually expecting to be arrested, and the meanness of a neurotic already in prison, guarding his contraband from the Daddy. Little things like having a piano or a drum kit on the premises of a recording studio he regarded as laughable extravagances. He charged you for hiring them in, for carrying them up, for unpacking them, *for renting you a mic stand.* 'I'll hold the fukken thing,' Fran told him one day. 'Can't,' replied the wizened one. 'Musicians' Union rules.' Like a lot of rat-faced, balding men, he was always going on about insurance. He couldn't possibly allow you to unload a flight case yourself. You might fall and break your coccyx, a word he enjoyed saying, especially to Trez, and where would we all be then? Fucked, that was where. 'Fucked five ways.' At the time I wasn't sure there *were* five ways to do that. But if anyone knew, he did. Fran's revenge was to secretly make a blithering fool of our host, which given the raw material wasn't hard. Near my home town is a stately manor called Luton Hoo, these days a luxury hotel. 'Hoo' is a Saxon word meaning the spur of a hill, but Fran gave it a meaning of his own. Asked by our tormentor what was his 'actual, Oriental name', Fran replied carefully, enunciating with scrupulous clarity, 'Lu . . . Ton . . . Hu . . . Say it with me?'

'Loo. Tawn. Hoo.'

'Harder. In the back of your throat.'

'Lwa . . . Tung . . . Hwa.'

'Very good.'

A plastic cup into which you might pour water cost 25 pence. As a favour, he'd sell you the water. He couldn't permit 'outside refreshments' to be brought into the Santa Monica. They might damage the equipment or short out the circuitry. He'd standards to maintain. Standards meant rules. Beginners like Mr Hu mightn't be cognisant of 'best practice in the industry', but he was happy to clue Lu in.

His malignity and balderdash notwithstanding, we started into the work unfazed. It was a relief to be playing again, and our progress was solid. I can't say that either of Trez's songs was the finest she'd ever pen, but the fact that she'd penned them at all signalled steadiness of intention in her, a more useful thing than genius for a musician or anyone else.

In she'd come with sheets of lyrics tidily typed on her Amstrad, ideas for harmonies and kickers. Often, she'd worked them up a bit in advance with Seán, and they'd unveil the effort with a shyness I found affecting and lovable, like kids showing you starfish they'd picked off a beach. Fran's singing amazed me. He'd no *right* to be so good. He'd shamble up the stairs like a bad caricature of Marlene Dietrich, late, unkempt, bollock-eyed with exhaustion, ripped to the bonce on his chemical of the week; accompanied by the nice but excitable Ecuadorian boy he was seeing at the time, a *muchacho* that would cause him some pain. But when Fran opened his mouth to sing, a presence filled that shabby room. We did Trez's 'Seven Kinds of Vinny' and 'Can't Face My Homework', my 'Ripping Up the Papers', Fran's 'You're a Sweatshop' (later amusingly misprinted by the *NME* as 'You're a Sweetshop') and his 'Fighting in the Chinatown Pub'. Startling to see yourself materialise through the lyrics of a song. Seán had a little but hummable thing of his own, Otis Redding meets the Wailers with a splash of the Clash. If it didn't totally work at the time, 'Loving Hot Cities' would turn out to be a memorable song. You know it from the Virgin Atlantic advert.

As to our sound, at least we had one, or were close to unearthing it. The Kinks were a touchstone but so was Marc Almond. Our aim was to blend the shimmer of the high-octane torch-song with romping, sixteen-wheeler guitar. Trez gave us depth. Fran gave us drive. Seán gave us an ability to go nought-to-ninety and back. It was important to all of us that the lyrics would be, as Fran put it, 'unusual'. That seems, and probably was, a strange ambition, yet you knew what he meant at the time. Our ideal would be a song that raised your eyebrows while making you need to dance. Sometimes we got close. We'd get closer.

But it was obvious, at least to me, that there was a hole in our repertoire: we had nothing resembling a love song. Raising this subject with my fellows could result in unease. Seán and especially Fran felt the theme had been exhausted, and in any case was unsuited to the New Wave genre, in whose slipstream we found ourselves swimming. Trez drifted between camps, saying she wouldn't overrule me if I could come up with an original approach. I was hobbled and dumbstruck. There seemed nothing to say. The hardest thing about writing is knowing what to write. Finally, painfully, I managed to get a verse of something down. My approach to any song at the time was to imagine one of my heroes singing it. In this case, I went for Tom Waits. It was a number I titled 'Wildflowers' and I played it to Trez in the kitchen one night, to see if she thought it worth bringing to the boys. My Waits-style growl was a thing I was working on. I tried to get the sandpaper going.

Stirring the ice cubes
Alone once again
Reasons you went
And the cry of the train
Hank Williams lonesome
I'm writing this song
Livid with wildflowers and
Overly long
Very pretentious
Extremely unplanned.
You'd rather not hear it?
Of course.
Understand.

Trez found it difficult to lie, especially when she was fond of you. Gently, carefully, she told me it 'wasn't great'. She felt I might do better. 'Rework it.' Somewhere in the writing I'd 'got a little lost'. Well, she wasn't entirely wrong on that point. Had she read the opening letter of each line in a downward sequence, she'd have seen just how lost I was.

There's an old blues that puts across in ten plain words of honest sorrow what it took Dante 42 chapters of *La Vita Nuova* to say: 'I love my baby. But my baby don't love me.' That song was on my mind a lot in those days. I knew the bluesman's pain, and there are many songs on that theme. But they'd all been written before. I sometimes wished I didn't know her. That would have been easier. Sharing close quarters with the person you think is the other half of your soul isn't easy when you're young and she doesn't feel the same way but still wants to be your mate. To stumble into our kitchen and see her washing her beautiful face. To join her on the sofa. To be treated as her girlfriend. ('There's a hair in the *middle of my forehead*. Can you pluck it for me, Rob? The mirror's confusing my tweezers.') Walking with her in Hyde Park on an impossibly gorgeous wintertime morning, when the sky was fierily vivid as the things I wanted to say, I was further from home than I knew. Once, boarding a bus, she briefly held my hand. Queensway was Paradise that night.

When she stood close to the mic in the Santa Monica, I envied it. I could barely play for wanting her. I'd talk to myself on long trudges by the Grand Union Canal. Her violin would tremor and purr like my hopes. We'd frowst away an evening pretending nobody noticed, and I'd resolve that before morning I'd have knelt to declare my obeisance again. But it somehow never happened. I think I know why. The idea that I'd force her out of my life was too terrible. Some say youth is wasted on the young, but I can't second that emotion. I believe I was wise. Faced with a difficulty that has kyboshed many friendships we managed to keep ours going. I turned twenty that year. I'd made few good decisions. All my life, I'll be grateful for that one.

Ten

O n sailed the Ships. The Santa Monica rocked. At the
end of a fortnight we had more than enough for a
demo. Eight solid songs, maybe nine. The mixes were rough
and the playing was raw, the arrangements so basic that
Trez felt we'd wasted our time. I thought she was wrong
but I feared she was right. She said we should start all over.
To placate her, we laid down a skittery version of one of
the few numbers by anyone else that all four of us unques-
tioningly liked, an album track by the Boomtown Rats called
'Living in an Island'. One night back in Luton I'd taped it
off a telly show called *Rock Goes to College* when I should
have been studying for the A Levels. It's a prizefighter of a
song, although no critic ever mentioned it at the time. From
memory, it was Fran's idea to record it. Maybe it was Seán's,
though that seems unlikely to me now. Perhaps it was the
bald little bastard's.

A specialist in passive-aggressiveness, he'd try to upset
us whenever we took a break. This he did by claiming close
association with the esteemed personages of pop-rock whose
images adorned the studio's walls. Marc Bolan had been his
discovery. ('Poor kid. What a waste.') 'Mick' was a mate.

'Muddy' was a buddy. 'Cliff' once bought him a bible. U2 were not yet as huge as they'd soon become, but already he was referring to Bono as 'Paul', often the sign of a monster. He'd communed with the greats and you weren't among them. Particularly loathsome was his smirking silence or tactical reticence if the name of any female rocker was uttered. Janis Joplin? 'Oh dear. Mustn't go there, young friend. Could tell you a thing or two about Jannie.' Grace Slick of Jefferson Airplane? 'A gent don't kiss and tell.' Joan Baez? 'Fakkin wildcat. Move on.' Every woman in the history of music was a notch on his bedpost. Had you mentioned the Andrews Sisters or Dame Vera Lynn, he'd have claimed they once blew him in the back of a Roller.

But having an enemy can sometimes be useful. The more he wrecked our heads, the harder we worked. His indifference became our instrument, and we played it. It came to be my favourite fantasy that every time I strummed a minor seventh it caused a fierce and spectacular pain to shoot up his anus. He'd listen to my solo, then smile tolerantly, a little sadly. 'You know who *could* play? Jimi. Makes you think. Twenty-seven when he left us. What a talent, what a talent. And I *said* to him, Jimi, that dope's gonna kill ya. But fuck me five ways, could he play.'

Trez and I researched the matter of where to send the demo. But as is the case with all research, our knowledge contained gaps we didn't know about. There turned out to be little point in inviting EMI to sign you for four million pounds when you hadn't a regular gig where an A&R could come to check you out; if in fact you'd never played London and had no immediate plans to do so. For days we traipsed around Soho, delivering our masterwork up staircases. The same whey-faced young woman reading *The Face* or *i-D* was behind every desk. She smiled, indicated the in-tray, and didn't call the stupidity police. The jiffy bag, as well as carrying our cassette, contained a Photostat 'press release' that was four and a half pages long, i.e. too long by four and a quarter pages. Seasoned with lines from Samuel Beckett and other noted humorists, its tone of unearned superiority now makes me want to bludgeon it with a mallet. I have a faded copy on my table as I write, but not faded enough.

We sent our parcel to every radio and television station in London, to every branch of the BBC, including the World Service, Fran having contended that as a 'non-British group' (a what?) we might stand a chance of getting heard there. Seán and Trez, native Londoners, and your chronicler, a Lutonian, listened, enthralled, to his attempted redefinitions. Desperate, you're open to persuasion. 'Ah'm fookin *Vietnamese*, me,' he would thunder, in his Yorkshire-Irish brogue. 'That's got t'be worth *summat* off these BBC bastards!' I exaggerate the accent, but the point proved moot. The World Service, for whatever unfathomable reasons of its own, appeared not to regard Irish-Britain or British-Ireland as eligible for the ether. 'I understand you're from Luton,' the producer wrote crisply. 'It isn't the Côte d'Ivoire.'

FROM FRAN'S FINAL INTERVIEW

This Ireland-versus-Britain thing. I don't buy into it, man . . . In the past, that's different . . . But not now . . . I know things were done . . . I've read all the history . . . History of Ireland's gonna crack your heart in two. But to me, England and Ireland, it's practically the same place . . . It's mulatto, to me . . . If you look at it again . . . A mate of mine used to joke, we ain't British or Irish, we're from Brireland. That's where millions of people live, quietly inter-marrying and ignoring all the bullshit and getting along with the neighbours. And that's where my band come from . . . We weren't English *or* Irish. Who'd settle for either? We were the Ships in the Night. Stick your passport . . . When I sing, I'm Vietnamese, Mississippian and bloody Bolivian if I want . . . A Cajun Billy Fury, a West Indian punk . . . Like, our drummer loved ska and we weren't no ska band, but we'd stir it all in, let it mix. And me, I liked soul. So I gave it full Aretha. You're gonna sing a song, man, you give it all you got. Why would you tie yourself down? Ninety-nine per cent don't do. So don't wrap me in no flag, man, not when I'm singing. Flags are for parades. They're foolishness. Singing's my nation. The only country I ever had. The place I felt safe, where it mattered what I thought. Give you a vote every three minutes, not once in four years. I'll stand and salute the cover of *Never Mind the Bollocks* but run up the Union Jack or the green, white and orange, I'm sitting right down . . . Means nothing . . . Not to me . . . Flags are for children . . . I don't mean no disrespect. Whatever you're into. But I believe in the People's Republic of Song. That's my land. Never lived anyplace else . . . Being honest, it's why I got into a band as a kid. You're young, you know, all the arrogance of that . . . You don't have all the answers but no other sod has any. If our group achieved anything, which is open to fair comment, we never spouted nonsense or reverse-racist codswallop . . . You can look at our songs . . . We always had dignity . . . And I'm proud we stood up for the Brirish.

The Beeb's army of security porters accepted our packets with perfect courtesy, before setting fire to them in a skip out the back. As for the late John Peel, it would only be a small exaggeration to say that we stalked him. Trez heard that he occasionally supped a pint in the Lamb and Flag near Broadcasting House. We sat there every night for a week, left packages for him behind the bar, marked URGENT AND PERSONAL or MESSAGE FROM THE UNDERTONES ENCLOSED. Famously, Billy Bragg once sent him a mushroom biryani as an incentive to play a record. We sent bhajis and pohas and palak paneers. I don't know what we'd have done had he ever entered that pub. The scene would be frightening and violent.

I think we paid for 300 copies of the demo. Seán says more, Trez less. What is certain is that when we got down to the last box of ten, we realised we were wasting our time. Without a gig and an audience, we wouldn't be signed. Christmas came. I skulked home to Luton, returning to London on New Year's Eve because Fran was alone in the flat. He was very, very down. I was glad I'd come back. January '84 was cold.

Trez and Seán were cheerful. We started again, approached the neighbourhood pubs that sometimes did music. Nobody wanted to know. I tell a lie, there was mild interest at one

Irish-themed establishment of the kind then beginning to appear in London – posters of Michael Collins, agricultural machinery hanging on the walls – but when they asked us to put together 'a night of ballads, good air-punching stuff', we felt the fit was wrong. We'd be supporting a trio called the Jacket Potatoes, the landlord explained. You think I have invented the name of that band, but on my life, they truly existed. I'm behind the curve on what the Irish scene in London would be like these days, but in the middle 1980s the potato's unfortunate role in matters Hibernian was perhaps over-frequently sung about.

The brothers who managed the Dutch bar in Chinatown asked if we could play anything 'smashed Australians might like'. This was a facer. Fran began suggesting.

'Punk?'

'No.'

'Funk?'

'Not really.'

'Soul?'

'They're Australian.'

'Oh.'

Unable to figure out what the Oz-boys required, we were forced to admit that we lacked it.

Trez went to Dublin for a weekend and came back with a possibility. Her aunt had reminded her that a second cousin of the twins was studying at Leeds Poly and was Entertainments Officer there. Seán rang and asked if he could help. He said he'd stick us on the bill with a visiting Jamaican reggae act with the improbable name of Lady Di and Dark Star that was doing the college circuit at the time. Up the M1 we bussed that wintry weekend, through a storm that blackened the skies. Arriving late, the Ships in the Night went on at half past nine, without sound-check, cuppa, shower or refreshment, to a predominantly white audience out of its face on ganja and the excitement of higher learning. My tranquilliser of choice had a Russian name, Smirnoff, and I was perhaps over-thoroughly medicated. We didn't play well. Not that it mattered, since nobody but the twins' cousin was listening. Alas, ten minutes in, they started to. That was bad. When I remember the evening I'm reminded of a comic Victorian music-hall number that Jimmy used to sing when under the influence of happiness.

> *They made me a present*
> *Of Mornington Crescent.*
> *They threw it one brick at a time.*

About Lady Di and Dark Star, I can tell almost nothing. I was pig-faced by the time they slouched on in a tornado of drums and thunking bass, Leeds Poly's single strobe-light working hard to justify that week's hire-purchase payment. Trez and I watched for a while, then betook ourselves out the back of the exam hall where among the coupling couples and pyramids of empty beer kegs we tanked a bottle of gin and had a little bop and did some but sadly not all the things boys and girls do. Laughed. Mocked. Danced again.

There was a moment when we realised we were looking in each other's eyes. She blew her hair from her forehead and smiled.

'Let's get stoned,' she said.

'Sure,' I replied.

From her pocket she pulled a little lump of Haile Selassie for which she'd paid a law student ten pounds.

'Get that intya, Cynthia,' she said.

'Heavy-duty,' I slurred. 'They don't muck about up north.'

Trez was not normally a devotee of the magical smoke. But I didn't ask questions. Off we went. There was a little of the old electricity crackling in the air and perhaps she might cop off with me out of pity if sufficiently spaced – so I told myself. We passed the dutchie, inhaling in sibilant sucks. Even through the rainstorms of hard-liquor drunkenness, I thought it tasted unusual. But onward we toked, peering up at the stars and speaking of art and beauty. If Trez had a wild side, I wanted her to walk on it. And I'd stagger along beside her.

This was the life. *This* was rock and roll. Fools who toiled for the System would envy us. Them with their silly little mortgages. More gin? Okay. The *time* the wage slaves waste. And anyway, what is *time*? Another fukken . . . weapon . . . in their flaccid . . . ideology . . . Let's roll up another. *Course* I've done this before, Rob . . . Hey, the car park is revolving! . . . I feel sick . . .

The 'Moroccan Black' turned out to be an Oxo Cube, a fact Fran established by the expert means of looking at it briefly before administering a tentative lick. This was shortly before the tarmac began rolling like a wave and I swam all the way to unconsciousness. I don't know if you've ever smoked a product intended for the making of gravy. But I wouldn't advise you to do so. Not only is there great and ineradicable shame, but your wee smells of casserole for a week.

The only good thing about that night was that it led quickly to more college gigs. Perhaps we weren't as bad as we thought. Certainly, we offered the qualities most Ents officers wanted: cheapness and availability. Hatfield Poly was next to receive us. Then Aston University, and Manchester and Bangor. We started getting paid actual money; not very much, not enough, as Jimmy put it, to put herrings on the spuds, but sufficient to procure a bag of bottles for the bus down the motorway, and maybe a good pinch of that aromatic herb not purposed for a *coq au vin*.

Seán and Trez went home to Luton one Sunday and returned with his car, a '71 Hillman Hunter he'd bought for three hundred nicker at a police auction. Enterprising and ambitious working-class boy, he'd figured that his career and his social life might be aided by having his own vehicle. He'd kept it every bit as clean as you can keep a rustbucket frequently employed for conveying leaky washing machines to the workshop. In London it became employed for conveying musicians. We were not as leaky, true, but we were noisy and ungrateful, like a carload of screeching chimps. Fran in high spirits did his amusing imitation of a tumble dryer on rapid-cycle containing 'George Michael and a spanner'. Seán was a good sport about this and many other distractions, but there's no doubt they added to his burdens. Our non-driverhood allowed us to drink, which we copiously did, while our chauffeur pretended to content himself with orange juice. But soon it became clear that the car, not being all that large, was unsuited as the band's personal limo-cum-goodswagon.

'I think we should get a horse-transporter.'

'For the gear?'

'For Fran.'

'I will not be fucking *transported*,' Fran replied, like a foul-mouthed Queen Victoria, if such a travesty could be imagined. Rich, from a fellow who by now was much of the time on another planet, a realm where the Horse loomed large.

To save money while on the road, we slept in the car, more precisely in the car-and-accompanying-transporter, 'two up the front and two in the horsebox'. This was a phrase Fran enjoyed saying. It reminded him of the title of an educational videotape he'd purchased in King's Cross with helpful subtitles from the original German. But the sleeping arrangements gave rise to difficulty. It was hard to know which two should go where. In all chivalry we felt that no woman could be asked to sleep in a horsebox. Thus Trez's berth in the car was a given. But what to do, then, so proprieties would be observed? It seemed a bit much, even in rock and roll, to require adult siblings to sleep together. Seán must be accommodated down the back in the straw. But whither boy Fran and your scribe? Fran was no molester, don't get the wrong idea. I never once saw him put the moves on anyone who didn't want them put on. At the same time, he was what he was. Seán felt that a bisexual druggie with a porn habit and few early-morning inhibitions wasn't necessarily an individual you'd want waking up beside your sister. Down the back Fran was sent, making a pillow of his fun-furs and a blanket of his unending complaints. This meant that I would be up front, on a reclined leatherette seat, fewer inches from Trez than were usual. We'd have a laugh before rolling over, a midnight tête-à-tête, and there was no one in the world more interesting to talk to. We'd listen to the radio for a while, or play poker, at which she usually beat me. She was a cruel and cunning poker player, utterly ruthless, but since we were playing for matchsticks or fags it didn't really matter. I was fond of the little togetherness. We'd share a secret nightcap: a mug or two from the winebox we'd hidden from the lads. If she was working on an essay, she might read me an extract, or I'd read her a bit from the *NME* while she took off her make-up and modestly prepared to retire. But things could be difficult, particularly on sultrier nights when the removal of exterior clothing became necessary. One's impeccable non-sexism could be put to the test. You'd find yourself praying for a blizzard so she'd have to sleep in a tracksuit and overcoat, but the gods of the weather were unkind.

After a couple of weeks, I couldn't stand it any more. Well, I could. But it hurt to be trying. Her habit of muttering nocturnal endearments in the dream-drifts of sleep was coming between me and my rest. She'd enfold her precious limbs around one or more of my own. She'd be cuddling up, half undressed. Merciful reader, I was young and a male of our species. I needn't go dwelling on details. Suffice to note that Viagra is not targeted at twenty-year-old boys, since Eskimos don't buy snow. In a state of flamboyant and ardent arousal, I awoke one sweltering morning on the outskirts of Hull, not a metropolis universally associated with epiphanies of the erotic, to the sight of a bared and purple nipple, her T-shirt having ridden up in the night. It's hard to know what to do at a moment like that. One of the things I wanted to do was get out of the car. Thankfully, that's what I did.

For a brief time thereafter, the permutation was three

boys in the horsebox, another phrase Fran enjoyed saying. But this arrangement, too, proved problematic. Seán was a light sleeper, especially after a show. It's a frequent complaint among musicians. Being on fire is a lot of fun, but you have to put yourself out. Depart a strobe-lit stage where you've made loud noises for a couple of hours and you won't be nodding off soon over cocoa. Encouraged by all of us, Fran was trying to get himself off the poppy dust. As a result, he could be a little jittery by pyjama-time. His twitchings and rustlings and scratchings and burblings would drive Seán into paroxysms of hectoring. Pumped by the gig, nettled by Fran's restlessness, cold, hungry, resenting the smell of horse-piss, he'd sit himself bolt-upright like the vengeful corpse in a horror flick and switch on his torch and start shouting. This led to him stomping from the horsebox, venting by moonlight, before trudging off resentfully to kip in a field or wherever else he might. His departure and its valedictory fanfare of obscenities left Fran and me alone and awake. Sometimes there was tequila, Fran's favourite tipple at the time. Sometimes there was vodka, my own. He could get a bit flirtatious. He'd be giving you the Grin. Well, boys will be boys. Why deny it? Once or twice, we had an enjoyable meeting of mouths. I've no regrets. He was a sensational kisser. His persuasive skills, also, were extensive. But those occasions, fun as they were, mainly served to establish in my mind that the love daring to speak its name, indeed rarely shutting up about itself, was ultimately the one I was after. This being explained, he accepted in good heart. Fran would never take it personally that you weren't in the mood. He'd have made a wonderful spouse.

Soon we ran out of colleges and began playing in pubs.

Poole, Braintree, Slough (twice), Rottingdean, Staines, Shitterton, Gravesend. My diary confirms what I already know, that few of southern England's offputtingly named towns were unvisited by the Ships in the Night. It is a country I love deeply, and I've lived there many years, but it's easier to love England when you're not seeing it from the back seat of a rustbucket or dreaming its dreams in a horsebox.

Pub audiences? Yes. I had better describe them. The dog-faced landlord and his slipper-wearing missus. The teds of the locality, in drainpipes and Brylcreem. The cider-fucked gloomies who'd only ventured on to the premises to tank up before going out burgling. The odd pubescent girl smuggled in by the barman intent on defloration down in the cellar, among the mousetraps and crates of pale ale. Glass-washers. Lunatics. Contestants at Pacman. The stripper who'd be on later. The grinning 'old lag'. Spouse-haters, gallows-birds, wreckage on legs, lobotomies, dipsos, automatons. Men the colour of nicotine. Women with smoke-wreathed nostrils. Fiends of indeterminate gender shrieking at the Tom 'n' Jerry pinball machine while slapping its day-glo flanks. Urinal-vommers, skinheads, the religiously disturbed. If I give you the impression that they had any interest in us at all, except possibly as food, I have failed.

Onward we apprenticed, up and down the motorways, through the violently cold March of '84 in Albion, a kingdom of sleet and dismal little caffs and an acne of gorse on the hilltops. Cold chips for breakfast and baked beans for lunch, and bubble 'n' squeak for to sup on. England does not have motels in the American sense, but if we happened to be in funds we'd put up at one of those small-town B and Bs where the sheets give electric shocks. A 'toilet duck' in the bathroom the only item of decoration. The landlady's bra on the washing line. Slice of toast? Thirty pence. Microwaved soup. Pot Noodle as room-service menu.

Mostly we slept in the horsebox, which, in truth, was not so bad. Seán kitted it out with inflatable mattresses and sleeping bags designed for the Arctic. ('I am going out,' he'd intone, on departing for a pee. 'I may be some time. Carry on.') If you zipped two of them together and shared body heat with your colleague, and you didn't mind the beating of rain on the roof or the whiskey-fumed befuddlements that passed as pillow talk, there was a sensation of consolatory fellow feeling, such as undergrounding Londoners are said to have known during the Blitz. When young, as previously noted, your stupidity is bomb-proof. But you can fall asleep anywhere. That's the upside.

For all the privations, we were learning our trade. There was joy to be squeezed from the struggle. One night, at a gig in Stoke, Seán did a tiny thing out of boredom, reversing the snare pattern on the middle eight of Fran's song 'Mullarkey', so the accent fell on the second beat, ska-style. The change was a lightning bolt, sudden and random, and the song burst out of itself like a fruit. To be young and in a band that is stumbling towards its own sound, messily, slowly, with all the infuriation of hope, is to realise what it feels like to be alive. When a gig went well, the fierce, besotted excitement would buzz through your blood till the dawn. Uplifting any audience, even a tiny crowd in a bar, is an addiction you'll never get over. At Fran's generous insistence, we started swapping lead vocals, the rest doing backing, even Seán. I always tell my daughter, I learned to sing by singing. Trez sang too, with presence and attack. Fran's guitar-playing, meanwhile, was beginning to astound us. He'd wrench screams from a Strat, raise wails of plane-crash feedback, pull a Chuck Berry duckwalk if the mood was upon him, but if you wanted an anchoring shuffle-time chug he'd supply it with scrupulous discipline. He retuned my old Ephiphone to an open B-flat, in which he'd jangle away contentedly at the back of the stage, nodding us in turn towards the lead mic. Seán by now had taught me to drive, a thing I enjoyed and was good at. Those motorway nights I'll remember all my life. Four kids in a scruffy car, facing into a rainstorm, punk on the radio and a hundred miles ahead. No drug comes close to that elation.

It was Seán who came up with the idea, probably through impatience, that we 'release' the demo ourselves. He'd shopped around and come up with a factory in Essex that would produce five thousand cassettes for three grand. We'd been playing the songs for a few months now, seeding them into our set of not overly known cover versions, like apologies into a conversation with a person you're about to break it off with, and it had started to happen occasionally at the end of a night that a punter would ask if we had a tape for sale. Fran was reluctant but we won him over. Various titles were thrown around, many of them a bit pompous or defensively facetious. In the end we went for *The Thrill of it All (And the Worry Afterwards)*, which had the advantage of being pompous *and* facetious. Trez and I condensed the ghastly four-and-a-half-page press release into 'liner notes'. In the passport booth at Paddington station on the rainy Sunday morning of 8th April 1984, we took twenty pictures of the pair of us, Fran and Seán having refused to get out of their beds, and that became the cover photo. My daughter tells me that if you have a playable copy of that cassette today, it's worth 900 quid on eBay, 7K if signed by Fran, eleven thousand if possessing the liner notes. I wish I'd stashed a box for my dotage.

Fran, having provided the subsidy that was keeping us alive, now decided its administration was beyond him. Every organisation is helmed by a leader who sometimes seems bizarrely opposed to it, and such was the case with the Ships. He had backslidden and was by now spending excessively on his favourite hobby. Entire villages in Afghanistan and rural Colombia were being funded by Fran's enthusiasms. One imagined the ringing of bells when this week's order arrived, and the cheerful folksong of goatherds. In the search for enlightenment, he could be recklessly experimental. He'd have snorted the ashes of martyred Joan of Arc if nothing more traditional were available. We said it must stop, and he promised it would, but up his nose or into his person by sundry other routes had gone a truly astonishing sum. A meeting was convened to 'elect' a Chancellor of the Exchequer. Trez, obviously, was chosen. Confronted with the exigencies of keeping us a step from starvation, she responded with frightening zeal. Indeed, she was to prove a ruthless monetarist. 'We will live *within our means*.' 'The books *must* be balanced.' 'The spending simply *cannot* continue.' She disbursed to each of us on a Friday evening the sum she'd calculated as necessary to sustain an adult human for one calendar week, less 5 per cent. Following an incident in which Fran claimed not to have received his allowance (from what was in fact his own money) Trez tried to institute a system whereby we *signed* for our dough. At this we drew a line and italicised it with blasphemies. I'm not saying she was heartless, but she could be steely and purposeful. She had something of the Grocer's Daughter.

Funny old time, the 1980s in England. I am fond of my adopted country's palette of restful greys, but things got a bit black and white. The electorate, or part of it, had imposed on us as Prime Minister a union-crushing, self-avowed admirer of General Pinochet. But there were important cities being governed by designer-suited Trotskyites who named municipal playgrounds after Sandinistas. When the centre fails to hold, opportunism sprouts, and from it we weren't immune. A flag of convenience can sometimes be useful. Three of us in the group realised that construing ourselves as a 'left-wing Irish band' – which, by some definitions, we were – might result in a little harvest of apologetic money and sympathetic embraces from the populace. After all, it was only proper to have a feeling for the motherland. ('The what?' Trez said, astonished.) A long time had passed since the Great Irish Famine. But boy, were we still upset about it.

At Irish festivals and Militant rallies the length and breadth of the kingdom, speaker after speaker excoriated England, her cruelties and extortions, her invasions and annexations, historical, contemporary and allegedly planned, her back-catalogue of pitiless tyrannies. Let's face it, there's a lot of raw material. If you played in a university attended by upper-middle-class students, the ante was that much higher. Jude and Willow would want you to bring your guitars but also your ideological firmness. Anything short of outright support for the Red Brigades or the immediate necklacing of Education Secretary Sir Keith Joseph and you were regarded as a bit of a splitter.

On Merseyside, say, and in certain boroughs of London, we'd be handsomely remunerated for appearing on a bill that even Ho Chi Minh might have found a bit unnerving. For all that, in many of England's less assertively Marxist towns – Bath, for example, or Leamington Spa – you tended to keep your Irishness muffled, lest it result in a burning crucifix. Seán was useful in this regard, since he spoke in the tones of south London. Not ideally what one would want to hear in the Nell Gwynn tearooms, but better than perceived bombers such as Fran or me. A dose of blarneying invective from that gentleman's mouth and the smelling salts or the West Midlands Crime Squad might have to be summoned, and where would we all be then.

We returned home to the flat late one summery night in a state of nearly catatonic exhaustion. We'd driven the 400 miles down from Aberdeen in one go, a gruelling and sullen nine hours. My diary tells me it was Sunday, 27th May. We'd racked up eleven dates, and while the gigs had gone okay, we were sick of the road and sick of the songs and heartily sick of each other. There was never decent food or anywhere to shower. It was an eternity of peanuts and rinsing your pits in a sink and trying to get paid and taking less than you were promised and sniffing a facecloth before using it. The almost total lack of physical privacy was irksome to us boys; for Trez who complained least it was hardest. Being the only young woman in any group of young men is a trial, and the privations of touring made things worse. More than that, the little squabbles that attend close bodily proximity were starting to curdle and fester. The rows grew bad. We'd go at it like boiling water. Trez could be crabby as her final exams approached, Fran quite impossible, contumelious and fault-finding and unendingly negative, an embittered Reverend Mother whom the novices dread. A nimbus of suppressed rage seemed to glow from his face and you feared what would now be termed his mood swings. He was off the Shanghai Sally again but the worldview of people fighting addiction remains insular, even when the anaesthetic gets abandoned. I know what I'm talking about. I point no finger. The least capable musician, I loved the group most. The others had options I hadn't, and that scared me to false glee. I feared they would sack me soon.

Drink was helping me develop strategies to parlay my dread into a cheeriness they must have found exhausting. As for Seán, he had a girl in London he didn't like missing. With Seán, there was always a girl. Inability to stick the sight of your colleagues is the reason most groups break up in the end, not that we knew at the time. But we did know, I think, that we couldn't go on as we were. It was notable that on any occasion when we returned to the flat all together, we'd each of us head immediately into a bedroom alone and, short of an earthquake, stay there.

This, I supposed, was what would happen on such a night. Trez lit a cigarette off the toaster, gathered her notes and retired without comment to the bath. Her finals were to start next morning and she was hoping for a scholarship. But life on the road doesn't marry well with study. There was a sense that a junction was fast approaching. I could see she was worried and down.

I put together a pear crumble and got a simple pesto going, because I knew that she liked it and I wanted to give her a treat. A spider was scuttling in the sink but I spared it a watery demise. Let the ugly flunt live. Who cared? I imagined myself seen through his numerous eyes, a kaleidoscope of failure and geekery. Bills had arrived in our absence and I opened one or two. Among the mail was a statement from the outfit we'd hired to put around our cassette. It announced that we'd sold 141 copies in total. You might think it would be a consolation that there were 141 fools willing to buy the fruit of your labours in a country of sixty million. But I personally had bought 11, so there were only 130. At a push, you could have squeezed our entire British fanbase into Jimmy and Alice's house. I murdered the spider. His death didn't help. Violence never does, so they say.

Fran came into the kitchen with a shocked and haggard look. He asked if I would listen to the answering machine. Control freak that he was, he insisted the flat's only telephone be kept in his bedroom, lest any of us use it to escape. He'd listened to the message himself. But he wanted someone else to hear it. He was naked but for his underpants, which were surprisingly conservative. Away with him I trudged, too weary to be alarmed.

Into that cavern of taffeta and lace and non-returned library books and poppers and fag ash and wet-wipes and lipsticks, a realm where the daylight was never permitted to enter, came a ray of Wirral-born sunshine. Any music-lover of my age would have recognised the voice, which pretended to be sardonic and just about succeeded. I'd heard it under blankets in the bedroom at home, and as I wept with my back to the runway lights of Luton Airport, counting up years, or smoking out the window, wondering why the Christ of lies had murdered my sister and if she could hear it too.

'Evening, it's John Peel here at Radio 1. Just to say I got

your cassette. Excellent stuff. Playing a couple of tracks on the programme tomorrow night. Thought you'd like to know. Be in touch.'

Fran was at the sewing machine. I sat down slowly beside him. He was weeping. I held him. We cried.

Eleven

In June '84, with our cassette getting noticed and the group about to record a session for Peel, Fran told us he'd been unhappy and was quitting. We were in a boat on the Serpentine when he gave us the news. The paddle back to shore was quiet.

He wouldn't be persuaded, was taking himself to Dublin, a city where he claimed to have friends. Seán and Trez did their best. I gave it everything I had. Thinking him desirous of flattery, as was sometimes the case, I flannelled and pleaded and blandished. Then fearing something was wrong with him, I worried. There was no need, he told me. He simply had to go. The London of his heart was not the city we were living in, and the group had 'made things worse'. He didn't want to be a professional, dreaded the thought of compromise. I'd always reckoned this a pose. Now he swore he was serious. Fame was an enemy. He was off.

'Fame?' This was slightly premature. A two-paragraph review in the *NME* doesn't lead to the paparazzi rummaging through your bins. But his mind was made up. It didn't matter what we thought. Elvis was leaving the building.

I could say I was surprised, and I imagine I did, but that

would be a little disingenuous. There'd been moments of memorable adventure, yet things had been uneasy for some time. On stage or in the studio, we were carefree enough, but playing music is the sex life of being in a group, the pleasure and intimate companionship, the young lovers' way of talking. Other dimensions of the affair were not what they might be. We'd become a bit married, which can happen in a band.

It was also a problem that Trez's intentions were unclear. She adored playing live but the grim-faced truant officer of her academic career was always beckoning sternly from the wings. She was cleverer than all of us put together, which Fran, also clever, tried very hard to like but failed to. And it must have felt odd to him, as it did to me and the twins, that the group was being subsidised to such an extent by his money, which had dwindled to the last four grand. I managed to get an occasional morning with a removal company that paid cash off the books. Seán chipped in, too, whenever he had it, but neither of us could afford much more than a bag of groceries or booze. Trez earned a little by proof-reading for a publisher, but you don't make the rent by proof-reading. British citizens, she, Fran and Seán were entitled to draw various benefits, but they didn't regard themselves as 'available for work', which you had to be in order to claim. Fran sometimes 'signed on', and for a while so did I, but the authorities gave me grief because I was still a registered full-time student and told me I'd have to stop. Stopping gave Fran power, and that was uncomfortable too. Every time you bought a set of guitar strings, you'd be aware of who was paying. It stung. I don't know why.

I have to place on record how gentlemanly he was about

the subject when he decided to go, refusing to accept whatever by then remained of the only inheritance he could ever hope to receive. We were to think of it as a loan. It could be repaid when we had it. Trez, who could be witchy in the acuity of her insights, used to say it was his way of continuing to control us through indebtedness. His attitude discomfited her and always had. She'd go hungry rather than accept it, and that had caused its own problems. It was her view that inexplicable generosity outside of a family, and sometimes inside one, can be a form of establishing jurisdiction. At the time, I regarded this outlook as harsh and misanthropic. Later, I came to feel she was not quite right but also not quite wrong. Every band likes to think it is creating its own pictures, but often there is a figure, not necessarily one of the group, who is using its members as paint. Trez wasn't someone you told what to do, by words or by silences either.

The night came when we planned to see Fran off at Euston station for the ferry-train to Holyhead, but he never turned up at the concourse pub, as all four of us knew he wouldn't. A postcard depicting Robert Johnson arrived from Dublin a couple of days later. 'Goin' wake up in the mornin'. I believe I'll dust my broom. Good luck. Keep at it. Your number one fan. Thanks for some lovely times.'

We missed him. Who wouldn't? Fran was our captain. And it was obvious we were a lesser group without him. There's a moment while you're writing a song when you get hopelessly lost, when your confidence melts like snow off a rope, and you gape about the room seeking any sort of milestone. For me – I think for all of us – the signpost was Fran. He'd know what to say, whether the thing was worth saving. He'd come up with the chord that might pull it from the ashes. Trez would know the chord was called 'F-sharp half-diminished'. Her knowledge was astounding and so was her grace. But Fran was the one who could feel a way towards it, knowing nothing of the name and feeling no need to baptise. He'd lean over the piano and vamp out four notes and you'd feel the dying song start to breathe. Seán used to say Fran was like the sculptor who knows his David is somewhere in the slab. But that wasn't quite right. Fran was blind. He'd know *something* was in there, if something actually was, and he'd make you keep chiselling as long as you could, or as long as you were interested, which isn't always the same thing. He could write in any of our voices, better than we could ourselves. And he'd know when a song should be abandoned as a lost cause. He was ruthless about that, and he'd hurt you by his tactlessness, but he'd always, *always* be right. It's hard to love anyone who is always right, but we did. We got more work done after he left, but it was high level mediocre. We were punctual and organised. The flat was a lot tidier. Fewer arguments happened. So what?

Onward we paddled, Franless and brave, through the hot, loud nights of our schooling. In a way, his absence was so good for us that it was almost a presence. Being a quarter of a quartet means there are places to hide onstage: not many, but you learn where they are. A member of a trio has no such nooks, especially if the instruments are guitar, drums and cello, an uncommon enough line-up for a rock band. And we were gigging in the kind of pub where they'd never seen a cello, except maybe in the *Morecambe and Wise Christmas Special*. You'll find it surprising to be told that Trez, a future *Rolling Stone* Musician of the Year, was in those days so doubtful of her abilities on the bass guitar that she'd only play it at the sound-check, if there was one. We'd shuffle on in the Hangman's Arms or the Bride and Hammer, Leighton Buzzard, to a tsunami of indifference or hostility. The cello she could afford at the time was a respectable old dear but a few dusty years past retirement. It took an age to tune up in the back room but the moment it inhaled lager or encountered the flashing lights of a pinball machine, it wilted like a quiff in a sauna. Trez would retune. And we'd wait.

Men with rat's-tail hair, girls with Lugers for eyes. Stares as inviting as last night's condom. Individuals you could imagine having piercings through their toes. Pockmarked, human dartboards. A single attempt at harmony or any sort of nuance, a lyric not *directly* about fighting or sex, and you'd better have a spit-proof umbrella. The only option was to blast them, and we learned to blast them good. Our thinking was akin to that of one of the era's standing army of non-sexist socialist comedians, Ben Elton, who often remarked in interviews that he'd developed his rapid-fire style of onstage delivery so as not to give the hecklers a chance to mock his spangled jacket or, presumably, his non-sexist socialism. We played fast, loud, tight as a gnat's arse, said little, got off quick, hid the instruments. But I'd have stress-nightmares the night before a gig, where I was naked in a crowd. I'd be about to go on in some vast auditorium of hayseeds with the neck of my banjo apparently made of rubber, and no set-list. Whenever that happened, I drank.

Summer continued. We were skint. It will surprise the reader to learn that London in the middle 1980s, era of slobbering yuppiedom, was still a city you could be poor in. It wasn't like London now, where the unfortunate beggars must ask if you can spare them seven pounds for a panini. Big Maggie made 'United Kingdom' a savagely ironic phrase and the legacy of the greed she fostered is the Second Great Depression, but it took New Labour's touchy-feely ferment of Chardonnay Stalinism to cleanse the greatest metropolis in the world of non-millionaires. Our needs were few enough. Food wasn't expensive. At the Friday market on Queensway I could get reasonably fresh vegetables for almost nothing. I'd an understanding with the Italian butcher on Praed Street. Not by any means the cuts you'd be offered in Soho's finest eateries, but if you knew a little of cooking, even a basic tomato and garlic sauce, you could make something nourishing and filling. The Iraqi fishmonger on Paddington station would give you a quart of prawns or a whiting and parsley stock for two quid if you pitched up as he was closing. It's not hard to bake bread and there's pleasantness in doing so. You feel – I don't know – a little blessedness and rightness in making something for your friends to eat. The warm aroma of a loaf coming out of an oven is perhaps not that far from a song. There was a public swimming pool near us, Porchester Baths, where for 20 pence you could have a hot shower and put yourself together and even rinse your smalls if no one was looking, which a lot of the time no one was. They had a basketball court where Trez and I would often shoot hoops or play a little one-on-one. We were clean, fed and happy, and liked living together in the flat, which we managed to make a home.

The idea of, say, starting a pension or ever owning a property wasn't so much as the faintest blip on the radar.

Perhaps privately so for Seán, but he never spoke of such things. If in your own case it was different, then I salute your prudence, from the ghost estate of my own inadequacy. We'd have decried such notions, had they ever been raised. Alas for blithe youth and the cost of its liberties. It didn't click with me that today's mortgage-feeding wage slave is tomorrow's carefree oldster banging his balls around the golf course.

As the Peel session approached, we started feeling anxious. Seán was despatched to Dublin to see if Fran would talk, but returned a week later saying it was pointless. Our founding father had 'given up music' and was 'writing a novel'. He planned to go to Nicaragua on the coffee-picking brigades and in the meantime was working on a construction site to support himself. The image of him hefting blocks and swinging a pick was vivid. You hoped he wouldn't attempt it in his hot-pants.

In August, now resigned to remaining a trio, we went into the BBC to record the session. Things didn't go the way we'd expected. It was an uneasy day, for several reasons. Trez received her finals results that morning and they were good enough to drop a bomb. She'd been offered a scholarship for postgraduate work at NYU, to start in October or November. Having lost Fran so recently, we might now lose Trez. Since Seán was still at the point of not considering himself a full-time member of the band, that would leave me alone in the water.

Peelie wasn't about, and while it was foolish to have imagined he might be, his absence rather took us aback. Seán was having difficulty, a bad tendonitis in his left hand. Trez was off her game, too loud. We'd agreed that she would take all lead vocals for the day – a sore throat was irking me – and she was more than competent at that. But she knew she couldn't match the singer whose glories had scored us this opportunity. Neither could I. No one could. Christ, even *Fran* wasn't as good as Fran some days. There'd be those accidental moments when he'd sing you through the roof. Without him, we felt anodyne and overly slick, like actors impersonating a rock band in a West End musical. As for me, I'd fallen out of love with my usual guitar, a '72 Rickenbacker that had cost Fran two grand, a beauty with bullet truss rod and three-bolt neckplate, but we weren't seeing eye to eye. I borrowed an instrument left in Peel's studio from that morning's session, a custom-green, quilted-maple Telecaster, but whatever way I amped it the treble was harsh, and I dealt with the problem by persisting too long in trying to solve it when I should have crawled back to my baby and begged forgiveness. I don't know. It was one of those days that never gets going. We put down three tracks of our own, then 'Groovin' With Mr Bloe' by Cool Heat, Trez doing the harmonica solo on fiddle. The engineer complimented us. We complimented each other. But we knew we'd fallen short and the realisation was crushing. By the time we got back to the flat I was hoping the session would never be broadcast – as indeed it never was. It's a cold feeling to know you gave only a hundred per cent. That isn't enough. Not in music.

With the last of Fran's money, we pressed up 600 copies of a song of his, 'Glimmertwin Buddy', with a thing of my own called 'Ash' on the backside. It sank like the *Titanic* only without the attendant publicity, selling 47 copies and receiving no media mention that I know of, except in the photocopied in-house newsletter for employees at Whipsnade Zoo, which pronounced it 'a smashing achievement by young people'. I've long had my suspicions as to who penned that anonymous review.

It was at this point that the lobster-faced old fraud called Fate took a hand. The Karma Police were at work. Trez got a call from Robert Elms, a journalist she knew. He told us, in some amazement, that the peerless Philip Chevron, leading light of the Radiators, had heard our cassette and was interested in working with us. I was convinced this was a piss-take, probably got up by Fran, but it turned out to be the unbelievable truth. To us, Philip Chevron was God's representative on Earth, the greatest thing to happen to popular music since Cromwell outlawed Morris Dancing. He came to our flat and seated himself on our bean-bag. When he went, I remained awake to the dawn. He left a couple of albums he wanted us to listen to, including a spellbinding thing called *This is Madness* by the Last Poets, but his presence shot out my lights. The man who wrote 'Kitty Ricketts' stood in our kitchen. I handed him a cup of tea. And a biscuit.

We had nothing to offer except our continued adoration, but we agreed, with gulping gratitude and no small disbelief, that we'd spend a couple of days in the studio together when next he was in London. It was in Greenwich, that studio, and it cost 900 quid plus VAT for eight hours – the sum was paid by Philip, peace ever be upon him. On the day, I was badly hungover and also suffering from bronchitis, for which I downed a veritable smorgasbord of medicines, not all of them legal or wise. So I'm unable to tell you much of The Great One at work. I seem to remember a conversation about possibly Marvin Gaye? And a checker-board shirt Mr Chevron was wearing? We recorded four songs: two efforts of my own, then a strong thing by Fran called 'Dreaming in Red' before making a further stab at the Rats' number 'Living in an Island', reggaefying it a bit more than we'd done on the cassette and sticking in barking guitar like the Kinks. I thought we'd made a hames of it, but the Chevvy mixed it beautifully. And the fact that he liked it pleased us. You can be pleased by realisation that you've not been a gobshite. You turn the accident into a decision.

I spent the rest of that week in bed, buzzed on cough syrup, downing strong, sweet tea, the latter a favourite cura-tive of Trez for any of life's woes. To my bronchitis, worsened by smoking, was added a double-ear infection. I had never known physical pain so crippling. The twins conversed frequently about the session and the pleasure it gave them, playing me cuts we'd apparently made, which I couldn't recall. Chevron phoned at some point, to say an independent label he knew, Johnny Too-Bad Records, wanted to sign us immediately and release 'Living'. The infection now entered my lungs and I got double pneumonia, with shaking chills, chattering teeth and a fever of 102, in the end causing my admittance to hospital for five days. I celebrated my induc-tion into contractual rock and roll by having Trez, Seán and the white Rasta from Johnny Too-Bad toast me with a bottle of Asti Spumante they'd bought in a garage on the Bayswater Road, while I sweated out the last of my illness. I wish I could remember more.

Things started speeding up. 'Living' came out on a Tuesday, was played by Janice Long on her Radio 1 programme every night that week, and the phone we had in the flat only because British Telecom hadn't got around to disconnecting it started ringing like Quasimodo's bells. We entered the chart at 98, between Alphaville's 'Big in Japan' and Depeche Mode's 'Master and Servant', both of which were on the way down. Somewhere folded among my books I still have the three-line review from *Melody Maker*: 'Luton's vaunted Ships in the Night blend a wicked melody with the chilli-hot skank of the Caribbean. It doesn't quite work, yet it actually does. Sting, be afraid. They're coming for you, rudeboy.'

More journalists called. U2's management got in touch to offer us five support dates in the north of England. Larry Gogan on RTE Radio interviewed Trez. The following week we were at 87, a position that disappointed me a little. Having spent many hours neurotically disliking our version of the song, hearing every fault and foible, every misconstrued bit of instrumentation that even Chevron's skill couldn't conceal, I'd convinced myself that the public, for whatever unfathomable reason, would be in the mood to buy it. It's one of the most maddening hurts of the artistic life, that the outcome you'd have been prepared to hail as a triumph seven days ago is now the slap in the face of your hopes. We wrote appreciatively to Janice Long. She played us again. The new chart was released on the Sunday afternoon and we were floating at 87 once more. Around us were Feargal Sharkey's 'Listen to Your Father' and Lionel Richie's 'Penny Lover'. It was obvious that both were heading one way. Elvis Presley was at 72, a club remix of 'Suspicious Minds'. I will always be a loyal and loving subject of the King, but to have a person who is actually dead be doing better than you in the charts is not without emotional complication.

Astoundingly, giving no notice, Fran came back. Trez and I returned from the gym on a rainy Monday morning to find him stood outside the flat with a suitcase. 'I had to get out. Couldn't stand the stupidity any longer.' He looked fantastic, bright of eye, was clearly off the gear. On Janice Long's show that Tuesday night, he appeared as special guest. He was witty, mercurial, flirty and elusive. 'Would you say you're battling demons?' Janice gamely asked. '"Battling", no. Though it's such a gorgeous word. Perhaps lightly shooing them away with a fan.' The next day, we got a call from BBC 1. I thought my heart would burst.

If you're a music-lover of my era, *Top of the Pops* was your childhood salvation. It's hard to get across just how little popular music featured on the telly in the 1970s. The idea of round-the-clock videos, or downloadable albums, was the stuff of science fiction. Without *TOTP*, you starved. You'd anticipate with religious yearning its arrival on the screen in your living room. Thursday was the night on which it was broadcast in those years, and you dreamed of that arrival, organised your life around its approach, endured the purgatory of Monday, the agony of Tuesday, the asphyxiated and soul-murdering midlands of Wednesday, for the glitterballed, hip-wiggling Newfoundland. The opening theme's reenactment of Led Zeppelin's pile-driver 'Whole Lotta Love' riff meant your teachers were wrong about everything they'd ever believed. Your pimply little existence was not a prison of loneliness but a passport to a world of tight codpieces. Alice Cooper might materialise, strangling an anaconda with his thighs. Strange boys dressed as ladies would pout in thick slap. Pan's People would butt-shake and groove. *Top of the Pops* was where you smouldered to be. To have someone from their office speak to me over the telephone in our little flat of shadows – impossible, wonderful life! They were introducing a new segment, 'the breakout' section, in which a record in the lower realms of the charts would be featured. Perhaps we might be interested in appearing this week? I guess you'd call it English understatement.

FROM FRAN'S FINAL INTERVIEW

For me, it was music. Not even the music itself. Because a lot of it, you know, in the mid seventies, it was shite. But looking at *Top of the Pops* you got glimpses of yourself. That's how I'd put it. Like a mirror. There's a black guy in Showaddywaddy playing the drums. Romeo Challenger from Antigua. And that's his real name. And you felt, okay, they ain't the New York Dolls. But here's a black man who lives in Leicester playing the drums. And he's nobody's minstrel. You know? Errol Brown from Hot Chocolate, a Jamaican-born frontman and he's having these massive hits. Because you never saw a Caribbean person on English telly back then. Totally unreal, the portrayal of England. And then the gender thing, too, it was like every band had a guy who came on like a girl. Mud. Slade. Sparks, Sweet. Playful. You know? They smuggled it in. So, to me *Top of the Pops* was a political show. You watched it to be reminded you weren't alone. That's why there's music. Right there.

I will never forget the day of the recording. The BBC sent a car, and we traversed the couple of miles across slate-grey west London feeling godly and excited and terrified. Arriving at Television Centre in White City, I felt I might weep. To the bemusement of the security guards, Fran solemnly knelt pope-style and kissed the very steps on which Bowie and Bolan had walked. Young women with clipboards were waiting for us. (Clipboards! For us!) We were shown into dressing rooms that had our names on the doors, and fruit bowls and bottles of beer. Would we care to take a shower? Had we names for the guest list? If the end of the world had been announced for later that afternoon, I wouldn't have minded too much.

Ian Dury was on the show that day. Should I write that out again? IAN DURY came in to say hello, joshed around, uttered kindnesses, signed autographs, wished us luck, went away. The reggae band UB40 conversed with us about Delroy Wilson. Status Quo let us borrow their anti-dandruff shampoo. ('You washed your hair in *Francis Rossi's* Head-n-Shoulders?' my brother later gasped. 'You jammy little undeserving BASTARD.') At two o'clock we were led out to take a look at the studio, a room far smaller and somehow *lower* than you'd long envisioned, with cameramen and coolsters with walkie-talkies hurrying smoothly about the floor and lining up shots and fades. 'You're the Ships?' a young woman asked. I could only nod that we were, following her pointed finger up the steps she was indicating and on to a small square stage. Where would we like to stand? Would Fran be moving around? (Er, yes.) What colours would we be wearing, had we questions? And it was

Trez, of all people, who dashed the cold water. You'll have heard it said many times that at the last minute we refused to mime. To this day, people still congratulate me for the courage of our stance. But that isn't in fact what happened.

Trez was not in the studio, being at that moment in Aldergrove Airport, Belfast. A seminar at Queen's University had brought her to that city for a couple of days. We'd agreed she would taxi directly from Heathrow to the BBC. We paced. We worried. Then the message arrived. The most reliable and sensible person on the face of God's earth had managed to miss the flight.

Seán advised calm, as was his wont. All was not lost. She was coming, he said. Mustn't panic. We suggested to the BBC that we wait for her, and play live. The Assistant Director flipped into kindliness mode. *Top of the Pops* wasn't a live show.

The air seemed slowly to drain from my head. I felt as though I was leaking sand. It was conceded that from time to time a Premier League band might be invited to play live. The Style Council, perhaps. Duran Duran. But this wasn't the show's normal practice, as everyone knew. It was expensive and time-consuming to get something like that set up. To be honest, it wasn't even what the viewers wanted. Your *Top of the Pops* audience was interested in *seeing* a band on the screen. They wanted the sound to be perfect, the way it was on the record, and obviously you couldn't guarantee perfection if you shot the performance live, particularly when the group were newcomers. In that case, Fran asked, could we be shot as a trio? The producer was summoned to the floor.

Danny Saint-John or maybe Jonty Saint-Dan, denim of jacket, leather of filofax, with the goatee, perm and blow-dried suavity of a person who has been on many strategic breakout sessions. He looked like the bearded man in *The Joy of Sex* but a little less joyous and a little less sexual, lightly coloured in by tan crayon. You could see he was busy but he could not have been more amiable. What seemed to be the pwoblem, he pleasantly enquired, shaking our hands and clapping our shoulders and generally getting down with the kids. He spoke like a comedian imperson-ating an Etonian Classics Professor cum Spitfire pilot, even though he was only about thirty. 'Hmm,' he kept saying, as Seán and I went through our difficulty. 'Quite. How unfawtu-nate. But time is wawther shawt.' By now, Fran was speechless, a rare enough thing. He stood there in the full-length ruched Zandra Rhodes evening gown he'd rented specially for the occasion, reaching down from time to time to cup his balls through the silk. Dan nodded a lot and sucked the arm of his spectacles. Quite. Quite. One understood how we felt. But we couldn't perfawm as a twio.

'We can, Dan! We can! Dan, we can! Can't we, Dan?' Pleading like seagulls for the scraps from a trawler, we followed as he began walking away. We didn't actually say, 'We're desperate, Dan.' But I think he must have known all the same.

'Musicians' Union wules,' Dan pointed out sadly. 'There's a cellist on the wecord, so we need one on the stage.'

'But we haven't *got* a cellist,' I said. Because we hadn't.

'In that case,' Dan said, 'Yaw fucked.'

Out we were cast, encouraged by Security. Alison Moyet got our slot, a woman with a powerful and truly exquisite voice but I can never hear it without screaming in self-hatred.

Her appropriately named single 'All Cried Out' went to number 8 the following week, our record label dropped us, Fran got hepatitis. Drunk on seven pints of panic, we made the idiotic mistake of covering up Trez's accidental non-appearance by claiming in an interview for the London *Evening Standard* that we'd 'refused to mime on principle'. Jimmy once told me that a squid will gnaw off its own limbs if bored. I could gnaw off my own with shame.

Over the course of the subsequent month it was made known to us by the very winds of the night that no tentacle of the British music industry would ever touch us again. We were the imbeciles who had blown an appearance on *Top of the Pops* by declining to move our mouths to a beat. Who did we think we were? Bruce sodding Springsteen? Lighting would not strike twice.

Frantic, we put out an EP ourselves. *Talking in Bed* did the decent thing by dying. I feel it's important to state that throughout these days of guilt and horror, the person showing greatest gentleness to Trez was Fran. If I raged and accused, he would insist on my silence. When I fought with her, he demanded I stop. Her own brother spewed torrents of ridicule and hurt. Fran never did. He stood loyal.

Freud says there are no accidents. Perhaps he's correct.

Sans Fran who was still recuperating, we did the five shows opening for U2, but they were by no means enjoyable occasions. Providing music to which an audience is finding seats isn't easy. I can't blame them. They were there to see a group fast becoming the biggest in the world, not a troupe of baboons that had wrecked their own chances. Also, there was a ghost on the road.

Trez told us she was accepting the NYU scholarship. We

could find another cellist; London had many. Pointing out that she'd always been straight with us about study coming first – well, somehow that made things worse. I begged her not to go. She said she was going. Immediately following our last show with U2, we drove all night down the motorway from Birmingham to Heathrow. It took us seven hours because something was wrong with the car. We breakfasted sullenly. Everything was broken. Trez became the only person in history to run away from the circus and join school. Right to the moment when she walked through the gates, I was convinced she'd change her mind. She didn't.

My diary goes blank. I was drinking like a fiend. But I can tell you that ten days after our cellist's departure, Seán, Fran and I locked up the flat that was my first adult home and took an Air India flight to Newark. We each of us went as a mail courier, which meant our flights cost almost nothing, but you could take no luggage at all, except for one bottle of water. So we arrived at Trez's student accommodation without even our guitars, malodorous, unshaven and hungry. 'We missed you,' we happily said. Imagine her surprise and delight.

'At least you're out of London,' Jimmy told me down the phone. 'New York is like Luton. Just bigger.'

Twelve

Trez had a room in an NYU block, but it was the size of a monk's cell, with a narrow single bed, a rudimentary desk, and a cupboard of meagre capacity. Her dresses were hangered on a pole that was bracketed to the ceiling, and her other clothes were folded into piles, giving the room something of the ambience of a very small laundry, perhaps in a story for children. One flapped one's way in, through the skirts and the shirts. One moved a shoebox of pants to sit down. On the bed lay her cello, as though recovering from the crossing, unimpressed by the colonials' ways. The books Trez was already amassing were stacked in turrets about the floor, increasing her knowledge while decreasing the space in which scholarly talk might be had. Overnight guests were not permitted by the authorities, and if a Nelsonian eye was sometimes turned on the realities of student life, that wasn't a room in which four adult humans could live without someone being obliged to notice. Seán had enough cash to get bunks for the three of us in an all-male hostel near the Bowery. There, we resided a week. When the readies ran out, we had no other option than to spend a night or two al fresco. I couldn't call it 'sleeping rough' because I never once slept. It was more 'sitting rough until dawn'. Like characters from Henry James, we had an address in Washington Square Park. In our case, third bush near the syringe-pile.

November '84 in New York saw relatively mild weather. Still, the outdoor life can be unnerving. Fran seemed unfazed by nights beneath the stars but Seán and I were uneasy, knowing little of the city except that its nocturnal armies were worth being afraid of. We owned nothing of any value, yet the night-people couldn't be expected to know this. Some of them were gentle enough, but many truly frightening. We saw that we'd need to do something. So we did.

Trez introduced us to a person she had met in an East Village bar. He looked like a man who had once been overweight but was now almost skeletally thin. Saggy, wet-eyed, drug-fucked, *loose*, like one of those celebrities you see in the tabloids now and again whose fat has been sucked out by machine. His name need not concern us. He was a gentleman of the streets. Agreeable, philosophical, an artist of sorts – is there anyone in the East Village who is not an artist of sorts? – he understood we had a problem but we were not to despair. A solution might be found if we could see our way clear to helping out an old soldier with a buck. 'May ye die in Ireland,' he added softly, 'as Yeats once said.' I'm fairly certain that was Bing Crosby but I didn't press the point. We gave him ten dollars. He gave us an address.

The squat was on the third floor of 114 St Mark's Place, a hundred-year-old derelict tenement house. The apartment, for want of a better word, had no functional front door, that luxury of middle-class life having been smashed as a prelude to burglary. Pity, or admire, the optimism of such a burglar. Brother, more power to your jemmy.

Someone, maybe several people, had lived there before. There was evidence of heroin use all around. Nor had occupancy been confined to members of the human species. A carnival of Manhattan's smaller creatures had taken up tenancy.

Egress and entrance were effected by means of a curtain fashioned from a draped and smoke-stained American flag, each of whose discoloured stars had a cigarette burn in its centre, a feat that must have taken some ravaged junkie a whole night on the acid to accomplish. That gallant Stars and Stripes had been hideously befouled in other ways, too. I didn't like picturing its sufferings.

A New York realtor would have called the house 'airy' since a good many of its floorboards and windowpanes were missing, as was the entire staircase leading to the property's upper rooms. Weirdly, the bones of its banisters lay raggedly piled in a corner, a funeral pyre waiting to happen. Lower down, some of the ceilings had sagged or entirely caved in, following the rough removal of the tin ceiling-pieces old Manhattan dwellings used to have. Some doorways were bricked up, shards of shattered pipe-work strewn about. City Council notices advised in several languages, and with pictograms of skulls, that trespass upon this property was dangerous. Unless mad, blind, and lacking all sense of smell, you had likely come to that assessment by yourself. But still, every little experience can teach us something useful. I learned the Spanish word ¡PELIGROSO! from those posters.

If you could imagine Ozzy Osbourne's mind turned into an apartment – and I counsel you never to attempt any such thing unless accompanied by an understanding nurse – you wouldn't be far from the Pit. Even Seán's habitual cheeriness was slightly dented by first sight of what would become our Manhattan base. But Fran, to his credit, made the best and bucked us up. It was better than nothing, he said. And by a whisker, it was.

On the landing reeked a bathroom, more accurately, a fungus room. Description I will spare you, if only because describing it would result in such a plethora of censoring asterisks that this page would look like a map of the Milky Way. You had the impression that the urban hawks that often settled on its windowsill were afraid to peck their way through the glass.

Seán is now a citizen of the United States. Fran does much of his work there. It could create problems for these gentlemen were it to be admitted in a book that they ever breached the terms of a tourist visa by working illegally in America. For that reason I make no such admission. At the same time, shall we say, it was known among undocumented immigrants one might meet in Irish bars about the city that there were ways of getting one's hands on a few bucks without a green card: hotels that might require a washing machine to be fixed, restaurants with a lot of vegetables to get peeled before lunchtime. Seán, Fran and I did no such work.

Our headquarters had a roof and four bare walls, and we avoided the holes in the floor by placing stolen traffic cones around them, but the place could seem dark by four in the afternoon and that would lower the spirits. Clearly, we did not illegally tamper with the disconnected electricity supply in order to provide ourselves with basic light, still less did we manage to get the stopcock going. The main difficulty was the cold, which was unrelenting and vicious. At one time the house had boasted a furnace-fired central heating system, but even if Seán and I had broken into the basement to look at the boiler – which obviously we didn't – we'd have seen that it was long rusted and quite beyond repair and that squirrels were now living in its innards. But frostbite is the mother of invention. We improvised.

Not far from us, on that stretch of the Bowery that intersects with Delancey, was a line of bargain warehouses that sold enormous fridge-freezers and other equipment from failed restaurants. One of us, I think Fran, discovered the happy fact that the cardboard boxes enwrapping the plywood crates in which these mausoleums of refrigeration were shipped could be used as sleeping partitions. On a chilly night the bubble-wrap might be employed as a blanket, if you didn't mind an orchestra of poppings. A sack of Styrofoam marbles made a passable pillow. You could call it a policy of recycling, indeed we did call it that, which demonstrates, among other things, that we were creative.

We were fond of lighting candles so as to give the place a bit of homeliness. Doubtless, the situation was a fire hazard as well as a moral one. You crawled into your cardboard casket, accompanied or solo – sometimes, in Fran's case, severally accompanied – and a certain degree of privacy might then be experienced. The situation, as may be understood, was far from ideal. My own tendencies when it came to the erotic were fairly vanilla. But the full 57 flavours were available in the Pit. Fran's particular thing at the time was the wholesome, down-home type, the person whose previous experience might have been confined to a Saturday night make-out in the back seat of Mom's Volkswagen somewhere in rural Ohio. His persuasiveness in the Pit became honed. Seán, less ambitious, was nevertheless a popular and handsome boy and his search for love was conducted extensively. Then there were the hangers-on and fellow travellers of which the Pit always had such a profusion. It could be a startling experience to totter home in the early hours of, say, Sunday morning, a bit the worse for refreshment, or disappointedly sober, and see six of these love-coffins twitching and bumping, alive with the ebullient cries and fervent machinations of newfound downtown friendship. Alone, you'd be irked by it, or saddened, or made jealous, as you tried to locate the miserable quadrant of rotting floorboard where you'd lie, resenting your comrades to the dawn. If accompanied by the darling of that night's ambitions, you had no small challenge on your hands. Attraction would need to be unusually intense to survive the suggestion, no matter how subtle, that it be given expression in such surroundings. The phrase 'share my bed' may be tenderly uttered. The phrase 'share my box' not so much. The young of the East Village were experimental of spirit in those days, but the invitation to come back to what was in effect a filthy indoor shantytown was a somewhat risky overture. A bit of adventurous slumming is one thing. The Pit was another. There might be a lobotomised street-person in a corner torturing an electric guitar, a couple chewing at one another's privates in the gruesome quarter we called 'the kitchen', a sophomore from the Tisch School of the Arts fighting the mouse-infested sofa or spliffing up to celebrate recent induction into the Fran Club.

And yet, the place was rarely empty of swains and

maidens, particularly at night, when the punk rock raged, and the nothing about which there is much ado was vigorously and unselectively practised. It was as though the apartment had been featured, with a starred review, in some frightening underground publication about Gotham-based vice dens where few questions were asked and none answered. You walked into this armpit of sordor and you could almost smell the smouldering hormones, along with what I suppose must have been Teen Spirit. Recreational sex, in my birthland, was constitutionally prohibited, except for politicians, certain lady novelists and bishops. But the keys of the Manhattan candy store seemed to have been handed over and we made whatever use we could contrive of them. A gift horse is not to be looked at in the mouth, or, as Fran put it, anywhere else. Usually, we ourselves were the horses. Thinking back, it was the era when AIDS began decimating New York. You'd think we'd have known. We surely must. Seán tells me we all discussed it, were aware of safe practices. I'm sure he's correct but in truth I don't recall. What I remember is an increasingly chemical separation from realities, and not minding much about that.

You will feel I was unhappy. I should have been. But I wasn't. It was a strange and murky and abandoned time, one of those eras around which a carapace appears to be forming even while you're going about the business of living it. Perhaps every life contains one or two of those, or it would, were it not for the gas bill. We weren't so much going off the rails as ignoring them completely, or hacking at them with the crowbars of our recently realised pointlessness. Back in London, we'd had what a kind person might call the beginnings of a career. We stamped on it, hard, and twisted our boots, worsening the calamity of *Top of the Pops* by putting out an EP of songs we knew not to be ready. As for why, I can't tell you. A psychiatrist would have theories. Perhaps we were afraid of what would happen if success came in the door. Or else we just drank too much. There are teenagers who spend a gap year backpacking around Australia or learning Chinese or doing good works. I wish I had been one of those, but apparently I wasn't. I spent it getting out of my head in the East Village of New York. That winter is indeed a gap.

As a parent, I'd love to tell you that I wept with inner emptiness, that I longed for something meaningful to fill my God-shaped hole. But that wasn't the way I felt at the time, and there may be little point in dwelling on why. Phil Spector said he approached every song as a challenge to say something memorable in three minutes. The longer it was, the worse it would sound on the radio. But there are seasons of every life that can't be expressed in three minutes. I got through mine alive, for which I'm grateful to happenstance. A lot of kids don't. I've known some.

Abutting the ground floor of our tenement was an oldsters' dirty bar, in which the patrons watched sports and semi-legally bet on them: baseball, football, the ponies. Occasionally a drunken cheer would erupt from below, making you feel strangely happy on a wintry and self-anaesthetised evening with New York howling in through your windows. There was a Polish church on the next block with gorgeously sad bells, deep toned and sonorous, as though Chopin had forged them. For me, that sound will always be the music of Christmas 1984. Cubans and Puerto Ricans drank on Avenue C, a part of the Lower East Side sometimes known as

'Loisaida'. Not far from us was the synagogue, with a mournfully beautiful music of its own that would drift into the Friday evenings, entreating and praising. To this day, I carry a map of those streets in my soul, a cartography of New York song.

In love with a dung heap, you wouldn't notice a broken straw. At the same time, things had to change. Doing absolutely nothing is tiring and depressing, almost as much as hard work. Trez would never join us in the dark ways of indolence. Indeed her absence from the Pit became a sort of rebuke, and slowly we copped ourselves on. She had her old cello, Seán acquired a snare drum, and there was usually a guitar lying about among the squalor. Sometimes, around noon, we'd busk in Washington Square Park, a surprisingly pleasant experience. Often the same people came by, students, hangers-out, lunch-breakers who worked in the neighbourhood, and they were generous when we passed the hat. We did rockabilly stuff, with an occasional ballad. I'd been teaching Trez guitar, just the three-chord trick, but you don't need much more for early Elvis or Eddie Cochran. On a good day, if you got a pitch beneath the monument arch, the takings would buy a couple of pizzas and a bottle of Rough Rider gin. Fran and Seán liked flirting with the crowd. There were days when we drew a couple of hundred punters. They started asking if we'd be here tomorrow, they wanted to bring friends. Would we gig at a party? Could we play at Hunter College? Music is the most merciful blessing in the world. It was turning us back into a band.

After a while, we noticed a particular man would often come by, a tall and rather nondescript-looking midfifty-ish gent with some quality that made you look at him anyway.

He dressed like JFK on a Hamptons weekend and consequently seemed out of place among our crowd. Sometimes he'd come alone, occasionally with a dark-eyed, beautiful woman we later learned was his second wife. Once, he stopped by with the poet Allen Ginsberg, a figure you often saw downtown. Ginsberg nodded along as we cracked out an old Bessie Smith tune, 'Need a Little Sugar in My Bowl'. Then he gave us beefy hugs and introduced his companion. He was Eric Wallace from an outfit called Urban Wreckage Records, a small label he'd set up primarily to record American poetry, though he'd diversified into blues, experimental rap and loft jazz. One bitterly cold January afternoon Eric invited us to the Waverly diner on Sixth. That was a coffee that changed our lives.

Eric was fantastically serious, like a prophet in a movie. I don't think I ever saw him smile. He led us into the Waverly, requested 'the usual' from a waiter, who shook his hand and addressed him in Spanish. We took a booth near the window and he started to talk. He liked what we were doing. What was our plan? That didn't take long. We didn't have one.

He explained that his label was small and wasn't seeking new signings, and, in any case, wouldn't be the right home for our sound. But he wanted to give us a piece of advice. What we needed was to tour. Get out of the park, start building a base and earn what he called 'the chops'. If we wished – no strings attached – he'd make a few calls on our behalf. Down the years he'd sent his acts on a beginners' circuit to develop them, bars and clubs in the south, college venues in the Midwest. There would be no upfront money. This was made clear. We'd get 60 per cent of whatever door-takings accrued on the night; the remainder would go to the venue. 'For good luck' he would front us a grand in cash for expenses and he'd hire us good second-hand instruments. 'I'm fond of the Irish. Pay me back when you're stars.' Consider it? We did. For all of ten seconds. 'Okay,' Eric said. 'Let's eat.'

We started out across the river in the dives of Jersey City, where they stood about the sticky dance floor in threes and fours, an archipelago of slightly drunken and strangely resentful islands hoping for reunification. We did our best but it was rarely good enough to make even the most twitching of slovens dance. One kinder soul, occasionally, might manage a little gibber before being stilled by the glares of his fellows. Playing music to a sparse audience who don't really want to hear you is like trying to kindle a fire in the rain: if you're lucky, a twig catches here, a coal smoulders there, and soon the assembled logs join in with the blaze, having no other option but embarrassment. But we ignited few fires on those chilly nights in Jersey. Often, we put them out.

Occasionally, as in the varsity town of Princeton, there was a local promoter who claimed intimacy with the scene, but his idea of advertising a concert by a totally unknown group was to hand out twenty fly-bills to winos in the park or students who dressed as though Banana Republic ran the world. A poster in the window of a bar in Point Pleasant Beach once read 'The Ships – From England – Pool table!' On another haunting occasion, in Scranton, Pennsylvania, a coachload of old people turned up from a suburban retirement home, convinced that the name of the band would mean a pleasant evening of shanties about whaling. Believe me, had we known any, we'd have done our utmost to please. But their nurse took one look at topless Fran in his chains and satanic tattoos before leading her confused charges busward. We weren't 'the right fit', she nervously confirmed. Scranton had a Cultural Studies Group, and that night we played to seven of its faultlessly welcoming members. The best I can say of the evening was that a dog on the street outside the town hall seemed to like us, to judge from his appreciative howlings.

The following Friday night found us on a Greyhound bus to Virginia, where the bar gig did not go well. America's a trip in any sort of city. But out in the tall grass, things can be different. I'm fond of the new American South – which music-lover isn't? – but an apparition like Fran was a pretty big ask. Tolerance for a person of his particular look was not what it might be in, say, a nightclub in Phuket.

The response of any sane person would be to rein in the fun-furs and butch it up a little for the indigenous peoples, at least until you're north of the Mason–Dixon Line when you can return to expressing the fabulousness of your existence through the medium of tart-red lippy. Fran would have none of it. He became petulant, then reckless, avid with the rock-ribbed, fire-eyed arrogance that many insecure people get good at fronting up. Give him a top, he'd go over it. Soon as we rolled into Anytown, Georgia, he'd start referring to it as 'a godforsaken outpost of Darwin's waiting room'. Then he'd make for its thrift store, returning, an hour later, with armfuls of controversial garb. A buccaneer's hat. Diamanté drop-earrings. On one occasion the laced skirts and petticoats of a local flamenco artiste who died when struck by lightning. All he needed was the pineapple balanced on his head and he would have been Carmen Miranda. Reason with him? No. You were wasting your time. As well attempt to make a football out of raindrops.

It wasn't at all that the tour lacked successes. In the college town of Oxford, Mississippi, a gracious and most hospitable place, we got the barroom jumping. And in gorgeous bluesy Jackson, 170 miles down the highway, encores aplenty were bestowed. Our problem was consistency. We couldn't string it together. When a gig went well, we partied too hard, which meant that the following day, with its four-hour bus ride, would be encountered through the agony that even Dante never dared to conjure, the pain of a Jim Beam hangover. If Seán had lingered late with a belle of the South, he didn't like leaving at all. Fran, on the other hand, always wanted to go. Mornings found him sulky, endlessly complaining. The room was too hot. You couldn't get 'proper tea'. The lady in the drugstore had regarded him strangely when he asked if he could try that eye shadow before purchasing.

Requested by a pleasant reporter from a local paper in Alabama to suggest two useful tips for the visitor to that state, Fran expressed himself with uncharacteristic economy.

(a) Think of something you like doing.
(b) Don't do it.

This particular sort of attention-seeking isn't without risk. The few punters such publicity attracts to your gig tend to be carrying marlinspikes and hammers. As is often the case, in any walk of life, a person's most admirable quality is also his flaw. It would always be a difficulty, Fran's refusal to compromise. Argument merely encouraged him.

It was only our literal begging that dissuaded him from going on, in Centerville, Texas, wearing leather jeans out of which he'd painstakingly cut the arse, using Trez's nail scissors. (Down this part of Texas they hunt wild hogs, for fun.) In a South Carolina burg, an old cove in the bar turned to me looking stern. 'I mo say this wun time. That' – he gestured with his head – 'better nut be a mayun.'

I assured him it wasn't, that our Fran was a girl.

'That a fact?'

'Absolutely.'

'You KNOW that for a fact?'

'We're married,' I said.

'Ruther yewn me, son.'

Let me conjure the St Valentine's Night we spent in Hickman, Kentucky. This attractive part of the world is solid bluegrass country and the punters expected any visiting troupe of semi-Irish musicians to be offering reels and jigs. But that's not what happened. Fran sashayed on in a heavily sequinned mariachi outfit, with perhaps unwise maracas and knee-length tight pants of the sort worn by bullfighters. '*Traje de luces*,' they're called. His flamboyances were met with hooch-cooked silence from what technically must be named the audience. To add to the general sense of the problematic, Trez had bussed back to New York for an inescapable meeting with her NYU supervisor, so we were performing as a trio that night. Something went wrong with the microphones and PA, so that Fran's falsetto came out as an assemblage of incoherent burblings punctuated by vicious clicks. Also, it was a mistake to do 'I'm Just A Girl

Who Cain't Say No.' I said it would be a mistake. And it was.

In the McDonald's after the gig, we were seated in deep-fried failure, Fran and I, he casting gloomy aspersions out the window at what he insisted on calling the Mrs Shitty River, when a coven of drunken youths began jeering us.

'You girls British?'

We said nothing.

'Naw. See, one of em's Chah-neese.'

They exchanged the usual stupidities, miming what they felt to be oriental *ah-so* noises, one lout using his fingertips to refashion his eyes. Then their random neural firings continued expressing themselves in language. 'Hey, ladies? Whyn't you come over here'n suck on ma milkshake.'

'We don't want trouble,' I ventured, which was the literal truth. But stating it only seemed to goad them. Empty Coke cups were tossed at us. We made the mistake of not leaving. The Human League classic 'Don't You Want Me?' was playing. The answer, one felt, was no.

'You gurls English with that accent?'

'Irish.'

'Say whut?'

'Give us a break, guys? We're busy.'

'Oooooooo,' the boys brayed, as some boys are wont to do on these occasions, out-camping each other as a means of asserting their straightness, but I didn't feel like exploring the paradox. By now I was eyeing the exits and wondering how fast we could get to them. Fran looked red and angry as he chewed.

'Let's blow,' I said.

'I'm finishing my dinner.'

'They're gonna mill the fukken shit out of us. Come on.'
'Let them try.'

'*Mah granddaddy wuz Arish. You pinhead liddle faggots. And if mah granddaddy wuz here, he'd cut off your dick.*'

Whereupon Fran turned around and stonily replied: 'If your granddaddy saw my dick he'd beg to suck it.'

I needn't describe what ensued. The tinderbox of thwarted imbecility met the spark of Francisco El Loco. Punches got thrown. Jabs and cruel pucks. Handfuls of someone's supper – a Happy Meal, ironically – were smeared in our infidel faces. Fran's hours in the boxing ring as a lad proved useful. Also, let's face it, surprise was on his side. You don't expect a southpaw in a boob tube. The uppercut he detonated before being stormed by superior numbers was a cruncher. It levitated its recipient, resulting, I would think, in a windfall for the dentist of the town. I gave what little I had in the way of retaliatory gouges and self-defensive head-butts, but ended up on the tiles, someone's boot on my throat.

In a McDonald's, plastic chairs are screwed to the floor. Otherwise we would have been brained with them. As it was, a machine – for floor-polishing, I think – was seized from a bewildered Mexican member of staff, its flexes and extensions and heavy-duty hosepipe all put to use as flails. Somehow, in the melee, the wretched thing managed *to switch itself on*, and I remember its terrible buzzings. Our assailants called us offensive names, indicating that had grandfather not departed to the Ireland in the Sky, he would stick the vacuum-nozzles into several parts of our persons. A wheel came loose, about the size of a table-tennis ball, and one of the affronted set about attempting to stuff it down my gizzard with a calm and appalling seriousness. He got it into my mouth and began forcing closed my jaws. In the long and tragic annals of rock and roll deaths, my passing would be a footnote or a pub-quiz question. Brian Jones died in a swimming pool, Otis Redding in a plane crash, others amped on coke while 69ing a debutante or speeding a Lamborghini off a pier. I would meet my own maker with an omnidirectional rubber wheel jammed down my gullet, abashed, perhaps bummed by a hoover.

I can't say I actually remember the arrival of Seán with a brace of very heavy-looking local police officers, night-sticks out and sleeves rolled high. But I learned, in the jailhouse, on that haunting night, that Southerners shouldn't be stereotyped. Our arresters were not pleased with us, and strong language was used, but they saved us a month in traction. Releasing us next morning, they gave us bacon and biscuits, and pointed us to the restroom – 'You gents might wanna wash up a little.' We were musicians? Mighty fine. Typa music exactly? Had we heard of the Howlin' Wolf? Now *that* was the musician. Six foot four, three hunnerfifty pounds. They drove us in their Black Maria to see the club he'd once gigged at. Mercy, that bigman could moan 'Smokestack Lightin'. Come up from the town of White Station, Mississippi. His blues went the whole world round.

They posed with us for photos, let us try on their shades, and the captain gave us a piece of sound valedictory advice as he dropped us off at the Greyhound depot. 'You boys lay off the hot-doggin', y'heä? So long. Yawl comeback soon.'

FROM FRAN'S FINAL INTERVIEW

See, when you don't look like none of the other kids in the class – that's hard when you're young. They exploit it. They'd be calling us 'a chink' or a 'ching-chong Chinaman'. Kung Fu on the telly was big at the time. They'd be calling you 'glasshoppa'. Just to taunt you . . . Toys were all made in Hong Kong back then. You'd come in on Monday morning and they'd ask you what toys you made over the weekend, Charlie Chan . . . And your parents, you know, they don't look like you neither. And the kids know they ain't your real parents . . . And so then, you get to thinking there's two ways you can go. And mine was, I'm gonna best you. Every day. Every minute. Have a good long laugh, cock. I'll best you. You box? I'll box better. I'll beat you out the ring. This English you tell me I can't speak? I'll speak it better than you. I'll read every novel in the library, every poem, every play, and I'll make them mine and screw your head off in the process. Keep calling me a chinkie, keep demeaning yourself. I'll best you from here to Saigon. Via Dublin. And when you finally come to strangle me, you're gonna lose out. I'll die like Oscar Wilde. It's all good.

Thirteen

The tour was gruelling and it lasted nine weeks. By the end, we were tight and buzzed. We'd ventured north as far as the Chicagoan suburbs, back down to Baton Rouge, to many points in between. And we'd learned how to win over a smallish American audience, perhaps the most demanding task in rock and roll. But back in New York, Eric didn't return our calls. We persisted, but the day came when his assistant told us he was 'indefinitely unavailable'. That seemed to be that. The rebuff hit us hard. Square One was beckoning horribly.

Unlike some I won't name, I didn't do heroin. New York was an opiate in itself. The difficulty was that the Pit was getting out of hand. At any moment, this accommodation, about the size of two normal bedrooms, might contain Fran, Seán, me, a visiting Trez, various acquaintances and disciples and deacons and acolytes, an assortment of ruined creatures who were, or thought they were, or wanted to be, our friends, and whoever Fran was pursuing that night. This wouldn't be a problem if the weather was kind, for one could take to the streets for respite. South of Union Square was still entrancing back then, a quarter with a little vivifying grime beneath its fingernails. To walk the blocks of downtown was a trip and a half, funk pumping from the clubs and salsa from the bars and ragga from the punk boutiques. A gay men's choir used to rehearse in a coffeehouse on Avenue B and I can never hear Handel's *Messiah* without remembering again the fierce joy of their Hallelujah Chorus. Down on Mott in Little Italy you heard Puccini from the pavement trattorias while the last of the mobsters, womanly old men pretending to be mad, muttered the rosaries of Sicily. The fish stalls of Chinatown buzzed with Foochow Radio, an orchestra of spangling, glittering vowels and susurrations of disco-beat boombox. On the corner of West Broadway and Houston a trio of bobbysoxers channelled Motown, finger-snapping, lissom in sloppy Joe sweaters, sha-la-las and shang-a-langs raising whoops from the crowd. By the church of St Mark's in-the-Bowery, among panhandlers and junkies, a flautist did 'Purple Haze'. On the sidewalk by CBGBs I saw Lou Reed emerge from a limo, leather-jeaned, sullen, mop of ebon-black curls, horn-rim specs like a literature professor's, shoulder-padded white jacket reckoned deathly cool at the time. Along the block was Amato Opera, a one-time Mission House now an endearingly grungy little theatre where for three bucks you got Verdi sung live. Sometimes I'd head up to Matt Umanov's guitar store on Bleecker, a place that opened late, where they were tolerant of browsers. In the Rarities room was the most gorgeous thing I had ever seen: a 1955 two-colour sunburst Fender Stratocaster, signed by Keith Richards. One night, when the store was quiet, they took it down from the wall and let me play. I've always found New Yorkers kindly and amenable, undeserving of their reputation for rudeness. Hit a power-chord on that guitar and it grunged like a monster. Flick the switches and pull a solo high up on the neck, bending the strings, just *touching* the tremolo, and it cooed in sweet-sad soprano. 'Kid, I'm seein' a love-connection,' said the guy behind the counter. 'Talk to me. I'll do a good price.' Alas, the midnight Romeo must go home from his darling. Back I would trudge to the hovel.

We were often very poor. I was twenty and male. You'd think the squalor wouldn't matter. But it began to. You can only turn your clothes inside-out for re-wearing so many days before pining for bourgeois fripperies like laundromat money. One day, very low, I begged on East Houston. The thought of Jimmy and Alice scalded me with shame. But I couldn't go on in my filth. If the German girl who helped me outside the subway is reading these words, I want to say, without exaggeration, that you may have saved my life. You'd be my age now. I hope the years were kind. I don't pray very often, but every time I do, I remember your gentleness and tact.

I was diagnosed with chronic asthma, given a prescription for steroid medication. Some weeks, I couldn't afford it. Darker memories of that time are rapping on the door, but let's move this along. The past is the past. It was nobody's fault but my own.

In the end, it was the twins who sorted us out. Well, really it was Seán, but encouraged by his sister, not that he lacked much courage. I returned one Tuesday morning in April from a long weekend spent I don't remember where, to find the pair of them attired strangely, in rubber gloves, shorts, Doc Martens and leather aprons, faces glowing with sweat and purpose. The addition of only a fun-fur and a lick of mascara would have made them look like the New York Dolls.

Glancing blearily about the Pit, I saw they'd been busy. The boxes were gone. The 'kitchen' had been cleaned. The refrigerator shone like a mother's accusation. Inside was actual food, things like lettuces and carrots. On the floor were four sleeping bags, in ruthless parallel. The American flag had been laundered. Trez was moving in. There were plants on the windowsill. We were buying a door. We were going to stop drinking. Christ.

Seán explained that a Rubicon was reached during my absence. An overnighter nobody knew had proved highly unpleasant, a scene involving dirty needles and apparent psychosis, eventuating in the flourish of a switchblade. Seán and another had been forced to eject the troublemaker, and while Seán, like many a lad hailing from south of the Thames, was well able to look after himself in any sort of affray, he had a hatred of physical violence. From now on, there would be rules. They would have to be kept. He handed me a piece of paper.

1: Nobody stays over if we don't know their name.
2: Everyone does a share of cleaning and tidying.
3: You go back to doing music (that's why you're here) or bugger off home to Luton.
4: You water us once in a while. If you don't, we will die.
Signed – yours truly – the plants.

What I admired was the way he'd smuggled in rule number 3. But I wondered how Fran would take it. He'd been absent from the Pit for a couple of nights, was rumoured to be trysting with a Bolivian tranny who worked in a cabaret near Times Square, and had grown unapproachably surly when confronted with questions, not that we confronted him often. In the end, all he did on returning hollow-eyed from his sweetheart was point out that rule number 1 was ungrammatically expressed. I took it as his way of confirming that he wished the group to resume. So it proved. We got going again.

We agreed we'd give it three months, six at a push, then we'd hang up our boots if we had to. There were a number of background factors, some of them important. Seán, to buy us new instruments, had gone heavily into debt. To see him prepared to do such a thing was to realise something I knew already: that he wasn't along for the ride. Also – and I have never spoken publicly of this matter before – there was Trez's personal situation. I don't mean her studies, though those were important too. But there was another meter ticking and it wouldn't be stopped. Seán's stakes were high. Hers were higher.

She had always been one who said little of her private life. But you certainly knew that she had one. I've asked permission before writing of it now, and had it not been granted, I'd be maintaining my silence. Privacies remain, and I want to respect them, but it's a part of our story, and I've been given her agreement to tell it. The fact is that Trez was pregnant.

The situation, if difficult for her and the father, was in the process of being worked out, and that is all I wish to say. Except to add that the Italian-born student with whom Trez fell in love in New York became her husband many years later, in 2006, on their daughter's twenty-first birthday.

So that's where we were. Not quite as portrayed in a number of colourful chronicles of the group and our bohemian Manhattan adventure. Trez made it clear that the band's days were numbered, she'd be returning to England when she was seven months along. We could use the time remaining to do something useful or we could continue pissing ourselves away. Up to us.

Remarkably, we copped a break. A bar called the Moon Under Water opened right there on our block. It was run by a Scot of Italian parentage, Paolo Cafolla, who was a lover of any sort of rootsy music and wanted his place to feature new acts. On his third night in business, we played to maybe sixty customers. We gigged again that weekend, and the following Wednesday. It was the start of a residency we'd end up keeping throughout the most uncomplicatedly happy time we'd ever know as a group, a season of peacefulness and learning.

The Moon had been named for a slightly wistful essay by George Orwell about the perfect pub of his imagination. Paolo's grubby establishment didn't look like the Victorian inn of the essay, but it had a particular atmosphere you didn't find anywhere else in New York, a sense of itself as a club for non-belongers. There was a sign in its window: NO TELEVISION HERE. Pete Hamill and Jerzy Kosinski often stopped by, as did Mike Scott of the Waterboys, the Breton-Welsh singer Katell Keinig, and many other musicians. There'd be actors from the little theatre at 80, St Mark's, with Irish kids working in Manhattan, refugees from recession, and out-of-towners along for the peek. It didn't have a door policy, or any kind of policy I could see. The only rule was laidback tolerance. This was enforced by the fact that Paolo, a former mercenary in the Congo, so it was whispered, was six foot two and imperially fierce of demeanour. Troublemakers, homophobes and the over-assertive would be told, rather quietly, in chilling Glaswegian, that they'd enjoy themselves better 'in a fukken sports bar'. Anyone else was welcome. Artists, talkers, punks, neo-beatniks, Rastas who lived in a commune just across the street, hacks from the *Village Voice*, slum-bunnies, ladyboys, drag-queens, balladeers, even sometimes an older resident of a neighbourhood that had always been edgy, back in the Moon not so much for nostalgia but to see if the East Village still had any night-people and what they might be up to if so. The food was not good. The bathrooms were a challenge. It never stayed open quite as late as Apichart the Thai barman promised you it would. Paolo and Apichart were in fact a couple. What a wonderful place it was.

It's a bit much to say we became 'the house band' at the Moon, a thing I've seen written by people who should know better. It wasn't that kind of establishment. Officially, we played a couple of sets there once or twice a week. But if you happened to be on the premises in civilian capacity and someone else was gigging and invited you up, you'd have your guitar stashed in the kitchens just in case. A home away from home, I guess.

We'd stroll down around five, have some not very good food, drink a beer, set up, start playing. Sometimes just Trez and I, acoustic guitar and bass, while we waited for the lads to arrive. Fran might sing in French or blow a mean blues harmonica. He could wail it like Sugar Blue Whiting. Seán was always late because of a girl. The audience had all the roof-raising enthusiasm of a New York crowd but none of its high expectations. Some nights you took requests for a cover, or tried something new, others you played only songs with a colour in their name, or a day of the week, or a country. Seán made up a dartboard with a song title in every segment. He'd invite a punter he fancied to throw nine darts, and thus we'd shape the set. Touring had been our school, the road our college. But in the Moon we came to master a difficult thing: how to be the Ships mark two. One midnight I peered out through the purple fug of cigarette smoke. There, in a corner, sat Eric.

As usual, he wasn't smiling. But his presence was enough. After the gig, which he said he hadn't completely enjoyed, he explained that he was thinking of signing us. He handed Seán a foolscap envelope containing ten thousand dollars in cash 'for whatever little expenses you guys might be having. Nothing's attached. Living in New York isn't cheap. It's a gift from my wife and me. I'd like you to meet her.' With my share of the windfall, I went to Umanov's and made a down-payment on that Stratocaster. It took months to pay it off, and I often went without. I'm no fetishist – I bought that guitar because I adored the sound it made when you fed it through an old Marshall amp. But the first thing you ever worked hard to buy brings a strange pleasure all its own. I've loved many guitars but none as tenderly as that one. How could something so gorgeous be mine?

I cannot praise Eric Wallace enough for his gentlemanly mentorship. He'd invite us to his and Maria's apartment on Elizabeth Street, feed us, have us stay over, play records he felt we should hear, give us books or poetry journals. He and his wife were one of those couples you want to be around, generous to one another in company, never sniping or pulling faces, each listening when the other was speaking. They collected art in a quiet way and had a great respect for the fact that Trez was studying it, on one occasion giving her a beautiful Sol LeWitt lithograph she'd happened to admire in their hall. From his grandfather, a Lithuanian immigrant, Eric inherited a certain brand of sardonically expressed stoicism and half a considerable fortune gained by the extermination of agricultural pests. He was wealthy in his own right, having been a Wall Street trader, and had set up Urban Wreckage at the age of forty-three, following a fairly serious heart attack. He was in every way the opposite of the predatory figure that appears in many young bands' biographies.

Eric knew his music, could quote you chapter and verse on the blues. He owned a harmonica once the property of Blind Willie McTell and to hear him name the great blues players was a jazz riff in itself: Junior Wells, Hubert Sumlin, Robert Nighthawk, James Cotton, Snooky Pryor, Hound Dog Taylor, Earl Hooker. He'd been a cantor at his synagogue and worked with a major act or two in his time, including Run DMC and Grandmaster Flash. Unusually for a person in the music business, he was privately rather religious, a fact I only learned much later. He was one of those lucky souls to whom creative ideas arrive like the birds to St Francis of Assisi. Unfortunately, in the case of the Ships, the birds crapped on him.

The second wave of hip hop had hit by 1985, much of it emanating from New York. And Eric, bless his soul, loved rap. Any mixture of the spoken and the percussive excited him. One day he called Trez with a 'left-field idea'. There was a young producer on his books, an aspiring rapper and

MC, Stone Fever, whom Eric reckoned a talent, the next Coke La Rock or Afrika Bambaataa. That was high praise indeed. We listened to a couple of his mix-tapes. Trez was a little uncertain, feeling the territory was too far from our own, but Eric pressed us and we agreed to meet.

He turned out to be a skinny and studious-looking French-Canadian, a youth who might have weighed 150 pounds when wet. Wikipedia tells me his given name was Antoine de Canonville Lefèvre, that he attended a shockingly expensive private boarding school in Hartford, Connecticut and was technically a count back in the old country – Le Comte de Saint-Germain – but he hated to be reminded of any of these facts. A devotee of *Star Wars*, he slouched into the studio on that fateful morning wearing a Darth Vader T-shirt and belted jeans so baggy they could have accommodated Mama Cass. He was a nice guy who overdid things a little.

Eric made the introductions in customarily polite manner, Stone Fever nodding at the floor as his CV was summarised to us. He'd heard our demos, so Eric confirmed, and felt we had potential if we were willing to work. Perhaps he'd like to say something himself? A mere handful of years older than us, it must have been hard for him to assume a position of sudden leadership. But he gave it his best and we listened.

'Thanks Eric. Wuzz up. Y'all some bad Irish outlaws. Hey Trez, love that cello. Beautiful playing. My man Fran. Good to meet. Let's talk.'

'Do we call you Antoine or Stone?'

'Call me Tony.'

Eric went away. Tony continued talking. Our stuff was

'steamy and loose', he loved the ska and reggae elements, but we could do with some 'tightening up'. I sounded, at least to myself, weirdly upper-class British as I responded. 'A song is a sawn-off,' was one of his sayings. 'Cut it short, more damage gets done.' You'd the feeling he had never shot anything, except perhaps a brace of grouse on a relative's estate in the Camargue, but he wanted you to think him a Man With a Past. He was fond of the loaded silence.

It would be easy to satirise a person like Tony and I'll try to resist cheap temptations. The fact is that he proved an assiduous and immensely talented producer, singing interesting jagged harmonies, playing volcanic licks on a wailing Hammond organ. It must be added that he was hardworking, arriving promptly every morning and remaining far later than he was paid for. He seemed touched by Fran's wish to learn the basics of production and he explained them with care and thoroughness. But if anything Tony was a tad on the conservative side when it came to the vision thing, and the surprise of this realisation disconcerted me. I don't know what I was expecting. But it wasn't this *stylishness,* this sense that a record was finally an artefact rather than a recording of people playing music. Every track had to be brought home in three minutes thirty or less, which is obviously a good idea an awful lot of the time, but if you'd said it to Bob Dylan we wouldn't have 'Like a Rolling Stone', which some might feel would be a pity. He didn't want Trez to improvise solos or even to play electric bass, preferring to work carefully with her in early-morning rehearsal, to make her sound 'less wild but more powerful'. Occasionally he'd permit her to 'cut loose with the crazy' and she'd saw at the poor cello as though trying to cut it in half, but always he followed these flights with a demand for strict arpeggios or tightly controlled pizzicati.

'*Si, Mama*,' he'd mutter, hands on his ear-cans.

Local success and having a story to tell are often limiting in a male, since they can lead to unearned licence and silly remarks, imperviousness to proprieties established for a reason. He appeared to find Trez's playing arousing in ways that were not merely aesthetic. 'She make that cello *moan*.' We grinned with obedient cowardice, Fran and I. Seán would fall strangely silent. An odd energy enters the room when a collection of young men are brought to the realisation that the young woman they have tended to construe as one of their own is desirable to the interloper. Once that genie is released, it rather flaps about, and it's hard to get it back into the bottle.

Over that fortnight we got through five or six tracks without too much violence being done to them and we learned a useful thing for anyone in the arts: the skill of the slightly forced smile. It was undeniable that Tony was taking our efforts and turning them into actual songs, entities you could imagine getting played on a radio, possessing verses and choruses and snazzy little bridges, and that wasn't by any means unexciting. If your dribble could be made into a sonnet, you'd be happy to take the credit. Yet I wasn't. Ted Hughes writes somewhere of Sylvia Plath's artisan-like approach to a poem, that if she couldn't make a table she'd be happy to make a chair, or even a toy, and that's all very well, indeed an admirable resourcefulness in any poet, but I guess I'd grown fond of our tables.

We didn't say much. Tony did the talking. We'd cluster about him in the booth, amid the beer cans and the bunts, the Rizla papers and speed-pills and packs of Gauloises, the discarded bits of turkey-and-jalapeño sandwiches from the Korean deli on East 9th, and we'd listen to the playback, agreeing like mad on its phatness, its superiority to anything contemporaneously attempted, but I had the uneasy feeling that a dog can be trained to admire its own farts, that we were straying pretty far from the point. I didn't know any more if the Ships possessed any point. But if we did, I wasn't certain this wasn't it. There is nothing more glorious in music than rap done by a master, and nothing worse than rap done anaemically by extra-cultural forgers, invaders who don't know the nuance. As with everything else, it's a matter of earning your stripes, not renting them from the fancy-dress shop for the evening. The more Tony praised a take, the more forced my smile. It came soon to the stage where if I had to smile any harder, my eyebrows would disappear into my hairline. The grammars of hip hop were exhilarating, to be sure. There was intensity and muscle and *brashness* in his approach, but I couldn't help wondering if the fit was right. It was as though Emmylou Harris had announced her intention of joining Def Leppard. She'd be *able* to do it, no doubt about that. And you'd be interested in seeing it. Briefly.

I kept my own counsel. Well, you do when you're flustered. I should add that there was always a lot of tequila flowing about that studio and it proved a ten-ton sedative. But the feeling grew among us that we were being a little shoehorned, hemmed in. Small things at first, but Tony could be contumacious and brusque. Also, there was occasionally a loftiness about his manner, and no young person likes uppishness, which was all this was – snobbery dressed as taste. Trez suggested we might use a concert harp to colour a track called 'You Can't Have Both'. He nixed the idea immediately, said 'orchestral was over' (Christ!), a dismissal so sweeping that it rather took us aback, and of course, like everyone avowedly rebellious, when confronted with superior force and the emission of false confidence, we trounced each other in acquiescing. I was no Sir George Martin or Daniel Lanois, and he was gentlemanly enough in pointing that out, but cross-fades I might offer got quietly forgotten, often in a verbal formula that began to annoy me: 'That'd be one way of doing it, yeah.' I discovered that I didn't like him, that his repudiations disconcerted me. He could in fact be a bit of a comte.

I was afraid of him, of course. All of us were. Having ballsed our career in England, he was the elusive second chance. Giving power to a leader you disrespect creates the Petri dish of mediocrity. In it, we bubbled and fumed and retrenched. We'd tell ourselves he was well-meaning, that he couldn't be the control-obsessive he appeared. 'Nobody could,' Trez said.

But there arose an unspoken tension between Tony and Seán. Our producer appeared to feel that a drummer was a bit surplus to requirements, that no group needed a human to supply what a drum machine could be programmed to supply more reliably. Seán was a charming boy, by far the most open-minded of us all, a youth as utterly devoid of ego as you could ever hope to encounter, but no musician likes to feel he's being tolerated as a favour while they're wheeling the ironmongery up the stairs to replace him. It was a question of subtlety, and Tony had little. He was one of those people who make an impressive show of listening to your every word, as a means of ultimately dismissing you. At the same time, we were all aware, Fran especially, that Eric saw providing him to us as a sign of Urban Wreckage's commitment. Tony's services were not cheap, as he daily found a way of reminding us. The atmosphere began to curdle.

There was a particular track that was causing us concern, for we feared what Tony would do to it. It was called 'Eleven City' and had been written by Fran, with a couple of ideas from Trez. They wanted to use a Low D Irish tin whistle on the bridge, but we knew Tony wouldn't permit it, under his sternly non-folk statutes. How, then, to manage the problem?

Fran had stolen a book from a store on Second Avenue, about the film director Billy Wilder. He was taken by a story of how Wilder once wanted an actress to appear topless in a scene during which she would awaken in bed beside her lover. From memory it was Marilyn Monroe, but my daughter says Shirley MacLaine in *Irma La Douce*. Anyhow, it doesn't matter. Knowing that the conservative studio bosses would hit the roof and keep hitting it, Wilder contrived a plan by which he would alter the script to include a sequence of his leading lady 'naked and sensuously embracing a tree'. The executives duly revolted and the topless shot was admitted as a compromise. It's a time-honoured negotiation strategy, used by everyone from the Ancient Greeks to Sinn Féin. In the hands of the young, it's dangerous.

Having refused to outline the details of his scheme in advance, Fran announced to Tony that he wanted to record 'an improvisation' as the opening track on Side B. He would bang randomly on the piano keyboard with both fists for a while, this to be followed by a period of eleven seconds 'precisely' during which none of us would play anything at all. The result would be 'coloured air', a concept much explored by Stockhausen. The track would be entitled 'Stockhausen Shuffle'. So would the album, perhaps.

Always, the tiniest detail is the one that seals doom. The suggestion that Tony would permit any record bearing his credit to be titled in such a way turned his expression of tolerant bemusement to a scathing scowl. Stockhausen was important, Fran foolishly went on, and his ground-breaking experiments in musical spatialisation were 'a major influence' on the Ships. Seán didn't actually look at me and ask what on earth Fran was talking about. I suspect he didn't need to.

Tony drew the line. Fran drew his own. These impasses are always worsened by the presence of an audience, and the room was forbiddingly small. It was clear that a grave error of judgement had been made. Tony was tiring of our disobedience.

'You guys,' he said darkly, 'are wasting my time. I think we're all through. See you round.'

Well, Fran started into a peroration that even Philip Glass would find incomprehensible, full of references to 'aesthetic breakdown' and 'sonic toxic shock'. On the way, he referenced the works of the noted experimental composer John Cage, an eminence he admired for writing a piece entitled '4'33"' comprising four minutes and thirty-three seconds of silence. I am told it is popular in the Benelux nations. Tony, alas, was no Belgian.

'You figure a lotta people gonna pay fifteen bucks for a record of fuckin silence?'

'Music without silence is sex without tongues,' Fran said.

This went down like a bomb in a nursery. Tony was not a person you lectured about the many ways of love. He looked at Fran like a man who has decided to let a calculated slight go but is storing it up nonetheless.

'I'm going across the street and eat me a sandwich,' he said. 'I come back here and you're still talking nonsense, you need another producer. That clear? I mean it, Fran. I'm out.'

'It's just an idea,' Fran said. 'Don't flounce off with a hole in your tights.'

Again, the choice of imagery was imprudent.

Tony wafted out in a miasma of wordless outrage, the rest of us too shocked to set upon Fran and beat him. In fairness, he looked shaken himself. His solo run had achieved nothing. Worse, it attracted fire. I feared that it had turned our producer, who should have been our staunchest ally, into an enemy who would be self-protective and cunning. I hadn't the smallest doubt that if Eric got to hear of our antics, we would be condemned as ungrateful, indulgent gobshites, and that Tony would save his own skin by leading the prosecution.

It was a difficult hour. We argued among ourselves. Tony arrived back from enjoying his sole meunière at the Yale Club.

'I sense a disturbance in The Force,' he said bleakly.

We came clean and explained that we had in mind to use a tin whistle on the track.

Seán, unwisely in retrospect, produced the said instrument from his bag and feebly blew a note, perhaps an E-flat. By now, I felt unwell. Tony turned to him.

'Want me to hit you up with a leprechaun, cabrón?'

'Sorry?'

'The fuck is this shit? Saint Paddy's Day? In the ghetto? Day I gotta *flute* on my work ain't here, Bro.'

'It isn't a flute,' Fran pointed out.

'Gettin professor on me, now? The gay Alan Lomax? Who's supposed to be in control of this record? Me or you?'

'That's offensive,' Trez said gamely. 'Don't talk to Fran like that.'

Now he resorted to sarcasm, the C-major scale of the satirist. 'Oh no? I *offend* you? Please accept my apology. And there I was, thinking I'm a record producer. So sorry, Miss Sherlock. Truly am.'

The rebuff was sharp. It resulted in silence.

'I work eighteen hours a day for you. And this is what I get. Fluteboy here. Is that what you want?'

'Ah, here,' Trez said. 'This is gotten out of hand. These are *our* songs, Tony, you'd want to cop yourself on. We're not your raw material. You're hired to be helping us.'

He turned to her and uttered an obscene and hair-raisingly misogynist remark. The working environment of a recording studio can be a little rough and ready, and in those days, particularly, you heard language of a decidedly seafaring stamp. But the unprintable sentence spoken by Tony was many steps too far.

'Say that again, mate?' Seán said quietly.

'Leave it, Seán,' said Trez.

Mild mournfulness in her eyes, she crossed to where Tony was standing. Gently she placed her fingertips on his shoulders and leaned in to peck him on the lips. 'I'm sorry,' she whispered. 'For letting you down.' And that was when she kneed him in the bollocks.

He sank slowly and heavily, making small woodland-animal sounds. And that was when she punched him in the head. You mightn't think that being punched in the head by a cellist would hurt very much, but believe me, they can get pretty muscular.

Seán opened the door of the studio. Tony limped away. He stood unhappily on the landing for a moment, then Trez followed him out with icy calm. One hand clutching the belt of his baggies and the other clutching his bobble-hat, she swung him once – twice – thrice – then down the stairs he was thrown, with a strange and terrible quietness, culminating in a faint, sad 'merde'.

Trez returned to her chair and picked up the bass guitar. Seán closed the door and sat down. Somehow, in the fuss, the metronome set itself off.

'That went well,' Fran said.

And you won't believe that over the next nineteen minutes we wrote the first draft of a song many people would love, 'St Mark's Place'. But we did. That night, Trez and I went down to the Moon Under Water, and we sat there sipping green tea, and scribbling. She'd write out one line. I'd offer the next. We remained there till three in the morning. She'd give me a lyric. I'd give her one back. It's maybe the best song that I ever had a hand in and we never got it right at the time.

Over the months, it was redrafted. It was always too long. Eric disliked the arrangement and we didn't do it live. Through all that remained of our career, we never once played it on stage. But somehow, that song found a life. Included on our debut album in an orchestration we didn't like, it nevertheless began to get played on radio here and there. A DJ in Ontario, Canada, featured it a lot, as did our old pal, Janice Long, back in London. It's been covered a few times. But the reason I loved it was private.

To see those two names in the same brackets was something.

(Sarah-Thérèse Sherlock, James Robert Goulding.)

The closest we ever came. That comma.

Fourteen

In early summer of '85, we got a helpful write-up in *Village Voice* and it was syndicated pretty widely around the East Coast and Midwest. Eric had sent us out on the road at the time, and we played seventy gigs in three months. We'd finished recording the album, but he wasn't content with the mix. In truth, we weren't either. His thinking was to fish around for the right producer, 'maybe a European, let me sit with it a while'. In the meantime we should get out of the studio and return to building a base. He felt it wasn't good for any band to stop playing live. Off we went again.

For me, it was the best tour we'd ever do. The venues were right – 500-seaters, established clubs – and by now we knew the songs in every tiny nuance, so we were able to focus on the playing. Publicity was handled well. Full houses became the norm. Proper sound-checks, professional crew, basic but comfortable hotels. Also, there was an impetus to life on the road. The album was coming. These punters might buy it. We worked hard all that summer, ate sensibly, cut the booze, in part because Trez as an expectant mother was living even more healthily than usual, but also because it was time. Fran rationed himself to a single quiet smoke or two every evening and seemed not exactly happier but grounded and accepting. Amazingly, he took up the habit of jogging. A boy habitually reluctant to arise from his sheets before noon was suddenly up with the linnet. And the tour included the most memorable visual image of my entire career. In Detroit, we were booked to play an outdoor festival, but monsoon-like rain began just before we went on. The field emptied in thirty seconds as punters hurried to their cars, which were parked in tidy ranks in a meadow behind the stage. The promoter insisted the show proceed. Fran suggested we tear down the backdrop and face out towards the car park. After no small debate, this was reluctantly permitted. We played to seven hundred cars, in the teeming downpour. Instead of applauding at the conclusion of every number, touchingly they flashed their headlights.

TREZ

Being pregnant on the road isn't a bundle of daisies. In one way I didn't mind. Because it gives you a distraction. But yeah, very tiring. I wouldn't do it now. Certainly wouldn't advise it, but you know, I was young. I suppose, to be honest, I saw it as goodbye. See, I'd made up my mind I was quitting the band. Going home to mum. All that. So I guess, have a last bit of adventure before going. And the boys were really supportive, I have to say that. We'd be going through these books of babies' names on the tour bus. Yeah. A good laugh. Really was. Fran was amazingly fascinated by everything to do with it. Asking me every question, you know, about pregnancy. He was actually very kind. People didn't see that side of Fran. He knew it was hard, you know, with no partner. The night I told him I'd like him to be godfather . . . he burst into tears . . . I'm welling up now, just thinking about it again . . . Sorry . . . And Rob wrote me the gentlest note before our gig in Seattle. 'Dear Trez. We all love you. You'll never be alone. Don't be scared. You're the greatest. I mean it.' What can you do? Yeah, I had a little weep. Because you're happy about the baby, she's the greatest thing ever happened. But you're saying goodbye to a part of your life. And that's why I went on the tour. Not many musicians retire before their album comes out . . . [*Laughs*] . . . I did everything the wrong way around.

Major producers were approached for the album but nobody bit. In the end, Fran remixed it himself, with the aid of a good engineer, Jimmy Reilly, who'd worked with Talking Heads. It was good of Eric to allow this, but we'd wasted much time and I felt he was losing interest. Suddenly it was Fall. The record still wasn't ready. Eric felt we couldn't release in December because the stores would be stuffed with the big names and 'all that tinsel would choke us'. He slated it for January. There were other things on our minds. The end of the band in its current incarnation was approaching. The sadness of autumn was sharper that year. Central Park seemed a mournful cathedral.

In late October, eight months pregnant, Trez finished her MA and returned to England. It was the last week the airline would allow her to fly. Eric and Maria drove us to

JFK to wish her farewell. Many a tear fell that night. She permitted us the hope that she'd return to us eventually, maybe in a year, if the band still existed, but we knew she was being kind, trying to let us down lightly. She didn't quite say we'd still be good friends. Perhaps even this was in doubt.

We auditioned new bassists but my heart wasn't in it. New York is always plentifully supplied with dazzling musicians, but I didn't want to be dazzled or even impressed. Dispiritedness was unleashing a strange neurosis. I found myself hoping nobody skilled would turn up for a try-out, that every candidate would be a dud. Such was the madness. In the end, we took on the wonderful Stuart King, a laconic, witty Chicagoan and a wizard of the bass, but after a fortnight he had to go, for the undefeatable reason that whatever way you regarded him, he wasn't Trez.

There was also the difficulty that we were sitting on our hands. Somewhere along the way we had lost the teenager's useful ability to contentedly do nothing but sit in a room. Without Trez, we became a bit hag-ridden by the idea that we were getting away with it. The songs seemed mediocre. Playing the Moon was little better than busking. And it worried me deeply that we still hadn't toured enough, a concern Eric could do little to allay. Usually he'd want a band on the road for two years before putting out an album. We all of us knew it. He wouldn't tell us lies. Eric would reassure you in any way that didn't involve dishonesty, which was an unusual approach in the music business. But there were other approaches than relentless touring to try. His plan was college radio, local stations, start small. Every college town in North America had a music station whose listenership was discerning, and every station had a rock show on which new material might get played. College radio had openness, wasn't run by the play-listers. It might work. We'd need luck, whatever happened. 'I wouldn't go putting a down-payment on your mansion,' he said. 'But maybe it's a start. Let's see.'

He and I began to fight a bit. I felt we should put out a single. 'Usually, sure, but there's nothing ready to go. A single that tanks could kill us stone dead. Be patient, Rob. Okay? This is worth getting right.' We'd ended up somewhere, but it wasn't the destination I'd wanted. It's a kvetch you see now and again in the artistic type, and in everyone who sleeps odd hours. There's a sense you've entered the wrong door, found yourself in the dark and learned to call it light because you have to.

You read sometimes that a group fell apart because of 'musical differences' or a couple had to separate owing to 'irreconcilable problems'. With us, I often think it was the other way around. We only got together out of the desire to convince each other of something. I don't mean to be glib. That's really how it seemed. The differences were the glue and the grit. Listening to the album – then and even later – was an unhappy experience, at least for me. Fran's production was tooled and slick, in many ways admirable. But there were moments when it seemed at war with itself. It had chilli from the blues, salsa spice from reggae, a sprinkle of lemongrass and a wine-glass of Guinness, but the whole had been drizzled with a mid-Atlantic nothingness. Any juice we'd ever possessed was squeezed out.

To me, making the record came to feel like an end, not a beginning. Trez was gone. Eric was busy at the label. He was a fair-minded man, but no business person wants to haemorrhage money. I felt he'd print up the album in order to satisfy decency but release us from our contract when we failed to make a mark. Worse, there was the prospect that he might 'sell us on', unload us to another label where we'd have to start again. Gentlemanly as he was, he didn't fear tough decisions. No New Yorker does.

A fire at the Moon closed the place, supposedly for a fortnight, but in the event it never reopened. By December, Seán, Fran and I were no longer living together and we'd pretty much stopped hanging out. I don't know how you define the break-up of a group. But by certain definitions, that had happened.

I came home for Christmas, played my brother a cassette of the album. He did a touching job of pretending to like it. Since I didn't like it myself, we had nothing to say. Mum thought it 'brilliant', of course. It was good seeing Trez, besotted with the baby, a big-eyed, adorable black-haired girl, Elisabetta. We took her out in the stroller, got ice cream, talked. Trez told me she was happy. I believed her. A small incident comes back to me now, of that Christmas Eve walking Luton. In grey St George's Square, where Fran and I first busked, a drunk shuffled over and begged the price of a coffee. You could see he half recognised Trez, and he asked 'Are you someone?' She replied 'No, I'm not. I'm no one at all'. The calm joy in her voice as she said those words. Music was over, she told me.

On Boxing Day morning, I awoke from a nightmare. I've no words to describe the sensation other than to say what it was: a literally physical sense of impending danger. I'm not superstitious, and I don't believe in spooks. But I knew with strange certainty that someone I loved was in peril. It was 7 a.m. The house was asleep. Three thousand miles across the Atlantic, as I sank a vodka in Alice's kitchen, Fran was walking towards death.

There's a section of Lower Manhattan that looks like an Eastern European city: the vast 13th Street electrical substation, 1970s public housing – and it was Fran's habit to walk there late at night. He'd make his eventual way to the banks of the East River, where there was a long-abandoned basketball court, vandalised, chained up. Don't ask me why he liked it. I couldn't begin to tell you. But sitting in the wrecked bleachers, smoking a joint, looking out at the waterfront lights of Brooklyn in the distance was a thing he often did during our months in the East Village. He'd tell you he found solace in 'closeness to the ghosts', that the desolation of that place gave perspective. You didn't pay him much heed. He always loved ruins. Byron on silence and heroin.

Christmas night, spaced on whiskey and his trouble of old, he tottered woozily along towards his dreamland kingdom of rusted gantries, when fate arose to greet him.

A young woman, he later told me, was being bothered by an 'auld lecher', a scrote of perhaps sixty who'd had too much to drink and felt the world owed him a Yuletide grope. Fran intervened on her behalf, as was his nature. He could be a bully and a coward, and his default mode was selfishness. But as is sometimes the case with those who were beaten as children, bullying was something he despised with a white-hot fury, and he'd take any risk in its defeat.

Fran was a tough kid, let no one believe otherwise. I've seen the CC footage of what happened that night. He walked up to the man and the girl, swung a fist, dropped back, and then hit the guy again, in the chest. Maybe the second punch was too much, perhaps even the first. A threat might have been enough. I don't know. A knife, a handgun, was something you saw in New York at the time. He must have had his reasons for going in hard. But soon after the young woman fled, the situation turned worse.

The oldster got a punch in, knocking Fran down, then pulled a bicycle chain from his pocket and got swinging. A lot of damage can be done with a weapon like that, particularly when the victim's on the ground. Fran took a beating. To think of it appals me. Even now, I don't know how he managed to clamber to his feet but somehow he did, and the fight went on. He was bleeding, gashes in his face, and had lost several teeth, but they got into it again, all the ugliness – the old guy bit him – when two men who claimed to be off-duty soldiers came on the scene. Like Fran, they were badly drunk.

Assuming the old guy had been attacked by a mugger, an assumption the old groper did much to stoke up, they set upon Fran and kicked him almost senseless before throwing him into the river. He was only rescued when the girl he'd saved, watching from her towerblock window, called her brothers and 911. She was a Nicaraguan called Eneyda Martinez and you could say she saved Fran's life. But in fact she witnessed the last moments of the sweet boy I knew. For many years afterwards, I could never look at the East River. I felt it was where the spirit of my friend had died, and that something of my own had died there as a result. Foolish. But that's what I felt.

Sober, you don't want to spend time in that river. Drunk,

stoned, in freezing darkness, losing blood, with four cracked ribs and a punctured lung, your chances are statistically zero. He'd lost consciousness by the time they found him and fished him out, the situation worsening when they sped him over to St Vincent's. His heart stopped for twenty seconds in the elevator to Intensive Care. They told me later that his eyes never closed.

Eric called me at eight that morning. I'd better get back to New York right now. He wanted to know Fran's religion; a minister might have to be summoned. Jimmy drove me to Heathrow, chain-smoking, frightened. Somehow, the ghost of my sister was in that car, with the ghost of a boy from Vietnam.

Seán was at the hospital. Fran was out of surgery. They'd shaved his head to get at a scalp wound; his jaw and lower face were bandaged. He was jocular at first, in a weird, intense way, his left foot in one of those modern plaster-cast boots, the rest of him in serious traction. He said he was embarrassed to be seen wearing the paper hospital gown. 'Don't you hate the fukken colour? It makes me look sick.'

If there was a moment when things began changing – well, there were a lot of those moments – it was what happened to Fran that night. Seán went to call Trez. Fran and I talked. He asked about Jimmy and Alice. How was Shay getting on? Had I pictures of Trez's baby? Oh, I didn't? Silly flunt. Suddenly he started to weep.

I'd seen him weep before, but not like this. I tried to hold his hand but he motioned me away, beckoned for a glass of water, which I got. A minute or two passed and he seemed more collected. And then he said something strange.

He told me he was 'glad' about the way the attack had

ended, 'relieved' the two thugs arrived when they did, 'thankful' he'd been thrown in the river. How could anyone be glad? What did he mean? I'll always remember the words and the chilling calm with which he said them. 'I'd have slit his throat slowly. I mean it. That rapist. I'd have made him fukken beg before killing him.'

A violence such as this doesn't come from out of nothing. Fran could be cutting, sarcastic and thoughtless, but I had never heard him express the kind of savagery he felt towards that sexual aggressor. Gates opened in the silence. Fran looked away. There was little need to say more, and he didn't. Nor did I. But I saw in those words, and in his looking away, that his childhood was even more terrible than I'd known. He was drying his eyes. But I couldn't stop crying. Not only for love. For my blindness.

They let him out by the end of the first week of January. He recuperated at Eric and Maria's. He was on sedatives, reading novels, never touching a guitar. He spoke to Maria of returning to college, of giving up music. It was around now that he began talking of going to Vietnam. Eric said he'd arrange it, would accompany him if he wished. He had contacts in the Peace Corps. They'd be able to help. Visas were applied for and inoculations endured, but, as things turned out, neither would be needed. It's been noted that God has a mischievous sense of humour. Mysterious ways, indeed.

In this murkiest of times, our record was released. Eric titled it *Five Flights Up* after an Elizabeth Bishop poem Fran liked, and it debuted at 97, climbed quickly to 61. We got airplay we'd never dreamed of. College radio went nuts.

Reviews were strong but early sales were sluggish. Then came the Sunday morning in February when we were five-star reviewed in the *New York Times*. You rarely have a day when you know your life is about to shift gears, but that Sunday was one of those.

STRONG DEBUT IS LYRICAL, SLEEK

. . . Mr Mulvey's voice is an instrument of remarkable beauty but it also has blowtorch intensity. Add to this the jagged lyricism of a young Irish poet, his unusually structured but highly persuasive songwriting, and the sizzle soon starts to glow. "I mean business," he sings on Devil It Down, the punk-reggae-tinged track that opens the album, as dynamite opens a safe. "Don't make no mistake. Start running.". . .The theme is recapitulated on Flag of Convenience, a slice of neurotic tongue-in-cheek brilliance . . . Banks of shimmering choral guitar meet stabs of pouty brass, while the fiery violin of Sarah-Thérèse Sherlock adds gorgeous cinematic tonalities. Classically trained Ms Sherlock proves adept on slinky bass and is credited as co-author on three of the twelve songs, the catchy Eleven City, Why Can't You Forgive Me (For Loving You), and the less successful St Mark's Place. Her brother Seán provides illegally thunderous drumming. Mr Sherlock, a former electrician's apprentice, knows a thing or two about power. In this glum, benighted era of synthesizer percussion it is wonderful that his playing is defiantly acoustic . . . *Five Flights Up* is imperfect. That is its greatness.

Perfection would be uninteresting to Mr Mulvey and his shipmates, one imagines. This is a flawed, occasionally elusive, sometimes maddening album, the most thrilling debut this reviewer has heard in fifteen years. If you have ever loved pop music, put this newspaper down. Go get this exhilarating record. Now.

Eric hit the phones, begged Trez to come back. Childcare, nannies, round-the-clock help, he'd shell for whatever she wanted. We were going to hit big. There'd need to be a tour. Come work for a month, you'll make a hundred thousand dollars, enough to buy a house, he'd advance her the cash. Think of your baby. Come *today*.

We were aged twenty-two. It was less than three years since Fran and I had left Poly. The last entries in my diary cover scraps of the tour. Ludicrously overwritten in some places, too sketchy in others. Three might be worth your attention.

On train. Awake. Yellowed lights dim, a few passengers talking quietly, but most of them asleep, open paperbacks on chests. Fran across the aisle from me, Seán in the Pullman behind. Looking out at distant city that must be Chicago, evanescence of amber light misting into the darkness. Rain on the window, droplets drawn sideways by the speed. One of those watertanks they have over here, alien craft on stilts.

An hour ago, Trez eased in beside me. Could feel heat from her, also tiredness. Seven hours to Boston. Someone's screwed up the flights so we're taking the train.

'Night owl,' she goes. 'What you listening to?'

'A book on tape.'

'Rock and roll, baby. Is it good?'

'*Wuthering Heights*.'

'You far in?'

'About a hundred miles.'

'Do you think I've feet like a hobbit?'

'What?'

'Fran saw me changing my socks earlier. He says my feet are ugly. Like a hobbit's.'

'You can show me if you like.'

She shines a weary smile.

'Do you ever think we're mad, Rob?'

'Every day of the week.'

'Seriously, though. *I* do. It's a ridiculous life. You think we'll look back when we're white-haired old gannets and wish we'd gotten jobs in an office?'

'Gannets don't have hair.'

'Answer my question, rudeboy.'

'There aren't any jobs in offices. There's a recession going on. Anyway, I can't see Fran in an office, can you? Maybe the one where they give prisoners back their stuff before releasing them.'

'Comedian,' she goes. 'Can I sleep with you? As it were?'

'Sure thing, Bilbo,' I said.

Leans her head against my shoulder. Chicago going past. Looking out at the moon, yellow in the rain. Don't want to wake her. Goodnight.

Hello, bastard diary. Don't look at me like that. Spare me your white-faced, unfillable grin. Emptiness don't impress me.

In horrible mood. I know what you're thinking. 'New town every day, room service, howling fans – it sounds like a wang-dang-doodle.' Let me tell you what it's like. You ignorant book. Look at you. Blank. Saying nothing.

Need to be up before dawn for the flight. So you drink your way through, fall asleep on the bus, awaken on the plane in yesterday's clothes, not entirely sure how you got there. In a time zone of your own, you limp to the limo. Through streets you don't know. Head glinting with pain. In through the truck-dock behind the hotel. Down a corridor of half-finished trays awaiting collection, tonight's room is the same as last night's. Strange loneliness, hunger, anger, melancholy. Dull coals of lust. Stomach problems. Try to get an hour's sleep. Flicker. Weird fantasies and playbacks. Mind-burps. Mental indigestion. That novel you were reading? Left it on the plane. The matchbook on which you scribbled that cool girl's number? Who knows. In the Hilton, St Louis. You'd go out for a walk but you don't know the streets. Read the Gideon bible but the print is too small. Lost key-cards. Clanking lift-shafts. Weird noises next door. You're Job in a suite. Quit complaining.

Room service trolley like a hospital gurney. Fish tastes like toilet roll. Water reeks of chlorine. Strange humming sound. Don't know where it's from. Heating duct? Pipes? Somehow you sense it's raining outside. Go to the window. It's not. Twenty storeys up. See a river seven blocks away. In the dream – when you jump – you can fly from that ledge. It's why you stay awake. You don't want that dream.

Four hours before sound-check. You fear it. Despise it. Everyone talking in road-code. 'Bobby gone for tea' means Fran's shooting up in the toilets. Bobby gone for coffee:

cocaine. Run out of Rizlas, tear the pages from the bible. You wouldn't get drunk? Wouldn't do drugs? You'd abandon self-pity. Love that halo. Not even joking, right? Falling apart. Wish I was at home. Dread the gig.

Los Angeles. Four thousand punters. Had dinner with Fran after show. Stoned out of his face. Made a carefully built scene at the restaurant. Everyone looking when he stumbled in. Sunglasses and cane. Waiter comes over, nice kid.

W: I'm Lance, I'll be your server tonight. Can I start you gentlemen off with some cocktails?

F: You're a handsome brute, Lance, sit down and have a drink?

W: . . . I wouldn't be allowed, sir.

F: What a shame.

Waiter a bit thrown. Didn't know what to say. Told him I'd like the lamb.

W: That's actually my favourite. Great choice, sir.

F: You box, Lance?

W: I'm . . . sorry, sir?

F: I'm guessing you work out?

W: Not really. I swim. And I press a little bench.

F: Lucky old bench.

W: Sorry, sir?

F: You've plans for later tonight?

W: Yes, I'm seeing my girlfriend.

F: Call me later and we'll party. Bring her along if she'd like? The three of us together. I'm at the Chateau Marmont. Don't worry about old Robbie, he tucks up early.

W: I have plans, sir. Excuse me a moment.

Waiter goes away. Fran skulls gin. 'Christ, I'd suck his

balls like Turkish Delight, wouldn't you? And I'm betting the girlfriend's a model.' Told him he was being an asshole, embarrassing the kid like that. Said he didn't mean it, was just 'being friendly'. Manager comes over. Is something unsatisfactory? Server is new, been assigned to another table. Didn't know who we were. No offence. Lance didn't understand 'the European sense of humour'. Such a pleasure to have us. Huge fans of our music. Dinner tonight will be on the house, of course. Would we care to do the signature kobe beef? Chef would be delighted. All of us delighted. COW would be delighted. So's his mum. Special cut from the Tajima strain of wagyu cattle, raised in Hyogo Prefecture, Japan. Fifty dollars an ounce. No charge tonight. Very special dish. We'll enjoy.

Food starts coming. Fran silent and sullen. Eyes with the coke-red stare. Says 'You need to watch your drinking. You're slaughtered too often. That shit's gonna kill you. It's a drug.'

'You're lecturing me on drugs?'

'Yeah, I am. You're fucked up. Only a mate would tell you.'

Starts talking about Vietnam. Wants to go there next year. Says I don't realise what it's like, no mother or father, he's an orphan nobody cared about, no one at all, and I'm trying to listen if only to shut him up, but I realise I don't give a fuck. Sick of it all being MY fault or Eric's or Trez's. He barely spoke to Seán at the theatre tonight, been seeing 'a psychic' back in NYC. 'Recovered memories' of 'a brother'. Told him Christ's sake, Fran, who the fuck forgets *that*? You want to go to Vietnam, so go. Says how could he. 'You think you'd last a week, this so-called group? Think anyone gives a shit without ME in this band?' Then apologies and vodka. 'I'm sick. Didn't mean it. Get me some ice, Rob? I'm burning.'

Four staggers to the restroom in less than forty minutes, to ensure everyone sees him, then complaints of their staring. Lights up at the table, though we're sitting in non-smoking. Manager brings him an ashtray. Special *grand cru* vintage. Sommelier's recommendation. Only two bottles left in stock.

Fran says, 'Bring them both. My companion's an alcoholic.'

Leaves three hundred dollar tip. Collapses in the foyer. Syringe falls out of his pocket.

Through the window, I see the paparazzi. Cameras at the ready.

And I realise he's called them himself.

Fifteen

Fran started getting help but it didn't last long. He told us he thought the psychiatrist 'bossy' and self-important, 'too old and he talks too much'. Others of that profession were seen and dismissed, but Eric found a counsellor whom Fran agreed to see, an Indian woman who practiced on the Upper East Side, and their sessions seemed to calm him a little. She told him he'd have to get clean. He resolved to try. He began to go swimming in the mornings in the pool at the Y, sometimes with me or Trez, often alone. By now there was a palpable tension between Fran and Seán, and, if I'm honest, it never truly disappeared.

It's a strange thing to be in a group that's only remaining together because of its success. But that was the hand we'd been dealt. I guess it's like a couple deciding to stick it out for the sake of the children. But the children aren't earning people a lot of money, of course. That isn't the point of children.

Our single 'Why Can't You Forgive Me?' was released in early March '86. Trez returned from England again, with her mum and the baby. Eric hired a fleet of round-the-clock nannies – 'handmaidens', he termed them, in his sardonic style, which Trez was beginning to resent. By the time she and Eric began to quarrel about it, the single was at 4 in the US charts. A week later, it went to 2.

As the album got bigger, the unit sales became mind-boggling. In a two-hour window on Saturday 22nd March 1986, it sold 56,000 copies in the United States alone. One of the weirdest things about suddenly having money, more than you ever imagined, is that everyone gives you stuff for free. Guitars, designer clothes, jewellery, food, booze, their thoughts, and, of course, drugs. A SoHo gallery sent me a signed limited-edition print by my idol Patti Smith. Books. Furniture. Flowers. Records. When poor, we knew we couldn't go out on a Saturday night in New York without thirty bucks each, the utter minimum. I swear, when the album hit big in America, I didn't carry cash for a year.

We went on the road again. Personally I found it healing. I swore off the tequila, which meant I could hear the songs. Through the milder haze of red wine and a couple of beers, they sounded stranger and better than I remembered. To play music you wrote in your bedroom and hear thousands sing it back to you is a fierce and startling pleasure that every musician should have at least once. The hotels were five-star. Stretch-limos at the airports. The suite they gave me in Boston was larger than the house in which I'd been raised, so big that I couldn't sleep and had to ask Seán if I could kip on the couch in his room

I didn't have the coolness of one or two of my colleagues, who were able to look at a line snaking five city blocks for us and not be wowed by the sight. Punters roared for the songs. They sang along with the choruses. They bought T-shirts I'd never been shown, emblazoned with images of our faces. They bought the record in tens of thousands. Fran climbing the stage scaffolding. Mosh-diving. Spraying beer. A crowd of fifteen thousand bouncing as one, hands raised high towards the sweeping beam of the spotlight, and THE SHIPS in scarlet neon.

Fran, always a diva, started making demands. Catwalks to be built into the audience, special lights, bigger amps, dressing rooms re-carpeted, 'crushed-velvet white curtains', and for the *tickets* to feature artwork by Keith Haring or Basquiat. It was around this time that his onstage behaviour began to disturb me. He'd always seen himself as belonging to rock's more theatrical lineage. You got used to him going on in 'corpse paint' and wielding a chainsaw, gimmicks I found tiresome in a singer of his gifts, but suddenly things got darker. He'd want to perform 'a suicide'. Trez absolutely forbade it. Roadies are of a hardy brotherhood, not easy to shock, but the images Fran wanted our effects-guys to project across the backdrop resulted in a walk-out strike. Photos of Vietnamese children, napalm burns, amputations, intercut with extreme pornography. We forced him to back down, but he resented us for doing this. We were halfway through our show in Boulder, Colorado when he started tearing at his face, raking it with his fingernails, as though he wanted to do serious damage. He was smoking heroin to help him sleep, and we turned a blind eye – without sleep he could be impossible to deal with. To wake himself, or perform, a couple of bumps of coke were needed. It became his thing to go on wearing a balaclava or a Mexican luchador's mask, or to do long sequences of the gig with his back to the audience. In Dallas, he scrobbed so hard at his face that he appeared to tear the skin, rivulets of blood raising screams of joy from the billies. Backstage, he told us it was just an old wrestler's trick. Before showtime you slice your earlobe with a razor blade and cover the cut with sellotape, ripping away the tape so 'the burgundy flows'. We put it to him that the audience didn't want tricks or burgundy. What we meant was that we didn't want them ourselves. He talked of getting a gun.

It's been written that at the Summit, Houston, Texas, I walked out of the gig. Not true. I never walked on. Three minutes to showtime, I took off my guitar, slapped Fran across the mouth just as hard as I could and threatened that if ever he spoke to Trez so insultingly again I'd put him back in fucking Casualty. Had a direct flight been available from Houston to London that night, I've no doubt the band would have ended. As it was, Seán found me, drunk in the airport, waiting to fly to any city on the North American continent that wouldn't contain Francis Mulvey. We sat there till dawn. They'd done the show without me, which was a poisonous little epiphany of its own. We'd have been sued if they'd cancelled. But their playing that show meant nothing was ever the same. To realise that your worst fear is grounded in reality, that actually you're *not* needed, the show happens anyway – not only does it hurt but it thieves your last card. I apologised to Seán, said it wouldn't happen again. But he knew that it would. And it did. In Oakland, then Atlanta, again in Detroit. I told them I couldn't stand Fran's behaviour on the stage, his apparent contempt for the audience, which stoked them even higher, and this was true enough but it wasn't the whole truth. I walked because I wanted him to ask me to stay. And some nights I walked, just because.

Persuaded by Eric, we all moved back in together. We weren't to worry about money; choose anywhere. Trez found the place on elm-lined Bedford Street in the West Village, beside the townhouse in which Edna St Vincent Millay penned those increasingly meaningful lines about burning both ends of the candle. The realtor explained that Trotsky and Auden had frequented a bar in the neighbourhood, 'though not at the same time. That's a sitcom, right?' Like half the population of Manhattan's downtown at any moment since about 1980, he was writing scripts and 'hoping to direct'. The rent was astronomical. It was paid by the record company. Everything was 'a deductible', apparently.

The room Fran commandeered was up in the attic, the most studiedly bohemian garret I have seen. You expected to find a soprano stoically dying of consumption beneath the oak rafters, on the assiduously distressed chaise longue. We didn't get invited. He spent days there, alone. By then, we left him to it.

Trez and the dote were in an apartment of their own, down in the basement, a place I never liked, dark and low-ceilinged, like a cabin on a coffin-ship, but she beautified it by spending great fortunes on wildflowers and throws. There was a room for her mum, who detested New York and returned to Luton after two months. Two nannies moved into the room; Irish students, as I recall. You'd hear them singing and sweetly laughing as they moved through their realm, clucking at the little one in quack-quack merriment as the ecstasies of bath-time approached. A youngish professor at Columbia would visit Trez from time to time, paying court, as I supposed, or simply offering adult company. From my window he seemed handsome, always impeccably dressed, bearing flowers, a bottle of wine, little gewgaws for the baby, chocolates for the hot-and-cold running nannies. Reluctant to meet him, I finally asked if I could. But by then he'd been dismissed, back to Columbia or the suburbs, where he lived with a wife who got depressed on Sunday nights, a lady he'd not only neglected but neglected to mention. 'She's an orthodontist,' Trez told me. 'He'll be needing one.'

There was a tiny garden out back, through battered French windows, leading to a courtyard where you could sulk in the evenings if the weather was too hot and you felt like considering the strange twists of Fate over a sweat-stained glass or a joint. As for her brother and your scribe, we took the ground-floor bedrooms, since we were drinking like bastards in those days and didn't want to deal with stairs, especially not the spiral version that ascended all the way up the house like a corkscrew in a dipso's nightmare.

The best thing about the place was that we made a rehearsal studio right there on the premises, in a sitting room we didn't need because we didn't do much sitting any more, at least not the four of us together. Eric sent guitars, a keyboard, a drum kit, a nifty little 16-track recording machine, which Seán, thank God, figured out. Some of my favourite Ships numbers were demo'd in that room, often late at night, when we had to play quietly on account of the neighbours' dogs. Fran would slink down from his eyrie or in from his roamings, blow harmonica, strum a chord, or just sit there. Sometimes he'd make a pot of tea and listen to us a while. Another night he'd float an idea, very quietly, like it mattered, and he'd stand to the mic with his eyes closed hard, and the words seemed to come out of the air.

Trez might have a sheaf of lyrics or the smoke-ring of a melody, even just a cluster of chords. I don't think I ever heard her play better than in that room of forgivenesses. Because the walls were so flimsy, I started learning mandolin and uke, instruments you get more out of with gentleness. We'd play all night long, exchanging hardly a word, shuffle out to the Italian café on Bleecker when it opened at six, then drift home and try to sleep a couple of flickered hours and open that morning's mail. Invitations and fan letters, and, pretty often, cheques. The sedan would arrive to take us to the airport. Unbelievable days. But they happened.

Looking back, I think we knew they wouldn't last. But nothing was ever said about that. It's amazing what you can hide by standing out in the open, especially if you're holding a guitar. It was obvious that for Trez and Seán things were not stacking up. Perhaps they were afraid to come out with it, as was I. But life on the road alters your factory settings. It's a matter of getting through.

In court proceedings that would happen much later, Fran denied on oath what I am about to say. I don't want to call him a liar. But I know what I saw. I went into the kitchen one dawn to find him sitting at the table. He was in silent mood. On that table was a pistol. I know what I saw. So does Fran.

He knows that I sat with him, that we didn't say much, that after a time I picked up that weapon and walked to the 6th Precinct Station House on West 10th, where I lied that I'd found it on the sidewalk. It was loaded, they confirmed. I shouldn't have touched it. A Glock semi-automatic. Illegal in New York. Eleven K cash, black market. 'Here to tell you, you prevented a couple murders by handing this in,' the NYPD detective told me. 'Tell your grandkids. Good job. I suggest you make tracks, pal. Before questions occur to me. Hit the bricks.'

Soon afterwards, Fran flew Concorde to London without telling us he was going. He'd been booked to appear on a talk show over there. In fact the producers had wanted the four of us to come on, to perform a couple of acoustic numbers in the course of the programme, but Fran never told us we'd all been invited. I didn't find out for years.

You may remember what happened: the fuss, the head-lines. He got into a squabble with an audience member, threatened 'to take it outside' and the police were later called to the studio.

The ruction caused comment, for obvious reasons. But for us, there were private unrests. Fran performed a new song, which none of us had heard, called 'Stop Holding Me Back', a thought-provoking title. He followed it with a number I knew he'd been working on for a while, a devastating thing called 'Running in the Fields'. His plan had been to record it with a full concert orchestra and Vietnamese folk musicians. But that night he did it alone, a single acoustic guitar, played bottleneck style, heavy echo. It was simple, two chords, wrenchingly direct. No make-up. No mask. No Ships.

> *Save your sordid sorrow*
> *And the pity it conceals.*
> *You'll eat three times tomorrow*
> *While she's running in the fields.*
>
> *Flags upon the altar*
> *Where the murderer kneels.*

I see my mother weeping
As she's running in the fields.

Cleveland, Aspen, Vancouver, LA. The venues grew larger. Philly, New Orleans, up to Detroit, from there over to Houston where we opened for Joe Strummer, Trez and Fran joining him on stage for the most magnificent encore I ever heard, 'The Guns of Brixton' played acoustic. The people we gigged with were our heroes, our Titans. Sly Dunbar and Robbie Shakespeare in Santa Monica, California. Nick Cave at Jones Beach. Brian Wilson in Raleigh. For Christ's sake, *Tom Waits* in Charlotte, North Carolina, with Trez playing cello on 'Downtown Train', seven thousand cigarette lighters ablaze. Sinéad O'Connor in Toronto. B.B. King in Baton Rouge. On 5th July 1986, we opened for the New York Philharmonic at a Central Park concert for the re-dedication of the Statue of Liberty. The *Post* put the audience at 800,000.

Japanese and European mini-tours, headlining at that year's Glastonbury Festival. On the night of my 23rd birthday, k.d. lang held my hand and sang a song for me, Roy Orbison's 'Crying Over You', in a sake bar in Tsukuba, Japan. Elvis Costello bought me a margarita while we discussed Ray Charles, his use of the E-minor 7th on 'What I'd Say'. I saw the name of the group scrawled on walls, jeans and schoolbags. Paul Weller named us in an interview as his favourite young band. Neil Young said on television that we were 'a pile of lame hairdo's' with 'a guitarist who couldn't play shit'. The fact that he was even aware of my existence was like winning a Pulitzer Prize.

In October our single 'Devil it Down' went top ten in

seven countries. We were booked to play Croke Park, the biggest stadium in Ireland, where Jimmy once took me and Shay as kids to watch the hurling. I was able to buy Jimmy and Alice's house for them, and a cottage in Scarborough, a seaside resort they loved. Then came the moment, in December of that year, when the last teenage dream burst true. In the town of St Clair Shores, Michigan, a little north of Detroit, Seán and I knocked on a door.

We waited in the snow. The door was painted black. It was opened by Patti Smith.

I cannot describe her. I'll try. But I can't. She looked gorgeous, a little weary, as though she'd only recently woken up, beautiful as an autumnal Sunday in an American city, when the dust and the traffic noise have receded for an instant, gentle as the gaze of a very old friend who knows all your secrets but forgives you. She blinked at us, grinned, stepped into the porch, said nothing at all but held out her arms, which seemed long in the frayed, grey cardigan she was wearing. A hundred years passed and I took a step towards her. A cop-car whoop-whooped on the street behind us and a cat blinked up from the gutter.

I was not, had never been, a boy who wept easily. But I was shaking, close to tears, at that moment. I have no explanation for the pictures that were forming in my head: my sister in a Dublin park, my parents and Shay. The image of my teenage bedroom, picture of Philip Lynott on the wall, ripped from the *Daily Express*. A pile of scratchy 45s in the wardrobe near the window. *Led Zeppelin IV* on a turntable. I was thinking of hissy cassettes recorded off the radio, the moonlight italicising the dusty venetian blinds, a copy of the *NME* I'd kept for seven years for its photo of

Patti Smith on the cover. Time had faded its crow-black to grey. But I hadn't thrown it out. I couldn't. Somewhere in my dad's attic it was waiting for me to come home. Maybe it's still there now.

She led us into the house, past a room of many guitars, up white wooden stairs, to a kitchen. There were paintings on the walls, stacks of art magazines on a bare floor. Near a fireplace hung a black-and-white photograph of Dylan circa '66, looking cool in mirror-shades like a punk. I remember her telling us that there'd recently been a flood in the basement. She was concerned about her books, among which were a signed first edition of Auden and rare monographs on Virginia Woolf. It was shockingly cold that day, the way it gets in a Michigan winter, and I was wearing a parka, one of those enormous American efforts like a duvet with sleeves, and the realisation suddenly assailed me that I looked like a fool. You don't meet Patti Smith in an anorak and spectacles. I don't know what you meet her in. But not that.

I was babbling, incoherent, a bit shaken up. She sat on a stool near the window. She loved Christmastime, she said, the best season in any city, but in New York they did it like no place else. Yes of course she missed Manhattan but was 'a happy mom' these days, and that brought a nightlife of its own. Give her regards to Broadway. Had I children? I should. They were a blessing. 'A child is a song'.

She asked about the group, about Fran in particular. Every photo of him she'd noticed in a magazine showed him smoking. I must tell him to quit. It was never too early. A singer couldn't smoke. Nobody could. Were we writing new material? Where in Detroit had we gigged? Did we know such-and-such a club in Berlin, and the Flèche d'Or in Paris? We were to call up the booking managers and mention her name. Would we care for a herbal tea, or a glass of port, perhaps? There was a bottle she'd been saving for a special occasion. It had been given her as a wedding gift by a fan. She started telling the story but broke off after a moment. She would find it and we'd share a Christmas toast.

The fool in the parka sat gibbering in the kitchen, while the heroine of his youth went rummaging in the cupboards and rinsed the small, blue glasses. The woman who wrote 'Dancing Barefoot' and 'Birdland' and 'Free Money'. Seán helped her open the bottle.

How was 'beloved London'? What did we think of William Blake? Of Kerouac, Rimbaud, the Who, Bessie Smith, of the Bhagavad Gita, the Animals? Had we visited Jackson Pollock's house out on Long Island? My accent was cute. She loved European voices. Would I read to her a while in the studio? From a shelf over the washing machine she took a yellowed edition of *The Wild Swans at Coole* and as we descended the stairs she switched on a lamp. It was darkening outside. I could see the houses across the street, the dusk coaxing Christmas lights on in windows. We sat on a battered couch, Seán, I, and Patti Smith, and I read to her from Yeats while the night came down on St Clair Shores. Sometimes she took a tiny sip from her tumbler of port. At one point, she picked up an old Guild 12-string that had seen a few fights. And that's all that happened. She played a chord or two while I read. Seán and I walked back to the Holiday Inn through snow, where a limousine collected us and brought us to the airport and we took the midnight flight to Newark.

At home, I couldn't sleep. I walked all night. West Broadway to the Battery. The empty streets of SoHo. Up the Bowery to St Mark's. The East Village of New York. You wonder if I've lived, if I've any regrets? Have mercy. Don't confront me.

Sixteen

Seán and I bought Harleys. Trez bought a Saab. Fran, who by now could be close about money, bought art, though I never saw much of it and wondered where on earth he was putting it. I wandered out to Trez's courtyard one morning, drunk as a boiled owl, to find Fran in fervent conversation with a young man introduced to me as 'Dave'. Turned out to be David Wojnarowicz, the artist and film-maker. He was thin, clearly ill, full of bright, brave talk but with a gloriole of hurt around him. A wry, funny storyteller, bless his troubled soul, he looked like a younger version of the farmer in *American Gothic*. He'd come around now and then, with his sketchbooks and tear-sheets, was fond of shooting the breeze with Fran. One of the happiest memories I have from that time is of a night when David happened to mention he'd never been on a motor-cycle. I drove him all the way to El Barrio in Spanish Harlem, 116th Street and back, in the New York dawn, through the empty canyons of Broadway, as the lights forming the elec-tric ticker-tape across the marquees of Times Square spelled out the national deficit. Of such impossible recollections is that city made. He died of AIDS-related complications in

1992, too young, aged only thirty-seven. Years later I gave my daughter his beautiful nude of Fran and a charcoal portrait of Trez.

Invitations to openings and installations were delivered by the sack-load. Private viewings in Hell's Kitchen. Grad-shows in former abbatoirs. Exhibitions of 'radical work' in the yawning warehouses and one-time sweatshops near Union Square or the Garment District. Fran and Trez often went. It wasn't my scene. I flew Jimmy and Alice out to see us gig in San Francisco, a city they'd long wanted to visit. It was a fundraiser for the orphans of Chernobyl – the explosion had happened that April – and so Dad delighted in scolding me that the first-class tickets were a criminal waste of good money. He'd be happier in a truck-stop motel where a person *might* get a decent cup of tea than in the Four Seasons, where 'people like us' didn't belong. He adored disapproving of the breakfast buffet, clicking his tongue in admonishment at the kumquats and the egg-white omelettes, before trousering extra croissants for his lunch, to Mum's wailing mortification. This refusal to enjoy himself was his Irish mode of enjoying himself, and I was happy to have given him the chance. For many months afterwards, to the neighbours back on Rutherford Road, he would decry my profligacy and decadent wastefulness. It was his endearing form of boasting.

'It's after going to his head. Forty dollars for a breakfast! And a *mint* on the pillow and half the waiters daisies. For people like us! It's shocking.'

There were other varieties of happiness, too. A couple of months before the album came out, I'd met someone after an acoustic gig we were doing down in Brooklyn. She was a Canadian engineering student called Juliet, or Jools, and we started kicking around together. There was a seriousness about her I liked. She was well-read, into poetry. We'd go to the Public Library for readings or concerts, idle an hour around the Frick Collection at the weekends. She had a part-time job as a docent at MOMA, showing children the special exhibitions. New York is a wonderful city in which to fall in love. I realised I cared for her when little jealousies would nip me from time to time. There was a boy she liked at college. And there was also Fran. One night we all went to a salsa club in Alphabet City and I wasn't too crazy about the two of them dancing. She teased me about it. She was great.

Plans were put together for a year-long world tour – Asia, Australia, Europe, South America, the States, then back to Europe, finishing at Slane Castle in Ireland. Eric wanted us to play 200 gigs that year. I was up for it. Why not? It would give us something to do instead of murdering each other. Alas, things weren't so simple.

We were 'a self-managed band'. That isn't too wise. At Eric's noble insistence, we'd signed with a bookings agent and a lawyer. But then Fran got himself his own manager. Which was fine, I guess. But somehow we weren't prepared for it. She was an amiable and immensely capable woman who cared about music. Yet it sent out signals all the same.

Letters started arriving from attorneys to congratulate us on the 'fantastic success' of the record, but pointing out that something called our 'business situation' would now need to be 'legally formalised'. I'd no objection to that, in fact I thought it a good idea. Jimmy, back in England, had from time to time asked if the band was a properly incorporated company, and while I'd often scoffed at his nagging, or put it down as inquisitiveness, I secretly felt he was right to point out the obvious. But there began to be what I can only term a slight loftiness about the letters from Fran's lawyers, a subtle sense that we were all being done a favour by the maestro, even that he was in essence our employer. Seán, in particular, would often take offence. And he wasn't a boy got offended.

We should have said something. I don't know why we didn't. Perhaps we were afraid that the implications were true. Or maybe we just didn't want a fight. To be fair to Fran, he didn't hide what he was doing. But not hiding is the best way of hiding.

I've read accounts in which it's been stated that the band 'stopped speaking' at this time. That isn't true. How could it be? Not talking to the people with whom you're making music on a stage five or six nights a week – it simply isn't feasible, if you think about it. It was more that the chilliness of perfect courtesy seemed to enter the room when Fran did. It used to be that Seán would slag him to his face and be polite behind his back. Now it was the other way about. As Jimmy used to put it, there are two ways to call a guy 'sir'. The first shows respect, the second contempt. The voice has many inflections.

Then there was Trez. I don't know what to say. An odd change came about in her as the audiences grew. She could take a gig hard. She'd be pallid, dredged out. In truth I believe she stopped enjoying music. It was hard to understand in the Sarah I'd known, a girl who'd cross

London on foot through a snowstorm to play for six drunks in a pub. Had I been a parent myself, I'd have read the picture better. But at the time, I wasn't empathetic, to my shame.

Trez and I grew apart. The fault was all mine. Remaining in the group, fighting off the inevitable, took every atom of effort I had. We spent most of '87 touring. In November of that year we came back to New York. We'd played Milan, Paris, Berlin, Rotterdam, Glasgow and Barcelona, in eight exhausting nights. A bootleg exists of the Barcelona show but I've only listened to it twice. It was a gig where Fran did an awful lot of closing his eyes and touching his wrist to his forehead and melodramatically pulling the sky down into his soul, but his voice, shot by coke, isn't something you want to hear. 'I can't rape myself every night for them,' was an excuse he'd started offering by then. The three of us let him get away with it.

Jools and I Harleyed out to Montauk for the weekend, with Seán and his then girlfriend, Ivelisse, a beautiful Puerto Rican who worked in a barber's on East 7th to support herself at Baruch College, where she was studying Business Law. If you've ever been to Montauk, you'll know it's got an atmosphere all its own, a sand-blown, windy lonesomeness that isn't quite charm but isn't desolation either. The town is way out at the north-eastern tip of Long Island, nothing at all like the Hamptons. Montauk's the kind of burg where you could imagine an old Scott Fitzgerald, shipwrecked by whiskey, slowly dying in a motel that's been closed for the winter. Seán and I loved it. (His solo album is called *Montauk Sound*.) My ex-wife lives there now.

The Stones and Andy Warhol got it on there, back in the day. There's a lighthouse that's said to be haunted. Minke whales, even an occasional blue, can be seen from the cliff-tops. Trawler-men with switchblade tattoos spit and gamble outside slightly forbidding bars, or whistle at the waterfront beauties. There can be – what shall we term it? – a little unease among the locals about the outsiders who flock into the town every summer. You know, I think, the sort of behaviour I mean. Some trusta-farian lights up a spliff and thinks his designer sandals excuse him and quotes a lot of Trotsky at the barkeep. An Upper East Side liberal earning twenty million a year on his granddad's investments says flying the Stars and Stripes in your yard is a sign of xenophobia. ('These pinheads should be *ashamed*. I mean, George *Bush*? Like, come *on*.') We found that if you minded your manners and didn't get in their grille the Montaukers would be tolerant and welcoming.

We booked the rental in Eric's name because we didn't want attention. There'd been profiles in the New York tabloids, we'd appeared on CNN. Montauk had a used record-and-book store, a nice bluesy little place, adorned with posters of Fats Domino, Big Mama Thornton and Studs Terkel, and our album appeared in its windows the morning after our arrival with a handwritten sign reading 'Welcome, The Ships'. I'd notice in a clam-bar or dawdling the antique shops with Jools and Ivelisse that people might be looking or nudging. There's a way of making a firework display of your inconspicuousness, but we tried not to indulge in such a kickable form of attention-seeking. Seán or I wouldn't don sunglasses indoors unless at gunpoint. If a kid approached for an autograph, we'd give it and make pleasantries, then go back to the seafood chowder.

The Sunday morning came. I remember it was grey and drizzling, the way it gets in a Montauk wintertime. We'd half planned to catch a movie in East Hampton but decided not to bother. Instead we lazed around the house, played a record or two, cooked a big lunch of crayfish, opened wine. The weather cleared a little. We read. Ivelisse had a college assignment to finish so we left her for an hour while the three of us went walking at Gin Beach on Block Island Sound. When we got back, she told us Fran had called from New York and had sounded 'a bit freaked'. Could we call him back urgently? Like, now.

I tried, but couldn't raise him. The answering machine at the house was switched off or wasn't working. I don't know. I was worried. It wasn't like him to call. In truth, I hadn't realised he even knew where we were. Seán shrugged off my anxiety, said it was typical of Fran to make a problem, he'd be afraid we might be happy without him. But I could see that Seán, too, was a bit concerned. And I'd a fair enough notion as to why.

I will never in my life say a word against Trez, but the fact is that her behaviour had been troubling. Whether it was the tension between the rest of us that was getting her down, or the strain of combining single motherhood with ludicrous amounts of travel, she'd become a person of intense privacies, and it was unlike her. She'd spend hours in her basement, where she had a phone line of her own installed, and if you happened to drop down you'd hear her talking quietly to someone whose name she wouldn't mention. Asked to come out to the island with us, she said she didn't want to get in the way, the weekend would be 'too couply', and anyway she was busy with the little one. There was some wooer knocking around, as there usually was, and she planned on spending a day or two at his place. For some reason, I didn't believe her. Neither did Seán. But by then she wasn't a person you questioned.

By mid-afternoon, Seán managed to raise Eric's PA, a nice guy whose boyfriend lived on Perry so he often hung out in the Village at weekends. He said he'd call to the house and see if Trez or Fran were there. Neither of them was. That scared me. I put it to Seán that we should leave immediately, head back to New York, but he said I was overreacting and Jools said the same. Probably Fran had called because of some major domestic crisis like not being able to figure out how the microwave worked. They both had a chuckle at that.

I wouldn't call it an argument, but a kind of edgy squabble arose between Seán and me. He was smiling when he came out with the stuff, but he came out with it all the same. I was wedded to fukken Fran, was behaving like 'his wife', would never realise what a treacherous prick Fran actually was. It boiled up, as these things do when tired participants have been drinking. Jools and Ivelisse looked uneasy. I said a couple of things in Fran's defence, which was probably unwise, not because I didn't mean them but there's a time and a place. I didn't understand why we were talking about him at all. Now, of course, I do.

'You'd want to hear what he says about you, Rob. You wouldn't be so concerned. This bruv-affair of yours might be over.'

'What does he say?'

'Never mind.'

'No, come on. Spit it out. What are you, the fukken expert?'

'Seán,' Ivelisse said. 'Let's not go there. Okay?'

'I think we should cool it,' Jools said.

It was like being in a bad Woody Allen movie all shot in one room. Well, you don't like the feeling that everyone's in on the secret and you're not. Seán went out on his bike and didn't come back for a while. Ivelisse said she didn't want to talk.

At about six that evening we happened to be sitting on the deck, Jools and I, playing chess, when we noticed a helicopter in the distance. That wasn't a totally unusual sight. Sunday evenings, the skies around Montauk would buzz like a hive as the weekend bohos choppered back to Manhattan. But this helicopter didn't seem to be making for the airstrip. It hovered for a couple of minutes like a malevolent hornet. Then it turned and took a course right towards us. It landed on the baseball diamond directly across the highway from our rental. You've guessed who stepped out. You're right.

He told us Trez was okay, just 'strung out and tired' and had returned to England with the baby for a few weeks. He was in a very strange mood, wouldn't come into the house. I felt the cause wasn't drugs this time – his eyes were clear – but he was jumpy, a bit suspicious, watching over his shoulder. He asked if I'd go for a stroll with him. There's a public beach called Ditch Plains near the town, and that's where our last walk happened.

It was a cold November evening and the waves were grey

and high. We must have talked about Trez, but I don't remember the details. Was I doing okay for money? Had I thought of seeing an accountant? I should get myself 'straightened up bread-wise'.

Then he said he was buying a hotel 'as a business investment'. *That* one, he told me, pointing across the back lots at a dilapidated inn that was indeed for sale that winter. It was a beaten-up ruin, a surfers' hangout from the fifties. The price was three million. He had it 'in cash'. It needed renovation, at a further cost of 'four or five mill', but he hoped to have that amount soon. I tried to hide my shock, and I believe I did a good job. I'd seen him in many masks and disguises down the five years I'd known him, but Fran as property developer was a tough ask.

An hour later we were drinking margaritas on Gosman's Dock, the seagulls flapping about us and occasionally pecking at our bowls of nachos, when a song came on, one of that season's biggest hits. I knew the song. You know it yourself. You'd dance to it, even now, if you were tipsy at any birthday party or wedding where the music of the eighties might be played. It was by the telegenic East London sextet Böyzll-b-Böyz, a gruesome number called 'Big Strong Luvvah'.

These days, experience has coaxed me into the mildly accepting tolerance it is wise to observe in the face of realities you can't do anything to prevent. Even the early Beatles released teenybop material, perhaps aware that if you can reduce an adolescent to smouldering mists of arousal it might set you up in time for 'Hey Jude'. Irving Berlin bought several mansions from the rhyming of 'moon' and 'June'. Elvis wasn't averse to a hiccuping croon about puppies when the Colonel put his balls in a vice. And if something as innocent as music makes the listener fleetingly happy in this lonesome vale, who are we to complain, after all? At the time, however, this wasn't how I saw things. I regarded the harmless Böyz as an affront to civilisation. I detested the nöise they emitted.

Their cover of Bill Withers's 'Lovely Day' had spray-gunned a Monet with syrup. The wrecking ball had been taken to Suzi Quatro's 'Devil Gate Drive', and, horror of shuddering horrors, Marc Bolan's 'Get It On', a masterwork they transformed from its sexy dirty sweetness to a clean, shorn mutant that only an anaemic virgin could dance to. But 'Big Strong Luvvah' seemed to me evidence that humanity was beyond redemption. It topped the chart in eleven countries around Europe, went to two in the UK, four in Australia, three in Japan and Brazil. Thank God, it was banned in Communist China, a fact that had me reaching in gratitude towards the Little Red Book. As a lover of popular music in all its multifarious forms, I find it hard to unremittingly dislike any song. But this was like listening to an assault on a well-meaning octogenarian nun who doesn't quite know where she is.

Up it loomed at Fran and me from the restaurant's outdoor speaker-system, booming and pummelling to disguise its lack of soul, *luscious* with a disco bass-beat robbed from Nile Rodgers and Chic that went all the way up its undeserving, hairless legs to its pert little synthesised butt. Jayo, Joey, Jason (the quiet one), Justin, Dustin and Darren. I wish every one of them a happy retirement on the pro-celebrity golf course. A böy got to do what a böy got to do. But back then, I was a Partisan, and I loathed them.

I'm your BIG STRONG LUVVAH
And there'll nevvah be ANNUTHAH
So come over and DISCOVAHH
All the luv ah got for YOU.
Coz the other night I METCHA
And I never can FORGETCHA
So come over and I'll LETCHA
Do the stuff you wanna do.

The hen party in the restaurant were gittin on down, stabbing their fluttering fingers at the gleeful bride-to-be, who was miming the lyrics into a lobster she was clutching to her lips and shaking her puff-skirted bootie. In my recollection, which is obviously suspect, the wait-staff were singing. Even the *lobster* was singing. A conga line began, and my will to live left me. Nice maids of honour pirouetted, flashing their garters, boogieing with the barkeeps, doing the bump with the maître d'. I didn't like to see drunk people having fun, especially if the fun was mildly sexual or transgressive, which fun by definition often is. It made me feel I was missing out. No prig is happy. He smiles once a day to get it over with.

'You look like Maggie Thatcher sucking piss off a nettle,' Fran said. 'What's your problem? It's only a song.'

I don't know, but his insouciance shot out my tyres, the way a bullet you don't expect always does. I started into the usual default-mode guff I propounded in those days, the craft, the art, the necessary doom, something about Jim Morrison and Rickie Lee Jones, something about Randy Newman. After five or six margaritas, I could become more intolerant than I felt, especially if I had the idea that someone was getting on my case. It was a frequent stratagem of Fran's to try and screw you up by arguing a cage-rattling standpoint you knew he didn't believe. In truth, this was his *hobby*. Arguing was his bingo. The only way you could score a victory was not to play the game. But that left you with the reduced options of the guy who walks off the field with the ball. I remember wishing Seán or especially Trez were with me right then. They'd have known what to say. They'd have said it with style. Maybe it's better they weren't.

'It's a song I don't happen to like,' I said. 'There's enough shite in the world already.'

'Reckon our stuff is better?'

'I guess so. You don't?'

'Better's a word. A song is a song.'

'Thanks for the clarification. I'm grateful.'

He chuckled into his drink. A new number came on. The hen party sat down to affectionate applause, the kind you sometimes hear in America for people who pretend they're crazy characters. Fran wasn't clapping. He looked at me.

'That song you reckon you're above? Got summat to tell you. I wrote it.'

'Go piss up a rope,' I laughed.

'I did.'

'I don't believe you.'

'Don't give a toss what you believe. Believe what you want. But I wrote that song. Took me twenty-two minutes. And it's gonna buy me a hotel. So fuck you.'

'Terrific,' I said. 'I hope you enjoy it.'

'Write me a hit, Rob, then give me your thoughts. Till then, keep 'em up your arse. You fukken passenger.'

We managed the next hour, and a couple more drinks, I think because neither of us wanted to lose face. Also, and it's not a small thing, we loved one another. I don't think I'd ever felt as close to him as on that night when he cut me to the core, strange as that might sound. We talked about a song we'd recorded the previous fortnight. It was close, Fran felt, but wasn't quite there. We'd remix it the following week. He'd value my input. We talked of the new album, the tour we'd been planning, 97 dates, all over the world, kicking off at the Bernabéu Stadium, Madrid in January. We'd need to ensure Trez had all the help she needed. Being a mother must be tough. We should care more.

I gave him a ride to the station on my Harley. Or we walked. I don't remember. I was drunk by then, so perhaps I didn't take the bike. But the last sight, I do remember.

He hugged me, said he was sorry for having spoken unkindly about 'that other thing', said he'd see me in New York at the rehearsal session when I got back on the Tuesday, and went into the station quickly because the midnight train was hooting for departure. I recall him waving from a window as the train pulled away. Perhaps already in his pocket was the statement that would be released to the press next morning, saying the tour was cancelled, ticket sales would be refunded, the Ships were over, 'if they ever existed'. There would be no rehearsal on Tuesday. He was in Los Angeles with his lawyers. I didn't see him again for nine years.

Next time I did, he and I were in a courtroom in London, where he was suing me to give him back copyrights on songs he felt I hadn't helped him compose. Eric was dead by then. Seán and Trez gave evidence in my favour. I don't think Fran looked at me once throughout the two weeks it took to hear the case, which I lost on a contractual technicality.

By his side as the verdict was announced was his wife of some years. The mother of his three children. Jools.

PART TWO

A Day in the Life

Final words? Don't have none. Said enough already. I'll say goodbye with a story about Thomas Moore, you know, the great 19th century songwriter? Him and Lord Byron are sat by the Thames. Beautiful summer morning. Everything's quiet. Then this pleasure-boat goes past and it's chock full of day-trippers, all singing away, one of Moore's Irish Melodies. Poor old Byron turns to Moore with a wistful look. 'Ah, Tom,' he says. 'That's fame.'

FROM FRAN'S FINAL INTERVIEW

November 2012

There are people who reverence pop music and observe its important dates. The birth of a major songwriter, the death of a guitarist. This year marked the fortieth anniversary of Roxy Music's first album, the fiftieth of 'Love Me Do', the sixtieth of the Gibson 'Les Paul', the twentieth of the passing of those Chaucers of the blues, Willie Dixon and Champion Jack Dupree. Ten years ago this Christmas, Joe Strummer left us, encountering in that otherworld of beautiful imaginings a trio of then recently departed champs: Waylon Jennings, Dee Dee Ramone and the Who's John Entwistle, most mesmerising bass guitarist ever born. I knew those three gentlemen slightly and like thinking of them jammin' with Joe. I envisage Paradise as a bit like the town of Carshalton in Surrey – nice, neatly mown, ever-so-slightly dull. But that's a foursome could rock Heaven's golf club.

Pop is not a religion, but it has a little canonical calendar of its own, the moments when we remember the thunderous icons and lesser-known prophets, the shouters and pouters and heroes and whores who walk the tattered storybook of the devil's own music as the fishermen once walked another scripture. What's the Bible but a clutch of rants about wastrels who wouldn't do what they were told, God's *Exile on Main Street* or *Blonde on Blonde*? Well, the chilly month in which I write sees another small milestone, hardly worth noticing, for which few candles will be lit.

It's been twenty-five years since the Ships went down. Quarter of a century. Rest in Peace.

I'm now forty-nine. Welcome to my houseboat. She's a twenty-foot barge on the Grand Union Canal in west London. Pull yourself a cushion. Take the weight off. There's Thai tea in the pot, over there on the stove. If you feel like a smoke, no one's looking.

I've a settle-bed inside and you're welcome to stay. It's ancient but unbelievably comfortable. There's a pleasant walk I was half thinking of doing in the morning, from here along the leafy towpath, past Regent's Park Zoo. See how you feel. I might just make breakfast. My coffee's pretty good, and I bake my own rolls. You've not lived until you've savoured an omelette on a Sunday morning canal in London, the moorhens whistling and the silence of traffic stilled. Sunrise is beautiful here.

A word on my respected neighbours. They tend to have a story. How shall I put this so you'll understand what I mean? Say few of these pasts would be centred on a double-ring ceremony and a bungalow in the unimpeachable suburbs. John, two moorings down, is seventy and tends gardens in Maida Vale. As a young man in Wales he served seven years for armed robbery. I would trust him to babysit my child. Indeed, I've done so. Mary and Mary wouldn't mind me telling you they were at one time nuns. Paul and Dennis met in the army. They're both carpenters. We have neighbours who work in offices and bicycle shops and cafés, but they're of that particular stamp of reserved English non-conformism that prefers not to sleep in fixed places. We look out for each other. It's a pleasant place to live. Perhaps the knowledge that by nothing more complicated than the unfastening of a knot you can be gone to new moorings in a matter of hours is the reason why nobody leaves. Impermanence seems to have fostered that awful word, community, a word no one around here would ever use. Invited to become an officially registered Housing Association, which no doubt would bring advantages among the snowstorms of paperwork, we voted unanimously not to. There's a set of written rules but no one's seen it for years. Everyone knows what they are.

Here I washed up, when my life hit the rocks, to this archipelago of old longboats not far from central London. Shelter from the Storm, as Rabbi Dylan once said. I found mildness in canal water and the nesting of swans, the scrupulous tact of quiet neighbours.

There are things I don't want to say about my post-Ships years, matters for which no thesaurus has enough varieties of regret, having mainly to do with my drinking. But you'll need at least some of the background facts if the day I'd like to tell you about is to make any sense. Fran used to say: lay the bass-line first. I'm no Entwistle. Who is? But let's go.

In 1991, I married the smartest and most forgiving person I've had the honour to know, Michelle Marie O'Keeffe, a Tennessean. We moved to France, where she worked for an international realtor, and downed sticks near the town of Mougins in the Alpes-Maritimes, an hour's drive from the border crossing at Menton. Music was over. I hated even hearing it. We'd no stereo in the house, a seventeenth-century water-miller's cottage that needed more work than we'd heart for. No radio in the car, no tapes. If a Ships track happened to come on, in the supermarket, perhaps, or in the bar down the village where the jukebox was long behind the times, I'd walk right out that door. There was too much pain, and no drunk can stand pain. That's why he's drinking. For immunity.

For some reason that I didn't and don't understand, I couldn't part with my guitars, mostly Guilds and old Martins, but I stacked them in the barn, didn't open those flight cases, ever, and one night, bitter with drink, went to take an axe to the pile, Michelle stopping me at the last, dark moment. A neighbour called the town's gendarmes, who, sadly, knew their way all too well to our door. I was arrested, then hospitalised, and underwent psychotherapy at a clinic back in Chelsea, London. For me, it made things worse, since poking at the past stirs up old poisons.

But no unhappy marriage was always unhappy. The house was dark and old, its decrepitude oddly calming. We'd sometimes drive into Italy, just to hear the people speak. Lake Como in winter is beautiful. The hurts you brought into a marriage because there wasn't time to push them out don't bloom with the ferocity of youth's cartoon hearts, but there never were two lovers at war every day. We'd cook. Walk to Grasse. Talk futures.

My plan – God help us – was to own and run a vineyard, the equivalent of a heroin addict wanting to own a poppy farm. France, a gorgeous country, is not a good place for an alcoholic. Norway, where a beer costs a ransom, would be wiser. Or Iran, as Michelle used to joke.

Seán moved to southern California the year the band

split, as did a 21-year-old Mexican nursing-student, Consuela Villagomez Saavedra. They met while swimming at Zuma Beach. This Christmas will be their twenty-third together. In 2010, Consuela was ordained a minister of the Baptist Church, an organisation not universally associated with salsa dancers as extremely sexy as the Reverend Sherlock-Villagomez – but I guess the times are a-changing. Above my door is pinned a card she sent me at a tough moment in my life, with a text from Psalm 108, her favourite. *Cantaré alabanzas, aun con mi alma.* 'I shall sing and make music with all my soul.' They own several small businesses in downtown Los Angeles, including a bakery, a bookstore and a Mod boutique (I swear), the last being the most profitable of the lot. When not selling parkas to the groovsters of Rodeo Drive, Seán teaches music and composition in the California prison system. I must also mention his Jamaican-style ska band, Seán Sherlock and the Sheiks, which in varying incarnations tours the American college circuit and the Caribbean festivals every summer. He's asked me to say, they work cheap.

Fran, you know about. His star burned brighter the further it moved from us. Seán's album, *Montauk Sound*, and Trez's, *Sure Thing Bilbo*, were warmly reviewed but didn't sell. Fran's *Glitterball Farewell* went triple-platinum in the UK, the States and Japan. He wrote for Bowie, the Kronos Quartet, the Berliner Philharmoniker, Rod Stewart, Tina Turner, Mick Jones. Video was something we never did properly in the Ships. Given the budgets he now commanded, Fran's own videos were astounding – sump-tuous, usually animations, always self-directed. His album *The Hardest Part is Waking Up* was the first to have a video for every track. It sold seven million copies and won in nine categories at that year's MTV Awards. He didn't attend the ceremony.

By the early nineties his rate for a song was said to be a hundred grand advance plus royalties of 4 per cent above standard. Like a lot of wealthy people who don't work full time, he became ardently, perhaps obsessively litigious. He brought prosecutions against his managers, agents and lawyers, and a libel action against a tabloid that had described him as a bad role model to his children. Soon afterwards he disappeared from view, continuing to write, record and produce, but refusing to engage in publicity. He hasn't given an interview or played a gig in twenty-two years. Winning Grammys, Ivor Novellos, and, twice, the Oscar for Best Soundtrack, he didn't turn up to collect them.

In June '94, when Michelle and I were still together, I travelled from France to say goodbye to my mum. She died of oesophageal cancer. That a woman I can't remember ever doing a deliberate wrong could be taken in such a way – it was crueller than I was able to stand. I'd been clean for a while, reluctantly, resentfully, but after the funeral there was unseasonably violent weather all over the south of England and Heathrow was closed for some days. En route to the ferry, I took a side-trip to London, and there my old trouble found me, along with some new ones. I'll be honest, among the maelstroms of inchoate anger, I was furious with Fran for not attending the Mass. My mother had shown him no small compassion. The self-importantly flashy wreath he'd had his PA send to Jimmy fell short of the respect that was owed. In Soho my rage and I went drinking. My, we had a high old time. After several nights of pontificating at flicker-lit strangers and ghosts, I was arrested for possession of cocaine and assaulting a police officer. In a remand cell at Pentonville Prison a warder gave me the news that Michelle had given birth to our daughter.

A change of subject is often eloquent, saying more than words might do. It isn't that I wish to plead the Fifth. More that these years were so wounding to those I loved, and still love, that cataloguing my every failure would hurt them again. Also, my recollection is clouded, for obvious reasons, one of alcoholism's very few mercies. Bottles hidden in the toilet cistern? I can even tick the clichés. Terrifying the mother who was breastfeeding our child. Talking midnight shit-and-vengeance to the mirror. I spent a few weeks in several hospitals, pretending to listen to counsellors and psychiatrists. All it ever taught me was a particular sort of tolerant silence. The kind you hear in the audience when the musician whose classic hits they've paid to hear says 'Here's some of the new material'.

Trouble was, I wasn't mad. I wasn't even sad. Not always, and rarely while drinking.

When Michelle threw me out, I staggered back to England, divorce papers in pocket, signed into rehab, stuck it four days, and stayed for a time with poor Jimmy. Slaughtered by grief, he lost weight and got ill. We'd sometimes go to Scarborough, where I'd bought them the cottage, but he couldn't bear seeing it any more. Christmas of '94 he went to New Zealand to visit my brother, remaining three or four months in the end. Jimmy gone, I picked up the friendship with Trez, who was teaching at UCL by then. We'd go to theatre, do a gallery, tool around Hyde Park at weekends. She was single at the time – she and the Italian were 'on a break'. You gathered that the relationship was intermittently stormy but it was one of several matters you knew not to raise. Another was the band. She'd never want to go there. Her line was that we'd all been innocent urchins 'cast into a freakshow', and outcasts get pushed together. She helped me find my houseboat, even signed as guarantor. Occasionally she'd show up with a suitcase and the kid. Elisabetta was nine by then, a mop-topped Botticelli cherub, the second-loveliest child I'd ever seen.

'*Buonasera*, Zio Robbie. My parents fight again.'

'All friends sometimes fight, pet. I wouldn't be worried.'

She'd give a small shrug. '*Non importa.*'

The neighbours thought Trez and me an item, which gave us quite the kick, since by then we were more like an insane defrocked monk and his sister. My former teenage obsession wandered the boat in baggy tracksuit and moustache cream, irritated with the kid, stirring baked beans, marking her students' essays, which were often not good, and filching my disposable razors to deal with her legs in prep for a forgiveness-date with the Italian. My wardrobe, such as it was, she regarded as her own. My T-shirts and sweaters, my socks and gloomy boxers – all were summarily borrowed. Off she'd wend into London, while I lullabied Elisabetta and emptied the ashtrays Trez's anxieties had filled. Most nights she'd come home but the odd night not. Questions weren't welcome, you felt. I was happy to have the company, and, since I didn't like conversation, her silences were easy to live with.

Trez would hate me to record it, but record it I must: without her, I couldn't have stopped drinking. I've read and thought about alcoholism a great deal over the years, unsure as to whether it's really an illness or just a branch of the leisure industry, but the one thing I can say, now I'm on the other side, is that what most drunks need is someone to talk plain sense. Even as a teenager, Trez was a scrupulous listener, not inquisitive but with a sort of settled curiosity. In her thirties she still had that skill, honed by time and tough lessons. But if you committed the mistake of uttering a single syllable of bullshit, she'd call you out, and fast. Nobody understands you? Get over yourself, babe. Why should you be understood when no one else is? Life didn't go as planned? Has anyone's, ever? 'You've a child,' she'd say. 'It isn't too late. Get on the phone. Right now.' Writing those words makes her sound impatient, and she certainly wasn't always a saint in the lava-lamp glow of my addict's self-fascination, but she spoke even the harsh things with a celestial calm that made them impossible to ignore.

I started going to France, to see Michelle and our Molly. That's what I did for five years. I'd go over once a month, maybe kip in the barn. We'd spend Christmases or Easters together. It was over between Michelle and me, this was made clear often enough, but as long as I stayed off the rotgut I was welcome. It was a careful and generous accommodation, for which I'll always be grateful to Michelle, but we knew it must be temporary too. A work opportunity came up for her in Montauk, of all places. She wanted to return to the States. I didn't stand in the way. Indeed I drove them to Nice Airport on the morning they left, Michelle and I tearful and putting on smiles, the seven-year-old Molly oddly calm. We promised we'd manage. And somehow we did. It wasn't always easy. Which family is?

I went to Montauk a lot in those strange, aching years.

By the time Molly turned twelve, I was missing her more, and I think she was missing me, too. Then, thanks to Michelle's extraordinary gift for decency, Molly started coming to London in the summers. A child was permitted to fly unaccompanied at the time, if an adult put her on board and another met the flight. I'd look at this girl, this unfurling young woman, so insolent and insouciant and up for a scrap, so avid for the world and all it might throw, and I'd think Christ Almighty, I'm not nothing. She was a restless little shark, wanted bites of experience, like everything I'd once wished to be but wasn't. She had all her mother's gorgeousness and a scathing wit of her own, but something in the particular meld of those often-warring traits allowed for the possibility of more. This was a kid who would never need to be in a band. She was a band of her own. The full Clash.

One day, on my boat, she found a yellowed old page in a shoebox of clippings I'd forgotten to throw away. It was dated '86, from one of those questionnaires you see in magazines. I remember her pointing out that it said everything about the Ships. Looking at it again, she was right.

Q: Imagine you win thirty million dollars in the lottery. What would you do?
Sarah: Give it to my mum.
Seán: Buy an island where inner-city kids could have a vacation and see wildlife.
Robbie: I'm not sure.
Fran: Nothing.

A normal person would get something like that framed and hung in his loo. But that would mean seeing it, so I didn't.

27th July 2012 is a day you may remember because it saw the opening of the London Olympics. It was Jimmy's seventieth birthday. He and I were in Dublin. It being an Irish summer morning, there was a thunderstorm. We left the city not long after dawn and drove down to Enniskerry, a pretty village in north County Wicklow. It was a place we used to visit when Shay and I were kids, in the summers before we moved to Luton.

We'd a long day coming. I reckoned silence medicinal. The trees along the roadways had shed the occasional branch but the storm clouds were giving way to sunlight. A narrow country road at five of a July morning, with the hedgerows dreeping and the alders forming a tunnel, can be a place where you'd feel the presence of something. But I'm not going to start. You could also feel nothing. Forgive me, Mr Wordsworth, shut the latch on your way out. I am older but I've not forgotten your crimes.

We didn't say much in the car. Jimmy hadn't slept. For reasons I'll share in a while, reporters kept phoning the hotel until almost midnight, and no matter how vehemently he denied I was there, the hacks refused to believe him, poor Jimmy. Eighteen years had passed since the death of my mum, but he still hated the telephone ringing at night. I felt bad for having caused him upset.

The news came on the radio. He switched the channels fast. Tony Bennett was crooning on Radio 2 and Jimmy doo-be-dooed along. It's a while ago now but I remember efflorescence over the turrets of an old Protestant church. Rooks on a gatepost. A jogger in a high-viz. The apple-crisp sweetness of Ella Fitzgerald's voice. A signpost had been twisted in the wrong direction. By 'gutties', Jimmy said.

'Mam always loved Powerscourt House. Will we take a run up there?'

'They'd be closed,' I said. 'It's too early.'

'The waterfall, so? Sure they can't close a waterfall. Not even this blueshirt government.'

We headed up the sodden lanes, the pair of us quiet as swans on a brook. The rain came on again and he cursed it beneath his breath. 'Bloody thunder. In July. Shouldn't have gone messing with Tara, I tell you.' For Jimmy, the motherland's economic crash and dismal recent climate were caused by the decision to build a motorway through the Boyne Valley in County Meath, a place of pre-Christian archaeology. Age has not withered nor custom staled his fondness for the unusual theory.

He'd brought bread and slices of beef from last night's carvery. We ate them in the car park at the waterfall. 'I won't give them seven euros for a sandwich,' he said. 'It isn't the way I was raised.'

We got out and walked a while, up to the falls, then around the winding track that circles back on itself, Jimmy naming the birds wheeling by the spruces. Larks. A moorhen. A couple of dirty seagulls – 'Sandymount Snow Whites', he called them. A grey bedraggled fox trotted out from between the recycling bins. Jimmy clucked in greeting and I swear the damn thing smiled.

The sun grew stronger. Everything was quiet. We came to the stream where there's a bridge made of planks and we stopped there, a custom of old. He plucked a web of matted ferns from a clump near the signpost and crumpled them slowly, tossing them into the water, and we watched them float away. When I was a kid, he'd always tell me to make a wish at this point. But he didn't say it today. I wanted to tell him he could. But the moment passed, like the ferns.

'The world's gone mad,' he said to the stream. 'You wouldn't know which end is the sleeves.' I offered him a chewing-gum and he accepted it with a nod. His hand was shaking a bit.

'Well, there we are, anyway.'

'There we are,' I confirmed.

'Ducks in a row, Rob?'

'Ready to rock.'

In less than thirteen hours, I'd have a date I didn't want. You'd think I'd be scared.

I was.

The spring of 2012 had proved a difficult time. Michelle went through a cancer scare. Her dad was diagnosed with Alzheimer's. Old misunderstandings with the taxman were causing me chewed fingernails. I was broke as a pox-doctor's clerk. A couple of months earlier, I'd had to sell the last of my guitars, my '55 sunburst Strat. A rarity such as this, you can double your bid. Go again a few times. Add noughts if you're expert. We're talking a candidate for the glass case.

I'd had it reconditioned in the old days by a master in New York, an ancient wizard in the East Village who didn't come cheap, because he was the best in his beautiful trade. Fingelstein was his surname but musicians were permitted to call him 'Professor', for the exquisiteness of his work and his reverence. 'You kids,' he'd chuckle. (Everyone under the age of eighty he regarded as a kid.) Solly's dead now, but he was a great man for a war story; in his time he'd fixed the lyre of Orpheus. To an outsider his shop appeared a graveyard for guitars: crates of necks and shattered bodies, rusted input sockets, webs of wiring. You wouldn't want to venture in while suffering the DTs – you'd get an attack of Hieronymus Bosch. Browbeaten banjos, burst lutes, wrecked Dobros, a defeated army of crippled ukes and stringless Flamencos, playing a silent, eternal symphony of the might-have-been blues, implicating you, somehow, in the loss.

Anyhow. Forgive me. I tend to digress. It cost more than my first car to have my road-weary Stratocaster put back the way God meant it. But the young woman in the London hockshop could only offer me half its book value, said I should hang back and give it a float in a big auction of pop memorabilia Sotheby's had coming up. The Olympics were on the way. London would be jammed with wealthy foreign visitors, their ardour inflamed by beach volleyball and beer. The Far East was going bonkers for old-school rock. Her strong advice was to wait.

I needed ready funds. When did I need them? Now was good, I told her.

I've never been a bread-head, but to paraphrase Woody Guthrie: if you ain't got the dough-re-mi boy, the world be a lonesome town. Michelle needed help with her medical bills. My case manager at the Inland Revenue, a connoisseur of fine Italian wines, is patient with a late-maturing Brunello di Montalcino but not with back-tax payments. And Molly was accepted by Princeton that month. The motto of that fine university is *Dei sub numine viget*; in English 'Show me the Money'.

I said some of this to the appraiser. I don't know why. She couldn't up her offer – the boss would have her eyes – but my acceptance seemed to open a newer conversation. There was a time when I owned 27 guitars. This was my last. A farewell's a farewell. A loving home was promised as she took it from my hands. I swear the damn thing was about to unspool its own strings and tendril them around me, pleading. She showed me photos of her boyfriend and talked away my clouds. A cool, clever kid. Sardonic and funny. Studying Sound Engineering at night, lived with her folks. Played accordion in a Zydeco band. She was eloquent and gutsy and attractively cantankerous. In truth, she reminded me of Molly.

Around that time, I got myself a second-hand laptop from a neighbour's kid on the canal, a smart and affable boy who'd hang out with Molly whenever she was in town, taking her to gigs with his mates. The old Toshiba that Michelle gave me was virused to death and I hadn't got around to replacing it. This smaller, nattier gizmo appealed to me, somehow. It was company, I suppose. Living alone, you get curious. Well, curious is one of the things you get.

Jimmy, like a perhaps surprising number of older people, is a tremendous fan of the Net. He took to sending me emails, alerting me to references on websites, to newsgroups about the bands of the 'eighties. Oh, I'd googled us before, don't be getting me wrong. I'm not devoid of vanity. But I'd stopped. The burgeoning of the internet coincided with a phase of my alcoholism when Memory Lane and its tenebrous cul-de-sacs were not my favourite haunts. But all of that was over by the spring of 2012. I'd been clean sixteen years, had work I didn't mind, teaching English as a Foreign Language in a college down on Queensway. I'd smoke a little weed with my neighbour Welsh John now and again, but nothing to frighten the horses. I was working towards an MA at Goldsmiths in South London, on children in post-war English novels. Music was no longer any part of my life, and to tell you the plain truth, I didn't miss it. There was bad stuff back there. 'Like Fran,' Molly said. That wasn't what I meant. Not entirely.

Well, maybe she was right. Fran was once my closest friend. I didn't want to see him, but it's important not to be a nutcase, especially when you're father of a teenager. Maybe the past and I could figure out an accommodation. Perhaps the past and I could be neighbours, or 'partners in a process', like the loyalists and the IRA.

In this spirit of tense détente, I braved cyberia again. I thought it might be character-forming. I'd sit in my house-boat like a lame old hoofer shuffling through her shoeboxes of faded reviews. The screen brought me grainy photographs I hadn't seen in twenty years. Youthful, angry faces, sweat-drenched bodies. Turned out YouTube had footage of us performing in the Paradiso, Amsterdam, at the Rainbow Theatre, London, at the Summit, Houston, Texas, an inter-view I once did with Fran on *Late Night With David Letterman*, a clip of us doing backing vocals for the Ramones at a fundraiser in CBGB's. Michelle would ping me from time to time, flirty little haiku, playful, nothing more. Had I seen Wikipedia? I was hot in that shot. I should set up on Facebook. She'd 'like' me.

Gruesomely, I image-searched. Who was this youngster

with all that gravity-defying hair, the vertiginous cheek-bones, the pout? Encountering your younger self can be sweet and amusing, but usually, if you're honest, there's also a hint of regret in the snow-globe you don't want to shake. Well, it mightn't be regret, that's putting it too strongly; more a pointless wish that you could corner that inexperienced flunt and subject him to the bludgeoning of your hard-won wisdom. Strange, when arguably he was wiser at nineteen than you are now, innocence being a form of intelligence. Maturity is only added time and the ability to be dull, perhaps with varicose veins.

Click the mouse and another old photograph would form. When the image was on video – your younger self in motion – the pang made your marrowbones throb. And if you've ever had your Warholian fifteen minutes, there is stuff in the nooks of the Net that astounds you. Directions and a map of how to get to the old watermill in Mougins where I lived with Michelle in the bad years. Our divorce papers were downloadable, with appetising redactions. Then there was the band. Accounts of our doings and undoings. Discographies, lists of shows, biographies of the four of us. If there were inaccuracies and outright howlers, they didn't bother me much. Well, some of them did. I won't lie.

I'd had the laptop six weeks when this story changed key. I'd been feeling kind of strip-mined for a while. My weight was where it should be, I went swimming or running every morning, but I was on meds for a blood-pressure issue inherited from my mum, and I found one of its side effects to be a stupefying sleepiness. Also, I was bothered by irksome bouts of bronchitis, a nuisance since my early twenties. The desire to sleep in the afternoons began to assail me, the strange red dreams of daytime. I've never liked the feeling of awakening twice on the same day. Now, it could happen three times.

I'd hear people passing my barge on the towpath above, children coming from school, old London ladies talking. It was the habit of two lovely young women, au pairs from the Philippines, to stroll via that route to the shops at Kilburn. Sometimes they might pause and look at the allotment I share with Welsh John – they were teaching me little phrases of the Tagalog language – but one day when I heard them calling I was unable to rise from my bunk. After my AA meeting that night I fell asleep on the Tube and was prodded awake out at Heathrow at two in the morning by a police officer armed with a Uzi. He was courteous, but London is not as relaxed as in former times. That's an experience you'd tend to remember.

In March, Molly visited for a fortnight and I shook myself together. We went hiking in the New Forest, hung out and cooked Thai. My neighbours on the canal loved her. She never asked them questions. For a girl raised in assertive America, her way of negotiating our little flotilla's nuances is admirable, and I missed her when she left, as I always do. By April, the dodgy chest was irking me again, and I changed medication, which helped me to breathe, but not quite as freely as I'd have liked.

I flew to Derry, Northern Ireland, early that month, for a convention of my old group's fans. 'Shipsters', they called themselves, dads and mums with a mortgage. Some brought teenagers. That seemed strange. I'll be honest: no atom of my body wanted to attend. I went as a favour to Seán, who was due to represent us, but he was grounded by a strike at

LAX. There were talks, discos, swap-marts for records. Two tribute bands played, so loud they hurt my teeth. The boys doing 'me' were spindly.

When you once were in a pop group, people are kind. And it wasn't that I didn't find it moving. You played 'Wildflowers' at your wedding? Well . . . thanks very much . . . Seán and Trez are great . . . Very happy . . . Both married . . . No, I'm not in touch with Fran . . . Didn't hear his new album . . . No, I don't do music any more . . . Enjoy your weekend.

A professor of something called Media Studies at a university in England gave a lecture on the influence of something called 'Celtic Paganism' on our lyrics. Since I'd never been aware of any such influence, I found his paper riveting. He was a small, obese, turbot-faced piece of work who seemed excited to veritable moistness about being in Ulster. I think he'd been hoping to run into a druid while visiting the Occupied Territories; at very least, a photogenic rioter. Some of the Shipsters took him for a Sunday afternoon spin into rural Donegal and he returned with the customary ecstasies.

On the Monday dawn Ryanair flight back to what we mustn't call the Mainland, he happened to be seated in the aisle just across from me. I'd supped late with the Shipsters and was regretting it. Something fried in batter had been consumed in the song-filled wee hours and was commingling uneasily in the chasms of my gut with eleven or so Coca-Colas.

Van Morrison's 'Have I Told You Lately That I Love You?' was stuck on perpetual replay in my head, an earworm that was causing me discomfort. The rhyming of 'I love you' with 'above you', the zizzing violins. I will horsewhip the cretinous infidel that denies the genius of Van Morrison, but I was feeling so rank that I disliked that song. Suddenly it seemed not beautiful or even pleasant, but like being locked in a paint factory with Vincent Van Gogh only to discover him daubing 'AЯSE' on a wall.

I realise – forgive me – that I am digressing again. Let me try and get my needle in the groove. As we disembarked at Stansted, I was sweaty and nauseous. But Stansted can do that to a person. I noticed the academic gentleman staring as we waited at Customs, and I wanted to tell him to stop.

On the coach for Victoria station, he was again across the row from me, and I felt, in all decency, that I couldn't continue ignoring him, as I'd managed to do all weekend. He was one of those Marys who have a way of *transmitting* themselves. Even their silences speak. Looking at them brings the feeling that a sort of sunburn is going to happen if you don't make the effort to avoid it.

'Enjoy yourself?' I asked, as we trundled out of the airport.

'Fabulous. Such an honour to be there.'

'Your lecture was fascinating,' I lied.

'Probably a little far-fetched and up itself.'

Faced with the oldest gambit, the self-deprecating appeal for reassurance, I failed to do the only correct thing and strangle him. We'd an hour or so to kill before arriving into London. I might as well kill it by false praise and disingenuous tripe, since the in-coach Wi-fi was down.

'No way, it was great. The punters were stoked.'

'That's gratifying to know. Put a lot of work into it, must admit.'

'I could tell.' Work was one of the things he'd put into it, undoubtedly. The contents of his bowels was another.

'Your stuff is so teachable,' he said. 'Do you tweet?'

All my life I've suffered an unmanly cravenness that pretends to be courtesy, the reluctance to call a spade a tool. Fran always said it would be my undoing, this refusal to shoot on first sight. The artist needs the heart of a monster, he'd tell you. What I had in my chest was a soggy lump of Weetabix. On this – on many points – Fran was correct. But we are what we are. God help us.

I found myself defending the criminalities the professor's lecture had inflicted, as though anyone would waste a single brain cell attacking them. Every ludicrous grandiosity, each preposterous gobbet of nonsense, I hailed as the glittering truth. I told him he was a perceptive critic. He told me I was 'a poet'. That's about the worst thing you can say to any failed professional musician, particularly one who has aspired to feed his family by attaching a key-change to his neuroses and calling the result a song. John Prine is a poet. Antony Hegarty is a poet. Morrissey, Polly Harvey, Richard Hawley, Joni Mitchell, they are all of them poets, if you must. I prefer to think of them as songwriters, since that is the highest calling, but demean them by misnaming should it please you. How belittled a medium is the one-time soundtrack of white America's nightmares, that it's been so poignantly re-baptised and told to grow up, having fought the law so long. Jim Morrison, the poet? If you think so. Go ahead. It's like terming Pablo Picasso a Spaniard. You're not *wrong*, but is your category the most relevant in which to place him? For three minutes of Emmylou Harris, I will trade you much of Lord Byron, with a barrowload of Pope and Dryden thrown in, and all of that vowel-hound, Hopkins. You like Stevie Smith? I prefer the McGarrigles and June Tabor. A.E. Housman? I'll raise you the Kinks. Any frontispiece featuring the words 'Collected Poems' has an invisible subtitle reading 'Hardly Anyone Has Read'. But enough. I shouldn't rant.

'Do you think you'll play music again? Professionally, I mean?'

'I very much doubt it. I don't have the interest.'

'Season to all things?'

'Something like that.'

'But you listen, I imagine?'

'Not as much as you'd think.'

'I rather like the Fuck Buttons. And the Vaccines are good.'

'The . . . ?'

'Vaccines. "Post Break-up Sex." And the National are interesting. Epic sonic washes and deeply bleak sensibility.'

'Fabulous,' I said.

'Well, sort of.'

By now the A1080 Roundway was going past our windows. I pretended to fall asleep.

We were almost into London when he slid into the seat beside me. 'Robbie,' he said, quietly, 'you really don't look well. I hope I'm not being personal. But don't you think you should see a doctor?' I was in a lot of pain as he spoke to me, so much that it was hard not to faint. My face was on fire. My lips and eyelids roared. It was a pain I wouldn't wish on anyone, not even my former accountant. I remember weeping and wanting my dad.

And this poor professor I'd silently disparaged came and held me by the hand. Asking no questions. And London arrived. I was thinking of the first flat I ever had in that city, the gracious, stately squares and grubby, shrieking squatlands, in the winter I turned twenty and I glimpsed John Lydon in a bar. The coach hit a speed bump. A stranger held my hand. I awoke in St Thomas' Hospital.

The doctor said I hadn't suffered a heart attack, merely 'a violent allergic reaction'. She was Scottish, in her thirties, and brisk. Had I done anything unusual? Something out of character? I confess that the north of Ireland is not my favourite place but it seemed unlikely to have induced in me a violent allergic reaction, at least not all by itself. Was I taking any drugs, legal or otherwise? I told her I was on meds for blood pressure and bronchitis. Had I varied the time of taking them? It happened that I had. Normally I would down the irbesartan last thing at night, the antibiotic on my morning walk to Porchester Baths. In Derry, a bit sleepy, I'd forgotten to take either. So I'd chomped down both at the airport.

'Might be on to something there,' she said, coolly enough. 'We'll keep you a day or two for tests.'

Like most of us I didn't, and don't, like hospitals. I have nothing but praise for the heroes at that wonderful institution, which wonderful though it is, is an institution. Noises in the night. Things done 'a certain way'. The perpetual redolence of disinfectant ought to be a reassurance, but for some reason it's usually a downer. Those gowns that show your bum. Slightly fearing the bathrooms. And also, let's be honest, the sick people. I mean no offence. But I was feeling a bit gloomy. If we truly liked watching members of our species facing painful, traumatic or merely upsetting experiences, we'd need urgently to be placed in a different kind of hospital, one with bars on the windows.

Apart from Welsh John, I didn't contact anyone. In all truth, I didn't want to be scolded or advised, which the excellent Molly and Michelle, if they have any faults at all, are sometimes inclined to do. I was also – I admit it – a little ashamed. You see, I smoke. Alas. Not much, any more. The odd one, on Sundays, or after a meal. But telling my daughter that you smoke, or even *think* about smoking, is to sign yourself up for a machine-gunning.

I was wheeled to Cardiology despite being well able to walk, then Virology, Immunology and the day room. I repeat – better care could not have been given to Her Majesty the Queen. But I didn't like that day room one bit. It gave me what acidulated hippies used to term 'The Fear'. I'm set in my ways, like to brew my own mocha, a read of the paper, the aromas from my stove. It isn't misanthropy: I like company, too. But there's something in being able to close your own door, stand on the deck of a moonlit old longboat and take a surreptitious leak into the Grand Union Canal while marvelling at the radiance of the stars. There were ill people everywhere, some distressingly ill. And being in any hospital, no matter how well run, is being in *every* hospital of your life. I've been in a few. Don't like thinking about them. I don't know if you've ever spent, say, a Christmas night on your own, or a bad New Year's Eve, when nobody called. For me, most hospitals have a wee touch of that. You can get a bit introspective, drawn to shadowy roads. Nothing at the end of them but the town called Remembrance. That isn't a town I like.

Then, there is the necessity of making conversation with strangers, a skill I wish I had, but haven't. An old man wheeled himself towards me and offered a bag of sweets.

'Did I hear you're from Luton, son?'

'I don't know if you did.'

'But are you? From Luton.'

'I am.'

'From Houghton Regis myself,' he exclaimed with no small delight, using the indigenous pronunciation 'Aayrton Regis'. I've nothing against this civil parish contiguous to the larger town of Dunstable, a mere bus ride from Jimmy's house, indeed I wish its people well. But I didn't want to talk about Houghton Regis at that moment, if ever. Still, what's to be done? He was a genial old man. All he wanted was a bit of company, and you can't say no. His son was in Birmingham. Daughter in Coventry. Wife dead a few years, 'lovely Irish girl, Roscommon'. No one had come to visit him, but he said he didn't mind. What broke my heart was that he didn't.

On the scale of these things, the specialist said, it wasn't a tremendously serious violent allergic reaction, merely 'an unfortunate cross-effect'. Which is a little like being told that your recent and highly painful stabbing in the face wasn't serious. Happy news but no voucher for Disney World. He wouldn't actually describe it as 'violent' at all. His colleague, the Scottish doctor, could be 'ebullient with language'. That's the ruddy Celts for you, he didn't actually say. 'We'll keep you one more night. Just in case.'

Life takes on colours, some of them intense, when you

spend a third night in a hospital. There's a lot of waiting around. You get ruminative. Fear, but mostly regret, in many lurid forms, all of them drawn by Ralph Steadman. The things you regret because you know you should regret them, and the things you regret because you do. They're sometimes not the same.

Then there are the failures regretted for other reasons altogether, if only you had the language in which to express them, which you don't, and you never will now. It's why we have songs. They know we're out of our depth. They get into the interstellar spaces between these ink-stains called words, living where there's no oxygen, collapsing all the distances. I found myself pining for that sweet drug of song. Gently, I slipped off the wagon.

I listened to the radio, which I hadn't done in ten years. And I'll tell you the truth: it helped. Hear 'You Make Me Feel Like A Natural Woman' or 'The First Time Ever I Saw Your Face', and you know that our species, for all our violence and vulgarity, aren't apes – that if there's vanity and hatred and frailty and lust, stupidity and cruelty and the everyday viciousness, there's also Bessie Smith and Cole Porter. It wasn't T.S. Eliot who noticed the change from major to minor, every time you say goodbye. That dry little thin-lips would have gnawed off a limb to have written a couplet so wrenchingly recognisable. But for me, he never quite did. Up the dial I found Adele, Keb' Mo', the Unthanks. I knew nothing of the charts except what I'd overheard from my Molly, but I ventured to Radio 1 and found myself cheered. There's vapid stuff, sure, but when was there not? Pink's songwriting amazed me. Emeli Sandé was fantastic. I'd long had a little thing for 'Bad Romance' by Lady Gaga, indeed for Her Ladyship personally. A programme broadcasting from Kerry, *The South Wind Blows*, reached me on medium wave. Vyvienne Long became my second-favourite rock and roll cellist. Seasick Steve howled the Dog House Boogie. One midnight, a Jamaican nurse came down the ward when almost everyone was asleep and peered at me in an unusual way.

'Mr Goulding, are you . . . *dancing?*'

'Just looking out the window.'

'You were dancing.'

'No, really. Just . . . moving.'

'What you got on them headphones?'

'"Boom Shak-A-Lak" by Apache Indian.'

'Man, I *love* that song.'

'Yeah, it's kind of infectious.'

'Can I listen just a minute?'

'Here you go.'

I handed her one ear-bud and listened through the other. The ward was dark and quiet, like a shadowed old ship, and the moon over London was lovely. She was nodding to the music. So was I. You can't not want to dance when you hear that song. It goes into your hips. Like a jig or a reel. Whatever inadequate bootie the Good Lord decided to give you, you want to start shaking it. Hard. In dressing-gown and slippers, I danced with Nurse J. Thirty seconds max. No more than a minute. It wasn't even *dancing*, just a shimmy and a shuffle. She held my hand aloft and I pirouetted like a flunt. Then she glanced at her watch and whispered sternly: 'Go to bed. Now.' Which I did.

I have danced with Chrissie Hynde of the Pretenders, and with Debbie Harry. In clubs in New York, San Francisco,

Barcelona, in Tokyo all night with Trez. But if St Peter should ask me to name the loveliest dance of my life, I'll have only one answer to give.

St Thomas' Hospital, London. April 2012. In a dressing-gown. Dancing in the dark.

The night they let me out, I came home to a worry, and it put me in strange, low mood. Welsh John told me that a tabloid reporter had called to my boat, asking tactfully worded questions about my health. Well, they'd started out as tactful but it was obvious what she was after. Was it booze or liver failure that had me in hospital? Would I maybe call her number? 'Just a quick, friendly chat.' She had then approached Mary and Mary, who told me she'd been 'a bit snooping'. I'm fond of my neighbours on the canal, of the particular peacefulness we enjoy together there. Some of them are elderly but there are also families with children. I don't like them being bothered or upset.

It happened that the next morning I had an appointment at the tax office, which I hadn't got around to postponing. On the Tube, I felt angry and tired. The meeting went all right, but I was preoccupied, a bit ratty. When your case manager at the Inland Revenue is telling you not to let silly little things upset you, you know you're sending out mixed signals. I didn't want the hassle of press or any kind of attention. Turn on that tap and it won't turn off. Better to leave it disconnected.

Back at the boat, there was a note from the reporter. She'd 'pop by tomorrow'. Hoped I was 'better'. Just a little colour piece. 'How's Robbie Goulding doing?' She'd bring along a photographer. 'Nothing heavy.' As a rule I do not throw litter into the Grand Union Canal. But this time I made an exception.

My experience of tabloid reporters is far from the stereotype. Generally they aren't grubby little wideboys in drool-stained raincoats but plausible, articulate, pleasantly mannered and calm, often highly educated too. That's why I am afraid of them. I can handle an enemy, but not when he's dressed as a friend. You invite him in for coffee. Oh, he deeply loves your work. Such a pleasure to meet you. Might he make a few notes? Would you say you fuck goats, Rob? Er, no, I bloody wouldn't. Tomorrow's headline will read ROCKER DENIES FUCKING GOATS: CLAIMS 'WE'RE JUST GOOD FREHHHHNDS.'

The only other thing I know about the red-tops is that they don't like to be bored. Jade them, and they go away. I reckoned the hack would find it mind-numbing to keep returning to my boat only to find it locked up and no one home. Walk out of the gig and the gig don't happen, at least not in the way they want. Anyhow, I was feeling a bit restless after my stay in the hospital, discombobulated and more turned-inward than I like. I gave keys to Welsh John so he'd come in and feed the cat, stacked whatever cash I could muster and cabbed to St Pancras; from there I caught the night train to Paris.

My plan, if I had one, was to drop out for a week. Put the head back together. Take stock. But that was a lie. I was planless. I traipsed around the 6th, went to galleries, museums. You can walk in and out of churches all day in Paris, lose yourself in the shadows and the afterglow of incense. There was a kind of dislocation. It's hard to explain. Once, on tour in Japan, I got trapped alone in a hotel elevator fifty storeys up, and my response was to think I was dreaming, that I'd awaken at any moment. That's what the days after my time in the hospital were like: a sleepwalk. Sudden thuds of weird dread – perhaps the reporter had gone ahead and written her piece without me? I found myself hurrying to the news-stand on Rue Jacob for whatever English tabloids were available, scanning them fearfully in the blaze of a Paris spring. What would she write? Should I call her after all? An elevator, stuck, looking down over the skyscrapers of a glittering city you don't know, only there isn't an alarm bell to press. Suddenly you're between the floors of a life. You listen to the thing you're not certain is silence, wondering if anyone is coming.

After a week, during which no article about me appeared, I dared to start feeling relieved. I spoke with Michelle and Molly in the States. There were tears. You can imagine. But there was anger too. Molly's fury inflamed itself into several varieties: I'd been ill without telling them, I'd gone away alone, I was *smoking*, she could hear me down the line.

'You had a heart attack, didn't you?'

'I *didn't* have a heart attack, Molly. It was a violent allergic reaction.'

'You're lying.'

'I'm not.'

'You saw a fucking *cardiologist*?'

'That's routine.'

'It was a heart attack.'

'Put your mother on the line.'

'You've upset her, you klutz!'

'Look, it's *my* heart, Molly. It's none of your business. I had a violent allergic reaction and *you're giving me another one.*'

'You're a sick puppy, Dad. You're a *douche*.'

It was only then I faced the fact that I hadn't told Jimmy. That was a tough conversation.

Next day was dark in Paris. I didn't get out of bed. I listened to the people passing by in the street, the cars, the trucks, the metal shutters on the shops. Night had fallen by the time I put myself together and went down. The city was alive. Couples entering cinemas. Pavement artists and buskers. Students. I went into a Turkish cybercafé on the Place des Vosges and killed a couple of hours on the Net.

The '55 Strat I'd let go for twenty grand made 82 K that morning at Christie's. 'An anonymous collector in the Far East market'. I'll be honest, it stabbed. But I'd needed the twenty. Twenty, when you need it, is enough.

There was no email from Seán, which took me aback. Later, I learned he was in Alaska on vacation, ice-fishing with the family, all devices powered down. But at the time I didn't know, and I guess I was cheesed off. Okay, so it wasn't a tremendously *serious* violent allergic reaction. But still. It might merit a shout. We'd long had a routine of calling every couple of months. Like all drummers, he's a creature of habit. But the arrangement had slipped and I hadn't heard from him in a while. I looked at the screen and a little miracle happened. 'Ping,' it said quietly. 'New message' popped up.

From: prof.sarah.sherlock-marinelli@exetercollege.edu

I'll be in the Place Saint-Sulpice at noon. Every day until you meet me. I'm patient. Love you always. Trez x

I went the next day at twelve, but stayed among the street-vendors under the arches of the church, where I knew she couldn't see me. If you're asking me why, I don't have an answer. Maybe you're not asking, which is also fine. All I know is that if there was a more beautiful forty-eight-year-old woman in Paris that day, she must have been Emmanuelle Béart. Trez looked like my father's idea of a French minister for culture: cool, elegant, in a serious pair of sunglasses, with the aura of one of those Parisian women who can dress like a movie star without looking like some imbecile's trophy. She was seated outside a café on the edge of the square, reading a magazine, or pretending to. And she was smoking, which surprised me. I'd assumed she'd long quit. From time to time she'd peck at her iPad or scribble on a place mat or exchange a couple of sentences with the waiters. I couldn't walk across to her. I hadn't the words. There's a David Byrne song in which he imagines Heaven as a place where nothing happens. That morning, I knew what he meant.

My phone rang. I answered.

'Do you think I can't see you?'

'Trez. How you doing?'

'Pretty good, *mon amour*. Are you coming over here or am I going over there?'

A greengrocer polishing apples. The *boulangerie* open. In the windows of the men's store across from the church were expensive-looking shirts on mannequin torsos. She peered at me and said nothing. I uttered her name. She was pressing her lips together hard like a person who doesn't want to weep.

'I've your mail,' she said.

'How'd you get that?'

'I went to the boat.'

'To the boat?'

'How you doing? This okay? Not pissed off I pitched up?'

'Why would I be pissed off? Don't be dense.'

She was tired, hadn't slept. It started to rain. There's an antiquarian bookshop in a winding lane nearby and we browsed a few minutes without speaking. When rain falls on Paris, it changes the light. There's peacefulness in any place where old books are gathered, but that day we had to reach for it.

You'll think it odd but we didn't talk about my hospital stay even briefly. We spoke of Elisabetta, the child I had often sung to sleep, now living in Madrid and making short films and 'having fun with inappropriate boyfriends'. Trez showed me snaps of her stepchildren, two girls and a boy, and we went for lunch in a Vietnamese near Shakespeare and Company, one of those touristy gaffs with photos of food in the windows. Orwell says when you're in Paris the cheapest restaurants are best. She told me about the university in Exeter where she's now Professor of Art History, her farmhouse in Cornwall, the monograph she was working on, provisional title *The Torch-song of Frieda Kahlo*. Her book on the Italian baroque painter Artemisia Gentileschi had led to a year teaching at Yale, and in 2010 she'd contributed to the catalogue raisonné. She still played cello now and again, was in a quartet with three colleagues from the college, but 'didn't bother' with the bass any more. I hadn't seen her in six years, not since her wedding. No reason. Just a drifting out of touch.

We talked about albums. She liked Björk, Ida Maria. I

played her a clip I had on the phone, Sarah Vaughan and Billy Eckstine doing Irving Berlin's 'Easter Bonnet', a lovely thing my daughter sent me. How was Molly? Entering Princeton? Had I a picture? Could she see? I found a clip of shaky video, High School graduation. 'That's a trip,' Trez said. 'She's you at eighteen.'

'She's prettier,' I said.

'Yes, she is.'

We sat there in Paris, Sarah Sherlock and I. The lunch crowd departed. Time passed. In the sunshine through dirty windows, she looked statuesque. After a while, she asked if I wanted to talk about 'the body situation'. I said I didn't, at least not for now. She nodded and glanced away, towards a street-singer who was doing Édith Piaf's 'Milord'. Then she looked at her glass without seeing it.

'What's the story for bread, Rob?'

'Grand. Why?'

'Don't be spinning me yarns. Fess up.'

Well, I spun them a while more but she didn't believe me. Anyhow, it made me uncomfortable, lying to Trez. Lies, for an addict, are notes in a song, and you need to watch out for that number when it starts. So I told her the truth, disliking every word: there was nothing going on but the rent. Any dough left after the divorce had been invested by my accountant, a genius who believed in Irish bank shares. The ninety grand I'd spent on those for my daughter's future security was by the spring of 2012 worth enough to buy a hockey puck. My fiscal sage had further advised diversifying into Eastern European property where it was 'literally impossible to lose'. So I was now the co-owner of an unfinished but already condemned block of apartments in Minsk, a city situated on the Svislac and Niamiha rivers, so I'm told. If you're ever there, say hello to my ruin.

'Could me and Gianni help you?' Trez asked, already knowing the answer. 'We're okay at the moment. Bread-wise I mean. If a couple of grand –'

'Bugger off.'

'Gianni asked me to tell you. We'll do anything we can.'

'What's this about, Trez? You're not talking straight.'

'I called up a friend, a cardiac specialist in New York. I'd love you to go over and see her. They've a different approach.'

'You've been talking to Molly.'

'She says you had a heart attack.'

'Trez, look – I actually didn't. Can I make this very plain?'

'That's good. Because you'll be needing your heart. I've a favour to ask.'

'What's that?'

'You'll agree?'

'Depends.'

'I'm putting together a gig. Some little place in Dublin. And I'd like you on the bill. What you reckon?'

She reached out with a napkin and removed what must have been a morsel of food from my face.

'You and me?' I said.

'Well, you, me and John-John. He's up for it. Whenever. And Napoleon if we can get him.'

'He wouldn't do it.'

'Never know till we ask.'

'If you think I'm asking that fucker for anything –'

'So okay. We're a trio. Relax.'

'I haven't played in twenty years. I'd be shit playing live.'

'I don't seem to remember that stopping you.'

The notion didn't appeal. I'd rather cocktail sticks got stuck in my eyes. Sleeping dogs, all of that. Old roads. We meant nothing any more. And I was cool with meaning nothing. Music had changed, which is what it does best. A lot of bands now have more talent and drive than the whole boiling of so-called past greats. Punk was full of energy? Hmm. Give a listen. You were full of energy yourself and that's what you heard: the riot going on in your head. Fran used to say there are always only four cracking groups, no more, no less, always four. It was true in the sixties, true of glam, punk and grunge, and will always be true until Gabriel blows the last horn and the four last bands get fried. My most recent annual royalty statement revealed the salutary reality that songs of mine had been played a total of fourteen times on the radio in 2011. Fourteen plays, in the entire measured world. You want the writing on the wall, there it is. Anyhow, there's nothing more pitiable than a long-busted group reforming. As a wise song said, Let it Be.

Well, she didn't see it like that, turned her smile on me like a lighthouse. 'There's days I talk to the washing machine. I don't want it talking back. Last trip to the well. Be a bit of a laugh. You *owe* me, babe. Pony up.'

'I sold my guitars.'

'We can hook you up with a guitar.'

'You're impossible.'

'And that's why you love me.'

I couldn't help laughing. 'Is that what I do?'

'Is that *not* what you do? Fickle twunt.'

We went in to a French movie, but the story made no

sense. Still, it was cool to sit in darkness and say nothing. Afterwards, we walked down to Notre-Dame and the island. As we walked, she linked my arm, quietly whistling 'The Coolin', a traditional Irish air I'd once tried to teach Molly on ukulele, not one of my wiser endeavours.

'You're on board for the gig?'

I said I wasn't, but thanks.

'So when are we rehearsing? I'll need a bit of notice.'

'Trez –'

By now we were in the doorway of my hotel in the rue des Canettes, one of those narrow Parisian walkways that have the curious effect of making you stand very close to the person you're talking to.

'My handsome,' she said. 'Sweet Roberto, precious angel. Do this one thing for me? Say you will.'

All I did was look at her. I could have done that all night. 'Precious Angel' is the name of a Bob Dylan song from his record *Slow Train Coming*. One evening a thousand years ago it was playing on a car stereo as Trez and I kissed. The only kiss we ever had.

'What's a girl gotta do to persuade you?'

'I've the bridal suite booked.'

'I was hoping you'd offer. Is breakfast included?'

'The *café au lait* is a smacker.'

'Lactose intolerant.'

'Ah. *Quelle dommage.*'

'Anyway, you wouldn't respect me in the morning.'

'I'd give you a rasher. Would that not do?'

'I couldn't sleep with a man who had a heart attack last week.'

'I'd die happy,' I said. 'And quickly.'

'Couldn't handle you, rudeboy. Never could. That's a fact. Call me. I'm getting guitars.'

'I'm not doing your gig, Trez.'

'Yeah you are.'

'No I'm not.'

'You know you really want to.'

'I don't.'

On the morning of the gig, I got to the venue around nine. Vicar Street in Dublin, a gorgeous clubby place. But if it had been destroyed by an earthquake the previous evening, I wouldn't have minded too much.

I returned to the underground and got into the car, gathering the togetherness required to get back out. Jimmy had wanted to accompany me but I'd managed to put him off. He needed to sleep. And I needed to be without him. A Bowie song came on the radio and I switched it off. It had been co-produced by Fran, who was playing guitar. Not something I wanted to hear.

I walked down to the river, got a coffee from a petrol station. The sky looked like the sky in the opening sequence of *The Simpsons*, blue as your aunt's hat, with neat white clouds. On a summer morning in Dublin the Liffey can seem pleasant, stretching like a mirror down towards Ringsend, the little smacks and cruisers all shining. Clusters of lads stood fishing on the walkway. A tourist boat was moored, her crew having breakfast on the quarterdeck. They looked peaceable, contented. Some were playing chess. One sailor, a shirtless black guy, was missing a hand. The scene was like something from a lesser known classical myth, a person who once failed Greco-Roman Civilisation might think.

Shortly before nine. Everything was quiet. There was a time I'd be drinking by now. A couple of Bloody Marys to lay the foundations of the day. There are places in every city where you can get a drink around sunrise. In Dublin I knew where those were.

A weird fantasy assailed me, to see if I could stow away. Anxiety about the gig was part of that, I guess. My stomach felt like a chemistry experiment, probably illegal, involving a jellyfish and a flagon of petrol.

Nearly twenty-five years since that night in Barcelona, our final concert as it turned out, the worst we ever played. Wish I'd known at the time that we were saying 'adios'. In truth, I can barely remember it.

On a hoarding outside a derelict pawnshop was a billboard poster of three teenage faces: Seán, Trez, your hero. THE MARITIME VESSELS – AND FRIENDS. I felt uneasily that the whole idea of the gig had never been much to do with me, that I'd gone along with it out of misplaced politeness or a sense of what was owed, like the bride who didn't cancel a wedding because the invitations had been sent. The cake was ordered. The tables were set. Stage fright exists for a reason. I didn't want to play, didn't want to hear the songs, was yearning to be back on the Grand Union Canal, phone switched off, tea brewing. I hate it when forlorn Americans say 'I am not in a good place', but the usage seemed strangely appropriate. My boat is a good place. I wanted to be there. But here I was in Dublin, looking at pictures from the past. Not a good place at all.

I tried doing a trick once taught me by Trez, where I'd mentally project forward a number of hours, to the aftermath of the show, the limo-drive to the hotel, the party that would follow, the drinking. But it scared me to summon the moment when tonight's gig would be over. I didn't like to think about that.

From my pocket sounded a bomp-a-bomp barrelhouse piano riff. I knew that ringtone. Meade Lux Lewis doing 'Sixhand Boogie Jook'. Some winter morning when you're finding it difficult to haul out of bed, try the Luxman. He'll give you the sundance.

'Hey, Dad,' said my daughter.

'Hey, Molly. What's the story?'

'Fucked up. I'm in Glasgow. The flight got diverted.'

'What the fuck?'

'Right?'

'Can they sort you with something else?'

'Hope so. It's crazy busy. Where are you?'

'At the venue.'

'Already?'

'I like to be early.'

'Someone's with you, right?'

'Yeah, yeah. Granddad Jimmy.'

'They're trying to get me on the eleven-thirty. But it's full right now.'

There was something she wanted to tell me, and I knew what it was. I found myself trying to think of a way she wouldn't have to say it straight out because I didn't want her taking anything on her shoulders that day. Eighteen is a tough age. Hell, all of them are tough. But she didn't deserve to be anyone's bad-news-giver.

'Look, I guessed Mom isn't coming,' I said, 'but don't worry. I'm cool with it. There's no problem. Okay?'

'You're really not pissed?'

'No, I'm not.'

'She wanted to. Seriously. It's just things got insane for her at work. You know Mom. She can't say no.'

'That's why I married her.'

'Stop changing the subject.'

'Honest, she never promised. It's all good.'

'If you're sure.'

'I am. So I'll see you lunchtime.'

'Cool, Dad. Love you.'

'Love you too, Mollzer. Be good.'

Well, then she was gone. I let it sink in. Michelle wasn't coming. There it was. Free country, I know. But you still have your hopes. The strangest thing – I'll be honest – I would have given a lot to speak to Fran at that instant. I've no idea why. We'd have fought.

I'd a powerful sense of him being in the same town, a few miles away from me, in Howth. Walking his gardens. Looking out at the sea. Moving through his rooms like the ghost of himself. I could be out there on the DART train in thirty, forty minutes. Telling you I didn't consider it would be lying.

Loss of face? I suppose. The loser begs his buddy. If you think I was pig-headed, I've no doubt you're on the money, but would you want to be the leper at the millionaire's gate? I was afraid of the self-abasement, the apologies and appeals, didn't want to be the ex who won't go away without a restraining order. God gave me many faults but I'm not a drunk-and-dialler.

I looked at the river, tried raising Seán but his phone was switched off, so I counted the seagulls and thought about Michelle and tried to get my thoughts to alight in the same tree. A man I took to be homeless shuffled towards me with a demented grin.

'Robbie Goulding, right?'

'That's me.'

'Name's Luke. They call me the Prof. Your sound man for tonight.' Dublin guy of my own age, with straggles of grey hair, like a former member of Jethro Tull. 'I'm heading up to the venue. You with me?'

He led me up the hill and around to the truck dock at the back of Vicar Street, where a scruffy long-loader was berthed. 'You're fierce early. Will I see if there's someone around? They'll be flying the lights. Like a cuppa?'

I asked if he knew anything about ticket sales but he didn't. 'Don't be worrying, we'll be jammed to the rafters. Smoke?'

'Cheers.'

'You're taller off the telly,' said the Prof with a mild grin. 'I saw youse once in London. Town and Country Club, Kentish Town. Special night, it was. Huge fan.'

By now, a couple of roadies had appeared on the forecourt and were unloading bits of the rig from the truck. Lighting-spars, speaker cabs, the Bechstein for Trez, wires, flexes, cables, effects-boards. The roadies must have been wondering why I was there at all. I guess I was wondering too.

The Prof led me upstairs to Catering and got me a brew.

'That Seán. He's some drummer.'

'Yeah.'

'And Trez on the bass. What a line-up.'

'I guess.'

'We'll have a great night. I won't let youse down. Honour to work with you.'

'Cheers.'

'Ever see himself these days?'

'Who's that?'

'The bould Fran.'

'Not in a while.'

'Worked with him once. Some character. Bit mad. But Christ, could he sing. What happened him anyway, to send him the way he went?'

'Long story,' I said. 'Wouldn't want to bore you.'

'Doesn't buy you peace. In't that what they say? The money, the fame, when you think of all he's got. Guy could buy Dublin. Does an awful lot for charity. But is he happy?'

'I wouldn't know.'

'Sit down over there.' He pointed to a bench. 'Make yourself at home. You're in your granny's.'

There were posters on the walls: Sinéad O'Connor, Neil Young. As he buttered bits of toast, he hummed to himself. 'There's a bicky around somewhere. Tuck in.'

'I'm grand.'

'Show you something? Give you a laugh?' He pulled a picture from his notebook, a photo of Fran, Trez and me, circa '85, snipped from a newspaper and folded so many times that its creases had worn a way through. We were on Camp Street in New Orleans, Trez wearing a leather twinset, Fran in ripped black bodice and trews. 'The wife give us that. Donkey's years ago now. It's autographed by Head-the-Ball. D'you see, in the corner?'

If there was one subject I didn't want to talk about, it was Francis Xavier Mulvey. But you don't like to be ungracious. I told the Prof I remembered the day, even remembered the photographer, a snake-hipped little oldster who'd once met Little Richard. It was taken during a three-weeker we did around the Southern states. This was back in the day, before we were known. The snapper was only there doing stock shots for a portfolio, but Trez informed him we were megastars on the slippy way up, and he laughed and pointed his Leica.

War stories. I got them. They floated around me. I spun them to Luke, the sound man at Vicar Street, as the cooks scrambled eggs for the roadies. He'd laugh from time to time, or shake his head in marvel. Trez and I in the Holiday Inn St Louis on the night she wrote 'Send it High', staying up until dawn, taking turns to get coffees from the machine in the lobby. Seán meeting Ginger Baker backstage in Chicago. Fran being photographed for the cover of *Rolling Stone*, garbed and made-up as Tretchicoff's Blue Lady. Our four faces on a Times Square billboard, Christmas Eve '86.

'Great days,' Luke said. 'Please God they'll come again.' It was a kindly way of letting me know that even a fan can hear enough. I appreciated the tact, the articulate gentleness you sometimes see in men that age. I talk when I'm nervous, an affliction of old. Would I like to see the dressing room now?

Up many stairs he led me. I lay on the couch. In a moment I was in the sailboat Michelle and I once owned. I wouldn't call it a dream, more a flicker of pictures. As I woke, I was blood-sugary and hot. When Molly was a kid she wrote a story about a fictional street called Parallel Avenue, where you lived your other life, the one you'd be living had you taken alternative turnings at every junction. A cop would be a robber, a beggar a merchant banker. She won a prize for it at school. The essay was dedicated 'to my daddy'. I kept it when her mother threw me out. A painful season. But the story tapped at the windows, that morning in Dublin. I found myself wondering what mine would have been, who'd be living in my house, or sleeping beside me.

You need to be careful when that old song starts. It isn't a help, and it's wiser switched off. Parallel Avenue Blues.

12:03

Seán was standing alone on the Vicar Street stage, staring at the Paiste crash cymbal he had in his hands as though trying to see his reflection in the brass. I knew he'd be there by noon. Creature of habit. Doing his own set-up was always a rite, even in the days when success meant you could have a techie for every drum in your stack and a different masseuse for each wrist. He liked and respected the roadies. He'd join them on the razz. But no one was permitted to build Seán Sherlock's kit.

I watched for a while. He pointed a zapper towards the PA. Nothing much happened. Then 'Message to You, Rudy' burst on. Fat parps of trombone and luscious harmonica. The Prof appeared from off-right, dancing with himself, in a dirty, too-small T-shirt whose slogan made me laugh. TOO OLD TO DOWNLOAD. TOO YOUNG TO DIE. Trez's grand piano getting wheeled up the ramp. Forests of clamps and mic stands.

Encircled by a fairy ring of Yamaha and Akai flight cases, Seán got down on his knees. Largest case first, then every other box in a sequence of decreasing size, next the packets containing the bolt-nuts and washers and tuners, and the quiver of sticks and brushes. Only when every piece was out on the floor would he commence the process of assembly. It used to drive Fran and me batty, his scrupulous insistence on performing any act in the right order. Watching him make a pot of tea or dress himself or shave could reduce me to arse-clenching rage.

He won't mind me saying he'd gained a pound or two down the years. The fortnight over in Dublin to rehearse the show had done little to lower the jean size. His phone rang and he answered it, now noticing I was there and beckoning me over with the cymbal. He'd done up a set-list, and I tried reading over it as he talked to his Consuela, who was calling from their beautiful home in Thousand Oaks, California, the only musician's house I know where everything works and light bulbs get replaced the day they die.

Nicotine patch on his forearm. His jaws mashing rhythmically, with the toffee-crushing intensity of someone who doesn't like the double-strength spearmint chewing gum he's pretending to prefer to a smoke. The shirt was sharp, Gabicci Vintage. Good pair of brogues, the whole bit. The sideburns tapered to a point that could cut you. A fat Mod granddad. Not uncool.

'All right?' he said. 'Connie sends her love.'

'Right back to her.' I nodded. 'You're early.'

'I'm actually late. Gimme two.'

He went back to his call, talking in a Spanish I found affecting since it was delivered in a strong Lewisham accent. His eldest daughter, Luz-Maria, had a baby last year and their first grandchild, Adoncia, brought great joy to Seán and Consuela. 'We was hoping they'd call her Beyoncé,' he told me at the christening, not entirely ironically, I felt.

Call done, he regarded me with amiable tiredness as he fingered the lapels of my anorak.

'You look like you woke up in a skip,' he confirmed. 'Call that a shirt? I ain't going on stage with no hobo.'

'Building your kit?'

'Want to help? Over there.' He gestured towards the floor tom and I went to pick it up. '*Gently*,' he chided. 'It's an instrument, not a coal sack. Guitarists. You don't know shit.'

Assembling drums is complex. We didn't say much. He was looking forward to seeing Molly – his and Consuela's goddaughter – and he asked about her plans for college. It always tickled him to think of her making do on my houseboat, a humble enough vessel for a girl accustomed to walk-in closets and air-con. 'That kid is gonna make one unusual lawyer,' he said, 'with her knowledge of low-life ways.'

He showed me a photograph of Adoncia, taken by her dad, then gnawed off a length of gaffer tape and fixed the picture to the top side of his bass, so he could glance at it now and again while playing. A touching thing about Seán was that he always went in for such totems while mocking the slightest belief in them.

Gaunt roadies were building his riser up-stage. They looked like the image of Christ on the Shroud of Turin, only with additional facial injuries. He asked them to centre it a little, which put them into a huff. I could have told them there was no point in resistance, he must be permitted to prevail; else he'd take it apart personally and move it the two and a half inches to the left that can make all the difference in show business. An impossible man. They did as requested. He sorted his colour-coded sticks.

It was cold in the auditorium. Cleaning-staff were hoovering. My headache was bad, and I hadn't put in my lenses, with the result that I couldn't actually make out the back wall in the distance.

The Prof checked his grid. It was tricky, but he had it all straight. Above us, in the flies, crew were locking off. Two young women who worked in the box office showed up backstage and came over to say hello.

Seán switched on the charm, Twinkle-Eyes in his XXL polo shirt. You'd wonder at the unfairness that makes some people have it, when so many millions don't and never will. He's fat but he's suave. That combination isn't legal. They shake hands and tell him their mums used to fancy him rotten and he's deploying his Bill Clinton aw-shucks grin and inviting them to have a bang on his snares, the bad bastard, and offering them coffee and buns. Now he's breaking my balls for being 'a filthy-looking scruff-bag' or, his worst of all insults, 'a rocker'. And they're laughing like sunbeams as he imitates my glower and my tight little knot of a smile. They're asking him for autographs. Would he mind a quick piccy? 'Huddle up, ladies, the glamour makes me thin. Now, smile at poor Rob. It confuses him.'

A bald Buddha who could use his belly as a parachute. 'It's the shoes, mate,' he says, with a slappable smirk. Just like the days of old.

Back then, you couldn't get Fran into a suit unless you tranquillised him first. But Seán, even when poor, spent every spare penny on clothes. He'd scrimp six months to buy a jacket or a pair of suede loafers. Twice a year he'd voyage to a Mod boutique in exotically distant Leeds, for the cult was always stronger in the northern regions. Once, he ferried to Belfast for a soul all-nighter. I didn't even know they *had* Mods in 1980s Belfast, an unwise city to be walking around with a target on your back.

Seán wasn't an admirer of ZZ Top, but he felt there was a truth in their hit 'Sharp-Dressed Man'. This was in an era when I regarded matched socks as not worth the drivetime and shoe polish as a cheaply available inhalant high. His habitual mode of turtleneck, mandarin collar and chessboard-pattern Ben Sherman sent Fran right out of his mind. 'The boy wears a *tie-pin*. What's he trying to prove? Cuban-heel boots and a crombie coat. Fukken reject from *Quadrophenia*.' Through all of it, Seán would smile peaceably with his ski-bum's white teeth or run a hand through his lustrous mop-top. Nobody had white teeth in 1980s England. I think he must have imported them without telling us.

'We'll get you a pukkah suit,' he'd say to Fran. 'Gonna degrease Robbie next and introduce him to soap.'

'I'm one fucker you won't Modify,' Fran would shoot back at Seán. 'You dress like a Mormon pimp.'

'We'll see about that, mate. We'll see. Don't be jealous.'

'Pill-taker.'

'Junkie.'

'Soul-boy.'

'Tramp.'

'Rev up your Vespa and bugger off to Brighton.'

'That dandruff or coke on your shades?'

It became their affectionate language, a code you had to understand. Feigned dislike was their form of closeness.

He turns to me, laughing, as the two young women walk away.

'All right, mate?'

'Bit nervous.'

'It's only a gig. All the same in the end. Pub or a stadium, don't matter. Main thing is face forward and try to look interested. And get yourself a shirt. And some shoes.'

'But Seán—'

'Ain't nothing to worry about. Everything's rosy. Trust me. Okay?'

'Okay.'

SEÁN

I was worried bloody sick, love. But I didn't want to say. Venue like that – yeah, it's only a thousand seats the way we've set it up – but you want everyone in the band with their mind on the gig. And Robbie was too in his head.

Know what I mean? Gone into himself. It's a thing he does sometimes. Drives me spazz. And Robbie's a guy with a lot of head to go into. It's big in Robbie's head. Massive. Vast. Throw-a-boomerang-massive. There's an echo. Lady Gaga and Justin bloody Bieber could play a gig in Robbie's head and there'd still be room for *Riverdance*. You know the way the Aboriginals down in Australia have to go on walkabout every now and again? That's what Rob does. In his head. Big mountains in there. Ayers bloody Rocks. Uluru, I'm telling you. He's walking about, looking. And you may as well tell your dog to go whistling Leonard Cohen as talk to Rob when he gets like that. Wasting your time, mate. He ain't gonna listen. It's like digging a hole in a lake.

And I'm having a shufti around, trying not to let on, and wondering how bad things can get. Rob-wise. You know. Things ain't looking too clever. It's like you're thinking of stuff to say to him and running out of words. And the Olympics is kicking off on the telly tonight, with every banger ever cut a record in the history of the world on the bill. McCartney, the Arctic Monkeys, Dizzee Rascal – that's a gig. You can see it for gratis on the telly-box tonight, sitting at home with the missus. Quite fancy it myself. Who wouldn't? So are the punters gonna show? Say if it rains? And we ain't played in so long. It's all on your mind. Might be a case of 'everyone spread out and look like a crowd'. Ain't the vibe you want for a gig like this. Ain't the vibe at all.

We're under-rehearsed. Fuck-all's agreed. I's worried about the sound. It's doing me in. Vicar Street's a lovely club but they've a balcony there, seats up above you, all round. You're bottom of a bowl. Punters upstairs, roaring down. Like putting your face in the well of a jet. I wanted Chloé Nagle or Ciarán Byrne, best sound engineers in Ireland as far as I'm concerned – no disrespect to the rest – but Chloé was working in Galway with Scullion, and Ciarán was down in China. The geezer we got was all right but he weren't no Chloé. 'The Prof' they called him. Good ears on the boy, don't go getting me wrong. But your sound-hog's an essential part of the show. And things've changed since the old days. Like, the young bands now, they don't have a monitor on stage. It's earpieces now, but Rob didn't want that. So we need to score monitors nobody's booked. Arse-ache, you know. It's a hassle. A gig is two hundred decisions all need to be right. Else the whole thing's gone Pete Tong. One fuse gets blown, one input packs in, you're up there naked as the day you was born but a fuck of a lot more hairy. It ain't 'put on a show in the barn' no more. It's a lot more professional now.

Tell the truth, I hadn't slept. Too many hassles. Lists needing checking and they're swirling all night. And Trez ain't no help. So it's you on your tod. We've these brilliant surprise guests pitching up but we can't put the names out. Nowadays, you've guests on a bill, that's the way it goes. See, they might be gigging next week in the same city, same venue. So their manager won't let you announce 'em.

I've spent a lot of time down the years backstage at a venue, coiling flexes, noodling about, you know, vibing up. You talk to the roadies, give a bit of respect. They're doing a job. It's important. To me, that's my workplace. That's how I feel. I'm happy back there. Want to know what's going on. But this wasn't no happy morning. Something ain't right. It's like smelling rain. Get your pac-a-mac.

Then in comes Roberta, looking nervous and grim, like a kiddie afraid of the circus. And he's smoking and looking about, at the lampies and the techies. Pillock's got blood pressure. He's smoking.

And he's yapping away about the tool-belts they're wearing. Spectating, you know? Not preparing. You want him talking about this song, that song, the harmonies he's got. Bit of smartness, you know? Chop chop. Turn up to the match, mate. Put the shirt on, okay? Lot of people would give their eyes to be wearing that shirt. You're playing for Chelsea. Look lively. But there was bugger all of that. Nerk's absent. I mean nada. You're looking in his eyes, it's like staring out a window. Asks me have I brought my naffing drumsticks like that's a surprise. No, I was thinking of playing the drums with me cock, mate.

Being fair: can't be easy, when he ain't played in twenty years or whatever it is. But he's focusing on the past, every story's about Fran. Stuck in Memory Lane. Which ain't where you want him. I've a very bad feeling. Not a happy camper. I'm feeling intensely dischuffed. I'm at the game long enough to know when Numpty's in his head. Grand Canyon between his earholes. Ain't kidding. And it wouldn't be unusual for the twat just to scarper. Blow the gig, sod the punters, I'm off, John. Done it once to us in Denver. Four thousand punters. Five minutes before the gig he's said he's nipping out to buy fags. Didn't come back. Not nice. You wouldn't think the quiet one's the walker in any band. But Robbie's a walker. Don't be fooled. Littlest aggravation or something wrong in his head, off he'll sod without shutting the door. He's essentially a twat. Which I mean very nicely. He's Olympics material for walking.

To distract him, I got him to help me do my set-up and prep. Then these girls come in, I hadn't a breeze who they was. Two nice kids from the box office. Just messing about. And that seemed to cheer him up a bit, he's come out of himself. So we've had a bit of a laugh with them and then they went away. But I can see he's all fingers and thumbs.

Trez wasn't about. She'd more sense, cunning mare. Tell a lie, she was at our auntie's, in Donnycarney, north of Dublin. Tucking into the Irish bacon sarnie. My auntie Carmel's idea of health food is fourteen kinds of cholesterol washed down with Holy Water and a grand auld cuppa tay. Nice old girl. Trez's gone up to visit. So that's where she was on the morning of the show. See, she'd never roll up to the venue ten hours before the gig. Bad luck and trouble. Mighty superstitious, our Trez. Had these routines and ways of doing things, the day of a show. If I told you, I'd have to kill you.

Nah, it was just she had her ways. A lot of musos do. You see it all the way back, in the blues and that. The black-cat bone and the mojo hand. I don't go for all the malarkey but Trez's a spiritual gal, straight up. She used to tell us 'Every time you play music for money, you lose a bit of your gift. So play it for something else.' That ain't the way I see money myself, never was. Give us the vig, mate. I earned it. But that's Trez. Another planet. See, musicians are spacers. Whatever gets you through the night. I don't judge.

And one thing she's right about. A show can

be cursed. Stuff gone missing. Rig's on the blink. Amp you tested all day, it's gone tits up in the water. You might think I'm talking bullshit but a show can get the hex. And that's the feeling coming over me that morning in Dublin. Bad Moon Rising. You know?

Like someone was out there, not wanting it to happen. And I knew who the someone was.

Seán and I went around to a café on Francis Street and got tweaking the set-list. He'd done his best with what was available. The opener would be 'Insulting Your Mother', a thing I wrote in our first winter in New York, having overdosed on Talking Heads. After that, 'Billy Fought Baz' and 'Nine Days Without You'. 'Ash' from our debut cassette was one of my babies. I found it hard to sing live, but we left it on the menu. Then, Trez's 'Send it High', and her 'Boy Marked by Winter'. I wasn't sure about doing 'Boy' so early in the night, since it would be a bit like marrying the audience before taking them out to dinner. I felt we should pace, maybe save it for an encore. Seán's cool kicked in. 'Throw it,' he said.

Silence came in and sat at the table. We knew there was a hole in the evening and nothing to fill it. If you didn't mind seeing the Mona Lisa with her entire face blacked out, we had just the right show to offer. What can you do? Onward we worked. He nodded judiciously as he looked over the completed list. 'That's a gig I'd wanna see. Some strong stuff there.' And he paused the tiniest instant before adding, as an afterthought: 'Punters don't always want the hits.'

He didn't mean it to hurt, and actually it didn't. But there was a mild, brief sting all the same.

Thankfully, we'd somewhere for the conversation to go. We'd guests on the bill and we started into the sequence: who'd open, who'd sound-check, who wouldn't. The nice kid doing Production Runner hurried into the caff. She had RTE Radio on the phone back at base. Would I taxi out to the studios for an interview?

Look, there's something on my mind. I've been asked to keep quiet. I'll be honest and say it's caused me concern. But on balance, I'm going to say my piece.

A month before the gig, I didn't want to do it. I was building up to telling Trez, when Jimmy emailed me to say Fran's people had called the house and wanted 'a chat'. My dear father advised caution, which is always his way when dealing with anyone who has 'people'. I should get myself a lawyer, a representative of some sort. I'd gone down painful and expensive roads with Fran and his people, journeys that were hard to come home from.

I called the number, which turned out to be Fran's record company in New York. They directed me to another office, in LA. There I spoke with an individual I'd never met or even heard of, who showered me with pleasantries while clearly doing something else, perhaps having his toenails filed by an intern. Would I be prepared to fly to Dublin next morning and come out to Fran's house in Howth? It was time 'to clear the air'.

They couriered me a ticket. A car would pick me up. Fran's chauffeur's name was Hakim. It would be appreciated if the summit remained confidential. Having sworn myself to Trappist secrecy, I hung up and immediately called Seán in California, telling him every last detail I'd noted.

I remember silence down the line, a few watery echoes.

'Up to badness,' he said quietly. 'I dunno. What's his play?'

I didn't sleep that night. In the morning, I went to Dublin, on the flight that leaves Heathrow at quarter to six. It was dark when we took off, getting light when we landed, the moon like a sliver of broken fingernail over the Wicklow Hills, and a mother of a wind off the bay. Hakim was in Arrivals, holding a sign. He asked if I wanted breakfast. I didn't.

Dublin Airport to Howth is only ten miles, but an accident caused gridlock and the journey took an hour. The newspapers, Irish and English, tabloid and non, were arranged on the back seat beside me. I've been inside Kyoto cocktail lounges smaller than that Lexus and less comprehensively stocked with booze. Wi-fi, a television, iPod dock, Nintendo Wii. It was a car you could go to on your holidays.

You may not know Howth, an old fishing village north of Dublin. Above the town is an enclave of mansions and hilly side-roads lined with wildflowers. Up several of the latter we purred, past many of the former, until we halted before a couple of black cast-iron gates the height of cathedral doors. A pictogram featured a snarling dog. Security cameras in cage boxes adjusted themselves in our direction. Hakim pointed a bleeper at a sensor on the pillar and the gates glided open like curtains.

We drove a narrow rutted laneway for about half a mile, then it widened to a newly tarmacadamed road. On our right was a paddock containing seven horses, all black, on our left, far below us, the grey expanse of beach. In the distance I saw the lighthouse where Fran has his studio. We passed a tennis court, a ruined chapel, a helicopter pad. The castle appeared through trees. I counted a row of twenty windows along the uppermost storey. Battlements. A dovecot. A bell tower.

A young woman in boot-cut jeans and an off-black T-shirt was waiting on the steps as though she'd practised that a lot. Her hair was blonde and braided, and she introduced herself as 'Amelia', shook my hand with professional conviviality. She had one of those spiderweb henna tattoos across her left wrist and wore expensive looking jewellery made to look cheap but failing to. Nice kid, she spoke in the throaty monotone of south Dublin's expensive schools. Oddly, she seemed familiar – perhaps from a newspaper photo? I found myself wondering if she was famous for something.

Buffets of wind came hard from the sea.

'Such an honour to meet you, Rob. I hope I'm not gushing. You get that a lot, right?'

'Not really.'

'Oh, you do,' she insisted. 'Robbie Goulding himself. Fantastic. You've been with us before?'

She knew I hadn't been there before but I didn't mind her dissembling. Well, you don't ask a person doing her job why she's doing it. She asked if she could get a picture, which took me aback, but in a moment her i-Phone was out and she was selfieing the pair of us. Hakim remained in the car.

'Cheers, Rob. That's epic. Will we head into the observatory?'

'The . . . ?'

'Observatory. You have *so* got to see it. It's awesome.'

I should resent how they talk, but for some reason I don't. The way they use the word 'like' as noun, verb and comma gets me buzzed to the nth. It's adorbs.

'We got it renovated last year by this amazing designer. Badly needed it, too, break your heart, chintz and velvet. Like, this *carpet* on the walls. I'm like *what*? All he didn't have in it was a piebald and a skip full of fridges, God forgive me.' Here she laughed. 'Follow me up the stairs, Rob? In we pop.'

I did as requested. Her perfume was lovely. Suddenly we were on a long landing lined with paintings of screaming popes.

The observatory turned out to be a vast room that didn't actually feature a hole in the roof. But it did have a telescope-on-tripod in a wall-length bay window, and many murals of constellations and comets. Amelia began identifying them, I think for my benefit, using a plasticised card of the type you'd see in a gallery, but pausing every now and again to repeat that meeting me was a privilege. No seriously, I was 'a legend'. She was 'totally blown'. Accepting a compliment is a talent, one I've never had. I found myself wishing she'd stop.

'Would you like something, Rob?' I thought I'd better not say what I'd like. Instead I asked for a glass of water.

'Fizzy or still? Oh, I think we're out of fizzy.'

'Tap would be grand,' I managed.

Well, off Amelia went, leaving me alone with Cassiopeia. At least, I think that's what she said it was. It was pleasant having it to look at because the old heart was beginning to whomp. Many moons had waxed and waned since I'd last laid eyes on Fran. The prospect of doing so now was a little intense.

It was quiet in the room. Indeed, the whole house seemed quiet, as though surrounded by several acres of snowfall. Money muffles facts. Money is anaesthetic. You can use it to buy peace or noise or insanity – believe me, I've bought my share of all three in my time – and Fran had used his to buy quiet.

I drifted over to the telescope and looked out at the bay. Sleet was falling. Two kids were fishing in a boat. I wondered why they didn't row back.

On the windowsill, among a stack of books, were two paperclipped sheets of A4 with a heading that took my attention.

MAOMM
INSTRUCTIONS FOR PUBLICISTS
PRIVATE

Who or what was MAOMM? A Death Metal band? One of Milton's many names for Satan? I have those strange and unsettling pages in my hand as I write, for I stole them – yes – you wouldn't have done so? Don't read if your conscience prevents.

- When Mr and/or Mrs Mulvey (MAOMM) travel, it is always preferable to use private jet. When that is not possible, they travel First Class.
- 'Business Class' is not First Class.
- MAOMM, when travelling, are accompanied by three (3) staff: Mr Mulvey's personal assistant,

Mrs Mulvey's personal assistant, and MAOMM's personal security operative. MAOMM may also be accompanied by Mrs Mulvey's parents. They are entitled to, and better receive, respect.

- No cabin crew will engage MAOMM in conversation other than that necessitated by professional duty. MAOMM do not drink alcohol and would prefer that it not be offered.

- The car conveying MAOMM to hotel to be unostentatious, e.g. jeep, SUV or saloon, **never** stretch limousine, but to have blacked-out windows and be private. Driver not to converse with, or look at, MAOMM.

- Hotel accommodation for MAOMM will be six-star, five-star (superior) at minimum. If five-star, the entire floor on which MAOMM are accommodated will be otherwise empty of guests.

- Michael Hakim Jamal, referred to above as MAOMM's personal security operative, is a former Colonel of Special Forces, US Military, and is a credential-bearing Private Detective under US Federal Law, licensed to bear firearms in all states and protectorates of the US. He will be given access to all records at hotel so register of guests can be checked.

- Suite in which MAOMM are accommodated to include sleeping area, living room, two bathrooms. Any TV and all alcohol will be removed in advance of MAOMM's arrival. All artworks to be removed. Bare white or off-white walls, no patterned curtains, carpets, throws, etc. Suite to be guaranteed noise-free and to contain the following:

(1)   One king-size divan-style orthopaedic bed. Cotton (not linen) sheets. High threadcount. One treadmill-style running machine. One set of basic free-weights and two sets of basic workout clothing. One 1972 Ovation Legend acoustic guitar ('similar' not acceptable), Black Diamond strings, N600XLB gauge.

(2)   No other musical instruments. No 'welcome note'. No flowers. No newspapers, magazines, books, brochures, travel guides, CDs or menus. The suite to be guaranteed free of Wi-fi.

(3)   Supply of clean drinking water, supply of fresh (not bottled or tetrapacked) orange juice, means of preparing tea, fruit bowl. The fruit bowl to contain no apples. Bananas to be ripe. All fruit to be replaced daily.

(4)   One yoga mat and supply of basic (unscented) candles of night-light type.

(5)   Notepad and ten (10) pens, five blue, five red (disposable is fine).

• The children of MAOMM, when travelling with MAOMM, and at all other times, will be treated like MAOMM. Anyone erring on this matter, or on any related matter, will find himself wishing he'd never been born.

• The personal staff of MAOMM will be obeyed without question.

- MAOMM do not grant interviews. MAOMM are not available for **any** public appearance or comment. MAOMM do not open events.
- The ambience around MAOMM will be drug-free at all times. NB: Marijuana is a drug.
- No photograph or visual image of MAOMM or MAOMM's children will be provided. Appearance in media of visual image of MAOMM will constitute breach of contract and those responsible will be liable to punitive damages.
- Fail to guarantee any of the above and MAOMM don't travel.
- Fail to deliver, you don't work here any more. Three months' wages will be sent to your account. Never turn up again. No exceptions.

If you've ever read a sadder document, I'm sorry to know it. Oh, my poor dear friend.

'Ready, so?' Amelia chirped, bottle of water in hand. I followed a ginger cat that was following Amelia down a long corridor where the burgundy carpet was embroidered with silver phrases in some language that might have been Sanskrit. I noticed Amelia was barefoot and wearing an anklet. But I felt it was wrong to be looking.

Along the walls were framed photographs of her employer with an assortment of world-improving luminaries. The Dalai Lama. Hillary Clinton. Aung San Suu Kyi. Cheryl Cole. Now and again there was a caricature of Fran from some newspaper or internet site, hung there to demonstrate to his cleaning ladies what a good sport he was. Platinum and gold discs in such unremitting profusion that soon they seemed to diminish each other. Fran with Vladimir Putin. Fran with Tony Blair. Honorary doctorates. Old wrestling masks. A framed A.S. Roma jersey. The mild eyes of Nelson Mandela assessed me as I passed. On his shirt were many parrots. He seemed to be saying 'hold steady'.

But it was hard to hold steady when we turned the next corner. There, in a glass case, was my 1955 Stratocaster. An anonymous collector in the Far East market? Clearly he was also a Dubliner.

Amelia led me into an office that had a view over the bay. Behind a very plain desk sat the most beautifully tailored suit I have ever seen. In it was a man. I'd no idea who he was.

'Mike McGoldrick,' he said with the offer of his hand. 'Good to meet you. Thanks for coming in.'

A well-preserved sixty. Frequenter of the Stairmaster. The accent Californian, those suntanned vowels. The hair George Clooney grey. His third wife was no doubt beautiful. I pictured them in matched sarongs on Malibu Beach, boiling lobsters but very humanely. There'd be some serious ocean frontage going down outside their bedroom windows. My pincers banged a little on the pot.

He gestured towards an *objet d'art* that I took to be a chair and raised no objection when I sat on it.

'You got water,' he said.

I confirmed that I had, lest he conclude that the transparent liquid in the bottle labelled 'water' that I was holding at the time was vodka.

'Your Irish water is wonderful,' he said.

That seemed an uncontroversial proposition. We nodded at one another and grinned. There followed pleasantries about the properties of water, its unmatchable capacity for the slaking of thirst, the inability of human (and other) life to sustain itself without it, the gratitude we all of us should feel for it. The room fell quiet again.

'You're probably asking why we wanted you to stop by,' he said. 'Before we start, let me tell you, we're grateful.'

'I'm sorry,' I interrupted, as peaceably as I could. 'I don't mean to be rude. But you're who?'

The eyebrows went up and down like caterpillars doing the Macarena.

'Fran's attorney,' he said. 'You weren't told previously?'

'No.'

He uttered a bitter sigh at the incompetence of whoever had been meant to tell me. 'I'm so sorry. Michael McGoldrick. DeWitt McGoldrick Management. I look after the personal affairs.'

'The . . . ?'

'Personal affairs of the family. Also the publishing and most of the philanthropy.'

'Ah.'

'I want to level with you, Rob. May I call you Rob? Thanks. We got a call from someone in the business about this . . . concert Trez is putting together. We thought we'd go over the ground with you. Informally.'

'Is Fran here?' I asked. Saying his name aloud was strange. I don't think I'd said it in years.

'Fran's in Vietnam for UNICEF, with his wife and the boys. We're building a children's hospital. In Quảng Ninh province. I can assure you, I'm authorised to speak on his behalf. I have full plenipotentiary powers.'

Hard to know what plenipotentiary powers might mean

in this context, but it was clear he got a kick out of having them. I didn't mention that I was so deeply conflicted about the idea of the concert that I had emailed Trez and Seán earlier that morning to say they should count me out. Instead I did what my daughter, a soccer fan, would perhaps describe as lob a speculative shot from the edge of the box just to see if it troubled the keeper.

'We were hoping, Seán and Trez especially, that Fran might join us on the night,' I said. 'Maybe do a couple of numbers with us. For old times' sake.'

'That won't be possible. I'm sorry.'

'It would mean a lot. I'm sure you understand.'

'I do understand, but we're otherwise committed. We're working with Streisand on a new album. Terrifically exciting. In any case, we have a couple issues I need to bring to your attention.'

'Sure.'

I switched my phone to record-mode and placed it on the desk. He glanced at it with mild disapproval but I insisted it would be staying *in situ*. This means that whereas my preceding account of our dialogue is reconstructed from memory, the exchange I'm about to report is 100 per cent verbatim.

'See, our primary issue is confusion, Rob. If I can put it like that. We're troubled that the audience might be confused as to what you guys are offering.'

'Why so?'

'We've had counsel look this over. I hope you don't mind. The opinion is pretty long but I can give you the takeaway. There's a legal concept known as "passing off". The precedents are established. The event can't be marketed as featuring the Ships or any iteration of the group. It's essentially a matter of trademarking.'

'We're three-quarters of the Ships.'

'With respect, no you're not.'

'Sorry?'

'We wouldn't want to get into precise quantifications – but we obviously don't regard our client's former project as having had what? Four equal contributors.'

'So give me a pencil. I'll figure my hours.'

He flourished a buttery smile. 'That's funny.'

'Delighted you think so.'

'No, but apportioning these matters, creativity, so on – there's no need to go there right now. What I'm saying, we'd need to watch wordings. This couldn't be advertised as 'featuring ex-Ships' or 'performing music by the Ships' or any formula of that nature. The public need clarity that this is a new entity. A trio, in fact. Could it have a new name?'

'Christ's sake,' I said. 'Fran can't copyright the word "Ship".'

'In this context, I assure you he has.'

'You brought me all the way from London to tell me we can't bill the gig as the Ships?'

'Well, for that and other reasons. This is difficult for us, Rob. We wish you nothing but the best, I can totally assure you of that. But I'm here to tell you, there's no question of this concert featuring property owned by my client.'

'By "property", you mean songs?'

'Songs included, obviously. Fran's work is his own. Also quotations, arrangements, co-written material, his personal image on merchandising items, photographic or videographic material, souvenir programmes, so on. All these are copyrighted. As I needn't remind you. Now, I've had my assistant compile an inventory of all the material at issue. I'm going to ask that you consider yourself formally served with this document. A copy will be couriered to senior management at Vicar Street this morning. So everyone has legal clarity.'

He handed me a sheaf of papers about half the thickness of the Manhattan telephone directory. Leafing through it, I lit a cigarette.

'We're actually non-smoking here, Rob? There's an area outside? It's down at the beach house? I can call a golf cart if you like?'

'I'm smoking,' I said. 'Fukken sue me.'

For a moment, he looked as though he actually might. I'm sure he'd sued people for less. But he decided to slide, which was wise. I was on the point of setting fire to his desk or strangling him with his necktie or shoving his monogram cufflinks up his almost certainly waxed ass.

'There's no law to stop us performing our own songs,' I said. 'Stuff written by the twins or by me.'

'Is that the intention?'

'Do we have any other choice?'

'There's a matter of some delicacy I hope I can raise. May I ask how many tickets you've sold?'

'I don't have the details to hand.'

'Because I made a call or two. Not intrusively, I hope. But I'm told you're not by any means sold out.'

'You're right. We're not. Fran's the sell-out here.'

Well, he let that one go, as a man with legal training would. They don't get sucker-punched and they don't fall for rhetoric. He looked calm as a person with nothing on his mind but the question of when he was next going to floss.

'Bottom line, we'd prefer the concert not to happen at this moment in time. We were wondering if you might be persuaded. I'm approaching with respect. I'm gathering from your tone that I've spoken inappropriately. If that's so, I assure you, I'm sorry.'

Well, I took a deep breath. And then I took another. I reckoned I'd be needing them both.

'Listen, Sausage,' I said. 'I've got blood pressure issues. You're jerking my chain. You're making me surge. If I die on that carpet, it's all your fault. So let's start this again? Understand?'

'The proceeds of the show – they can't be very large. Not in a venue that size.'

'Anything I make from it goes to my daughter's education.'

'So help me out. If you can. Meet us halfway. There's a compromise here, and I want us to find it. Could we maybe lose the recorder? No one's trying any spiel, swear to God. Let's you and me go off-piste a while and talk maybes. That work?'

What the heck. I switched it off. He thanked me. I waited. There've been times when I needed the benefit of the doubt. Innocent until proven guilty isn't a bad watchword, as they go. But in the music business, it doesn't go quite as far as you'd want, which was why I was feeling a bit guarded. When dealing with any lawyer, you need the wariness of an orphan. He pushed a piece of paper across the desk.

'Fran wants to reach out. As you see, the cheque is for ten thousand euros. Family expenses, your daughter's education, whatever. No one's talking receipts. I'm saying whatever.

Your obligations as a father – we want to help you honour them. And the concert goes away. Is that possible?'

'He's bribing me to stop the gig?'

'That's putting it very strongly.'

'How would you put it yourself?'

'An understanding,' he said carefully, as though he didn't like the word. 'No one loses face. Everyone is happy. The past is allowed to be the past.'

'Go on.'

'I'm saying maybe there's a press release. "Due to unforeseen circumstances." We can help you work up language. The show gets pulled. There's a private gesture in the background between a couple old friends. That's all this is. It's friendship.'

'Yeah?'

'If you feel you're being condescended to, that isn't the intent. I'm asking you to believe the motivation is sincere. All I'm saying, consider the offer.'

You're thinking I ripped up the cheque and flung the shreds in his face. But you know when I wasn't born? Yesterday. I've been burned enough times to know a play when I see one. One thing my dad taught me, and he learned it the tough way. I'm not the son of a union man for nothing. When the thief comes to get you, he doesn't wear a mask. Sometimes, indeed, he doesn't come at all. He sends his most utterly plausible, soft-spoken soldier, a thug in a beautiful suit. When you see that suit, keep your eyes on the road and your hands upon the wheel.

'I'd need a couple of days to sell it to Seán and Trez,' I said. 'But they won't be a problem. I'll fix it.'

'Of course. Understood. Totally take your time. Tell

you, Rob, I'm happy right now. And relieved. Really am. You think we have an agreement?'

'Okay.'

'Take Two was better today, right? Apologies again. Glad we got the chance to be clear.'

Coffee was summoned. We talked of the group. He'd always been a fan, loved Trez, loved Seán. His wife was a fan. I must meet her, I'd 'enjoy her'. His children were fans. His neighbours, his ex. I smiled and signed an autograph for his chiropractor in LA, told a couple of sexed-up road-stories. He was sweet when he laughed, like a boy on a first date. I almost wanted to hug him, but I didn't. The coming half an hour was forming in my mind. Our meeting would conclude with peaceable words. I'd put the cheque in my pocket, to buy us a little time, but would never demean myself by cashing it. Because a lot of things I am, but a whore I am not. It was the moment I decided the gig would happen as planned. Some silences Fran couldn't buy.

This is a vile reason to play a concert, as I knew even then. Making music to teach someone a lesson is a bad, cold idea, violent to the music, violent to the self, injurious to the spirit of hope and angry innocence that has placed a million guitars into teenage hands over seventy years and blessed the whole world by doing so. It's also an immensely stupid and short-sighted thing to do, like marrying on the rebound just to prove to your jilter that you could.

I hated myself for what I was doing that morning. And hate is the enemy of music. Don't talk to me of the protest song. I heard it all before. The most furious songs were animated by pride, not hatred. Belief in your own. The better way ahead. Nobody listens to hate.

But I was where I was. Fran could always do that. Put me in the place I despised.

'Man, I'm sorry he wasn't here,' said Mike as I left. 'I mean it. You deserved better. Really did.'

'Thanks, Bro,' I told him, bumping his fist. 'Cool we got to talk. Be lucky.'

But when you think you're out of the forest, the fairies step in to spin you round. That's what the fairies are for.

'Glad at least you got to visit with one of the kids,' he said. 'Fran will be thrilled you guys met. So special.'

'Say again?'

'What, you didn't recognise her? Amelia. Fran's daughter. Guess the resemblance is more to Mom.'

UNEDITED TRANSCRIPT OF INTERVIEW, RTE LYRIC FM RADIO, 27th JULY 2012

Kathy Conway: . . . if you would. Welcome back, you're back to us a few seconds early but welcome. My guest today is a gentleman I've admired for a long time, as many of you have. Robbie Goulding of the Ships, good to see you again.

RG: Afternoon, Kathy.

KC: 'Inundated', I think is the word for all the messages of goodwill pouring in. The screen in front of me here is lighting up like Broadway. I was saying to you in the break, the minute it got out that you'd be dropping in to us today, the team outside started taking the calls.

RG: I'm very touched by the kindness. Genuinely. A bit floored.

KC: Lisa texting from London played 'St Mark's Place' as the first dance at her wedding. Tom in Belfast says God bless you, the Ships got him through some tough times. Frank in Glasgow saw you at the Barrowlands, best concert of his life. And on and on. You're a hero to people.

RG: I was lucky to meet Trez and Seán. And obviously Fran too.

KC: I'm sure they wouldn't –

RG: No, what I mean is that I understand when your listeners say they were touched by those songs, because I would have been touched by them myself. You know? To be standing in a studio the first time Fran came in and played 'Devil it Down'. On the piano in the corner. I can see him there still. You'd remember a moment like that for the rest of your life . . .

KC: It's no secret that you and Fran had a falling-out in the end.

RG: Well, I wouldn't want to go there. Fran's Fran. That's all. He was a fantastic mate when we were kids, it's just I wouldn't want to see him now. I guess all of us have someone who you have to love from a distance. Whatever way it happened. It's a sadness.

KC: You're not in touch at all.

RG: We haven't been, no.

KC: When was the last time?

RG: That we talked? God, I dunno. Years ago now. We were in court at the time. There you go.

KC: There was a whisper in the press that he might

turn up on stage with you guys tonight? I should say to the listeners, you're gigging this evening in Dublin.

RG: No, Fran won't be along. I wouldn't want to mislead anyone. Anyway he's playing over in London tonight, at the opening of the Olympics. Which I'm probably not supposed to say. I'm sure it's a secret.

KC: That's amazing, I didn't know that. He hasn't gigged in so long?

RG: No, he hasn't. There you go. Guess he couldn't resist the Queen.

KC: So it's yourself, Trez and Seán.

RG: Three bad pennies, that's it.

KC: And it's a family affair too. Your daughter's dropping in? Molly by name?

RG: If she makes it over from Glasgow. Which is –

KC: Because I thought she –

RG: Yeah she lives in the States with her mum, but her flight got diverted coming over from Kennedy last night. Molly's a nifty guitarist herself; we do 'Where's Me Jumper?' by the Sultans of Ping as a party piece and we cooked up this plan that we'd do it tonight at the show for the laugh. We've been rehearsing on Skype the last few weeks. So everyone say a prayer she finds herself a flight over.

KC: And there's some incredible special guests. I'm just looking at the line-up here –

RG: Yeah, unfortunately we can't mention names but we can promise some surprises.

KC: We took the liberty of phoning around to their managements over the last hour or two when we knew you were coming in, and we're cleared to reveal the names, there's no problem. If you like?

RG: Oh that's . . . thanks. You're sure?

KC: All checked out. Fire away.

RG: Well, we've Philip Chevron from the Pogues, Camille O'Sullivan, Bob Geldof. You can imagine how knocked out we feel to have people like that along. Imelda May, Declan O'Rourke, the writer Colum McCann. Brian Byrne is conducting ten musicians from the RTE Concert Orchestra for us too, so that's –

KC: A Golden Globe nominee.

RG: Trez is thrilled to have Brian. Brilliant composer, arranger, pianist. It's amazing to think someone so talented was into our stuff as a kid. Because you never think anyone is listening when you're just starting out. He knows more about our stuff than I do.

KC: It must be wonderful to be making music again with Trez and Seán.

RG: It's strange, being honest. Not used to it yet. It's Trez's evening, really. She twisted the old thumbscrews. But good, yeah. Great to see them both. They came over, when was it, a fortnight ago, and we've been trying to rehearse. Catching up on old times. Like a get-together. Johnny still plays a bit, but Trez not so much. I mean there's songs we didn't even remember what key they're in any more. If we ever knew. [*Laughs.*]

KC: Well, give them both our love. And you're working on a book, Rob?

RG: How we met, got going, where the bodies are buried, all that. A couple of war stories people won't have heard before. My daughter's actually helping me put the whole thing together.

KC: People know you've had your battles down the years with a certain problem. You had dark enough moments.

RG: Sure did.

KC: But they're over.

RG: Well, nothing's ever over. You deal with it, I guess. I'm just one of those people who can't take a drink. One's too many and ten's not enough. So you just, you know – accept it.

KC: Okay, let's –

RG: The worst thing, as you'd understand, being a mum yourself. The hardest thing is when you're a parent – you let people down. Your wife. Your daughter. That shouldn't have happened. Because there's a feeling you're abandoning –

RG becomes emotional. Seven seconds of silence.

KC: I can see it's – take a . . .

RG: . . . Sorry . . . I don't –

KC: There's water there. Beside you. You okay?

RG: Yeah. I'm good . . . Sorry, Kathy . . . Funny old day.

KC: Would you rather . . . ?

RG: No, I'm cool now, honest. Carry on. I'm sound.

KC: Tell you what, I need to squeeze in a commercial break, so we'll take that now, back in a sec.

[*The programme goes to break. The transcript resumes.*]

KC: Welcome back, we're here with Robbie Goulding formerly of that fine band the Ships. Texts and emails coming by the dozen. If I went a bit far, Rob – I didn't mean to put you on the spot.

RG: No problem, you're grand. Just a ghost or two caught me.

KC: We got you to select a song, maybe one of your own from the Ships, but you've chosen something else. Tell us why?

RG: It's Joe Brown from the concert in memory of George Harrison. My late mum had a soft spot for George. So I'll play it for her – Alice Blake, Spanish Point, County Clare and Luton. Little thing called 'I'll See You In My Dreams'.

KC: Can I ask to shake your hand? Thanks, Rob. For everything. God bless you, and the family. Okay? You're a star.

RG: Thanks again, Kathy. Great seeing you.

After a late lunch, which I couldn't eat, Seán and I taxied down together to the rehearsal studio, a clean, bright cube in a cobbled backstreet behind the O2. Usually it was frequented by dancers, so there were full-length mirrors on the walls.

A fortnight of basing ourselves there had grubbied the place up a bit. Pizza boxes, coils of flexes, flight cases, empty cans, jars of jelly beans Seán bought in the duty-free at LAX, mic stands, amp cabinets, booms. We'd a notion of using a double bass on 'Wildflowers', so we'd hired one in. It was leaning on its side, near the piano stool in the corner, dust-sheet over its shoulders. A gracious old lady in her lovely mantilla, forgiving the noisy invaders.

Seán sat down at the kit, which was smaller than his own, and started rolling very gently on the snare. It pleased me to see him playing. He closed his eyes and brushed. I watched for a while. Light came into the room.

He nodded for me to get my guitar, but I didn't feel up to the guitar right then. Instead I went to the piano, an instrument I hadn't touched in years, and started into an old progression I'd sometimes used back in the day, D-major, G, E-minor, A-7th, then repeat the G and the A and bring it slowly on home, a gorgeous, simple sequence used in the Welsh chapel song 'All Through the Night'. There's a reason those chapel tunes last.

I sat at the piano and played old, sweet chords and closed my eyes for a while. I found myself on Denmark Street near London's Soho, a stretch long haunted by song-writers. Past a drinking den, a piano showroom, the 12 Bar Club, then a window full of saxophones – it always raises the heart – into an alley so narrow I could touch both walls simultaneously, before descending a rickety staircase, past a photographer's premises, into a basement that reeks of patchouli and mothballs. Through the curtain is a second-hand musical instruments shop called Heavyweight Sounds. That's where the chords chose to bring me.

It was good seeing it again. Shay was at the counter. And then I saw Trez was there, too. Talking about the mandolins and the beautiful guitars. Maple, rosewood, pau ferro, ebony. She took a Dobro from the shelf, shredded a sexy little blues lick, like something from Bonnie Raitt or Tony Joe White. I don't deceive or try to mystify when I tell you I heard that solo, that I glimpsed the wild smile it caused Shay. If you're a lover of music, you'll know what I mean. People call it a way of remembering, but that doesn't come close. It's a ticket to ride right back.

Dangerous, that drug. To be handled with care. But some-times you open old doors.

Molly walked into my head, her inscrutable grey eyes. A fight we once had in the café beneath St Martin-in-the-Fields, the church near Trafalgar Square. The Christmas she turned fifteen. A boy back at home. She was grown and she missed him, there was trouble at school. Up she came from the music, resentment smouldering from the cigarette she insisted on smoking despite my asking her not to, not here. I told her I was in a band as a kid, that she mustn't be too serious with this boy. Love can wait. Have friends. They're a family. Always around when you need them.

– Dad, I *had* a fucking family. Before *you fucked it all up*.

Hurtling through the crowds on the Charing Cross Road. Christmastime in London. She was gone. A cop outside the Hippodrome. Drunks in Leicester Square. Some fool recognised me from the old days and wanted a photograph. Onward, scared, through boys masked as hags, past the buskers of Chinatown, the peepshows of Soho, past the rundown guitar stores I'd shown to my child, and now here she was, in Denmark Street, alone, weeping in her fingerless mittens. And we didn't say a word but clung in the drizzle as the songwriters' ghosts walked by.

There's a street performer works Oxford Street, blowing car-sized bubbles. Molly used to find them entrancing. She'd follow them down the pavement, hypnotised, hands out. 'They're songs,' she once told me. And I knew what she meant. A song wraps you up, has a membrane you can see through, and it changes the view and the light. I went into A-minor, looked out at the storm clouds. Night we supported Dylan. Mad. Entirely mad. But a tune has a way of collapsing time, the way you feel when you open an old schoolbook found in an attic and inhale the lost rain of its pages. His face in a mirror backstage at the Carlton Theatre, Los Angeles, five o'clock shadow, the hooded, owlish eyes, and a rasped 'How you minstrel boys doin'?' Fran shaking his hand. Trez touching his guitar. Like a dream you didn't know you were having. He murmurs of Sonny Terry, Bukka White, Mama Thornton. He's asking if you know the Louvain Brothers' 'Satan is Real', if you ever bin to Clarksdale, Mississippi. Musk arising from his clothes. The glitter of his diamond earring. Can't you see him? I could. He walked out of a song, like the kiss of a long-gone lover. Watching from the wings as he stood alone in the spotlight for his encore, the *rage* in his howl and the audience howling back. His limo the size of a bus outside the stage door in the rainstorm, steam rising from the purring black hood. Trez weeping. We met him. It couldn't have happened. Seán, strong arm around her shoulder. And the strangest thing – in the memory, Molly is there too, although she wasn't yet born. Impossible.

We kept at the tune. Steady, four-four, an occasional little fill, nothing tricksy. Someone came in and went out, a roadie I guess. I didn't even look. Just played. A black Baby Grand, scratched and beaten, pedals bust, but sinking fingers into its keys sent a murmur of yes right through you, the way some old pianos will. Play the saddest blues ever written on an instrument like that, the audience will be uplifted all the same. 'Pianos remember everything,' Trez used to say. Somewhere in the recollection of ebony and teak, there's a whole lotta shakin' goin on.

Five minutes? Ten? Couldn't tell you. Don't know. That's the way it can go, playing music. Everything opens and everything closes and the things that don't matter flow away. I heard her before I saw her. A stream of violin like glittered smoke. She was standing there, by the door, fiddle beneath her chin.

Sunglasses. Raincoat. Gauloise in mouth. She's forty-nine this Christmas, looks seventeen when she plays. Trilby with a feather, bangles, many rings, dirty black docs, Pussy Riot T-shirt. Draws her bow across the strings, walks across to her brother, plucks a pizzicato that makes you want to shout at the roof for sheer joy, murmurs 'yeah', then shoots you a wink. She's up on her tiptoes as she hits the high A, like a superhero lifting off in a story.

Coaxes you towards something turns out to be Tom Waits's 'Downtown Train' and you go into that song for a while. It's like walking the aisles of a glorious old church, looking at its windows, like being stained glass. Sarah Sherlock is playing violin.

TREZ

. . . Sorry . . . I was lost a second . . . Thinking of a song . . . What did you ask me again? . . . I'm fine, just . . . you know . . . He comes into my mind . . . Tom Waits's 'Downtown Train' . . . Strange when that happens . . . I'll be grand.

. . . No I'd have got to the rehearsal room about two-thirty or three. I won't lie, Rob looked pretty terrible that day. Drained. Bleached out. He'd lost a bit of weight. You'd never in your life hear a word of self-pity from Rob, he'd be keeping up this front of bad jokes and all the rest, but we knew he hadn't been sleeping. His dad was up the walls about him. It was a thing about Rob that he joked when he was anxious. He wouldn't want you to think he was down, didn't want to go there at all. He'd have felt a responsibility to how you felt yourself. He didn't realise you were able to see through the act. He was a hard enough guy to talk to in any authentic way. And I guess I felt bad because the gig was my idea.

There was a lot of hassle going on. He was expecting Molly from New York but there'd been a problem with the flight. He was kind of invested in her being there, but she hadn't arrived by three o'clock. It was nobody's fault, the plane got delayed, and I guess . . . how to put it . . . I mean, Rob would never guilt-trip anyone, least of all Molly . . . But he was really looking forward to doing a number with her as an encore. I kind of knew it was the only reason he wanted to play the show. And it looked like that wouldn't be happening.

It was weird – I had the feeling he was going to do a runner. I'd say it was fifty–fifty. On the edge.

He kept logging on to the box office to check the seating plan . . . as though he was hoping the place would be empty and we'd have to cancel. I don't know why I felt it but I was certain he'd split. Say nothing, just go. You're in a band with someone all those years, you get to know him pretty well. Even his silences. And that was the feeling I had.

Yeah, we jammed for a while in the rehearsal space, just John-John, Rob and me. And it was beautiful seeing him play. Really good. Because obviously we'd been fairly rusty over the fortnight rehearsing. People tell you it's like riding a bicycle, you never forget – but that's rubbish, you actually do. John-John came up with the idea that we'd play our set with a couple of good young musicians, you know, like a backstop, to keep us covered. He'd asked around and got Darrel Higham, Imelda May's guitarist, and Tanya O'Callaghan on bass and then Aoife Ní Bhriain on fiddles, frighteningly talented kids, best I ever heard. The standard's so high now. Not like the old days. But Robbie wouldn't agree. Didn't want to 'cheat', so he said. But actually I think it was his way of making the gig harder. It was me, him and John-John, or nothing. That upped the bar big-time. And he knew what he was doing. Trying to make it impossible for himself.

He did a couple of things on the piano, then picked up my guitar. One of those old National Steels, a big, tough brute from the 1940s. I bought it years ago in Austin, never could get with it. You'd want the hands of a murderer to play it. Scrapper Blackwell used to play one. But an amazing thing about Rob, for such a gentle guy, he could master a National Steel. Fantastic hands. So we messed about like that for twenty minutes, and then John-John got out the set-list. We talked it over a while, moved a few numbers around. We started rehearsing 'Wildflowers'. Yeah. You know that song? I'd written new lyrics. 'Wildflowers 2012.' Let's see if I have it. It's got a little private meaning between Robbie and me. Little joke between mates. Gimme a tick. I wrote it in Paris, when I went over to see him that time. Scribbled it out on a menu and stuck it in his pocket so he'd find it when he went back to the hotel. We had a lovely day together, catching up, talking family. Flirting a bit. Like you'd do with an old mate. There's a way of reading the lyric-sheet that only Rob would understand. Little leg-pull hidden in there.

[*Now singing.*]

> *Feelin so lovely.*
> *Extremely beguiled*
> *Callin your phone*
> *Kissin numbers you dialled*
> *Off in the night*
> *Folks are driving their cars*
> *Fantasies warming*
> *Round flickery stars*
> *O babe see I missed ya*
> *But babe you ain't you*
> *Encore, une fois?*
> *Ring me soon.*
> *Till you do.*

And I played electric bass. Just with Seán on the tom. Bluesy, you know? Seemed to work. You can see Robbie's into it. Focused. Playing good. The whole fortnight we're rehearsing, his mind's somewhere else. But now, here he comes. Your fingers are crossed. It's like watching a ship slowly pulling up towards the quay. You're saying 'Come on, babe. Throw me the rope. I'll catch. But you gotta throw.'

The feeling in the room, with me, Seán and Rob – it's nice. You know? It's cool. He's settling, you can see it. Head in the game. Talking harmonies and bridges. Maybe we'll do 'Island'. The anxiety's going. He looks like a kid.

Then the Fran thing happens.

And Vesuvius.

It's all kicked off. Like you knew it always would.

We should have talked about it more. In hindsight. You know?

Do you mind if we stop a few minutes?

MOLLY

Yeah, my flight landed in Dublin and I called Dad from the plane. You can tell he's in a mood. Bad moment.

Something's going on. He doesn't want to say. But you know from his voice. Can't hide it. I'm, 'Dad, what's up? Spit it out. What's the matter?' I hear Seán in the background and he's shouting at someone. My cell cuts dead. Weak signal.

I'm walking down to Customs when Dad calls me back. Out of his mind with anger.

He's in the rehearsal room with Trez and Seán when this courier company calls. They've a delivery. Urgent. Can he tell them where he's at? So he gives them the address and thirty minutes later they show up. Dad's one of those Irish guys who takes a long time to tell you a story? You know, doing all the voices? Drives me nuts.

This oblong cardboard box. Maybe six feet long? A packing case, you know. And he opens it. Inside, packed in Styrofoam shells and all swathed up in bubble-wrap, there's his '55 Strat . . . The one he got in Umanov's all those years ago. First guitar he ever bought.

Beautiful thing. And this envelope taped to the neck. From Fran.

Dad's telling me this. And I'm slightly perplexed. This is bothering you, why? I'm, 'Hello?'

And he's, 'What do you mean, hello? What's that supposed to even *mean*?'

I'm like, Dad, what's the problem? Try to see it as something nice, he's giving you back your guitar. Tune it up, give it a clean, play it tonight at Trez's gig. Because a guitar like that was meant to be played. You don't like to think of it in a glass case.

And we're out of the blocks. Fran this and Fran that. It's 'charity' or 'largesse' and every other insane shit you ever heard. I'm telling him, quit reading everything the worst possible way but it's oil on the dadfires. Insanity.

Because I love my dad, you know, he's a deeply admirable guy. But he's a typical, oversensitive, slight-seeing klutz of an over-imaginative Irishman. Want to know why they were fighting all those 800 years in Ireland? Robert Goulding, that's why. It's a verb. 'Goulding' means remembering too damn long and not getting *over* yourself. Mom told me after he and Fran had the fall-out, you literally couldn't mention Fran's name. Turning off the radio. Wouldn't go into a record store for years. All I can say myself, there's usually two sides. When their marriage broke up, Fran was good to Mom and me. Bank drafts arriving. Always anonymous, but you knew. He paid my school fees for years. Christ, he paid off our mortgage. You couldn't say it to Dad. But it happened.

Sure, Fran did some bad stuff, there's no doubt in my mind, it's just that I don't believe in the demonising thing.

The guy had no parents. Look at his childhood. You think someone like that isn't broken? Little kid with no mother, beaten, abused – you'd like him to be perfect? How perfect are *you*? Easy for me to say; I wasn't the one he hurt. But he tried to help Mom and me in a really bad time. That's not everything. But it's something. Right?

I'm, Dad, take it easy. You've a show in three hours. So the guy gives you a guitar, so what's the big deal? And I'll always remember what he said, the Goulding Irish bastard.

'The killer just sent me my coffin.'

Well, then I see red. I'm, hold up a second. I'm back the fuck *up* with your shit. I just flew halfway across the world to see a show I don't even want to see and you're dumping your issues like a spoilt little brat, so spare me the hurt prom-queen act. You're not the babes in the wood, Dad. Some of this is your fault. Did you ever pick up the phone? Ever once make a move? And that didn't help. Didn't help at all. Okay, it's a little disrespectful to call your father a self-deluding, disingenuous prick, but as they teach you in pre-Law at Princeton University, truth is a perfect defence. So, by now I'm yelling down the phone and he's hollering back and he's 'you never understand' and I'm 'fucking SURE I don't'. I said Dad, you got your excuse. You wanted to wreck Trez's show. Well done. Only you. Congratulations. The Customs guys are staring. There's a nun in the line. Well, Sister heard some new vocabulary that day in Dublin. My family, we put the fun into dysfunctional. I let him have it. Both barrels. And he blasted me back. Like Fran is *my* fault. Or Seán's or

Trez's or *my mother's*. And he's 'Why are you late anyways? When you know this meant everything to me.'

I said Dad, you know what this is about? You wish he was here.

And I switched off my phone, walking through Arrivals at Dublin Airport. I was *shaking* with rage. Jimmy was waiting.

'I know,' he kept saying. 'I know, love. You're right.' I cried a bucket of tears and Jimmy just held me.

Impossible man, Robert Goulding.

Hey Sombrero.

It's myself. Been a funny old time. Put your eyes back in your head. Tear this up if you want. Well, don't for a minute. Still reading?

Sorry about the lawyer, day you came to the house. When I heard about the gig, I panicked, dunno why. Wish you well with it. Forgive me? Messed up. Knew you wouldn't cash the cheque. Dunno what I was thinking. Very, very sorry and ashamed.

What a beautiful guitar. I'm sending her back. I tried my best to woo her but she wouldn't be won. Tried reggae, the blues, and the twelve-bar boogie. Disco, Frisco, the pluck and the plectrum. She plays only one song: My Robbie.

I don't know what she sees in you, honestly I don't. It must be the red of your eyes.

Her second pick-up is loose. I gave her proper strings. Don't you *know* how to treat an eminent lady, you Lutonian flunt? I wouldn't string up Satan's dog with those useless yokes you had on her. Better off with barbed wire. You great booby.

I'm writing this in Vietnam. We've a house here now. It's fantastic because no one gives a cuss for who I am, i.e. nobody. They think I'm a returned Yank, or a weirdly silent local, which suits me right down to the slingbacks. I'm building a technical college, which is what they need most. I'd love you to see it. Dead proud. All my team, they're all locals – all born over here. The way we've set it up, I'm kept in the background. No 'Fran Mulvey' shite. No press. These kids over here, they're smart but they've nothing. Give them books and a teacher, they work all night. The only thing I said – don't give 'em a bar. Memories of the Trap! What a ratpit.

I saw you a few years ago in London with this beautiful girl. I was over there working, took a walk in Hyde Park. Synapses burning. Fried out. There you were – across the lake – with this vision out of Hardy. Took a moment to realise she must have been Molly. She's beautiful, Rob. You must be so proud. Wanted to go over. Should have.

I hear she's into music. That right? What a coolness. My own aren't into making it, which is fine, but they love it. Way I see things now, that's the main and only quest. A kid who really loves it, you're giving them a gift. What's making it? Nothing. We're sheet music, nothing more. It's the listener gonna sing you the song.

Hey Rob, I've a sister. Took seven years to find her. She's married and lives in Hanoi with her husband.

They have four gorgeous children, my nieces and nephews. Can you imagine such a thing as Uncle Francis. I never knew she existed until I started coming here in '98. They told me at the orphanage. Now, that was some day. Don't think I'll ever forget the morning I knocked on her door. She's a beautiful looking person, fragile, really serious, but speaks no English at all, and my Vietnamese is shockin mowldy, though I'm taking lessons now. Her name is Ho Xuan Nguyễn, not easy for a Paddy like me to say. Someone told me brothers and sisters in Vietnam share the same middle name, so I'd like you to address me as Xuan. Pretty cool, right? You know what a blessing it is to have something as wonderful as a sister. How terrible that must have been, for you to lose her, so young. How brave you were, Rob. And how stupid, the rest of us. When I think of how we never talked to you, or listened, or felt. Maybe music was your way of getting it out. You never knew there was no band without you, that you were the glue. At least I don't think so? Maybe you did. But the Ships was Robert Goulding and three of his admirers, and bugger all else, that's truth. Other songs might have been written. But not the ones got writ. If you ever hear 'Devil it Down' on the radio, remember this, hey? That's *your* song, compadre. No flunt else's. There's people who drive the train but they didn't build the tracks. No Robbie Goulding, no nada.

That time in '94 – I was so sorry to hear of your mum's passing, Rob. What a lovely lady she was. So mild and forgiving. It was a fucked-up year, I was back on the junk. Spent four months in rehab. No one knows. Didn't know whether to get in touch with you or not. Many times had the phone in hand. Suppose I was afraid. All I want to say – being a tiny part of your home's the only reason I'm alive. Should have told you back then. Never could. I'm talking literally. Plan around the months I met you was goodbye, simple truth. Jump off the bridge outside Luton station. Went there one night to do it, drugged up to the gills, pissed on cheap cider. Train roaring from London. That's a sound I remember. But you, and Rutherford Road, and Jimmy and Alice. Where would you find them? Tell Jimmy I said hello. I can hear him right now. ('Fukken daisy!') You saved a boy's life, Rob. That's more than most achieve. It's not everything. But it mightn't be nothing.

The littluns are well, and no longer little. Amelia's starting college. Wants to be a dentist. (A wha'?) She's inconveniently beautiful, so the brutish boys are all about her like wasps in a jam jar, little filthy snotty oily overconfident toadlike leering sods. Andrew's in Glasgow. He's studying theatre. Fantastic kid, spiky, dead smart. I've loved being a dad, way more than you'd think, mainly because the opportunities it presents for fascistic behaviour are so easily disguised as wisdom, don't you find?

James is named after you. I always preferred your first name, don't know why. 'Rob' sounds wrong. I don't think you're a Rob. (Maybe you're a Xuan? Just a thought.) He goes to Coláiste Eoin near Belfield, finishes next year. It's a bit of a journey but he loves it. You know what they're like at that age. Everything is mates.

They love him over here in Vietnam, he's so good with them, very gentle. You should hear him speak the language, he's fantastic. Honest, he speaks it way better than me. Funny when a kid from Howth is translating Vietnamese for his Vietnam-born old dad. He takes me to the football whenever Ireland are playing and I pretend to enjoy it but I don't. Have you and Seán acquired sense enough in your dotage to go off it? Twenty-two pampered ninnies chasing a bladder around a field and clutching their genitals and snotting. If normal people did it they'd be sectioned in an asylum. Honestly, you'd want to give them a spittoon. There's more refinement in a dunghill or a Michael Bublé album. Well, maybe not more. But it's close. James says I need to grow up and get over myself. He has a signed poster on his wall of Lê Công Vinh and Nguyên Minh Phương, who won us (Vietnam) the Suzuki Cup in '08 and who invest the wretched 'sport' with some chivalry. We beat Thailand 3–2 on aggregate, a word James had to explain. It was the politest night of soccer you ever saw.

Every time I say 'James', I think of you, Spatchcock. Well, not every time. Must be honest. I tell him he's named for the best mate a frightened kid ever had, the most gentle, sweetheart, generous boy, who I didn't deserve, because nobody ever could, that it was an honour to know him, that I wouldn't be here if I hadn't. I say he taught me guitar, gave me courage, lined it up. Told me I wasn't a piece of worthless, expendable shit, though not in so many words, because we didn't do words, right? We spoke in three chords. But hey, that's not hiding. It's a gain in translation. I say he taught me B-7th, A-major, to E. Which is pretty much the only logic ever made sense at the time, or before, or since, or ever. Taught me C-sharp minor has four sharps in the signature. Taught me Sam Cooke's 'You Send Me' is all you need to know, better than the Sistine Chapel or Newton's Laws of Physics, or Darwin, or the Great Wall of China. Einstein? Get ballsed. Gimme Sly and the Family Stone. And you know what James says? So, where is he?

I'm sorry, my Rob. For every hurt and hassle. Truly very sorry. For everything. If some time you felt like a walk on Howth's photogenic cliffs or a mug of dacent tay – we wouldn't have to unbosom, just maybe listen to an album or something? – well, think it over, hey? I know you don't want to.

I used to love being able to speak with you every day. With Seán and Trez, too, but especially my Rob. It's the only reason I wanted to be in the group. I liked you more than was wise. From the very first we met. Is it okay to tell you? Well, maybe you knew. I'd be so jealous of Trez – but then I saw she loved you. Not in any silly passing way, like wanting to be your girlfriend. That she cared. That she saw you were real.

BAD persons send me their bad albums and their VERY bad demos. You and I could assemble a bonfire in silent, menacing seriousness? I have discovered that a Coldplay CD, when attacked with a lighter, burns with a surprisingly beautiful and soothing sort of yellow-gold flame, the colour of a teddy boy's lapels. But the *funny* thing is, when you blow on it to extinguish the fire, from the resulting puff of smoke appears Bono! And he grants you a wish. This is fact, swear to God. Try it. I wished for world peace.

He's actually a good guy. Though you'd want to give him a dig sometimes. I'm working with the Tiger Lillies. Know their stuff? They're outstanding. Three-piece from England, singer sings falsetto, gorgeously gentle drumming, just a presence, nothing more, an old double bass, all acoustic. Got a beautiful song called 'Flying Robert' about a little boy gets lost in a storm. Everyone told him stay indoors but he thought the rain was lovely. Didn't want to be safe. Out he went. And the wind blew him away, till he couldn't find his home. Look it up on YouTube. It's a slayer, dead simple. I'd trade everything I ever wrote to have written that song. Just D, A and G. You'd love it.

Tell Seán to lay off the pies. He looks like a secretly bisexual Michelin Man forced to marry a librarian. Honestly, what's he *hiding* under all that tum-tum? His talent, I suppose. As usual.

You know I don't mean it. Tell him I love him, always will. Stoutheart. He's one in a million. Did you know they gave him an honorary degree at UCLA last year, for the work he's been doing with kids in prison? I bet he didn't tell you. Saw it in the papers over there. I've not spoken with him in years. It's fantastic he's happy. I got thinking the other night – he's the only one of the Ships was always in the band. We never did one gig without Seán. Funny, when he was only the temporary drummer. I heard he's a granddad. Imagine.

Much love to Trez. Isn't she gorgeous – sweet God. She's one of those women grow lovelier every decade. Imagine her at eighty. She'll still be the nazz. Thank Christ you two didn't marry. She loved you too much. But all of us did. You daft tit.

Tear 'em up, homeboy. Are you going to sing tonight? Find I can't sing those old songs of ours any more, they make me too sad. Put me back in the past. Admire you for being able to try.

Phi thường, bất phu, as we say over here. Nothing ventured, nothing gained, I think that means.

Oh, and stop that wicked smoking. Do you hear? CUT IT OUT.

What else? Don't want to go. I'm sorry, Rob. Truly.

Right I'm off.

Your glimmertwin bud.

X

Do you know what I'd love, above anything else? If some time – whenever – you'd come to Vietnam. There's peace here, Rob. You wouldn't think so. But there is. It's the most extraordinary place, you need to see the skies here. I wish you could see from my window right now, the red on the water and the fishermen coming in. And the people, even the kids, they've survived so much. They've courage. Generosity. It lifts you.

You and Molly might come, and Michelle if she'd like? I never met Michelle. But I know she must be lovely. Some time. Okay? Don't have to be now. In a while. Next year. I'd love if you'd come. All of us together. It's great we're still alive. We shouldn't be, y'know. But we are.

I know so many went away, far too early, too young. So do you, Flying Robert. So do you.

SEÁN

So it's coming on for six and we're onstage doing the sound-check, Trez and yours truly. No sign of Noddy. Ain't in his dressing room. Someone says he's 'nipped out for a walk'. Trez and me do the lot, drums, guitars, vocals. And that's a thing you want to get right. See, every band has its own way of handling a sound-check. Some of the young ones won't do it all, just a mic-test, keep it simple, get partying. But I'm old school. You want to do a sound-check. It's brushing your teeth before a date.

Sound's just a part of it. Big part, sure. But the other reason you do a sound-check is to get au fait with the stage. The singer needs to know how many steps to the mic, where's the sightlines, the flats, the monitors, the pit. How many steps to my riser? Where's Trezzie's water, her seat for the keyboards? You do a sound-check for fifteen hundred reasons. Where's the spotlight falling? You need the information. Too late when the gig starts if you ain't done your prep. Never in a million years would you face a gig like that with no sound-check. Own the gig. Or the gig owns you. Very dim idea, no sound-check.

I tell you this so you'll understand how we're feeling that evening. Ninety minutes to kick-off. We're running badly late. Guitarist gone AWOL. Probably pissed in some gin-shop. All day long, there's been every little screw-up you can imagine. Equipment gone missing. Pedalboard's wrong. Amps buzzing, you name it. This geezer, the Prof, who they've give us as sound-hog, he's turned out a diamond, professional, on the money, but he's had to work his nads off all day. Geldof's arrived backstage. Ready to go. I look at me watch. Five minutes to six. Doors open at half past. Time's badly short. And bang. The lights go out.

Power cut. All over the city. Then the generators fail. Most up-to-date club venue in the country, right up there with anyplace in Europe. The generators never failed, never once, couldn't happen. But it happened that day. Five to six. Like, you wouldn't want to be superstitious, you know what I'm saying? Bad fairies about. Bad scene.

The Prof's gone mental. Howling at the sparkies. Fix that effing rig you bucket of tosspots. Don't gimme no excuses, juice my rig else I'll cut you. The language is fairly non-Shakespearean, being honest. We've gone up to the greenroom, Trezzie and me. And there's Rob by the window. Smoking a sodding fag.

He don't look too happy. Ain't whistling a tune. But at least he's sodding here. It's a start.

Well, I don't say nothing. This is over to Trez. Noddy in one of his moods, that's well above my pay-grade. Also, there's a part of you don't give a shit. Tell the truth, I wasn't tremendously in love with him right then. I don't have the time, mate. Sorry to disappoint. But whole minutes actually pass when I'm not thinking about you.

She goes over and tells him she wants his help with a song. So they start working on a number, an old thing they never got right, from back in the New York days. Still faffing about with it all this time later. And I guess I didn't mind, because he needed the distraction. I recorded them on me phone. The two of them together. Nice. Like the Everlys. Beautiful harmonies. Aeolian. I ain't crazy about the song but they done it nice, have to say. Want to hear it? Got it here. Just a tic.

Down on
Saint
Mark's
Place
And there's midnight in the smile
Of the poets in the shadows by the park.
Ghetto Juliets go roamin with the Romeos from Queens
Making out beneath the doorways in the dark.

And the ghost of Johnny Thunders drifts from 8th Street
*   to the porch*
Of the shuttered Turkish bathhouse round the corner.
And he's starin' at the ruins of what was once
*   St Bridget's church.*
He was born in New York City, feels a foreigner.

For it's Christmastime is blowin down on Avenue B and
   Fourth,
All the fire escapes are draped in fairy light.
It's the worst time of the year to be alone, a poorboy
   thinks,
On a carousel of hurt and thirsty night.
Menorahs in the windows on Elizabeth and Prince,
For it's Hanukkah from Harlem to the Bronx.
There's a twelve-branch candelabrum done in neon on
   Times Square
Where a saxophone deliriously honks.

Down on Saint
Mark's Place
There's a crooked aspen tree
By a clam bar only closes in December.
For the owner, so they whisper,
Goes to Cuba for New Year's.
There's a love affair he can't bear to remember.

And a tumbleweed of tinsel blows through Tompkins
   in the snow
Patti Smith and Lenny Kaye are smokin' schemes.
Don't go.
Don't go.
Don't go.
Don't go.
I see you in the snowdrift of my dreams, my love.
I see you in the snowdrift of my dreams.

And just as they finish singing, I've looked out the

window. We're up top of Vicar Street, I can see everything clear as day. And the things I can't see, I'm imagining. Liffey in the distance, the city, the bridges. Tourist boat pulling down the river in this beautiful sunshine. I'm giving a squinnie. Just settling the head.

And right at that moment, I've looked down at the street. You know what I seen?

People.

They're crossing from the car park. Dozens, then more. Parents with kids, couples, gangs of mates. Trezzie's come over. Then Rob. Then the Prof.

No one says nothing.

The billies be coming.

I'm looking at them people. Gonna give 'em the best I got. You're with me, you're with me. You ain't, then you ain't. I've an idea what's gonna happen. And I'm gutted for Trez. Meant a lot to her, the show, all three of us together – but there's punters downstairs and I can't live someone else's life. But I'm fucked if I won't live my own.

I'm South-London Irish. Never back down. Make it tough as you want, I'm London. Play the gig every time. End of story. I'm the people tunnelled the Tube, mate. You got nothing to scare me. We fucking scared *Dickens*. We're a nightmare.

Only one thing I ever learned and I learned it from music. Own the show. Or the show owns you.

You ain't up to the fight? So, toddle on home.

M'say boom shacka lacka. Let's dancehall.

The fizz starts to boil in you. Waiting around makes it worse. You pace, drink water, tune your instrument again, gape at your watch, go out to the bathroom, run your mind over the lyrics, hum them at the mirror, and wonder if the cyclone roiling slowly through your body is going to cripple what's left of your mojo. In the old days, the fizz could literally make me throw up. That night, in Dublin, it was impish and mean. I was shaking like a foal with the staggers.

Camille did 'The Ship Song' and 'Sugar in My Bowl'. Geldof did 'Joey's on the Street Again' with a low, cutting menace, like an old bluesman you don't want to mess with. Philip Chevron did 'Faithful Departed' and 'Thousands Are Sailing'. By now I was getting the fizz like Samson got a haircut. There's a point up to which you can use it as emotional fuel. If you manage to throw yourself over it, you can ride it Harleywise into a gig and keep rolling. But the kickstart I needed wasn't there.

I stood in the backstage, looking out at the crowd, or the darkness where the crowd must be. Every time they roared, I heard a 747 lifting off. My shirt was so drenched I had to change it. Chevron finished his turn. They howled. Strobes raged. Declan O'Rourke and the Imelda May Band were up next, but I couldn't stay where I was. Too much. I went up to the roof alone and lit the only j I had. Maybe it would help. Maybe not.

Wicklow's mountains in the distance. The day's last light. A plane crossing sky. Many seagulls. My phone chirped a couple of times – Jimmy down in the car park having lost his ticket, Michelle over in Montauk wishing me luck. Now and again a thunder-roll of applause came rumbling up through the floors below. I was trying to put together what to say to Seán and Trez. Twenty minutes to go. Fifteen. Twelve. Suddenly Seán was beside me.

'There's some flunts want to see you downstairs. Nine hundred musical illiterates. Will I tell 'em you ain't available?'

I said nothing.

He took the j from me and sucked it. Gazed across at the rooftops.

'Camille was pukkah.'

'Brill.'

'Loved Geldof.'

'Epic.'

'Chevron was mint.'

'The best.'

'Rob, I know what you're gonna tell me. Don't beat yourself up. I've a session guy ready. We're covered.'

'Where's Trez?'

'Having a blow-dry. Says it calms her down.'

'A blow-dry?'

'Yeah. You want one yourself?'

'I don't have a lot worth drying.'

'Know what I always say? When I feel a bit fizzy?'

'What?'

'Drumming ain't nothing but dancing sitting down.'

'I'm not up to it, Seán.'

'Understood.' He nodded. 'Can't, then you can't. Ask you one fave?'

'What's that?'

'Split. Don't stick around. I'll say it to Trez.'

'*Listen*. I'm not up to it. So I'll need you to cover.'

'. . . How so?'

'Get the Prof-guy to sink me as low as he can in the mix. Drop 'Wildflowers' and 'Ash'. I don't want to sing.

Thirty-minute set, we bugger off out. One encore with Molly. And home. That's my best.'

He pondered. 'Okay. Was sure you was off.'

'I should be,' I said.

'So what's stopping you?'

'I don't want to let Trez down on the night of her gig. Get through the sodding thing, then it's over.'

'. . . Do what?'

'I know it means a lot to her. Playing this gig.'

'Trez don't need no *gig*, Rob. Don't be soft. She's Trez.'

'Then why are we here?'

'Ain't it obvious?'

'No.'

It's possible he turned away from me, but I don't remember that. What I remember is the words. I'll never forget them.

'For you . . . That's the reason . . . She wanted to give you back music.'

By the time I was able to look at him again, my face was covered with tears.

'People love you, mate,' he said. 'Honoured to be here. I say we go down and blow the doors off. Give 'em the goods. Anyone don't like it, there's a night bus.'

Backstage, Trez was waiting in a black and red Von Fürstenberg, tuning up her Fender P bass. I tried talking, but she wouldn't have it, and I was glad because I couldn't speak. 'Sex-bomb,' she told me, dusting off my shoulders and fixing my collar upright. 'Get your Strummer on, baby. And pout.' One of the videographer's seven screens was showing the opening ceremony of the Olympics in London. Fran and his band weren't announced but were suddenly playing. He looked trim, like a middleweight, hair dyed black. His musicians were all women, half my age, if that. Alto sax, tubular bells, drummer, bassist and DJ. Nobody sang, which surprised me. He moved around the stage like someone who didn't wish to be seen, often turning his back or lowering his head. The piece was strange and beautiful, full of arabesques and flamenco samples. He was wearing black jeans, black mandarin jacket, dark glasses: a man who wants to disappear while you watch. A roadie handed me a can of Coke and helped me don the guitar. It felt heavy, too big. Trez nudged me. On the screen, Fran had removed his jacket and was playing the synth. You now saw he was wearing a white soccer shirt with orange and navy trim. Few would have recognised it but Seán and I did. Luton Town FC, early eighties. Shoulder-swaying, nodding, he turned from the camera. Printed on the back were a number and a name. The shot moved in closer.

I

R. Goulding

Our stage manager came. It was time.

Someone had put together a back-projection of our early career: grainy footage of our shockheaded selves on Ireland's *Late Late Show* as kids, on Letterman, on Conan, at Glastonbury and the Albert Hall, with old publicity-shots segueing in and out of each other and slow-mo images of me arriving at Vicar Street that morning. It took me aback to have been filmed. I wasn't crazy about the fact. But the stage manager said the punters would need something to look at while the orchestra was getting on. Cellists and trumpeters passed me, raising bawls from the house as they made a quick way through torchlight to their risers.

We agreed before going on that we wouldn't be talking. No valedictions, acknowledgements or salutes. We'd be musicians making a sound and refusing to explain it. The Past wants you to talk to him, mention him from the stage? Not tonight. He ain't on the guest list.

I heard them chanting my name. Seán said, 'Let them chant.' Trez called for a bottle of water. She looked anxious and beautiful and I kissed her shaking hands. Seán drummed his sticks at the air.

Geldof shambled on as the house lights got killed. The roar from the audience made me choke. He waited for it to die, then smiled and muttered 'ah fuck off'. They laughed – the indescribability of a thousand people laughing – as he slid a cool hand in his pocket.

'Here's an old song by Shakespeare. Trez and Seán asked me to read it. What a piece of work is a man, how noble in reason, how infinite in faculty, in form and moving how express and admirable, in action how like an angel, in apprehension how like a god. Would you please welcome home – Robbie Goulding.'

Coronas of strobe, a flicker-storm of flashbulbs, the impossible constellation of iPhones on video-record, their dim blue Milky Way. Trez led me by the right hand, Seán by my left. We bowed at the front of the stage. The cellos and double basses were chopping out a march. The fat brass *blasted*, loud enough to strip the gilt off the walls. Seán clambered up on to his riser and hit the drums like he meant it. I was weeping as I plugged in. Someone threw me a flower. Trez slouched to the rifle-mic, left hand on her hip, and started into 'Insulting Your Mother'.

I was wearing the '72 Telecaster thighs-low, down at my

zipper like a punk. That's a guitar you need to get on top of, a monster and a chomper, otherwise you're riding Ahab's whale through a tornado of screeching feedback that'll blow out your spine at the volume I'm talking about. We were AEONS too loud. Brontosaurs were charging. But what the hey, you want Pete Townshend, I got him. Seán smashed at the snares and I gave it full windmill, toeing at my pedals to ramp up the fuzzbox and the shamelessly tasteless wah-wah. And I *milked* that naughty tremolo, zipped the plectrum down the strings. There's a time and a place for discretion.

I saw my daughter in the backstage, Jimmy behind her. Molly shot me a sullen glower. She looked gorgeous, like Shay.

Jimmy mouthed five words, the ancient motto of clan Goulding.

KICK.

THEM.

UP.

THE.

HOLE.

Trez pointed a hand at me. The crowd, oh the crowd.
I hit the hardest E-7th in the history of Dublin city.
Loud enough to wake the monkeys in the zoo.

The way a song ends can be the feature that makes it. The crescendo and impossibly long chord that finishes 'A Day in the Life'. The voodoo fade-out on 'Sympathy for the Devil'. And I'd love to give you an ending the story deserves. Yes, it's possible for a private jet to do the London–Dublin run in an hour. I've pictured Fran arriving with his minders just in time for the encore, strolling on coolly to the screams without a word, plugging in a Rickenbacker and letting rip. But that didn't happen. Never mind. I'd have liked to do Bowie's 'Heroes' with him, on two acoustic guitars. Maybe 'Be-Bop-a-Lula'. For auld lang syne. But I did it with Trez and Molly instead, and they tore that playhouse down. When we ran out of stuff we'd rehearsed, we did 'Twist and Shout' and 'Rebel Rebel', then 'Should I Stay or Should I Go?' and 'No Feelings'.

The high point, for me, was seeing Molly play lead on my Strat. She Slashed and Marred and Raitted and Blackmored. At one point I had the uneasy feeling she was about to Hendrix and smash it through Seán's kit, the sort of act you feel is dramatically pleasing when young. But, as I warned her backstage, that's the only trust fund she's ever likely to have. She's a sensible woman, like her mother.

We called Michelle after the show. It was gorgeous to hear her. Molly and I sang the Beatles song bearing her name down the line to Long Island, perhaps a first in transatlantic history. Then Molly went drinking with the Prof (huh?) and some of the roadies (WHAT?) and I talked a while more with Michelle. The east Tennessean accent is one for which I have a weakness. Down a phone line, in particular, it's what my ex's grand-uncle, a handsome Louisianan divorce-attorney, used to call 'one killin' thang'.

Jimmy said the gig had been too loud and not always in tune, on both of which scores he was right. I was hoping he'd call me a daisy but he didn't. He stole the soaps, comb and shower cap from his room in the Jury's Inn down the street and a preposterous amount of swag from the buffet. Next morning we returned to Luton and sat in the living room at 57 Rutherford Road playing WWE Wrestling on his Xbox. Annoyingly, he beat me. Every single time. He has taken to wearing trainers, which is quite the arresting sight, and he jogs, or sort of jogs, up to Lidl every morning, where he enjoys the range of invigorations you'd expect: complaining to the manager, defaming the Conservative and Liberal Democrat parties, and eating the boiled sweets he thinks I don't know about, when the doctor has commanded him not to. The persistence of many civil and political liberties in Britain, of legal, individual and socioeconomic rights, the non-beheading of rude people, the freedom of the press, and the existence of the European Union in any form at all, are matters Jimmy finds baffling. In essence, he would like to jail every human currently living on this planet, he to hold the only key. His friend, Mrs Simmons, would be one of few exceptions. Sixty-eight next month, she captains Luton's widely feared crown green bowling team, as the late Mr Simmons once did. I've warned Jimmy that I won't tolerate misbehaviour in a Christian home, that he mustn't make the mistake of treating it like a hotel, that Mrs Simmons is relatively young and impressionable. Occasionally I ramp on the immersion system when I drop around to visit. It drives him stark bonkers mental, which is good for his fitness. One night I'll turn the latchkey and creep into that house and he'll hurl himself from a wardrobe and attack me. He's going to Lourdes with a party of retired zookeepers in March 'for the fun'. No word in that sentence is a misprint.

As for Fran and myself, put it this way: we've talked.

'Quarrelled' is more accurate, but at least we've done it face to face. What is hardest to forgive is how funny he can be about the things we thought mattered, some of which did. He's asked me to play on his next album, *Live in Hanoi*, I think because he wanted to gift me the inestimable pleasure of telling him to sod right off. Maybe I'll tag along. Hard to turn down. He calls me late at night, pretending to be Bono, of whom he's a cruelly accurate mimic. Indeed, this led to an embarrassing encounter, when the actual Bono was kind enough to phone with gentlemanly wishes for my health. My reply – get knotted, you lip-glossed old slapper – took a little in the way of explanation.

If soon you happen to be in London with an evening to kill, I play the Bridge pub in Stockwell every other Tuesday night. Acoustic. Nothing fancy. Couple of mates might sit in, but usually it's me on my own. You pay what you want. No cover charge. I wouldn't call it a residency, just a gig I've been doing. I've six more left before I leave.

I'm writing this on a barge in the Grand Union Canal. Anyone wants to rent, it's available. I'm wintering in Montauk. Well, you never can tell. We're taking things gently. Who knows?

Acknowledgements

I thank my editor Geoff Mulligan and everyone at Harvill Secker and at Vintage, Fran Barrie, Beth Humphries, Bethan Jones, James Jones who designed the cover of this book, Declan Heeney, my literary agent Carole Blake and screenwriting/playwriting agent Conrad Williams at Blake Friedmann Literary Agency, London, also Jewerl Ross at Silent R Management, Los Angeles. I thank Peter Aiken and his colleagues at Aiken Promotions, Mike Adamson and his team at the o2 in Dublin, and the extraordinary musicians with whom I have been blessed to work in recent years. It's a pleasure to acknowledge a special debt of gratitude to Philip King, and to Robbie Overson and Sonny Condell. I thank my endlessly supportive sister Dr Éimear O'Connor and all members of the O'Connor, Suiter and Casey families, Ciaran Byrne at Cauldron Studios in Dublin, and Moya Doherty and John McColgan. For his gentle encouragement and immense skill I thank the maestro Brian Byrne. I thank my former Creative Writing students at Baruch College, Manhattan, especially Dave Feldman of the New York punk band Wyldlife, and Mary Williams and Giselle Lugo, for discussions about music lyrics and storytelling. The late Philip Chevron, to whom this novel is dedicated, was a deeply gifted songwriter and a man of remarkable grace. Robbie Goulding is a fictional character (as are all members of the Ships), and his opinions, dislikes and enthusiasms are entirely his own, but his profound gratitude for Philip's songs, and for those of the great Patti Smith, are shared by multitudes whose lives that music touched. I will always be one of that number. I thank Cliona Hegarty, Jane Alger at Dublin City Libraries, Sarah Bannan-Keegan, Head of Literature at the Arts Council, Ellen McCourt, Loretta Brennan-Glucksman and my kindly and welcoming new colleagues at the University of Limerick, especially Don Barry, Tom Lodge, Meg Harper and Sarah Moore. Above all I thank my favourite songwriter and performer, James O'Connor, my favourite rock drummer, Marcus O'Connor, and Anne-Marie Casey who deserves a Gershwin love song, a shimmering, gorgeous classic.

Joseph O'Connor was born in Dublin. His books include seven previous novels: *Cowboys and Indians* (Whitbread Prize shortlist), *Desperadoes*, *The Salesman*, *Inishowen*, *Star of the Sea* (American Library Association Award, Irish Post Award for Fiction, France's Prix Millepages, Italy's Premio Acerbi, Prix Madeleine Zepter for European novel of the year), *Redemption Falls* and *Ghost Light* (Dublin One City One Book Novel 2011). His fiction has been published in forty languages. He received the 2012 Irish PEN Award for outstanding achievement in literature. In 2014 he was appointed Frank McCourt Professor of Creative Writing at the University of Limerick.

www.josephoconnorauthor.com